Booksellers are raving abo

"*The Book Lover* is the name of a charming b   n
characters in this story of broken marriages, :   s.
The well developed characters and subject wı̣ı ....   ok
clubs."

ELIZABETH MERRITT, Titcomb's Books

"*The Book Lover* takes you into the heart and soul of the book world, with characters you will come to love. The most honest story about the world of books I've read yet."

ROB DOUGHERTY, Clinton Book Shop

"A compelling story of love, loss and survival."

TOM WARNER, Litchfield Books

"Book lovers everywhere will love this story!"

BETH CARPENTER, The Country Bookshop

"I've always found some character or situation in Maryann McFadden's books that reminds me of me and mine—this time she even nails my life as a bookseller!"

BETSY RIDER, Otto's Books

More praise for *The Book Lover*

"Oh, what a feast for book lovers! McFadden mines bookstores, writers' lives, publishing, and the rocky terrain of the human heart with equal grace and aplomb. *The Book Lover* is wise, knowing, and totally wonderful."

CAROLINE LEAVITT, NY Times Bestselling Author of *Pictures of You*

"Maryann McFadden takes you into the hearts and souls of two ordinary women, a writer and a bookseller, who find the courage to pursue their dreams, and the men they love. *The Book Lover* is unforgettable."

DOROTHEA BENTON FRANK, New York Times Bestselling Author

"Heartfelt and richly woven, Maryann McFadden's latest tells the story of love lost - and found again in an unexpected place. It's a valentine to book lovers."

SARAH PEKKANEN, Author of *These Girls*

Praise for *The Richest Season*

"Set in the fabled landscape of South Carolina's Low Country, The Richest Season takes us on a heartrending journey of discovery. Maryann McFadden is an exciting new author who writes with compassion, wisdom, and astonishing skill."

CASSANDRA KING, Bestselling author of *Queen of Broken Hearts*

"In Maryann McFadden's brave and carefully made novel, The Richest Season, two women set out on open ended odysseys, one to find her life, one to find meaning in her death. McFadden is out of the gate and on her way."

JACQUELYN MITCHARD, Bestselling author of *The Deep End of the Ocean* and *Still Summer*

"Beautifully written...Let's readers into the characters' thoughts and feelings as they struggle to understand how the past has led them to their present situations. In the process, a new person emerges, or perhaps it's the self each forgot was there all along."

ROMANTIC TIMES

"Skillful plotting keeps pages turning, and McFadden quickly has readers rooting for intriguing Joanna, on the cusp of change."

PUBLISHER'S WEEKLY

"A compelling debut novel that tells the story of one woman's courage to leave it all behind . . ."

FRESH FICTION

Praise for *So Happy Together*

"I can think of no writer I'd rather have sing me songs of the sea, even sad ones, than Maryann McFadden. The characters in So Happy Together will speak to you, and the best ones...have the ocean in their voices."

ANNE RIVERS SIDDONS, New York Times bestselling author of *Off Season* and *Colony*

"McFadden deftly weaves a story of three generations of women and the men who orbit around them. With a sure touch, she writes about the mother-daughter bond, the simple pleasures to be found in cooking, the pervasive nature of guilt, and the power of forgiveness..."

CHRISTINA BAKER KLINE, author of *The Way Life Should Be* and *Bird in Hand*

"So Happy Together is an honest book . . . that will resonate with many women who struggle to care for family members and themselves."

THE RALEIGH NEWS & OBSERVER

*The*BOOK LOVER

MARYANN MCFADDEN

Three Women Press
www.threewomenpress.com

ALSO BY MARYANN MCFADDEN

THE RICHEST SEASON

SO HAPPY TOGETHER

For information, address **THREE WOMEN PRESS**, P.O. Box 24, Vienna, NJ, 07880 or info@threewomenpress.com.

For information about special discounts for bulk purchases, please contact **THREE WOMEN PRESS** at 973-586-3247 or info@threewomenpress.com

Publishers's Cataloguing-in-publication data

McFadden, Maryann.

The book lover/Maryann McFadden. – 1st ed. – Vienna, NJ: Three Women Press, c2012.

p. ; cm.

ISBN: 978-0-9848671-0-3 (print); 978-0-9848671-1-0 (ebk)

Summary:
When small town bookseller Ruth Hardaway discovers Lucinda Barrett's novel, she takes the younger woman under her wing, showing her the book world, and sharing her secrets. But when Lucy strikes up an unlikely friendship with Ruth's son, an injured soldier, Ruth begins to question her judgment. And Lucy has no idea that her life is about to fall apart-- because of a little white lie.

1. Independent bookstores—Fiction. 2. Women authors, American—Fiction. 3. Self-publishing Fiction.
4. Paraplegics—Rehabilitation—Fiction. 5. Paraplegics—Sexual behavior—Fiction. 6. Parole—Fiction.
7. Libraries and prisons—Fiction. 8. Bird refuges—New Jersey—Fiction. 9. Divorce—Fiction. I. Title.
II. Title: Booklover.

PS3613.C4375 B66 2012   2011944660
813.6—dc23   1201

Interior Layout/Design by Dan Berger

1st edition

Printed in the United States of America.

15 14 13 12   4 3 2 1

To Michael and Joni Cassidy
Who helped me to believe again

"Books let us into their souls

and lay open to us

the secrets of our own."

—William Hazlitt

PROLOGUE

SHE SLIPPED OUT OF BED WHILE HER HUSBAND SLEPT, careful not to wake him. She'd hidden the letter in a stack of coupons and circulars in the basket on the counter, where she knew David would never look. It wasn't like she didn't know what it held. Her name and address in her own handwriting on the outside of the envelope was a guarantee: another rejection.

Slipping a fingernail under the flap, she opened the envelope and there it was.

Automatically her hands reached for her cropped hair, her fingers pulling, until she turned and caught her reflection in the glass patio doors—a small woman in an oversized t-shirt, her dirty blonde hair sticking up in comical rooster spikes, looking every one of her thirty-nine years. Looking more like a tired punk rocker than an author. Or the wife of an attorney.

She set the letter on the counter, poured herself a glass of chardonnay, and pulled a cigarette from the pack hidden in her tea canister. She opened the French doors, stepping out onto the patio. A blast of damp night air hit her. It was cold for November in St. Augustine, yet a crimson riot of bougainvillea still covered the concrete walls that surrounded their small yard. Most people didn't realize northern Florida had seasons, not like southern Florida, which was subtropical and what David preferred. But she needed seasons. A semblance of home.

She sipped her wine, then put the cigarette between her lips, tossing it in the bushes a second later as a movement caught her eye. The glass door opened and David stepped out in bare feet, then instantly stepped back in.

"Lucy, what are you doing? It's freezing out here."

She almost told him about the letter. That she was going to shelve her novel this time, as she'd promised. That he wouldn't have to see her heart broken again. And for a second, she felt a spark of relief. She had to admit, although writing had brought back so much joy these past five years, the constant rejection had also dimmed something inside of her. But if she told him, there'd be no turning back.

"I couldn't sleep," she said instead, which was partly true.

He looked at her for a moment, then closed the door.

Long ago, Lucy had learned that sometimes little white lies were the easiest way to avoid conversations which were not going to end up in a happy place. She knew David would never get how two cigarettes a day, just two, could somehow still her insides, blowing all her stress out on a long, thin stream of smoke.

David also no longer understood her need to write. How stories popped into her head, and characters had conversations as she showered or walked. How in those last moments of consciousness before sleep, when your mind was at its most pure, a thought would come and you simply had to get up and write it down. David had never experienced that moment of magic when you finally finish writing and a story falls into place like a jigsaw puzzle and your heart soars with satisfaction. You have created characters, an entire little world that rings as true as if it really existed.

As she thought it did in her novel, *A Quiet Wanting*.

Only now she was packing it in after thirty-eight rejections from literary agents, each one a little bullet in the heart. They were all different, but in essence, all said the same thing. *You're just not good enough.* And without an agent, she had no hope of getting a publisher.

She waited a long moment, sipping her wine, the scent of the bay just a few blocks away drifting to her as the air shifted, rustling the leaves of the magnolias and palm trees. When she was certain David was back in bed, she quietly opened the door and grabbed an afghan and the box in the closet of the spare bedroom, then returned to the yard.

Sitting at the table again, she lifted the lid off the box and picked up the top page: *You need to capture me on the first page and you failed to do so.* The next letter took an entire paragraph to praise her beautiful writing and well-plotted pages, ending with: *Alas, I just didn't fall in love with this.*

In the pile there were standard form rejections. *Of course another agency may feel differently*, these letters always ended, but so far, no one did. None of the letters gave her any clear reason why her novel wasn't deemed good enough. Many even contradicted each other. Hope, her heroine, was too nice, therefore not realistic. Then, another telling her Hope was a well-drawn character, but the story too quiet. There was too much description; there was not enough description.

But today's letter was the final straw because she'd really thought this was it. This agent had actually called her, something almost unheard of. Of course Lucy agreed to the three-week exclusive read, in which every day was an unbearable, endless stretch of minutes and hours of fevered anticipation— was the agent reading at that moment? Was she loving it? Was she crying at the end, when Hope leaves her house for the last time, as Lucy herself cried every time she polished that scene? She picked up that letter now and reread the opening sentence. *This is a wonderful book, but I was hoping there would be some humor.*

Had she ever mentioned there would be humor? It was enough to make you crazy and she knew that sometimes David thought she was. If he knew about today's letter he'd say once again: *Why do you keep torturing yourself?*

Because the other writers in a fiction workshop she used to belong to *really* loved it. And there were the raves from her boss's book club. And anyone else she'd had the nerve to share it with. *Where's your book, why isn't it published?* She heard that all the time. And finally, there was just that belief in her gut.

She pulled out the entire stack of rejection letters and set them on the table, and there underneath was her manuscript. She pulled it to her chest, remembering the long nights while the world slept and she'd buried herself in these characters' lives. This book had saved her, when she didn't think she could be saved.

Just then the wind kicked up again, tossing the pile of letters in the air. And in that long moment as they floated magically about her, then slowly fluttered to the ground to lie at her feet like a pile of ghostly white leaves, a thought that had been lurking in the back of her mind suddenly came into focus.

Lucy stood, scooping up the pages. Then she walked to the old fire pit on the side of the patio and tossed them in. She took the lighter and clicked it, touching the edge of a letter. It lit immediately, flared, and in an instant the rest of the letters ignited in a whoosh of flames. She began to laugh as every rejection she had received over the past three years burst into a raging bonfire, lighting up the entire yard.

Stepping back from the sudden heat, Lucy turned at a noise, relieved it wasn't David again. Once more she saw herself in the glass door, a deranged-looking woman smiling beside her towering inferno of rejections. Maybe she was a little crazy. But she was damned if she was giving up. There was no way she could keep that promise.

She would surprise David. She needed him to believe in her again. Besides, she'd already given up on one dream. How could she give up on this, too?

As she watched the fire burn out, the ashy remains of the rejections settling into a gray heap, she had no idea that the decision she'd made that night, a tiny splash, really, in the world at large, would in time send a ripple a thousand miles north of St. Augustine—would touch the doorstep of someone she'd never met before. Someone she would come to love. But who in the end would turn on her, because of a little white lie.

1

RUTH STOOD BEHIND THE COUNTER GOING OVER THE day's sales on the computer one more time, watching the woman from the corner of her eye. Ruth could have gone home; she knew the dismal numbers weren't going to change. But when the doorbell had tinkled ten minutes before eight, just as she was about to call it a night, she had sat back on her stool. The customer, with dark brown hair pulled carelessly back in a clip, had headed straight for the New Fiction section.

Ruth's calves, which had been complaining for hours, were screaming by then. The store was still technically open, though no one had come in since six-thirty. The new hours were mandated by the Warwick Village Downtown Revitalization Committee in order to compete with the malls outside of town. This could be more than just a single sale, Ruth told herself. This woman could end up becoming a regular customer, something Ruth couldn't afford to turn away.

She slipped off her low heels, and rubbed her left calf with the big toe of her right foot as she glanced at the blue envelope she'd slipped into her purse earlier. She was tempted to rip it open and read it right now. But no, she would wait, savoring it like a teenage girl. She would read it tonight, alone. And tell no one.

The woman moved to the shelf of bestsellers and picked one up, opening the cover, reading part of the first page, then slapping it shut. She did the exact same thing over and over, spending less than thirty seconds on four books as Ruth watched. She'd let her browse another five minutes, before asking if there was anything she could help her with.

Ruth turned back to the computer. The figures on the screen began to swim before her. Closing her eyes, she sighed. Once Saturday had been her favorite day of the week in the store. Nothing, though, was the way it used to be.

Reaching under the counter for her purse and sweater, she spotted the cardboard box which had arrived around lunchtime, and which she'd stashed before anyone else noticed it. My God, she surely wasn't herself today. How on earth had she forgotten the box? She smiled in spite of her exhaustion, now having two things to look forward to tonight.

She opened it on the counter, tossing a smaller box that also came in that day's mail inside as well. Maybe some things hadn't changed, she thought. A ripple of pleasure washed through her as she anticipated pulling out one treasure after another. Her daughter Jenny had been harping on her lately that she needed to get a life. But Ruth honestly couldn't imagine anything more enjoyable than the evening now ahead of her. So what if she would spend another Saturday night alone? She was used to alone. And she wasn't lonely, not really. Without her even thinking, a palm drifted across the top of the box, stroking it the way someone might caress a lover's cheek. There would be plenty of people to share her evening with now, of that she was certain.

CRASH!

She jumped at the explosion of hardcovers hitting the floor in the back of the store. Her heart leaped to a gallop in her chest. Oh Lord, she'd forgotten Colin. He'd been so quiet, as usual, organizing a clearance rack. Books that had not sold, that had outlived their shelf life, like poor, unpopular relatives who'd overstayed their visit and had to be gotten rid of quickly.

"No harm done," he muttered, loud enough for her to hear.

She sighed, and her heart began slowing to a canter. How was it she forgot about the accident at times? Was she really that scatterbrained? Not as scatterbrained as her friend Hannah Meeker, who was supposed to come in hours ago, but hadn't shown or called, as usual. Could it be Ruth's age catching up with her? She was sixty-four, although in her mind she still labeled herself middle-aged. But who was she kidding besides herself? She was nearly ready for Medicare, with an aging brain that seemed to tire more quickly, that was overloaded most every day.

"What do you say I throw the goodies in your car?"

She turned to see Colin coming up the aisle. She hadn't noticed before how handsome he looked, in pressed khakis and a button-down shirt the same light blue as his eyes. He had that knowing little smile. He'd been helping her in the store long enough to know how much the box meant to her. But it would be tricky for him. The carton wasn't heavy, but it was cumbersome and her car was across the street in the municipal lot.

She had to let him.

"You don't miss a thing, do you?" She handed him the car keys. "Just leave it on the front seat with the keys."

"You look tired, Mom."

She took a long breath. Had Jenny and Alex been talking to him? They really seemed to be on a mission lately.

"I'm fine," she said with more certainty than she felt.

She walked around the counter, toward the woman who was still opening and closing books.

"Is there anything I can help you with?"

"No thanks." She didn't even look up and Ruth decided to just get ready to close. She knew this game well.

She walked to the back of the store, her fingers gliding across the rows of books, as they'd done each night for nearly three decades. She washed her hands, and as she dried them, she stared at herself in the mirror, smoothing wisps of hair, more silver than black, into her long braid. Quickly she tidied up the bathroom, abused by customers and staff alike. Like her, this bathroom was in need of a makeover. It was a combination storeroom, nap place and dump for everything she didn't know what to do with in the store. Even if she had the time, though, she didn't have the money to fix up the bathroom. Or herself. The low heels she wore tonight had been an impulse buy, a silly indulgence. They'd been ridiculously cheap.

She closed the bathroom door. Right now, what she really needed was simply to soak for an hour or two in a hot tub. Her insides felt as if they were vibrating from exhaustion. She grabbed her coat, and as she made her way back to the counter, wondering if she had the nerve to be rude enough to tell the woman she was closing, she heard the bell tinkle once again.

"I'm sorry, am I too late?"

It was Hannah, breathless and yes, late, both of which seemed to be her habitual state of being.

"I'm sorry, I lost track of the time. My hot water heater exploded and of course all the plumbers are too busy to come right over. Not to mention Eddie's stuck at the store..."

Ruth felt a flush of warmth crawl up her neck, a stress-induced hot flash, and tossed her coat behind the counter.

As well as a lifelong crisis of confidence, her friend Hannah seemed to have a disaster every month or so. She'd been coming in for years, and Ruth knew her from their school days, although Hannah was a good five years younger.

Hannah hurried over to the Self-Help section now, just a few shelves because Ruth didn't have the square footage to devote huge amounts of space to each and every genre.

"*The Seven Spiritual Laws of Success.* You've read this?" Hannah asked.

"Yes, it's very good," Ruth said, slipping off the heels and sitting on the stool again. "He has amazing insight."

She watched Hannah read the book jacket, then frown.

"I don't know, Ruth," she sighed as she carried the book to the counter. "I'm not really looking for money. I just want to find that *thing*, you know? That I'm meant to do."

They'd been having this conversation for as long as Ruth could remember. At the moment, staring at Hannah's pale face, the fading dirty blonde hair, the worried brown eyes fringed with gold lashes, she realized that nothing she said tonight was going to make a difference, really.

"It might not be *the* answer, but I think you'll find a lot of really worthwhile advice here. And who knows? Maybe I'm wrong, maybe it will be the one."

"Okay. I need something to read this weekend anyway. I'm off for two whole days and Eddie has a sale at the store, so..."

"Why don't I just ring it up," Ruth said, gently taking the book from Hannah.

Hannah dug in her purse and pulled out a fistful of bills. "Sorry, my tips for today."

"It's fine, I can always use singles."

Ruth put the book in a bag, just as another book smacked shut and the woman headed for the door.

"Nice of her to paw all your books so she can go home and order—"

"Hannah, shush!"

"Sorry."

It wasn't like Ruth wasn't thinking the same thing.

As they walked out together, Hannah stood on the sidewalk, saying as she did each and every time she came in for a book, "You're so lucky, Ruth. Knowing what you really wanted. And making it happen."

Ruth just smiled, then shrugged.

It was mild for a March evening, although the downtown streets appeared deserted. They crossed Main Street to the community parking lot, where Hannah said goodbye and kept on walking home. As Ruth pulled out, she looked across at her store, the big front window so cozy with books lined up in the glow of a small lamp, and a poster of an upcoming signing for a local poet. Then she noticed the sign above the window, that the L from The Book Lover must have fallen off, although where it had gone to, she couldn't imagine. The letter was big enough that someone should certainly have noticed it on the sidewalk. Although she hadn't. But she knew how that was, when you saw something every day of your life, after a while you stopped *really* seeing it.

With a frown she read it again; now it was "The Book over." She shivered, then told herself not to believe in that karma crap. That was something Hannah would fall for. And that probably was why at nearly sixty, Hannah was still trying to find out what she wanted to be when she grew up.

* * *

LUCY OFTEN SAW HERSELF AS ONE OF HER CHARACTERS. Sometimes it was the easiest way to make light of a situation that might send her into a tailspin. Like now, standing in her driveway in her robe with the *St. Augustine Times* in her hands, staring at the bold black headline just above a smiling picture of herself: *DREAM OF BEING PUBLISHED COMES TRUE.*

Lucinda collapsed from embarrassment on the red brick driveway, praying none of her neighbors were watching. That somehow, today, no one would actually read the newspaper.

If only she could will it to happen. When she went back inside, she found David dressed and in the kitchen, standing at the counter with a cup of coffee. She handed him the paper.

"Front of the Arts section. That's great coverage."

She said nothing, waiting.

He put the paper down a few moments later. "You realize this makes it sound like you got a real publisher?"

"Well, when the reporter asked who my publisher was, I just said 'small potatoes press,' implying no one would have heard of them. Which is technically true."

"Yes, but you had to know that..."

David's voice faded. Her dream hadn't come true; she had published the book herself. But she didn't want people pre-judging it, and now it had all come out wrong. It was her own fault, really.

"Lucy, did you hear what I said?"

She looked up. David was staring at her. "What?"

"Don't you ever listen when I'm talking?"

"I'm sorry, I—"

"I just reminded you that I'll be home late. I have a deposition in Fort Lauderdale, then my poker game tonight."

"I remembered," she said, although she hadn't. She was doing that a lot lately, zoning out in the middle of conversations.

As he walked to the bedroom, she saw him pause as he passed the dining room, where piles of her book—nearly $1,000 worth—sat all over the table and floor. Yesterday he'd made a comment about the sink filled with dishes from the day before.

"Do you think you could find ten minutes today to straighten up?"

"I'm surprised you noticed," she said, trailing him into the bedroom, "since you're never home."

"Someone has to pay the bills."

"Jesus, David, that's a low blow. It wasn't so long ago the tables were turned and I was the only one working."

He stood there a moment and said nothing.

"What are we doing, David?"

He shrugged.

She took a deep breath, then walked to him and straightened his tie. "Listen, you've got a deposition, I've got a million booksellers to contact, plus the launch party is nearly here. We're both stressed."

He nodded, grabbing his wallet from the dresser. "I have to go or I'll be late."

"Are you having doubts about me doing this?"

"No, I think you need to get it out of your system. This is the first time I've seen you really excited about anything since..." His words died off and they looked at each other a long moment. Then he slipped on his suit jacket. "What about you, are you having second thoughts?"

"Not at all," she lied.

She went and put her arms around him, breathing in his cologne, the smell of his skin. He squeezed back before patting his pocket to check for his wallet.

"You just put it in there," she reminded him with a laugh. "Obviously I'm not the only one in la la land." But her attempt at levity didn't even bring a smile.

As they walked back to the kitchen, the phone in David's study began to ring.

"Aren't you going to answer that?" She realized it had been ringing when she walked in with the newspaper, before it was even seven o'clock.

"It's just Jason. I made a big mistake hiring him. He can't even handle a simple closing."

David grabbed his briefcase and gave her a peck on the cheek.

"Don't forget to invite your poker buddies and their wives to the launch party. I could use all the bodies I can get."

She watched him walk out and down the driveway. David was tall and thin, a bit stoop-shouldered like his mother had been. And despite being forty-five, he still had a full head of dark hair with barely a fleck of grey. He was an attractive man and right now as he got in his car, shut the door, then sat back and yawned, she thought he seemed like a stranger. And lately nothing she did could please him.

She went into the dining room and looked at the two hundred books. She picked one up and opened to the dedication page. *For Ben, For always...* She wondered how her husband was going to feel when he saw that.

Then she walked into the bathroom and stood in front of the mirror, staring at her ridiculously short hair. She picked up the cuticle scissors, held out a one-inch strand near her temple and snipped.

* * *

AS WATER RAN IN THE TUB UPSTAIRS, Ruth stood barefoot in the kitchen, the waistband of her long skirt unbuttoned. She reached for the box. Her dog Samantha, a mutt who'd appeared to be mostly beagle when Ruth rescued her from the shelter eight years ago, was miffed at not going to the store today and sat in the corner, ignoring her.

"Okay, girl, here we go," she said as she pulled the lid apart. She inhaled, and there it was.

Before there was a glimpse of a cover, the smell of the pages rose up to her. How did you describe the wonder of that scent? An odor that took her back in time to libraries, classrooms, clandestine hours beneath the covers of her bed, escaping to a world that didn't exist. Except in imagination.

She reached in and pulled out the first book. The cover was in muted shades of gray with the silhouette of a woman running away. Ruth set it on the table, reaching for another book. And then another, as well as the tiny box that must have come from a small publisher, and obviously held just one paperback. It was like Christmas, these shipments of galleys. These books wouldn't be released for months, but her orders had to be placed one or two seasons ahead. The publishers hoped she, and other booksellers, would fall in love with these books, order lots of copies, and then recommend them to their customers.

Handselling was the art of the small bookseller. Ruth loved being part of this process. In the world of bookselling, word of mouth was perhaps the most powerful tool to success, and Ruth knew that her word was gold to a lot of people. She would pick out a few for now, then bring the rest back for Harry, Kris and Megan to choose from.

She stared now at a pale gold cover, plain except for the distant image of a face. It was being hyped like crazy, with her sales rep telling her it could be the blockbuster of the year. Ruth held it to her breast, and then went to the fridge and poured herself a glass of cranberry juice.

"Well," she said to Sam, still lying in the corner, looking back at her with half-closed lids. "I'm going to take a bath."

At that, Sam, who also loved nothing more than spending a few hours in a warm, steamy bathroom snuggled on a soft towel beside the tub, swallowed her pride, rose to her four feet, and with a haughty shake of her ears, followed Ruth upstairs.

"Ummmm," Ruth sighed a few minutes later as her sore toes hit the warm water, and then her calves, her aching thighs, and the rest of her weary body. Lying back, she closed her eyes. A candle, the galley, and the day's mail perched on the windowsill just above the tub. She did her best thinking here, and some of her best work, referring to the tub as her "liquid office."

"Who says this isn't heaven?" she asked Sam, stroking the dog with her still dry right hand. Sam, too, gave a contented little sigh.

Then she picked up the book and began reading. By the third page, she felt her thoughts drifting and snapped herself back to attention. But then she began wondering what Colin was up to tonight. He was wearing a nice shirt and some spicy cologne. Was he seeing someone? Could it possibly be Gloryanne? She'd come into the store a few days ago when Colin was working. Oh, Ruth hoped so. She didn't want him spending the rest of his life alone. Shit! She'd just finished an entire page and had no idea what she'd read. Turning back a page, she forced herself to reread. Five minutes later, she dropped the book to the floor.

"I give up, Sam." She closed her eyes and splashed water on her face, holding her palms to her eyes. "There are way too many books out there to waste my time on this one."

There was a time when she would force herself to finish a book once she'd started. But years ago, inundated with galleys and review copies, she finally gave herself permission to stop. It had been liberating.

She looked at the stack of mail sitting on the window sill. There in the midst of bills and late payment notices, she saw the plain blue envelope she'd brought home from the store, with the slanted scrawl.

"Oh, Sam, I am a pathetic old woman, torturing myself with anticipation."

No one knew about these letters. Not Hannah, or the staff at work, and especially not her children. They would think she was crazy, or it was dangerous somehow. She wondered what Thomas was doing at that moment while she sat luxuriating in a tub of warm water, a lavender candle burning, an endless supply of books at her fingertips. Was he thinking of her?

She slipped a fingernail across the envelope and pulled the letter out.

Dear Ruth,

You were right about Gatsby. I like it. I'm reading it slow, like you suggested. When I got to the line "her voice was full of money" I had to stop. I remembered all of a sudden you telling me that phrase a long time ago, when you said it was your favorite book.

I can picture Jay Gatsby listening to Daisy. Feeling like an outsider. He just wants into that world, but you get the feeling he already knows he's not good enough. We'll see what happens, but I don't have a good feeling.

I thought about what your voice sounds like, after reading that. I used up an entire evening, which is not a bad thing, as I've told you how endless the nights are. Even if you can't see that it's dark outside, you know it, and there's a whole different feeling being in here. It should be worse when the sun is out, but somehow it isn't. Sorry, I'm digressing.

Anyway, Ruth, your voice is full of kindness. To me and everyone else you deal with in here. And for others, I'm sure. You're a good woman, I could tell that the first time I saw you here, nibbling on your lower lip, looking nervous. But here you are, how many years later? Five? Still coming. I'm glad.

I'll keep going with Gatsby. Maybe I'll have it finished when you come back in a few weeks. We'll see. I'll be counting the days.

She looked up at the ceiling and closed her eyes. She was counting, too, but weeks because there were just too many days. She turned the page over and was disappointed to see there were just a few more lines.

I almost forgot, my hand is getting better. Nothing broken, just sprained. Thanks for asking.

See you soon.
Thomas

P.S. Sorry, but I have to ask again, is there something wrong? I talked about your voice, but mostly I've been thinking about your eyes. When you were here last, your eyes were full of worry.

She read the letter two more times before folding it carefully and slipping it back into the envelope. And then she closed her eyes again, her hands sinking in the warm water, resting on her soft belly. She let out a humorless laugh at the pathetic state of her existence. How many women held a trip to a prison as the most exciting thing in their lives?

RUTH WOKE SUDDENLY IN THE MIDDLE OF THE NIGHT, needing to pee. A second later, her heart began to pound. Then it was as if the box of galleys she'd carried in hours ago suddenly landed on her chest. She could barely breathe. She sat up quickly, swallowing. Deep in her chest her heart still thudded against her rib cage.

She got up and went to the bathroom, her legs trembling so badly that her feet danced on the cold tile floor as she sat on the toilet. She then stood in front of the mirror, staring at herself. Jesus, was she having a heart attack? It couldn't be. It was probably the popcorn she ate right before bed, lodged in her esophagus. Yes, it was indigestion, she was certain. It had to be.

She went downstairs and found Tums in a cabinet, chewing two while her tea heated in the microwave. All the while the lines of an article she'd read recently kept popping into her head in big capital letters. How heart attacks are different in women. How they feel just like indigestion and it's better to be safe than sorry. But she was healthy as a horse, she kept telling herself.

As she sat at the kitchen table, she noticed that her hands were shaking now, too. The last thing she wanted to do was sit in an ER all night, only to be told it was nothing. And God only knew what that would cost. Her health insurance was bare bones, the best she could manage.

Maybe it was just her nerves. She'd decided today she was going to cut hours at the store—which seemed like an oxymoron since she was staying open later. Looking on the computer at what had come in during this last week of the month, which was always a tense week because it was her last chance to scrape enough together to pay most of her bills, if not all—well, the figures weren't good. Something had to give; she just wasn't sure what. She'd promised herself she wouldn't sell another piece of her mother's jewelry, no matter how gaudy it was, because it had been her mother's, after all. Still, if it bought her a little more time. But time for what? She didn't see anything changing in the weeks ahead. She'd been playing this Peter and Paul game for years now. The pressure in her chest shifted suddenly and she felt...something, she wasn't sure, in her shoulder. Her already pounding heart began to race. Stop it! She told herself. You can't panic.

She took a sip of the tea and felt it go down, hot and soothing. She took another deep breath, and another, her nerves vibrating throughout her body. The box of galleys still sat on the floor beside the table, and she reached in and pulled out another handful of books, to distract herself. She glanced at one after the other. Then she pulled out the tiny box that had come separately, and yes, it held just one trade paperback. *A Quiet Wanting* by Lucinda Barrett. She hadn't heard of it, or the publisher. On the cover, a woman sat on top of a picnic table with her back to the reader. In front of her stretched a circle of tall pines, a wall of green branches, but the woman was looking up, beyond the treetops.

Ruth opened the book, turned a few pages and came to the dedication: *For Ben, For always...*

She took another sip of tea and began reading.

She embraced her sadness like a secret lover she met each evening on her solitary drive home...

It wasn't until she sipped and found the cup empty that Ruth realized how much time had gone by. She looked at the clock on the stove. It was 3:40. She'd been reading for almost a half hour, and she was on page thirty-five.

And her chest...it felt just fine.

Relieved, she stood up and put the cup in the sink. "Come on, Samantha, morning will be here before you know it."

She picked up the book. More than anything she wanted to take it upstairs and keep reading. It was a haunting story of a woman trying to hold onto a marriage that was unraveling, yet she had no idea why. But she put it back on the table, deciding not to tempt herself. She needed the sleep.

But the book was astonishing. She wondered who this Lucinda Barrett was.

2

T HE DREAM BEGAN THE YEAR LUCY TURNED ELEVEN, the summer after everything in her life changed. Her mother got a full-time job, and Lucy was forced to watch her brothers, Jake and Charlie. Because she was so young, her mother made her promise to stay in the house or their tiny yard, in the old duplex in Morristown her father had rented before leaving. Resentful, expecting to be bored because they'd just moved again and she didn't have any friends yet, Lucy was surprised when something magical happened instead. Although she already loved to read, now, with little other diversion, she began to devour a book a day, while her brothers, who were six and seven at the time, played war, watched cartoons, and ran around the yard with water pistols.

She escaped in the lives and adventures of imaginary people who lived on those pages. On hot summer days, as she opened each book, discovering little nuggets of herself in these stories, it was as if a place inside of her opened up, one she hadn't known existed. The outside world faded, even the squeals of her brothers, until she'd hear her mother's key in the front door, and the real world came walking back in. It was *The Diary of a Young Girl* that gave her the courage to pick up a pencil and notebook and write her first story. It was as if every emotion she'd tucked inside her heart tumbled out onto those pages. And she knew with certainty what she was going to do with her life—she was going to be a writer.

Now, walking the streets of St. Augustine on her way to visit her friend, Tia, another writer, it amazed Lucy the twists and turns her life had taken, and that here she was at thirty-nine, still trying to achieve that dream. And how nothing ever really turns out the way you think it's going to. But she wasn't going to dwell on all that today.

As she turned onto Charlotte Street, marveling at the March weather which continued to be as mild as summer, she thought once again how lucky they were to live in St. Augustine. Back in New Jersey, March was a bitter month. Now Lucy savored the soft air brushing her skin like a silky scarf.

She had fallen in love the first moment she saw it, five years ago, soaring above the sparkling blue harbor on the Bridge of Lions, then descending into the small city, seeming almost too beautiful to be real—cobblestone streets and horse-drawn carriages, a town green with a white gazebo, stucco buildings dating back hundreds of years, picturesque streets lined with graceful oaks veiled in Spanish moss. It had taken her breath in a moment of complete surprise, unlike any part of Florida they'd seen.

How could she not agree with David when he said this was where they could start over? And what he'd left unspoken: where they could leave the past behind.

When they'd first moved, jobs were tight in the legal field and David had decided to open his own practice again. It took him a long time to pass the Florida Bar and he began joking about it, wondering if he'd break some kind of record. But neither of them was able to focus on much back then. Lucy had left an accounting career back home, but here she took a mindless job in housekeeping at a bed & breakfast, where she wouldn't have to interact much with anyone. When she got home in the afternoons, she worked on her novel while David continued studying, or took breaks and went to the beach with his new metal detector.

It was ironic that she couldn't focus on numbers anymore, yet she could spend hours on a particular word or phrase. When David passed the bar and opened his office—which took a year and a half—he insisted it was her turn, and she quit her job and finished the book, although they'd mounted considerable debt. And stupid her, she'd thought it would be scooped up by a publisher right away. Something good did come of it, though—she'd found herself going for long stretches without thinking of Ben.

She turned toward the old fort that jutted out into the water, constructed of coquina shells over five hundred years ago to protect St. Augustine from invading enemies. The oldest city in the country, it was now a place of history, beauty and art. And ghosts, her mother pointed out with dramatic disapproval, when Lucy told her they were moving there. But Lucy didn't mind ghosts. What writer would?

When she came to the south end of town, she stopped a moment before going into Tia's, staring at the shimmering marsh that stretched all the way to Anastasia Island, where the ending to her book had written itself in her head during those early days as she walked the beach. And where she had finally begun to heal. She savored the smells of fish and salt water, then turned to Tia's apartment complex.

It looked more like an upscale condo community than senior housing, the clusters of buildings in a buttery stucco, with arched windows and porticos to mimic the historic feel of the city. She'd met Tia, who'd introduced herself as Demetria, her full Greek name, at her first writer's workshop, shortly after moving to St. Augustine. At the time, Tia was still living in one of the assisted living apartments. Now she was in the main building, where she could benefit from 24-hour nursing care.

Lucy walked into the main lobby, signed the guest book at the front desk, and took the elevator to the third floor. Before even lifting her hand to knock, she heard Tia call to come in. Lucy found her sitting in a stuffed chintz chair beside a window with a magnificent view of the marsh. A view Tia was no longer able to see.

Tia was a small woman, but now she felt frail as a bird as Lucy hugged her, the long battle with diabetes taking its toll. She looked lovely, as usual, in a belted shirtwaist dress and stockings, smelling of her signature lilac cologne.

"Hello, my dear," she whispered, and gave Lucy a squeeze. "I'm so glad you're here."

"How are you, Tia?" Lucy asked, sitting in an identical chair across the room as Tia's eyes followed her. She realized the older woman must still be able to see something, shadows perhaps.

"Well, my hearing is getting better," Tia chuckled, "as you no doubt must have noticed."

"You really heard me out in the hall?"

Tia shrugged, then gave that little laugh that had such a lovely, musical quality to it. "I must confess, they do call when visitors are on their way up, but...yes, it's true, when the eyes go, your other senses seem to sharpen." She gave a little clap then, her way of transitioning a conversation. "All right, shall we get to work?"

Tia had written nine novels during the course of her eighty-four years, and actually had one published, which she'd brought to that original workshop group where they met, beaming with pride that she'd gotten it taken by a major publisher.

"That's not a major publisher," Regan, one of the others, had snapped. "They were minor at best, and they went out of business decades ago."

Lucy saw Tia's face freeze, as her own mouth fell open. Just as she was ready to lay into Regan, Tia, who was still able to see back then, gave her a look, and she stopped. But after that, they formed their own group with two others also tired of the bitterness and negativity. The others had since moved away, and it had been down to just Tia and Lucy for the past year, reading and discussing each other's work, although now Lucy read aloud for both of them.

"So what are we going to read?" Tia asked.

"I don't have anything new, but I did bring you a copy of my novel. I didn't want to tell you until I had it for you." She got up and placed a signed book on Tia's lap. "This is *A Quiet Wanting*, Tia. I published it myself."

Tia picked it up, her fingers sliding over the glossy cover, then touching the pages. "Oh, how I wish that I could see it. Could you describe the cover for me?"

"It's beautiful, exactly what I'd always envisioned—Hope sitting on a picnic table, the wall of green pines, the circle of blue sky above, where she seems to be searching for something."

"It reminds me of that one scene in the book."

"I know."

"So tell me, how did you do this? Was it very expensive?"

"No, back in November when I made my decision, I found this technology called Print-On-Demand that I'd never heard of before, and for $600 they made my book and designed the cover I wanted. I got two copies, and now any time someone wants a book, they can print one at a time, and it doesn't cost me a thing."

"Truly? Well, that's wonderful. In my day you had to pay a lot of money to a so-called vanity press if you wanted to publish your book yourself, because they had to print a minimum of several thousand books, which usually ended up in your basement."

"It is great, but the big downside is that the only place it's available for sale is online. And no one knows about the book, so no one is going to order it online."

"And what are you doing about that?"

"Well, I ordered myself a bundle of them, so it is costing me, but I've already sent copies to some small bookstores, hoping they'll read it and maybe want to sell it. You know all the real publishers send them galleys so they can order the book, so I've got to do the same thing. I'm getting another batch ready to send tomorrow."

"You know, I give you credit. This doesn't sound like an easy road, but I think if I were a bit younger I might try it."

"Tia, your novels are amazing. I can't for the life of me understand why they weren't all published."

"Publishing is not an easy business, my dear, and certainly not for the faint of heart. I've made peace with it," she said, waving her hand in dismissal. "And I had the one published, that was something, I must say." Her eyes were still for a moment, and Lucy knew she must be thinking back on that glorious time. Then she looked up again.

"I haven't written a thing worth reading since you last came," Tia confessed. "So what are you going to read?"

"Ironically, now that I published the book, that's taking all my time. I don't have anything new, either." They both laughed.

"Well, then, why don't you read me this?" Tia asked, holding up the signed copy of the book. "It's not a manuscript any longer, it's a book. And it always reads better that way."

"I'd love to, Tia."

Lucy took the book from her and opened it, reading the dedication as the afternoon sun set. It wasn't until she was on Chapter 4, pausing to turn a page, that she looked up and saw that Tia's head had fallen back on her chair, and she was asleep. Lucy covered her with an afghan, then grabbed her things, but when she opened the door, Tia said, "It wasn't the book, Lucinda, I'm just very tired. Your book is beautiful. I'm glad you're doing this."

Bolstered by Tia's words, Lucy walked home and decided it was time to do something she really couldn't put off any longer. Something that sent her heart fluttering. But if she was seriously going through with this, she had no choice. It was now or never.

* * *

RUTH SAT WITH HER STAFF AT THE WEDDING RECEPTION at the Chateau Hathorn, a stone mansion built in 1832 on the edge of Warwick Village. She looked at them, all dressed up, having a wonderful time, and dreaded breaking the bad news to them on Monday.

"Your hair looks really nice, Ruth."

She turned and smiled at Megan, knowing she was just being polite. Megan, who'd worked for her all through college and was now her only full-timer, was dying to get her hands on Ruth's hair. When Ruth was Megan's age, if she'd colored her hair, it was something you tried to hide. But there Megan sat, bright blue tips on her cropped dark hair, with a breezy confidence that

Ruth couldn't imagine at such a young age. At sixty-four, she wished she could channel even an eighth of it.

She patted her own wild mane self-consciously. After fussing for twenty minutes, she'd pulled the sides back in a pearl barrette. The long black skirt and velvet jacket were a staple, what Jenny laughingly called her "wedding uniform," while trying to lure her to go shopping. They were classic pieces that would last for years, she'd argued. To which Jenny responded, "Yes, but now it's time to retire them, Mom, they've had a good long life."

"Did everyone enjoy their dinner?"

She looked up to see Kris, beaming as mother of the bride. A mystery and women's fiction addict, Kris had come to work for Ruth about ten years ago, when her daughter, Cassie, started high school. Just then, the band started to play and Kris breezed off, as Megan and her new guy, Oliver, and Harry and Iris all jumped up to dance.

Ruth sat there alone, thinking as she always did that there was nothing worse than being an old woman alone at a wedding reception. She sipped the Cosmopolitan Megan had brought her and sighed, her earlier unease in the church returning. She'd been late, getting Jenny settled to help cover at the store with Colin, who was invited, but chose not to come, much to her disappointment. But it wasn't that, it was the moment they'd all stood, turning to the back of the church where Kris's daughter stood between her parents, that the odd feeling came over her.

Suddenly it was as if Ruth was seeing herself in that same vestibule, frozen on her father's arm more than forty years ago. Unable to make her feet move as a hundred and fifty smiling faces turned and waited. Filled with uncertainty and terror, her father gently tugging on her arm, until she looked down the long aisle and saw Bill wink at her and smile, taking her breath away. How was it that she—tall, plain Ruth Baldwin—was marrying handsome Bill Hardaway?

She shook her head now, dispelling the image, and took another swallow of her Cosmopolitan. Why was she suddenly thinking about her husband so much? But the answer was obvious. It was Thomas. And the feelings he was stirring inside of her.

At moments like this, she longed to have someone to be with. She imagined now what it would be like to have a man take her hand, lead her onto the parquet floor, then pull her close. For a moment she closed her eyes, listening to the music, feeling her head on his shoulder as they swayed to the slow rhythms. The fantasy never went further than that. It wasn't like she imagined making love to a man. It had been too many years, and something she put out of her mind long ago. It was simply the thought of being held, hearing the beating of his heart as she laid her head on his chest. It was Thomas that she saw.

He was a big man, well over six feet, and broad in the shoulders and chest, his brown hair shaved close, as Colin's had been in the army. When she'd first met him he reminded her of a big teddy bear, but she'd had to keep reminding herself that he was a prisoner. That despite his gentle demeanor and kind brown eyes, he'd done something terrible.

She jumped as a hand touched her shoulder, startling her back to the present. It was Harry. Behind him she saw Iris walking toward the Ladies' Room.

"Thanks for the rescue," she said a moment later, when they were out on the dance floor. They were the same height and she looked him in the eye.

"Don't be silly. I like to dance."

She smiled. Harry had been working part-time at her store for about five years. Ruth knew there were more lucrative places to supplement his income as a high school custodian, but Harry loved sci-fi, and he knew how to pick and hand sell a book. These days sci-fi and fantasy were very popular genres.

"So what's going on, Ruth?"

"What do you mean?"

"I don't know, lately you seem really distracted."

"Oh, let's not spoil a good time, okay?"

"Come on, out with it."

She hesitated, glancing over at Megan and Oliver, who were kissing at their table. "I'm going to have to cut hours."

"I see."

"I hate to do it, I just don't see any other way."

"I understand."

"I'm sorry."

"I know you are. How much?"

"As little as possible. It's just that I've cut out the radio ads, and I'm scaling back on the newspapers. I'm not sure what else I can do. Our revitalization efforts don't seem to be doing much."

"Maybe we need a big event."

"We're doing signings nearly every week now."

"No, bigger than that," Harry said. "You realize this is our thirtieth year coming up?"

"But we just had our twenty-fifth..."

Harry was grinning. "Yeah, it was four years ago, Ruth."

"Already? It doesn't seem possible."

"Yup, and it's time to start thinking about the thirtieth. It'll be here before we know it."

Ruth nodded and went back to dancing in silence. They had until November. She hoped Harry would still be working with her by then. For that matter, she hoped she still had the store.

She stayed for the cake cutting, then gathered her purse and shawl, saying goodbye to Megan, Oliver, Harry and Iris. She found Kris on the patio, sneaking a cigarette.

"I almost forgot to tell you," Kris said, "I finished that book, *A Quiet Wanting*. Oh my God, it was just beautiful, I couldn't put it down. That scene where she remembers being a little girl and her father tells her he's leaving, it just broke my heart."

"I loved it, too. It's funny, but I haven't heard a word about her, or her book," Ruth said.

"Why don't we get her for a signing? I could sell the heck out of that book. And I'd love to make it a 'Kris Pick.'"

Ruth agreed, then told her everything had been perfect, and slipped out.

Ten minutes later, she paused in front of her store, looking through the window at Jenny at the counter, her blonde hair behind her ears, reading glasses on her head, looking more like a coed than a high school teacher. It was hard for Ruth to believe at times that her daughter was in her forties now, like Alex. Colin wasn't far behind.

"Busy day?" she asked hopefully when she walked in.

"Not bad," Jenny said, looking up from a stack of books on the counter. "A few special orders. An elderly woman who bought ten books, which was great."

"God bless her." Ruth came behind the counter and turned on the computer.

"Oh, and we've got twenty-eight more copies of the Oprah book coming."

The title had been leaked that morning, and they'd scrambled to get as many as they could.

"You're a love. Where's Colin?"

"I told him he could leave early. I think he had plans." Jenny smiled. "Hopefully they're with Gloryanne. I have a feeling she's ready to go back with him."

Ruth said nothing, deciding she didn't have the energy right now to get into Colin with Jenny.

"You know, Mom, Dad's birthday is coming up."

"I know, honey. I haven't forgotten."

"It's a big one, sixty-five. I think we should do something, don't you?"

No, she didn't. Not really. "Of course."

Jenny grabbed her purse and jacket. "Oh, I almost forgot. A man called a few times. He said his name was Thomas. It sounded like a pay phone, and he wouldn't leave his number." She unzipped her purse and pulled out her car keys. "Who is he?"

Ruth stared at the computer. "I have no idea. He must be a customer, I guess."

"Well, he said he'd call back," Jenny said, then gave her a peck on the cheek. "I didn't know pay phones even still existed. Anyway, see you for brunch tomorrow?"

"Sure thing. Bye honey."

* * *

THE SCENE AT THE BOOKSTORE HAD BEEN A DISASTER and Lucy sat now with a big glass of wine, telling herself to forget it. But it was hard. She couldn't remember the last time she'd been so mortified.

After leaving Tia's, she'd gone home, gotten her car, and driven to Book-World, which was in one of the many strip malls that lined Route 1. Although she was sending review copies of her book out to small bookstores on the east coast, she'd yet to go into a store in person. The moment she walked in, a surge of nerves sent her heart racing.

She headed to the customer service desk.

"Can I help you?" a young man with short black hair, a goatee, and a diamond stud in one nostril asked without looking up from a computer.

"Yes, I'm a local author and I—" her brain froze.

"Oh, we love local authors," he said, looking up with a smile. "What's the name of your book?"

"*A Quiet Wanting*. I brought you a..."

But before she could finish, or hand it to him, he was typing on the computer again, and the book slipped from her sweaty fingers onto the floor. She bent to retrieve it.

"I don't see it here, who's your publisher?"

When she stood, he was looking at her, waiting, the diamond stud glittering from the overhead lights.

"I...it's a small press, actually." She handed him the book.

"So, you're Lucinda Barrett. Nice cover," he said, turning the book over.

See, relax, it's going to be just fine, she told herself.

"I never heard of this publisher."

"Well, they're actually a Print-On-Demand company in California."

He looked at her and his eyebrows shot up. "So it's self-published?"

"Yes, it is, but—"

"I'm sorry, but we can't stock self-published books, store policy."

"Oh, I..." She stood there, flummoxed. "I'd be happy to give you this copy anyway. Maybe you'll like it enough to perhaps change your mind?"

He stared at her for a moment. "Look, you have to realize how many people walk in here every week with self-published books. There's only so much shelf space, and we need to fill it with books that are going to sell, so we can make money and stay in business."

She heard a cough, then someone else whispering behind her, and she wanted to pinch his nose, like her mother used to do when her brothers got fresh. She wanted to tell him that her book was different, if he'd only give her a chance, but he was already back on his computer.

Turning, she raced past the other customers toward the exit, then stopped suddenly. She stood there, looking at the thousands and thousands of books sitting on those shelves, books by bestsellers, authors people had heard of with major publishers. Then she pictured the piles of books in her dining room, where she now sat in front of her laptop. She wished she had even a shred of the certainty and optimism she'd had when she was a girl.

Or was that simply the innocence of youth—that if you tried hard enough, you could make anything happen. Like she did to have a baby. *Oh Lucy, don't go there now*, she told herself. *Stay focused*. Because certain or not, she was plowing forward with this plan. And if nothing happened, then yes, she would do as she'd promised. She would give up writing. Just as she'd given up on having a child.

But the nagging scene at BookWorld kept playing in her head, her screen kept freezing as she continued trying to upload her book cover onto her website, and her frustration mounted, because in the background all she kept hearing was the phone ringing in David's office, like a shrill version of water torture.

She slammed her glass down, deciding to sneak a third cigarette out on the patio, since David wouldn't be home for a while. But the ringing started all over again and she marched instead to his office to turn the damn ringer off. The machine was blinking furiously. Walking around the desk, she saw there were...sweet Jesus, forty-seven messages. Her fingers began pulling through her hair as a weird feeling came over her. Something was horribly wrong. Why would someone keep calling this line over and over? Why wouldn't they call David's office, or his cell if they couldn't reach him? It couldn't possibly be Jason, his new assistant, not that many times.

She hesitated, then pushed the PLAY button. There was a long pause, and she almost hit ERASE before she finally heard a soft laugh, and then a voice so eerie it made her heart stop.

"You're a dead man, Barrett. You're a dead man."

She sank to the chair, horrified. Rewinding the tape to the first message, she played them all, each one a chilling repeat of the one before.

"You're a dead man, Barrett. You're a dead man."

Suddenly the edges of the room began to disappear and she leaned forward in the chair, letting her head hang between her knees as the blood rushed to her face, the beautiful colors on the Oriental rug swimming before her eyes.

3

FROM THE MOMENT SHE'D TOUCHED HIS FINGERS, as they barreled down a runway on the same flight back to New Jersey, when she'd closed her eyes, terrified, reaching for the armrest and finding instead a warm, reassuring hand, Lucy had always felt safe with David. He clasped her hand, a stranger's hand, holding tight until long moments later when she felt the plane level off. She opened her eyes, mortified, only to find a comforting smile.

He introduced himself and told her he was on his way home from a legal seminar in Atlanta. She was returning from a writers' conference in Marietta. He then ordered them both a glass of wine and began asking her all about it. Embarrassed, she confessed that she worked for an accountant but always wanted to be a writer.

"So why are you an accountant?" he'd asked with a smile in his hazel eyes.

"Because when it was time to choose my major for college, and the guidance counselor told me what I could expect to earn as a writer, well, let's just say the writing was on the wall."

David laughed, his eyes crinkling at the corners.

"Anyway, making a living writing fiction is like winning the lottery for someone my age, or any age for that matter. So I write on the side, whenever I can."

"I thought about being an archeologist once, but...I took over my father's law practice instead. You're lucky you can do both. Although I do get my kicks with a metal detector when I have time."

Before the flight was over, she learned he lived in Mendham, New Jersey, not far from where she'd spent much of her childhood in Morristown. He was an attorney with his own one-man office that his father had opened when David was just a boy. He was, perhaps, the most persuasive person she'd ever met. She wound up letting him read the three page short-short story which had won an award at the conference, as she stared out the window at a blanket of thick white clouds just below. She was thrilled by the award, but knew the market for short stories was miniscule and that she needed to start thinking about something bigger. A novel.

She heard him let out a rush of breath and turned. He was smiling.

"Jesus, this is really good."

"Really?"

"I have absolutely no doubt you're going to make it as a writer."

She laughed out loud as she looked at this stranger, David Barrett, not a handsome man, but attractive in his designer suit, his confidence and manner so refreshing from the guys her age. Six months later, when he got down on one knee, holding out an antique platinum ring that had been his grandmother's, he told her it was fate that had brought them together on that plane. He was just thirty, with a law practice, his own home, and a solid future. She was twenty-three years old, just out of college with a mountain of student loans, and still living at home. Of course she said yes.

David wasn't afraid to fly; his hand had just happened to be on the common armrest that day. Lucy often wondered, as she did now, watching the clock, waiting for him to walk in the door as he did every night, how her life might have turned out if she hadn't reached out in desperation and found him. Would she still be alone?

She got up and walked through the kitchen into the yard. The air was heavy with humidity. Just then the entire sky flashed with light. A few moments later, low rumbles of thunder seemed to go on for half a minute. Thank God he'd answered when she called his cell, because she'd nearly dialed the police. He didn't even give her a chance to speak, just quickly assured her he'd be home within the hour. She knew cell phones weren't allowed at the card games.

Another flash of lightning illuminated the house, and then it fell into darkness again. The low tile roof, the arched windows and bits of wrought iron were charming. "A piece of history," David had said when they first saw it and he'd fallen instantly in love. It had taken longer for her, numb as she still was, until it even felt like the possibility of home. Of course it was more than they were looking to spend, being in the heart of the historic district. But David insisted it would all work out and she hadn't seen him that excited in a long time. Maybe one of them being excited was enough.

Sometimes the loss of Ben, their years in Mendham, seemed surreal, as if it had happened in another lifetime. Or perhaps was something she'd read in a book. Six months after that loss, they'd moved here and David insisted that in order to really start over, they had to let go of the past. After a while, he wouldn't even talk about Ben, telling her it was just holding them back, dredging up sadness there was nothing they could do about. But she'd needed to talk, despite finding an escape, and a kind of healing, in her writing. She went for therapy, but David refused.

"Don't push him," her therapist had told her. "People cope in their own ways. Forcing him to come might make him resentful. He'll deal with the loss of your son in his own time. Trust me, you can't bury grief like this forever."

That was when she started smoking again, just two, like a hard-earned reward for making it to the end of each day.

Tonight, the thought of losing David, too, seemed very real. And made Lucy sit back and think about him, about them, for the first time in a long time. To examine the petty differences, the bickering, and distance that had grown between them. Yes, she'd been obsessed with her writing, but David used to admire her passion and drive. She'd accused him right back of being obsessed with building his practice, and she needed to stop that. He was still a relatively new lawyer in a town full of good ole boys, so of course he had to put in insane hours. But it was time they got their marriage back on track. David was everything to her.

And she would quit smoking again. She knew how much he hated it. His father had died of emphysema.

She heard the rumble of a car engine, then saw headlights sweep across the side yard as David pulled into the driveway. She raced into the house and nearly crashed into him as he opened the front door.

"Jesus, Lucy, you scared the shit out of me!"

"Oh, David, I've been worried sick, I—"

"And I told you I'd be home shortly. Guess what?" His face suddenly changed, filled with excitement. "I had a royal flush."

"David, listen—"

"I came in first, beating more than thirty people."

She stood there swaying with exhaustion, wondering if she'd imagined what had happened earlier, because not only did David seem so normal, but despite the fact that it was after midnight and he'd been up since dawn, he didn't seem tired.

"My first hand alone I had trip aces," he said, slipping off his jacket and pumping a fist. "Right then I knew I was on a roll. Do you know what the odds are of getting two hands like—"

"David!"

He looked at her, stunned.

"David, something horrible happened today. Remember your phone ringing before you left? Well, it rang all day and night. There are forty-seven messages on your machine! A man keeps saying 'You're a dead man, Barrett,' over and over."

"What?"

"I think we should call the police."

"You listened to my messages?"

She blinked.

"Lucy, it's just an irate client. You had no right listening to my messages. That's business."

"Are you serious, David? A man threatens your life and you're ticked because I listened to your private messages?"

He shook his head, then came over and put an arm around her, leading her to the couch. They sat and he took her hands.

"People get seriously emotional sometimes, and they want to strike out, and a lot of times it's the attorney they target. You know that."

"I understand, David, I'm not stupid, but this is different. I think you should listen to them. This is not just some pest."

"I will, okay, but believe me, honey, it wouldn't be the first time somebody lost it on me. And if I think it's warranted, I'll notify the police."

"Do you have any idea who it might be?"

He shrugged. "Could be the guy who lost custody in a divorce case last week. Or the brother who's fighting a will, hates his siblings, and thinks nothing in life is fair."

"But nothing quite like this has ever happened before."

He gave her a crooked smile.

"It has?"

"I've had threats, yes, but nothing I couldn't handle. Now forget it. I'll take care of it, okay?"

"Okay," she said, so worn out, so relieved, she just wanted to go to bed. And when she woke the next morning, it all seemed like a bad dream.

* * *

RUTH TRIED TO KEEP HER MIND from drifting as she drove to the lake, but as she made a mental list of all the little tasks ahead of her at the store later that day, like e-mailing Lucinda Barrett and inviting her for a signing, and submitting a rush order for Denise, the high school librarian, who had forgotten about an upcoming book fair, her mind floated off in the direction it always did on this trip: a rehash of her marriage, her failure as a wife, and the gut-wrenching guilt over the last night she had seen her husband alive.

Which was why she avoided going to the lake, because as much as she always tried to remember the good things about her marriage, for her kids' sake, somehow it was always the bad ones that came flooding back at moments like this. Once her friend Hannah had remarked that when Eddie was away on his fishing trips, she would begin to miss him so badly, that after those first few days, it was only the good in him that she could recall. The annoyances seemed to fade with each moment's separation. After all these years apart from Bill, Ruth wished she could say the same.

It was a beautiful drive, though, the blacktop road winding up and down hills and around curves that seemed to go on endlessly. The surrounding woods, littered with boulders and worn rocks, were bursting with new green leaves. You couldn't drive fast, and Ruth found herself remembering the first time she'd taken this drive with Bill.

She was still nineteen, he was nearly twenty-one, and he drove with one hand on the steering wheel, the other squeezing her thigh. The longing inside her had been a glorious ache that shot from her stomach down her legs. They couldn't wait to get there. Still, she kept begging him to slow down. She should have seen it then, there had been warning signs for sure. Bill was so full of life. And reckless at times. But she, quiet, ordinary Ruth, couldn't believe she was with this handsome, funny guy who could have had anyone. For the first time in her life she didn't have a stack of books beside her bed. Bill had burst into her life like a tornado and she never knew which way the wind was going to blow, but in her dull, ordered life, it had been intoxicating. She didn't have time for reading.

She hit the brakes suddenly as a deer wandered into the road, forcing her thoughts in another direction. Thomas. After the little ceremony at the lake, she'd be driving straight to the prison for her book meeting, and would finally find out why Thomas had called. Because he'd never called again. Her gut told her that something had changed, but she had no way of finding out. There'd been no more letters. And prisoners couldn't get calls.

The road narrowed then, veering left, and she slowed again as she approached the lake. A hodgepodge of houses cluttered the land around the lake, from beautiful chalets right on the water's edge, to tiny cabins flung like boxes across the surrounding hills, some of them added onto many times as they went from summer shacks to year-round dwellings. People were walking dogs and children rode bikes as Ruth navigated past the many side streets until she rounded the lake, driving toward the north shore, where the land was plentiful and sloped gradually to the foot of a small ridge of mountains. These were the old fish camps, properties that had been in families for generations.

Ruth wondered what would have happened if she hadn't come here with Bill that day nearly forty-four years ago. What if she'd gone to her class at the community college, as she was supposed to? But Bill had given her that wicked smile, his light blue eyes glittering. "Come on, Ruth, haven't you ever been bad in your entire life?" he'd asked. It was the way he'd said "bad," so softly, so suggestively that it sent a rush of heat through her, and she knew she was on dangerous ground. But it was thrilling, and yes, that day Ruth had been bad. But it had felt so good.

She neared the fish camps and the road pulled away from the water, as the houses were staggered on larger tracts of land. The camp, which had been in Bill's family since his great-grandfather had settled in the area, originally had three cabins, each on an acre. Over the years, two had been sold, until there was just the middle one left. When Bill had died she immediately thought of selling it, but the kids had gotten too upset. Each summer she'd had to take them out here for sleepovers, with fishing and bonfires, until they became teenagers and outgrew the phase. She barely ever came anymore.

Then, after his accident, Colin announced that he wanted to buy back the cabin next door, which Bill's dad had sold back in the sixties. The biggest of the three, it had fallen into disrepair over the years. She asked Colin why he would do such a thing, when she would have gladly given him the other one. He shook his head and smiled, telling her it was too small for year-round living. "Besides, that's Dad's place, and yours," he'd added, "and it always will be." What could she say to that?

She braked as she came to the cluster of tall pines at the beginning of the gravel driveway. Turning in, she drove through the tunnel of green branches and found her children's cars already parked in the clearing. There they were, sitting on the dock down at the water's edge, the three of them huddled close together. It seemed like just yesterday she was watching them jump off that dock, their shrieks of joy echoing off the mountains.

There were no shrieks of joy now.

* * *

RUTH GOT OUT OF HER CAR, glad that Jenny and Alex had come alone, leaving their children and spouses behind. She walked down the long sloping lawn to the dock, which was more like a wide wooden deck. Bill had rebuilt it when Colin was born, wanting it big enough for chairs and blankets and toys for all of them.

Her children turned at her approach, and Jenny stood and walked over.

"Hey, Mom." Her blotchy face was a sure indicator she'd been crying.

"Hi, honey." Ruth put an arm around her as they walked.

"We were just talking about that day you scattered Dad's ashes. How we were so upset and we thought you were crazy."

They stepped onto the wooden dock and Alex stood as well. "Yeah, we thought you were throwing Dad away," he said with a smile she knew was meant to be comforting to her.

"I was crying because I thought the fish were gonna eat him," Colin said with a little laugh.

They'd been so little, Colin just six years old, clutching Bill's battered field guide to birds. They'd come here then, just as they were now, the four of them.

"It was always his favorite place. And even though we'd never talked about it..." she began, and then stopped. Why would they talk of death? They were so young. "Well, I just thought it was where he'd want to be."

"Of course you did the right thing. It's so peaceful," Jenny said.

"Why don't we come out here more?" Alex said softly, almost to himself.

Maybe for the same reasons she didn't. It was just too painful. But in different ways for them.

"Speak for yourself," Colin said, in a teasing voice, to lighten the mood. "I'm here every day now."

Jenny locked eyes with her, and Ruth saw the message there. It had taken nine months for his house to be renovated, and now Colin had been living there for six, without incident. Still, Jenny thought it was a mistake for him to be so far from civilization. Or without neighbors nearby. In case.

Ruth took a deep breath. "All right, then. Why don't we do this."

They'd carried out this ritual several times before. When Bill would have been forty. And then again at fifty. And now sixty-five. A man she couldn't even picture, his face always frozen in time as he'd looked that night he'd walked out of the house for the last time, a handsome man in his early thirties, still in his prime.

"I have a Dad memory," said Alex. He was looking more and more like Ruth's father as he aged, tall and solid, his dark sideburns flecked with gray. "I was nine and he took me hunting with his buddies. I'd gone once before and I...I just didn't get shooting an animal and I started crying. I thought Dad would get upset, but he gave me a hug and told me there were lots of ways to be a man. And that he actually didn't like shooting anything. He just liked the partying."

"You're lucky, I can barely remember what he looked like," Colin said softly. "I have to look at pictures to really see him. But I think my clearest memory is of him whistling every morning before he went to work. It was such a happy sound."

Jenny smiled through her tears. "I remember he brought me a big Valentine one year, this huge red velvet heart-shaped box trimmed with lace. I ate one chocolate every day because I wanted it to last forever."

They waited. Ruth had forgotten, and now she had to think of something.

"I'll never forget how he used to get you all up in the middle of the night on Christmas because he couldn't wait until morning. I would be so tired, I'd roll over and complain, but he didn't care. He'd pick me up and carry me downstairs and then sit me beside the tree. He couldn't wait to see your faces."

"Yeah, remember riding bikes around the house in the middle of the night?" Colin said.

"How about the time I got a skateboard and we went outside while it was pitch dark in our pajamas and coats," Alex said, as Jenny cried softly now.

They made the sign of the cross and together said the Our Father and Hail Mary. Then Colin read aloud, in the same deep voice as his father, the poem by Emily Dickinson that Ruth had found and read at his funeral mass. It was an odd choice, but a desperate one at the time.

"If I can save one heart from breaking,
I shall not live in vain.
If I can ease one life the aching, or cool one pain,
or help one fainting robin unto her nest again,
I shall not live in vain."

When he finished, Jenny handed them each a single daisy, which they tossed one by one into the water. Alex popped the top of the can of beer, which echoed loudly across the lake.

"Here's to you, Dad," he said with a quiver in his voice, as he slowly poured the golden liquid into the lake, "and your favorite things: fish, family, birds and beer."

"Here's to you, Dad," Jenny and Colin repeated.

They stood there a long time, the petals separating from the long stalks of the daisies, a puddle of foam hovering on the surface. Then she heard Colin sigh.

"So what do you think he liked best," he said, "the fish?" The lighthearted tone was back.

"Nah, probably the beer," Alex joked back. "We were three little pains in the asses if I recall correctly."

Jenny had tears streaming down her face.

"It was his family," Ruth managed to say through the lump of grief in her throat. "You three were everything to him."

"You, too, Mom," Colin said.

She bent and hugged him. If only that were true. But what could her children remember? They loved their father, and she made certain they never knew what had really happened between them.

* * *

WHEN LUCY WOKE THAT NEXT MORNING, much later than usual, David had already gone to work. The terror and anxiety of the night before seemed surreal, thanks to his reassurances and the brilliant sunshine streaming in the windows. And once she opened her laptop to check her e-mail, all thoughts of that creepy voice evaporated when she saw the message from a bookstore in New York, one of the original dozen she'd sent review copies to. The subject line read: *Your Fine Novel*. She gasped out loud.

Dear Ms. Barrett,

Several of us in our store have read your fine novel and enjoyed it immensely. It's beautifully written and timely as well. It also hit home with me in a personal way.

If you're able to make it north in the near future for a signing, perhaps we can chat about it over a cup of tea. We'd love to have you.

Also, I'll be recommending your novel to several book clubs. Would you be interested in meeting with them, via phone conference? And do you have book club questions?

Thanks for sending a review copy to our store.

All my best,
Ruth Hardaway, Owner, The Book Lover

P.S. I was unable to locate your publisher through our distributor, could you please forward information?

Her euphoria faded. The Book Lover could certainly order copies from her publisher, the big drawback was that they'd be stuck with any books that didn't sell, unlike with real publishers, where they could simply return them. Lucy knew her only hope was to admit it was self-published and supply the books on consignment, and pray that the owner of The Book Lover wouldn't mind this arrangement. Or change her mind. But this was fantastic news.

She reread the e-mail a few more times, bouncing in her seat and laughing out loud. The store owner was suggesting Lucy's novel to *several* book clubs! It was unbelievable. She called David at the office to tell him the good news, and was surprised when he answered himself.

"I let Jason go this morning," he said. "He was completely unqualified for the job."

"Are you going to hire someone else?"

"Not right away. I can handle it."

"I could come in and—"

"No, no. I'm fine. Just focus on the book."

"Actually that's why I was calling. I've been invited to do a signing at a bookstore in New York, and I want to do it. Do you think that's crazy?"

There was a long pause.

"I know, it's just one store and it's so far away, but it's a start. And they love the book!"

"I think it's a great idea. How else are you going to get the word out there?"

"And David, she's recommending it to a few of her book clubs."

"That's great, Lucy. Listen, I have to go, I've got another line ringing and..."

"Okay."

She hung up the phone and stood there, letting out a small squeal of joy. Then she typed a reply: *Yes, I would love to come and do a signing at your store. Since my publisher is small and doesn't take returns, I'd be happy to supply any copies on consignment, if that's okay with you.* Hopefully that would do it.

Then she realized she didn't have book club questions. How could she have overlooked that? And she still had to finish the website. Suddenly she felt overwhelmed by everything she needed to accomplish by the launch. Her insides were racing, Ruth Hardaway's beautiful words playing in her mind over and over. This was her first big break.

4

L UCY ARRIVED AT SERENDIPITY AN HOUR EARLY to help her boss set up, but Kate already had trays of appetizers arranged on some of the fancy dishes they sold, and a cut glass punch bowl filled with champagne cocktail.

"Oh, Kate, it all looks beautiful."

"Well, maybe we'll start to move some of these items if people see how they can be used."

Kate looked gorgeous in a flowing chartreuse caftan, her hair pulled back in a chignon. Tall and slender, she had skin the color of caramel and was descended from some of the first slaves brought to St. Augustine.

"I hope the rain stops," Lucy said. It had been pouring for several hours and she knew that lack of nearby parking could definitely hamper her turnout.

"Let's have a toast," Kate said, while Lucy stood there looking out the window at the empty street, her insides racing with excitement.

Two years ago, Kate Viall had taken a chance and hired her after she'd finished the book and given up on getting it published. Lucy had no retail experience, but knew she needed something different. She'd been hiding from the world since they'd moved, first making beds at the B&B, then cloistered in the house writing alone. In this lovely gift shop, with a constant flow of people and Kate's easy demeanor, Lucy had felt herself coming back to life a little bit each day. She threw herself into creating window displays, rearranging shelves of stale merchandise for better eye appeal, and crafting press releases to introduce a new line or a special event.

Six months later, Kate had made her manager and opened a second store in Georgia. When she wasn't working, Lucy continued to write, trying to improve her novel.

Now Kate handed her a crystal flute, then touched it with her own glass.

"Here's to you, Lucy, and the success of your novel."

Lucy smiled and took a sip.

"Come on, you look like you just lost your best friend."

She shrugged. "Just a little nervous, that's all."

"It's going to be fine. We already sold two books."

Lucy couldn't help picturing the thousands on the shelves of BookWorld.

"Where's David?" Kate asked, as she flipped on more lights to combat the darkening skies.

"Working late, as usual. He'll be here soon."

"My niece used him for her closing, you know. She just loved him."

Just then a group of people approached the store and Lucy held her breath, but they continued by. What if no one came at all? Then the door opened and an older couple came in, huddled under a large golf umbrella. They stood a moment, looking around.

"Are you the author?" the woman asked.

"Yes, I am."

"I told my husband we had to come, no matter how hard it's raining. I picked up your book here two days ago and finished it this morning. I loved it."

Lucy had to restrain herself to keep from jumping up and down.

"I actually cried at the end, and I never cry," the woman went on, taking a copy of the book out of her bag. "Would you please sign it? My name is Laura."

As she signed and Laura chattered away, Lucy noticed a few more people walk in. She heard Kate tell them they were launching a new novel by a local author. As they sauntered over, Lucy handed the signed book to Laura, who thanked her. It was a thrilling moment! She was feeling like a real author now! One of the tourists picked up a book and stood a long moment, reading the back cover. Lucy wasn't sure if she should say something to fill the growing silence.

"It's really a good book," she said with a giggle, "and I promise I'm not biased."

The young woman smiled, and without a word put the book down and walked out with her friends.

Well, that was awkward, Lucy thought. Gushing about a piece of pottery was definitely easier than plugging her own book.

A short while later, Lucy's breath caught as another group walked in and she recognized acid-tongued Regan from her old writers' workshop.

"Hey, Lucy, long time," Regan said. "We saw the article and wanted to come and say congratulations. Nice to see one of us finally made it."

Regan had three novels and a memoir under her belt, all unpublished, and they were actually pretty good.

The short woman in the back picked up a book and said, "That's a great cover. Did they let you have any say in it?"

A hot wave of dread had been slowly growing in Lucy's stomach since Regan walked in. "Yes, actually it was my vision."

"I'm on my fourth novel and still can't even get a nibble from an agent," the other woman said, handing her the book. "Could you sign it to me, Valerie, and write 'good luck with your own novel?'"

She nodded and picked up her pen, not daring to look up at Regan.

"Did you submit it right to this publisher, or did you have an agent?"

"No, I didn't have an agent," she said, writing really slowly. "I...um... dealt directly with the publisher." Which was true.

When she finally handed Valerie her signed book, she could feel Regan's eyes boring into her.

"Did you publish this yourself?"

Oh, the hell with it, she thought. "Yes. I was tired of the publishing world telling me my book wasn't good enough and decided to take matters into my own hands. And I deliberately didn't choose one of the big self-publishers because I didn't want people to pick it up and..." she hesitated, searching for the right words.

"And assume it's no good?" Regan said.

"Actually, that's right. I want people to just read it, with no prejudice."

A slow smile broke out on Regan's round face. "Well, you had us fooled there. We were actually discussing the pros and cons of self-publishing at our last meeting. I mean, sure, you can self-publish online for free in some cases, but getting a real book printed, like yours, costs money, and in the end, who's really making the money? Not the writers."

Lucy looked right into Regan's eyes now. "I want my book out there. When you write, it's for someone to read, not just in a workshop. Not just your relatives and friends."

"But don't you get it? The only people who ever buy these books are your relatives and friends, because nobody else even knows about it."

"Actually, I have several bookstores already asking to carry the book." Well, actually one. "They've read it and like it enough to put it on their shelves and even recommend it to their book clubs."

They were all staring at her now.

"In fact, I've actually got a signing scheduled in New York and I'm putting together a book tour of my own." Again, partly true, but as she said it, she realized it was exactly what she needed to do. Orchestrate a book tour. If The Book Lover wanted a signing, why couldn't others?

"Well, I give you credit," Valerie said. "You must really believe in your book."

"I do," she said, then sat down at the table, because her legs were trembling.

Imagine her further shock when Regan handed over the book she'd been holding all that time. "I'll take it."

"Thanks for coming," Lucy said a few minutes later, letting her breath out as they headed up St. George Street.

But then she looked at her watch. There was just a half hour left. Where on earth was David?

* * *

RUTH PULLED INTO THE PARKING LOT AND TURNED OFF HER CAR. She sat there a moment, looking at the high metal fence, the double row of razor wire that ran around the perimeter of the prison, the high brick guard towers spread across the campus. It never failed to send a shiver up her body, no matter how many times she'd been here over the years.

She tried to imagine, not for the first time, what it must be like to walk into that cold, concrete building, knowing you wouldn't walk out again for fifteen years. She would probably go insane in a matter of weeks. But Thomas was so quiet. At times he seemed so...serene. It was an odd way to describe a prisoner.

She looked at the clock on her dashboard. Five more minutes. She wondered if Thomas, sitting in his cell, was counting the moments, too.

The idea to sell books to the inmates had been Jenny's. It was tossed out one Christmas brunch while Jenny and Alex carried dishes into her kitchen. Both had helped in the store over the years and knew the never-ending challenges of keeping the place afloat. Holidays were often spent talking shop for a while, throwing out moneymaking ideas, until Ruth brought it to a halt, usually as the food was being laid on the table.

They'd been discussing ways to get more people into the store.

"Hey," Jenny had said with a laugh, as she scraped a plate. "Who says you need to get them into the store? What about going out with your books, kind of like the Bookmobile?"

"And where on earth would I be taking my books?" Ruth had asked.

"Well...how about the prison?" Then she added with a chuckle, "They're kind of a captive audience, aren't they? My friend Andrea's husband works there. Maybe he can get you an in."

Ruth had dismissed it with a wave of her hand, then changed the subject. She didn't like talking about her problems with the kids. But a week later, when she saw a photo in the local paper of a student from a nearby college volunteering for a literacy program for inmates, the idea started to take root.

She'd come here that first day with a throat so dry, her first words were barely audible, as she walked in with a carton of books and a rehearsed speech. After a thorough vetting and some personal references, The Book Lover became the sole provider of books for these prisoners.

Her mind turned to her last trip to the prison to take book orders. She had sat across the table from Thomas and her eyes kept drifting to his bruised hand. When she looked up, he was staring at her. His look deepened and his face turned pink. Ever so slowly his hand began to glide across the table, until their fingers were barely an inch apart. Her own fingers trembled, but suddenly they were moving toward his, nearly touching, when the guard, who'd been standing in the doorway with his back to them talking on his cell, suddenly snapped it shut.

Thomas quickly reached back for the order sheet that was in front of him. Ruth began tapping on the calculator once again. The guard glanced at them, then turned toward the door and opened his phone once more.

After a few moments of quiet between them, Thomas said in a low voice, "Remember this one?" He slid the sheet over, and she took it quickly, not daring to repeat what had almost happened.

"Ah, someone ordered *A Tale of Two Cities*," she read and smiled back. It thrilled her that so many of them at least tried the classics. "I remember when you did. You weren't sure you'd like Dickens."

"Turned out I loved Dickens," he said, looking straight into her eyes.

"You read everything by him after that."

"Just like you did your freshman year of high school."

"You remembered that?"

"I remember everything about you, Ruth," he'd said in barely a whisper, his fingers slowly moving toward hers again. She watched transfixed as his hand lifted, as it was about to cover hers, and a wild longing soared in her chest. She closed her eyes, waiting...

Then she heard the guard close the door.

Opening her eyes, she found Thomas's hand gone. Her face must have registered disappointment, because he said, "Don't worry, next month'll be better, I'm sure."

She knew he wasn't talking about the orders.

Just then a prison clerk came out wheeling a cart, stopping at her car to load her books. She followed him inside through the security check, dumping her purse as well as her tote bag on a conveyor belt, then walking through the metal detector, something that was now rote for her. She deposited her car keys at the final checkpoint and was then led by a guard she'd never met before down a green cinder block corridor to the library, a small room with no windows.

She walked in, her eyes scanning the long table surrounded by chairs, landing on the one at the head where Thomas usually sat waiting for her. It was empty.

* * *

LUCY NOTICED THE RAIN HAD STOPPED and the street musicians had taken up their places on St. George Street again, one of them strumming a haunting melody on an acoustic guitar in front of the shop across the street. She marveled again at how good some of these people were who simply sat on a sidewalk all day with a hat on the ground for tips. And it hit her—was she really any different from him? How many people in the world have artistic ambitions and ever really achieve success?

"Well, I rang up four books so far," Kate said, coming up behind her.

"Better than zero."

"We've got a little time left, and the rain is over, so let's think positive, okay?"

She nodded, then spent the next minutes walking circles around the signing table, straightening shelves, looking at her watch and waiting for David to walk in. With a big bouquet of flowers and a face that begged forgiveness for being late. To buy a copy of her book, as he'd promised, and have her sign it. And finally read it.

Kate was considerate enough not to bring up David's absence as she locked up. Lucy gave her a quick hug in thanks.

"Good luck with the third store. And I'm sorry to abandon you at such an inconvenient time."

"I knew when I hired you it wasn't going to be forever. Besides, aren't we doing the same thing? Going after our dreams? I'm really glad you're doing this."

"So am I," Lucy said, and then managed a laugh. "I think."

"Don't do this halfway. You've got to give it everything, promise?"

"I will. I keep thinking of that woman tonight, Laura, who loved the book. And Ruth, the bookseller in New York. If they like it, how many other readers would fall in love with it, if only they had a chance to read it?"

"Atta girl!"

Then they turned and walked in opposite directions to where their cars were parked. A moment later, she stopped in front of the guitarist. He wasn't a kid, probably late thirties or even forty, and she saw a handsome face beneath the beard and the long, straggled hair. He began another slow, beautiful song.

"You're an amazing musician," she said, tossing the pile of bills from her book sales into his hat. He looked up at her and smiled. And she wondered, was this how David saw her?

It was nearly dark, wispy gray clouds skittering across the sky as she got in her car. She sat there a moment, then hit the steering wheel in frustration. She pulled out her cell and called the house. No answer. Then she called David's cell, which was turned off. Driving out of the lot she made a right, not toward home, but to David's office. How could he not have shown up, knowing how important this was to her? This wasn't like David. But she had to admit, so much about him lately wasn't like the David she knew.

Turning onto Cuna Street, she saw the white Victorian up ahead. His office, which was the entire first floor, was all lit up. She was so intent on David, she didn't notice at first the line of cars parked on both sides of the street in front of the building. As she slowed, she recognized a St. Augustine Police Department Cruiser with the lights off. A black sedan with lettering on the door was from the St. John's County Detective Bureau. She sat there in the middle of the street, her eyes travelling from the dark, empty cars to the long windows of David's office, where the shadows of men passed back and forth.

She couldn't move. She couldn't breathe. All she could think of was that eerie voice on David's voicemail. The soft laughter, the chilling words.

You're a dead man, Barrett.

5

RUTH PARKED IN THE MUNICIPAL LOT, and clipped on Sam's leash, and she could swear that Sam was smiling, her tongue hanging sideways out of her mouth. Sam loved spending the day with Ruth at the store.

First they walked up Main Street to Elaine's. Ruth was amazed she didn't even need a sweater today. For early May it felt more like June, and she hoped it would last. It wasn't unusual to get a frost in Warwick this far into spring. But the flowering pear trees lining the sidewalks in town were a stunning vision of white blossoms. The window boxes at Elaine's were bursting with yellow daffodils and purple pansies.

"Morning, Ruth," Elaine called over the counter as she came in with Sam.

Elaine had left a corporate job seven years ago to open the small restaurant. With leather booths and a long counter with round stools, it had the charm and character of a much-loved, and used, diner.

"You on for the meeting next week?" Elaine asked, as she turned for the coffee pot.

"Sure am. I just hope we get something accomplished this time."

The Downtown Warwick Revitalization Committee had been formed six months ago, but little progress had been made since, except for the longer hours to compete with the malls. Which didn't seem to be doing much.

Elaine handed Ruth a large coffee, then looked over her shoulder to make sure Hannah wasn't in earshot. "We just have to keep Eddie from blowin' steam for two hours and maybe we can. I know his appliance business is hurting from that box store opening, but hey, we're all hurting, aren't we?"

"I can't argue with you."

Then Elaine noticed Sam sitting patiently, her tail thumping the floor in anticipation. She knelt down and gave her a biscuit and a pat on the head.

"What's on your agenda today?" Elaine asked, as Sam savored her treat.

"Oh, the usual. Getting ready for an author signing next week. Then Megan's going to show me some ideas she has for My Face. Or is it Space-book?"

Elaine laughed. "It's Facebook and My Space."

"I know. She thinks I'm an old fart. She's always got ideas and according to her I'm always shooting them down. We're a bookseller, you know? I don't want things to get too complicated. Anyway," she said, "hopefully this heavenly day will bring people into town for a nice lunch and a good book."

"My idea of heaven is a good book and a chair parked at the beach."

"Amen. Only when was the last time either of us took time for something like that?"

"I thought just doing breakfast and lunch would give me a bit of a life after the corporate rat race. By the time we get cleaned up and prepped for the next day, guess what?"

"You're ready for bed. Sounds like my life."

Sam licked the last few crumbs off the floor, then looked up at Ruth, waiting.

"Ever think of retiring?" Elaine asked with raised eyebrows.

"Are you kidding? For what?"

As Ruth turned, Hannah came by carrying a tray loaded with pancakes. "Oh, hey Ruth," she called out, "I was just thinking about you. Can you wait a sec?"

Ruth sipped her coffee as Hannah delivered her platters, then deposited her empty tray on the counter. "Whew, my knees are screaming. Listen, I was going to stop by later and see if you might have some time this week to come over. I've got my class reunion coming up, and I wondered if you'd give me your opinion on an outfit I got."

"Sure, how about Monday?"

"Okay. It's a little different, a bit more daring, actually, than what I normally wear, but I thought Eddie might like it. I want to surprise him."

"That's great," she said, wondering if Deepak had instigated the bold wardrobe choice.

"Oh, I finished the Chopra book," Hannah said, as if reading her mind. "I did like it, but not all of it..." Her words trailed off as a customer began waving at her.

"I'll call you Monday. We'll talk about it then. "

Ruth walked up Main Street to her store, shaking her head. How was it she was always giving advice, to Hannah and so many of her customers, when she had no certainty at all regarding herself.

She unlocked the door, walked inside and flipped on the lights. Sam nestled into her doggie bed under the counter for a little snooze. Ruth checked the phone for messages, and found three, for special orders. There were also two hang-ups. Ruth listened to them again, trying to discern background noise as butterflies swooped through her stomach. It was five weeks since she'd gone to the prison and Thomas wasn't there. Not a night went by that she didn't wonder what had happened to him.

Just then, the lights in the store went out. Ruth groaned. Was it Hazel, their ghost? Or the circuit breaker again? She walked back to the bathroom/storage room, and Sam got up and followed her. Opening the electrical panel, she saw the main breaker had tripped. She flipped it once and the lights flickered on, then went out again. She flipped the switch once more, the lights came on, and she stood there waiting. They stayed on. But this situation wasn't good. And it was the third time this month.

Her landlord, Jeff, knew about the problem but had yet to send an electrician over, hoping that if he waited long enough she'd just take care of it herself, as she usually did. But then there would be the battle when she deducted it from his ridiculous rent. The phone began to ring and though she wasn't open yet, she ran to the front counter, grabbing it on the fifth ring.

"Good morning, this is The Book Lover. How may I help you?"

"Ruth?"

Her breath stopped.

"Ruth? It's Thomas."

Her hand went to her throat. It was so odd, actually hearing his voice on the phone.

"Thomas. I…I heard you'd called."

She could hear him let out a long breath. As if he'd been holding it until she spoke.

"I'm sorry I wasn't able to call back. You know how it is here." And then he gave a rueful little chuckle.

"Oh yes, I understand," she said, with what she hoped was a light tone, as well.

"I'm sorry I wasn't at the book meeting."

"I was worried."

"Things…" he paused, and again she could hear him pull in a long breath. "I was wondering if I could talk to you."

"Of course. I've got all the time you need, we haven't even opened yet."

"No, not on the phone. I need to see you. Can you come here? I've got scheduled visiting hours Monday."

"I..." She didn't know what to say.

"Ruth, I'd like to speak with you in private."

She hesitated again. Going to the prison to sell books was one thing. Fantasizing about an inmate as if he were a character was another. But going to visit him, one on one? What would her children think?

"All right, I'll come."

She hung up, staring out the front window across Main Street in a daze. What could he possibly have to tell her? Perhaps he would no longer be her book liaison. That would be awful. Or perhaps it was something more personal. She couldn't help thinking of how their hands had nearly touched the last time she saw him. Even now that memory ignited a thrill of anticipation, which was quickly dispelled by a rap on the door. Megan peered through the glass.

Get a grip, Ruthie, she cautioned herself as she went to unlock the door. *It's not like you're going on a date.*

* * *

"THIS FECKIN' COMPUTER IS SLOWER THAN MOLASSES," Megan hissed later that morning as she sat with Ruth, showing her the Facebook page she had created for the store. "No way you can manage a new computer?"

Ruth shook her head.

Ever since her trip to Ireland last year, Megan was into Irish slang, peppering conversations with it whenever possible. Feck wasn't as bad as fuck, Ruth knew, but still, it was essentially the same thing. She said nothing now. Megan was right about the old desktop, though.

"What about on a payment plan, you know, a little each month. Or maybe, leasing?"

"I'll think about it." No matter how much Megan understood about the bookselling business, there were some things Ruth preferred to keep to herself. She didn't bother reminding Megan about the hours she'd cut last month.

Finally the page loaded, a picture of the outside of The Book Lover prominently displayed, and under it the store's goal: *To be your destination bookstore. Find your favorite read, or experience the joys of a "hand sold" book, one personally recommended to suit your tastes by booksellers who actually read.*

"Maybe you should take out the word 'actually,' Megan. It sounds a bit, oh, insulting?"

"Whatever," Megan said quickly.

"Well, I think it looks nice, and hopefully we'll get something out of it. Now I'm going over to Shades & Shapes in a little while. Do you mind? It's been slow, and I'll run Sam home when I leave." After talking to Thomas, she'd called Dee at the salon, who told her to come in today.

"*Really*?" Megan asked dramatically, her eyebrows raised.

"Don't start," Ruth laughed. "Nothing radical, just a trim." And, she thought, maybe something to cover the gray. "Anyway, I've got all the new boxes placed near the shelves for stacking, if you could get that done. The ad for the Gazette is right here on the counter."

"Oh, that's right, Lucinda Barrett," Megan said. "I started her book. It's brilliant."

Brilliant was another word Megan had added freely to her repertoire since Ireland, the Irish equivalent of her generation's "amazing."

The bell over the door tinkled just then and Ruth turned to see Bertha Piakowski coming in with a large brown paper bag in her hand. Each month, Bertha came in for the latest canine mystery, always carrying a generous bag filled with her homemade pierogies.

"Oh Bertha, you lifesaver," Ruth said. For the past half hour her stomach had felt as if it were gnawing itself in hunger.

"You know I can't resist those, Bertha." Megan was on a special macrobiotic diet lately, and Ruth was pretty sure the ingredients of Bertha's pierogies were not on it.

"Oh, live a little," Bertha chastised Megan.

Ruth grabbed Bertha's special order from the shelf as Megan tore open the bag.

"*A Pregnant Paws,*" Bertha read aloud when Ruth handed her the book. "Is it a good one?"

"Kris says it's her favorite of all the canine mysteries."

Ruth bit into a pierogi and moaned in pleasure. They were crispy on the outside, with a glaze of butter, and the inside a soft explosion of potatoes and cheese. "Talk about comfort food. You could probably open a chain of pierogi shops and get rich."

Bertha laughed then held up the new book. "I spent my whole life cooking for a mob. I just want to read now."

As they savored her pierogies, Bertha paged through the novel.

"Okay," Bertha said, laying it back on the counter, satisfied. "Now, when you ladies are full, I need your help. Two books for birthday presents. And then, I have a baby shower next week and they're doing a wishing well where you bring in your favorite children's book. Isn't that a clever idea?"

Megan locked eyes with Ruth. "That *is* brilliant," she said. "We'll have to mention it in the newsletter. It hasn't gone out yet. And..." Ruth could see the wheels turning in her brain, "we should probably hang a poster about it back in the children's section, to give people the idea."

"It is brilliant," Ruth admitted.

Bertha smiled. "Don't you ladies just love your job?"

"We sure don't do it for the big bucks," Ruth said, and they all laughed.

"Ruth, I'll help Bertha, you've got to go," Megan said. "Your hair? Remember?"

"Oh, you're right."

She grabbed her purse and clipped on Sam's leash. As she walked out the door, she heard Megan call out, "Be brave, Ruth."

* * *

DEE WAS RUNNING LATE. Ruth couldn't complain, since Dee had squeezed her in. But after waiting half an hour, paging through books of ridiculous styles, she wondered what she was really doing there. Why should it matter how she looked when she went to see Thomas? Just as she was getting up to head back to the store, Dee called over to her.

"Ruth, go change into a gown, I'll be with you in just a few minutes."

As she walked back to the bathroom, Ruth watched Dee's eyes following her in the wall of mirrors, assessing her hair with a look of glee. Oh shit, she thought, as she unbuttoned her blouse and tied the black smock around her waist. Maybe letting Dee at her hair wasn't such a good idea.

But as she looked at herself in the bright, unforgiving mirror of the little bathroom, her unrestrained hair a long, wild bush around her face, she thought maybe letting go a little was just what she needed.

Having her hair washed and her scalp massaged was heaven, and she closed her eyes. But when it was time to assess the color, as Dee stood there explaining foils and glazes and highlights, Ruth began to get nervous.

"Let's just give it a trim."

Dee stood there shaking her head. "How about we take baby steps. What do you say to a temporary color, just to cover the gray? That's it."

Ruth hesitated.

"Jesus, Ruth, it'll wash out in eight weeks. It's no commitment at all."

Slowly she nodded.

The phone rang, and as Dee went to answer it, Ruth thought maybe that was her real problem. Except for the bookstore, when was the last time she'd made a commitment to anything? She looked at herself, imagining the gray gone, her dull black hair alive and lustrous as it once was, maybe a little bang, although with her curly hair, bangs were always a disaster. But every women's magazine said that after a certain age they were *de rigeur*.

She realized, suddenly, that Dee was talking quite loudly.

"No. No, she can't." A silence. "No, I'm not going to do that." Another silence. "Fine, but she'll probably never come back." Dee turned to her. "It's for you. The store."

She walked over and picked up the phone.

"Hey Ruth, it's Megan."

"What's wrong?"

"That author, Lucinda Barrett, is here, and she's freakin' out."

"What?"

"She thinks her signing's today. I told her she's wrong, it's not until next week, and she keeps asking where you are, but..."

"Of course it's next week, I just finished the ad, remember?"

"Can you hurry please? We're swamped all of a sudden with kids after school, all looking for things for some weird project, and now she's locked herself in the loo."

Sometimes Megan did act twenty-three. Ruth just wished this wasn't one of them.

"It's okay, Megan, I'll be there in a few minutes."

"But you have to promise me you'll go back and let Dee finish then?"

Ruth couldn't help smiling. Megan must truly be desperate to make her abort the long-awaited makeover.

She pulled her wet hair up in a clip, went in the bathroom and buttoned up her blouse, then walked back to the store, wondering all the way there what she was about to face with Lucinda Barrett.

6

L UCY CLOSED THE BATHROOM DOOR AND COLLAPSED on a worn brown couch, mortified, her insides vibrating as if she were still driving. Oh God, what had she done? What was she thinking even coming here?

She'd traveled a thousand miles over the past five days with The Book Lover as her goal. This event was a beacon, a tiny shred of sanity that kept pulling her north, because somehow she needed life to make sense again.

The night of her book launch, when she sat in her car in front of David's office, trembling violently, her first thought was that her husband was dead. That the mad man on the phone had gotten him. When a policeman came out to see who was stopped in the street for so long, he found her retching dry heaves. Gently, he helped her out of the car, sat her on the curb where she pulled in the cool night air. He kept reassuring her that her husband was alive.

It was only later that the rest of what he said, the truth, began to sink in. And as it did, her world began to slowly implode, like a skyscraper that crumples to dust in an unbelievable matter of moments.

If she'd tried to write that scene, and everything else she then learned, she'd probably be lambasted in a workshop: *that's not believable for that character;* or *it's too much; revise and take some of it out.* If only she could. Her bitter laugh rang out in the bathroom now as she thought of the old adage—truth is stranger than fiction. Which she should have known because her own childhood was littered with such incidents.

But David, her David...who would have thought he'd be capable of something like this? It was almost worse than him being dead, because this was deliberate.

There was the shock at first, brutal and numbing, as if you couldn't even feel your face no matter how hard you pinched it. She couldn't eat, sleep, write, walk, or do anything to function in the days and weeks afterward, except breathe somehow. Then, slowly, the numbness wore off and a brief—at times violent—anger set in, and there was something familiar about it. She recognized, eventually, because she'd gone through this before, the stages of grief from when they'd lost Ben. But this...this was a different kind of grief, one she couldn't quite wrap herself around. What he had done, all of it, a betrayal.

Staring now at the faded floral wallpaper in the bookstore bathroom, the tiny white blossoms began to swim before her eyes. She leaned back and took a deep breath. She closed her eyes and the room began to spin. Rubbing her temples, she wondered what on earth to do now. But she was too exhausted to even get up, much less make a decision. She'd thought no further than this day, this event, something she could control in her new future alone. Yet she knew that in the eyes of anyone who knew what had happened, this journey would have seemed frivolous and crazy.

She slid down on the couch, laying her head on one arm, resting her feet on the other. Her body felt as if it were still moving. She took another long breath and closed her eyes, and just as sleep enveloped her like a soft, warm quilt, she thought: *Thank God Ruth hadn't been there.*

OPENING HER EYES, Lucy had no idea for a moment where she was.

Oh sweet Jesus, she was in the bathroom at the bookstore. She bolted up off the couch and looked at her watch, horrified to see she'd been asleep for more than a half hour! Still groggy, she gripped the edge of the sink and splashed cold water on her face. These people were going to think she was crazy. Showing up like a ditz on the wrong day. Locking herself in their bathroom and falling asleep like some homeless person. If it weren't so pathetic she might have laughed at the irony, because she was sort of homeless, wasn't she?

She ran her fingers through her hair, spritzed herself with the calming lavender aromatherapy spray she kept in her purse now, and opened the bathroom door, praying no one would notice her.

A woman stood there, startled, her hand in the air as if about to knock.

"Lucinda?"

She opened her mouth, but nothing came out.

"I'm Ruth Hardaway," the woman said, smiling hesitantly.

She was tall with beautiful wide brown eyes that narrowed now with obvious worry. Her long hair fell halfway down her back in wet ringlets. Obviously she'd been interrupted at a bad time.

"I'm sorry, I...I..." Lucy felt her throat close.

"Are you all right?"

As she stared at Ruth Hardaway, Lucy felt a tear slip down her cheek, and then another tear, and in a moment she was gasping for breath as she tried to control herself.

Ruth took her arm and pulled her back into the bathroom, closing the door. Lucy sank onto the closed toilet seat, burying her face in her hands. In the weeks since her world had fallen apart, she hadn't let herself cry, except for that night in front of David's office. Even then, she had stopped quickly, not letting the policeman see her. And now, in front of this stranger, a bookseller she wanted to impress, she was falling apart.

Ruth's hand stayed on her arm the entire time, never letting go, which only made her cry harder. But the release felt so good, as every emotion that had been lodged in her chest like a balloon filling with air until she thought she might explode, drained from her body. Finally spent, she looked up at Ruth, who held out a tissue with a sympathetic smile.

"I'm sorry. I know I'm early..." Lucy said, shaking her head in embarrassment.

"Well," Ruth said, "I'd hate to see what would happen if you were late."

Lucy's mouth opened, and then...then she started to laugh, and so did Ruth.

* * *

AT FIRST SHE SAID NO TO RUTH'S OFFER TO STAY OVERNIGHT. But when the skies turned pewter and the wind began to howl and Ruth mentioned there would be storms all night, Lucy finally agreed. But as Ruth closed the front door of her old colonial, which hadn't even been locked, Lucy stood in the foyer in awkward silence, regretting her decision. It all felt so strange.

A small beagle trotted into the hall and sat at Ruth's feet, eyeing her suspiciously.

"Lucy, meet Samantha. One spoiled dog."

"Hello there, Sam." Lucy bent to pet her, but before her hand touched the dog, she turned and marched back out of the room. "Are you sure about this? I could easily find a hotel."

"Don't be silly. I have three empty bedrooms upstairs. And if you don't mind grilled cheese—it's what I usually have on Saturday nights because I'm too pooped to think about cooking—then it's absolutely no trouble at all. It's nice to have the company. Sam doesn't talk much."

"I don't think Sam's all that happy I'm here."

"Oh, she'll get over it."

Ruth was nothing like she'd imagined, not the small, prim, bookish-looking woman her writer's mind had conjured. She had a long face, a wide, thin mouth. Amber crystals dangled from her ears. Ruth was the best kind of character, a paradox—plain, yet attractive in her own way. The Earth mother, a character readers would love. Lucy looked at Ruth now, and it was then Lucy really noticed her eyes, a soft brown surrounded by laugh lines, or worry lines.

While Ruth riffled through her mail, Lucy looked around. Pictures covered the walls: a handsome son in uniform, a daughter on her wedding day, toothless smiles of grandchildren and then school pictures as they aged. They walked through the foyer, past a living room crowded with worn furniture, and then the dining room, where she stopped. On the sideboard enough white dishware was laid out to supply a restaurant.

"Oh, I have my family for brunch every other Sunday," Ruth explained and with a laugh added, "and there the dishes still sit."

"You must have a big family."

"If everyone makes it, my three children and all the grandkids, that makes twelve, give or take. My son Alex sometimes brings his mother-in-law, and my grandchildren might bring a friend or two."

"It sounds lovely, but it must be a lot of work."

Ruth shrugged. "It is, but it's become a tradition. I want to keep my kids close to each other, you know?"

No, Lucy wanted to say, *that's something I'll never know.*

As Ruth headed into the kitchen Lucy stood there, imagining the huge family crowded around the big oval table eating and talking, Ruth at the head, flushed with the warmth of what surrounded her. Then she walked into the kitchen. It, too, had a dated but comfortable feel—old pine cabinets, white Formica counters, an oak trestle table with four ladder back chairs with red checked cushions tied to the seats. Canisters with painted roosters on the front were lined up next to the toaster and coffee maker. This was a used kitchen. A loved kitchen.

Under the kitchen table, Sam lay with her head on crossed paws, eyes half closed, watching her.

"What can I do to help?"

"Nothing, it'll just take a few minutes. Why don't you go put your things upstairs? It's the first room on the right. Nothing fancy, but the bed's good."

Ruth turned from the stove. "Would you like a cup of tea? Or how about a glass of wine?"

Her hair had dried and she'd pulled it back at some point with a rubber band, but curling wisps of gray framed her face. Lucy imagined what her mother might say. After her father left, her mother had gone to beauty school and supported them working long hours in a beauty parlor. She'd no doubt cluck her tongue and say that Ruth was in desperate need of a makeover. But as Lucy looked at her, Ruth looked more like a Madonna—the luminous face, the kind brown eyes that curved down slightly. Her hair like a halo. Lucy wouldn't have changed a thing.

"Actually, I'd love a glass of wine. I'll just put my things upstairs and be back in a moment."

Lucy had never seen so many books in a house. They were everywhere, and when she went upstairs to the spare room, Ruth's door was ajar and she saw stacks of books on both nightstands, the dresser, and piles on the floor, as well.

She took a cigarette from her purse, then sat on the edge of the bed in the blue bedroom and looked around, putting it to her lips unlit, taking a drag, then letting it out as slowly as she could. The plaster ceiling was littered with cracks. The walls were navy, a dreary color, and the furniture was old and sparse. And then she realized it was the color of a teenage boy's room, remembering Jake's red, white and blue phase so long ago. On top of the dresser sat another assortment of framed photos, a blond boy with a fishing pole, and then older, in a high school football uniform; and there he was in yet another, on the porch steps of this house with an ice cream cone, sitting between a darker-haired boy, no doubt his older brother, who looked like Ruth, and then the blonde sister. She tried to imagine a younger Ruth here in this house with three children. She'd never mentioned a husband.

It was dark out now, and as she sat on the edge of the bed in a stranger's house far from home, a slippery feeling rose in Lucy's chest. She lay back on the bed and closed her eyes, imagining that she wasn't here in Warwick, New York. She was sitting on the beach on Anastasia Island. It was early morning, just before dawn, and she was waiting for the sun to break on the horizon. This was the game she'd begun playing since these bouts of anxiety started hitting her.

She could almost hear the calming lap of the ocean, the haunting cry of gulls. The waves, as you stared at them for long stretches while searching for dolphins, could be hypnotic, and she let herself fall into the rhythm of those phantom waves, willing her heart to slow down. She felt the grip of sleep pulling her again, as it had earlier, but this time she stood up quickly and slipped the unlit cigarette back in her purse.

She'd have a glass of wine, maybe two, then plead exhaustion—which was true—and go right to bed. She'd get up early and slip out before Ruth was up. An early departure would be excused, especially if she left a nice note.

After today's debacle, how could she possibly come back for the signing?

7

W HEN SHE'D NEARLY CRASHED INTO LUCY coming out of the bathroom at the store, Ruth knew immediately that Megan had misread her. Hadn't she seen that dazed expression often enough on her own face just after Bill's death? When the world as she knew it had been pulled out from beneath her? Worried about everything, from how she'd pay the bills to her children's emotional health. And worst of all, wondering if it had been her fault.

Now she sat across from Lucy, who was making polite conversation as she nibbled around the crust of her sandwich like a child with an old-fashioned pixie cut.

"Have you always lived here in Warwick?" Lucy asked.

"Yes, just a few miles out of town. My father was a dairy farmer, as was his father and grandfather. Our family was on that farm for generations. But although I used to fantasize about living in all the beautiful settings I read about, when I got married, well, this seemed like a great place to raise my own children. As you saw, we rarely lock our doors, plus my husband was from Warwick. After he died, I …couldn't imagine moving away with the kids. It would have devastated his parents."

"Did you want to?"

Of course there were moments she wanted to just run away from everything here, every memory, and start over somewhere else. "No, I knew this was the best place for the kids. They'd lost their father and I didn't want to take them away from everything familiar."

"Did you own the bookstore then?" Lucy asked, pouring herself a little more wine.

"No, I was what they now call a 'stay at home mom.' I had three children pretty close together and my husband worked long hours on the railroad, sometimes gone for a few days at a time. Back then, women were really just starting to get out in the working world. It's so very different now. After he died, there was some insurance money so I didn't have to get a job right away. But during those long hours when the kids were in school I started to go stir crazy."

Actually, she found herself admitting to Lucy, she had thought she was losing her mind. Alex and Jenny were coping, but Colin had worried her, barely talking, withdrawing from everything, even sports, which he loved. Despite longing to do something, she knew she needed to be there when they got home. So her days became lost hours at the local library. Like an alcoholic in search of a fix, she wandered the stacks and shelves looking for something, anything, to help her escape what wasn't supposed to be her life. And then, walking down Main Street one day, she saw a help wanted sign in the bookstore. Although it was just a few days a week while the kids were in school, it brought back a sense of order, something that had been part of her life since she was old enough to get up at dawn and help with the farm chores.

It wasn't just the reading, she went on. Being around others began to calm the tremors that had pulsed through her body from the moment she heard the loud knocking on her front door in the middle of that awful night.

"To be honest, I wasn't always this outgoing. Books were the only thing I ever really felt I was good at. And working in the store, discussing a novel, or recommending a biography or self-help book, well I finally felt myself getting over my shyness. People appreciated my opinion. And it was fun. I knew one day Betsy, who owned The Book Lover then, would retire, so I saved every dime and began compiling a list of books I'd want to carry. That was more than thirty years ago."

"What happened to your husband?"

"It was...a car accident." How simple that sounded. Accidents happened every day, didn't they? But nothing about it had been simple.

"I'm sorry, that was a rude question."

"No, don't be silly. It was a long time ago."

"Well, you must be very proud of your store. It's lovely, and believe me, I stopped at tons in the past five days on my way here."

"You drove here from Florida?"

Lucy nodded and then her face flushed. "I don't really have much going on in my life right now and I need to promote my book, so I figured this would be a good time."

"How many did you stop at?"

Lucy shrugged. "Maybe thirty or so?"

Ruth felt her mouth fall open. "You drove a thousand miles over five days and stopped at all those bookstores?"

"I just need something to focus on. I know, it's crazy, my life is just...in the crapper," she said with a little laugh, but Ruth could see from her face that there was nothing funny there.

Whatever precipitated this trip must have been pretty devastating. The way Lucy clammed right back up, it was obvious she wasn't ready to talk about it.

"Well, your book is wonderful," Ruth said, trying to bring the conversation back to something Lucy was comfortable with.

Lucy stared at her a moment, then blushed. "You realize my book is self-published, right?"

Ruth blinked. "I...I actually had no idea. I thought you were just with a tiny press that didn't really..." she shrugged.

"No, that's what I want people to think, so they won't assume it's awful because I couldn't get it taken. And that's why I've been going to so many bookstores, hoping they'll take a chance and read it."

"That's incredibly gutsy."

"Well, it started out pretty rough. I'd sit in my car all nervous and dread walking into these little stores, asking if they'd like to read my self-published book, sometimes catching the eye rolls. But I kept reminding myself I've been through a lot worse than that. Anyway, I have to say by the time I reached Virginia, I had a pretty good spiel down," she said and then laughed. "I worked in a store, you know, so I can sell, and I figured, why wasn't I selling the hell out of this book, right? So I mentioned you and our signing and that you're suggesting my novel to a few book clubs, that got them listening. Oh, and some reader quotes. So now I've got about ten stores that took review copies and I'm hoping to hear something soon," she finished with a smile that seemed almost too bright.

Ruth thought about the character in the book, the lonely little girl who grows up to be a lonely woman, struggling to hang onto a marriage that shouldn't have existed in the first place. "Lucy, it's a powerful book. I think anyone who picks it up can't help but be moved."

"You have no idea what that means to me, Ruth. I mean, you're in the business, you read tons of books and...well, it's kind of validation, you know what I mean?"

"I do, yes. So tell me what inspired you to write A Quiet Wanting?"

Lucy said nothing for a long moment. "I'd actually given up on writing. It just seemed pointless, as my husband started telling me after I gave up on a different novel, getting rejected over and over. And we were trying to have a baby, which was stressful enough, because we had to go through all that fertility stuff." She took a deep breath. "Anyway, I got pregnant but I started having contractions way too early. The doctor told me if I wanted to bring this baby to term I had to get in bed and not get up until I delivered."

Lucy traced the pattern of the lace tablecloth as she continued. "Can you imagine? Being told you had to basically sit in a room for months? Up until then I thought I'd do anything to have a baby, and I did, having one miscarriage after another. This was the first time I'd gotten to five months. But I began to get a dose of cabin fever after a week or so, kind of like you were saying before. One day I picked up a pen and one of David's legal pads and I started writing again. It was like I rediscovered a part of myself I'd simply forgotten about. The story just took off, and it hit me how lucky I was. I'd probably never have another chance like that, all that free time to devote to writing. Whoever has that? Especially with a baby."

"As the weeks went on and the novel grew, I was so excited. I was going to have a baby, and a book; I had a wonderful husband, a beautiful home. I was going to have everything I ever wanted. And then...just after my seventh month, I went into labor anyway. He was so beautiful, and so tiny. They told me lots of babies are born way earlier and survive. He struggled for three days, but there was something wrong with his heart and...we lost him."

"Oh, Lucy. I'm so sorry," Ruth said, reaching across the table and squeezing Lucy's hand.

"It's all right, it's been five years." She gave Ruth a little shrug.

Ruth knew it didn't matter how many years ago it was. Something like that never left you.

"Anyway, it took me another two years to finish writing the book."

They sat in silence for a moment, and Ruth poured a little more wine in her glass. Lucy held hers up, too.

"I nearly lost my son, Colin. He was serving in Iraq and got hit with one of those horrible roadside bombs a few years ago. He'll never be the same."

She wasn't sure Lucy heard her; she was staring at the lace tablecloth, seeming lost in thought. She reminded Ruth of a blonde version of Audrey Hepburn, with the chopped hair, the long, graceful neck, and the big green eyes.

"Do you think that's true?" Lucy asked her, suddenly looking up. "Do you think that nobody ever really gets everything?"

"Oh...I don't know, Lucy."

"My mother used to say that all the time."

Lucy went upstairs then. A short while later Ruth went up, too. She didn't think she'd sleep. It would be hard not to keep replaying the conversation with Lucy, who was nothing like what she'd been expecting. But then she remembered her visit to Thomas and her stomach gave a little squeeze. It was less than forty-eight hours away. But despite Lucy, and Thomas, the moment Ruth's head hit the pillow she fell into a deep and dreamless sleep.

* * *

BY FIVE IN THE MORNING RUTH WAS WIDE AWAKE and refreshed. She wondered if it was the wine. Maybe Jenny was right, she thought with a laugh, maybe she needed to drink a little more. She tiptoed down to the kitchen, let Sam out, and put up two big pots of water to boil for the seven pounds of potato salad she was making for brunch. She let Sam back in and poured food into her bowl, then filled the other with fresh water and a few cubes. Sam liked her water cold.

By then the coffee was ready and she poured herself a big mug. Slipping on her reading glasses, she stared at herself in the mirror over the sink. Years ago she had dreamed about one day having the money to put a window there. Now she looked at her hair, which was starting to look like Brillo. Maybe she could just trim the shredded ends herself. She opened the junk drawer, fished out the sharp scissor, and took a long lock, stretching it to snip a bit off when she heard a noise.

She turned and saw Lucy in the doorway, her suitcase at her feet, a piece of paper in her hand.

"Oh, I'm sorry, I didn't realize you were up," Lucy said, her face turning red. "I was just going to leave this note for you on the table."

Clearly Lucy was hoping to slip out without notice.

"No, no. I've been up a little while."

"Are you cutting your hair?"

"Thinking about it."

"Oh, your wet hair yesterday. That's where you were when I showed up. I'm so sorry."

"No, I'm actually glad. I think Dee was going to do something drastic, and truthfully, I don't want drastic."

Lucy put the note in the pocket of her jeans. "I could trim it for you. It's the least I could do. I feel awful, Ruth, about everything."

She hesitated. Obviously Lucy wanted to do something for her. Ruth handed the scissors over. "Trim away," she said, sitting in one of the ladder back chairs.

Lucy picked up the brush off the washer and began to pull it through her thick, wiry hair, no easy feat. "Your hair is beautiful. My mother was a beautician, so I know a little about this. She taught me how to cut her hair, too, so we could save money. I'm only going to trim the ends."

"I trust you," Ruth said, and she did. "I can't tell you the last time I had my hair cut."

She heard the first snip of the scissor and from the corner of her eye saw a tiny curl flutter to the linoleum.

"What's the occasion?" Lucy asked. Another snip.

"I'm...going to see someone tomorrow."

"A man?"

She nodded, and Lucy stopped abruptly. "Sorry," Ruth said. She held her head erect again. "Yes, a man. Actually..." she hesitated, and then, as Lucy continued cutting, Ruth began to tell her everything. That she sold books at the prison. That Thomas was the first man in more than three decades who sparked something inside of her. And she was afraid that after tomorrow, she'd never see him again.

Talking about it was a revelation, like the old cliché of a weight being lifted from your shoulders. But it was true. Hearing herself say Thomas's name out loud, and how over the long lonely years, there'd never been another man, sounded like something from a novel. The aged spinster throwing away her last years on a fantasy. The sorry satisfaction of having but a dozen hours a year to play it out at their meetings. Of course there were the letters. And maybe that was the problem, she confessed. At times his letters seemed so intimate there was a danger of reading between the lines, of concocting a person who perhaps existed only in her mind.

"But why do you think you won't see him again?"

"The last time I saw him he had a bandaged hand. And then he wasn't at our book meeting. He's never missed one in five years. And now...now he wants to see me, during visiting hours. I think maybe he's gotten into some trouble, maybe there was a fight, and he won't be doing the book orders anymore." She sighed. "No one knows about him. My kids would think this was all insane. And when I say it out loud, well, it does sound insane. But it's such a relief to talk about it."

"What did he do?"

"Actually, I don't know. It's ridiculous, I know, but back in the beginning, when I first began going, I knew the only way I'd be able to deal with them as real people was not to know what any of them did to get themselves in there."

"You don't strike me as the impetuous type, Ruth. There must be something about him."

She said nothing for a long moment, as Lucy continued cutting one tiny clump of hair after another, taking her time. "He's intelligent, kind and gentle. Doesn't that sound crazy? He's in for a fifteen-year sentence, that I do know, because he's been very open about it."

Lucy blew on her shoulders and brushed them with her hand. Then without even looking she snipped a strand of her own hair as she said, "And you would miss him if you can't see him anymore?"

Ruth looked at her a moment. "Yes, I would. I'd miss him very much." She stood up and walked to the mirror. "It's perfect, thank you. Me minus the ragged ends."

Lucy smiled. "You're more than welcome."

"Now, how about a cup of coffee, and maybe a corn muffin."

"I really should go."

"You barely ate last night, you must be starving."

Lucy put the scissor down. "I haven't had a corn muffin since college. I used to live on them."

"Sit down then, it'll only take a few moments." She opened the cabinet to pull out a skillet. "So tell me, where are you off to next?"

"Well, our signing was sort of the focal point of this trip. But I'll probably head to my mother's in Pennsylvania, although she has no idea I'm coming. And she's going to be…upset."

Ruth turned to her. "Because you're coming?"

Lucy gave her a rueful smile. "Because she doesn't know what happened."

"What did happen, Lucy?"

"Well…" Lucy gave a long sigh. "In the last month or so I've been like one of those clueless wives in a chick lit paperback who has no idea her life is falling apart until one morning it hits her smack in the face like a two by four and…let's just say I'm still digging out the splinters."

"Ouch." She knew Lucy was trying to make light of things, but she couldn't hide the pain in her eyes. Ruth could see that all too clearly.

"You're not the only one with a criminal in your life, Ruth. Although where David is going, or maybe already is by now, I'm sure is a far cry from where your Thomas is—one of those white collar prisons referred to as a 'camp,' kind of like where Martha Stewart went."

As the corn muffins burned, the coffee grew cold, and the pots of water boiled away, Lucy told her everything. That her husband's weekly poker games had apparently escalated into a huge gambling problem. He'd been stealing money from client trust accounts to try to pay off his debts, for which he was now going to jail. And he wanted a divorce.

No wonder she'd fallen apart.

"All this time I thought David was never home because he was building up his practice. That he was cranky and not himself because he was exhausted and under a lot of stress. Because if you knew him before, you'd have bet money," and she paused and let out a bitter laugh, "well, you'd never believe he was capable of anything like this."

Ruth said nothing. But of course she knew that people often did things you'd never expect of them. Horrible things. Things that destroyed others, and themselves. She knew all that first hand.

"My mother has always been a bit emotional. And she adores David," Lucy continued. "She always says he's the best thing that ever happened to me. To her, really. Ironic isn't it? But you have to understand something about David. He likes taking care of people. His father died young and he was an only child, very devoted to his mother, which I thought was wonderful. They say if you want to know what kind of husband a man would make, watch how he treats his mother...but now he's like this man I never knew."

"He's admitted everything?"

Lucy nodded. "I could understand him being ashamed but he's not, he's just so cold and...angry toward me."

"You know my son did the same thing after his accident, pushed us all away, and he seemed so distant, as you said, but I think maybe that's a natural reaction when your world is falling apart, you know? They tend to take it out on somebody close to them."

Lucy sat there shaking her head. "Why would he do this? Let himself get so caught up in something illegal. This was a man who four years ago found an emerald ring on the beach with his metal detector, and even though no one would have known if he kept it, he brought it right to the police station without thinking twice, because someone might be grieving over its loss. He was the one who insisted we buy my mother a car, and help finance her condo. I would have bet my life that David was the most honest, caring person in the world. It's the reason I married him. And I probably would have stood by him, if he'd let me."

Ruth waited as Lucy stared out the window. It was nearly light out now, and the raucous waking of the birds in her yard filled the air.

Suddenly Lucy shook her head, as if waking from a trance, and gave another little laugh. "This is strange, isn't it? How we barely know each other? How we're telling each other these secrets. It feels like—"

"Like a book," Ruth said, and Lucy nodded.

And it did. As if they were two characters, strangers on a train, or a bus depot, or in this case, in a house in Warwick, spilling their innermost thoughts to each other.

She smiled. "People are always coming into the store and telling me things. Things they say they've never told another soul. I think sometimes it's just a lot easier spilling our secrets to strangers."

"That's true. Someone who will just listen, and not judge. But you are a good listener."

"So are you." She smiled. "Now, how about we try those corn muffins again?"

Lucy nodded, returning the smile. Her face looked lighter, less troubled, and Ruth felt a shift in herself as well.

WHILE THEY ATE, THEY TALKED ABOUT BOOKS, the ones that had influenced their lives, the ones they still wanted to read. They both claimed Gatsby as their favorite, which Lucy thought amazing. But then Ruth told her it wasn't surprising, as it had been picked the number one book for the twentieth century, which Lucy hadn't known.

"In fact, Fitzgerald even mentioned Warwick in the book. I thought he'd just made up a name, but I did a bit of research and it turned out it was right here. Back then, thanks to the railroad, this town was in its heyday, where rich city people had summer homes. One of the characters, Jordan, had come to a party here and wrecked a car."

"That is so neat," Lucy said.

"Did you know when Gatsby came out it got mostly terrible reviews and one paper called it something like 'Fitzgerald's latest dud'."

"God, no wonder the man drank."

"It wasn't until after his death that his books began to really become appreciated. Oh, and one of my other favorite books in the past few years, *The Help*, was rejected by sixty-five agents."

"I loved that book. I guess that gives me a little hope."

"Then there's *The Bridges of Madison County*, which was originally self-published."

"I had no idea," Lucy said, clearly delighted.

"Don't get me wrong, Lucy. What you're doing isn't easy. Most self-published books aren't very good. I must get ten a month, and I don't have time to read them because I have so many others to get through."

"Then why did you read mine?"

"Honestly? I didn't realize it was self-published when I first began reading it. But you had me in the first chapter."

"I know this is an uphill battle. I just wonder sometimes if I really have the stomach for it."

"Oh, don't give up, Lucy."

"I'm not going to. Not yet, at least."

"And I'm glad you had a real book printed up, otherwise I probably would never have read it."

"I could have self-published it for almost nothing online, but I wanted a real book, something I could hold in my hands with a cover and pages and that I could see on a shelf in a bookstore. That's really my dream."

"Well, we're kindred spirits, there. I love a real book, too. Even the smell of it."

Just then the timer went off on the stove.

"Listen, I should really be on my way and let you get back to your life," Lucy said, getting up and carrying her plate to the sink.

Ruth walked over, touched Lucy's arm. "I have an idea. If you're not ready to go to your mother's, I have a cabin at a lake nearby. It's sitting empty, has been for years. If you don't mind rustic, you're welcome to stay there for a while. Until you figure things out."

Lucy began shaking her head.

"You have to come back next week for your signing anyway, and this way you won't be too far."

Lucy suddenly leaned over and hugged her, then stepped back quickly, looking a bit embarrassed.

"I don't think I've ever met anyone quite like you, Ruth. But I couldn't."

Five minutes later, she was gone.

8

L UCY DROVE DOWN WIDE TREE-LINED STREETS, with big old hous- es like Ruth's and spring flowers everywhere. She pulled over as she neared Main Street and the shops ahead and reached into her purse for her cell phone. She'd forgotten she'd turned it off yesterday when she went into the bookstore. Powering it on, she saw the voicemail alert and her stomach lurched, wondering if it could be David. If he'd somehow come back to his senses. Because in the past few months, it was as if an alien was inhabiting her husband's body.

But it was her new attorney, Carter Mayfield, letting her know that he was filing the divorce papers. There were only two grounds for divorce in Florida: the mental incapacity of one of the spouses for at least three years; or that the marriage is "irretrievably broken." That was certainly the easy choice, she'd told Carter at their first meeting. She just hadn't realized it.

She sat there now, drumming her hands on the steering wheel, thinking about the call she had to make to her mother. There was nowhere else to go, really. And she should have called her before she even left Florida, but she'd just kept putting it off, waiting, hoping that things would change. Her mother didn't know about David's arrest, or the fallout since. For that matter, her mother didn't even know she'd gone back to writing, much less that she'd published a book. Lucy knew better than to burden her with unpleasant news if there was a chance the outcome might change.

The year she'd turned eleven, when her father told her he was leaving one night after they'd moved into the duplex in Morristown, Lucy kept think- ing he wouldn't really go. It was just him talking after one of her parents' fights. Because he wouldn't just be leaving *her* as he always referred to her mother, he'd be leaving Lucy and Jake and Charlie as well. And he'd been so excited for weeks before, talking about the porch and yard, how she'd have her own bedroom in the attic. She'd never had her own room; they'd never lived in anything but small apartments, and her father had always talked about what he'd do with his own little "patch of earth."

That night she lay in her room too wound up to sleep or even read, even though she was almost halfway through her very first Nancy Drew book. Instead she stared at the sloped ceiling, the faded pink flowers, loving even the dusty wooden smell of the beams. She couldn't wait for summer, hoping they'd still be living there so she could prop the tiny windows open and look down at the world below. Or up at the stars. She wanted to somehow make a window seat, something she'd been dreaming about ever since she'd read Pollyanna.

When she heard the steps creak, an unfamiliar sound that startled her at first, she sat up, then saw her father duck, even though he was short, as he reached the top where the ceiling slanted to meet the wall.

"I love my room, Daddy, I'm so happy we're here," she'd said as he sat on her bed.

He'd smiled, told her he was going to pay up for a year, that's why he'd been working so much. But then he coughed, and as he stared out the tiny window, he broke the news that he had to leave. That he wanted to take her with him, but he'd be working a lot and of course the boys were too little and would be lonely without her. He went on, but she didn't hear much of it, except that they would all be better off, there'd be no more fighting...

"Let's just keep this our little secret for now, all right, Lucy Goosey?"

She'd said nothing to her mother, praying it had all been a bad dream. But a week later, when she came home from school, she found her mother in the closet in her bedroom, slumped to the floor, sobbing in a cloud of cigarette smoke.

"Did you know about this?" her mother had asked.

Slowly Lucy shook her head. Then she went downstairs to wait for her brothers to come home. She'd poured them cereal, turned on cartoons, and sat staring out the kitchen window at the little "patch of earth" her father had always wanted, her whole body still, as if everything of substance had evaporated within her and she was weightless. They were evicted three months later.

Now she rolled down the car window, letting the cool air in. Her mother loved David, and would somehow make this Lucy's fault. She sat there for several minutes, trying to come up with the right words. Then she opened her cell phone again.

"Hello?" her mother answered on the third ring.

"Hi Mom, it's me," Lucy said, after a little burst of static. "Can you hear me okay?"

"Sure, I can hear you. Why are you on the beach?"

"No, uh, actually I'm—"

"Oh, hang on a minute, Lucy," she interrupted, and then Lucy could hear the muffled sounds of her talking to someone else, obviously with her hand over the receiver. "Okay, I'm back. Now, you're walking on the beach? Isn't it raining? I hear you've got a tropical storm nearby."

Just then there was a loud noise in the background, as if something had fallen.

"What was that, Mom?"

"Oh, Lucy, you caught me at a bad time. I have...someone..." she hesitated a moment, seeming flustered. "Lucy, I've met someone. And he's moving in here with me."

"Now?"

"Yes, now. Artie is just wonderful. We met at a consciousness raising group. You remember, like the kind I used to go to?"

After her father left, her mother became a big fan of Gloria Steinem. She badmouthed men for so long that Lucy began to wonder if she liked women. Then she got a better position at a more upscale beauty parlor, telling them to call it a salon. Once or twice she went out on a date. If there was anything further that happened with a man, Lucy and her brothers had no idea.

"So, he's a nice guy?"

"He's like no man I've met before. In fact, he's so nice I assumed he was gay at first. He cooks, he cleans. He listens. And he massages my feet every night while we watch TV."

"Well," Lucy said, her mind reeling, unable to wrap itself around this major world change. "I'm glad for you, Mom. You deserve it."

"Hold on," her mother said, and then without her hand on the phone, she called out, "Artie, come say hi to Lucy."

A second later he was on the line. "Hello, Lucy. I just want you to know I'm gonna take real good care of your Mama. And one of these days, I'm bringing her down to Florida to finally visit you."

He didn't sound old. He sounded sweet and friendly, with a boyish voice.

"That would be nice, Artie. Or maybe I'll come up and see you two."

"It's been too long," he said, as if he were part of the last five years, where she had avoided her mother, her old friends, and everyone associated with the life she'd left behind.

"Well, I look forward to meeting you soon, Artie. I'm gonna run and let you get back to unpacking."

"Isn't he nice?" her mother whispered a moment later. "Now get off that rainy beach and call me soon. We'll make those plans for a visit."

Lucy snapped the phone shut, imagining the rainy beach in St. Augustine. Having no idea what to do now. She'd just assumed she could go to her mother's. The whole day loomed ahead, as did her whole life, and there she sat in Warwick, New York. She got out of the car and headed up Main Street, toward a diner she remembered seeing yesterday. She'd grab a cup of coffee for now and consider other options.

She'd forgotten how quaint the old northeast towns could be compared to Florida, where it seemed everything was new, except for St. Augustine, of course. Main Street and West Street were lined with the kinds of stores that used to thrive in downtowns, before the explosion of malls. Stopping under the marquee of an old theater, she looked up. The Darress, she read, thinking it sounded awfully similar to duress, which couldn't be a good thing. Peeking in, she saw that the lobby was a camera shop now. In its era, the theater was probably a focal point for entertainment in the area.

As she walked toward the bridge she'd crossed yesterday, she passed an appliance store, dog groomer, consignment shop, and Akin's Pharmacy, where she stopped and peered through the window. It was like a time warp. All it needed was the old-fashioned soda fountain. She was surprised it was still in business, recalling passing a CVS a few blocks outside of town yesterday.

She turned and kept walking, enjoying the mild May morning, the quiet of the downtown, the feeling that she could perhaps be anyone who lived there, enjoying a stroll. A block later she stood on the bridge, looking down at the creek rushing by. A family of geese coasted downstream on the current. In the deep, cool shadows of a sycamore a heron perched on a rock, waiting patiently. The tea-colored water was clear and shallow, and sunlight shone through to the rocks scattered across the muddy bottom.

It reminded her of the jigsaw puzzles she loved as a kid, struggling to find the right shades of brown, or green if it was a woodland scene, and slipping one piece after another into place until there was a whole. There was a feeling of satisfaction in that. Until her wild brothers tore it apart. It was the same pleasure she'd felt with numbers, too, solving one problem after another, like those puzzles.

Now here she was years later, and her life seemed like one of those thousand-piece puzzles tossed across a floor, as she struggled to somehow put it back together again. Once again this trip, the stops at bookstores, the focus of her existence now on nothing but the book, seemed like folly. And the delay in looking for a real job, a permanent place to live, seemed...insane. If she lived frugally, though, she'd have enough money to last a year, thanks to an old 401k account from her first job, which David hadn't been able to touch.

David had put them into a financial black hole. Carter had warned her that figuring out the entire financial picture could be a lengthy task. Of course he knew all about David when she'd called him a week after that awful night. St. Augustine was like a small town, really, and David Barrett was THE topic of the moment for the local legal profession. But she liked Carter, he was honest and a real southern gentleman, so she left it all in his hands.

She turned and kept walking, eventually reaching the bookstore, which wasn't open yet. She glanced at the big window. Just inside the door was a poster for her upcoming signing, and she wondered suddenly if she really would come back. As much as she liked Ruth, it was hard to imagine return-ing, or picking up the immediate intimacy they'd established. She noticed, then, a copy of her novel displayed in the window, with a row of hardcovers and other new releases. It hadn't been there yesterday.

She couldn't help but smile. Who was this woman? This kind stranger who felt a bit like a fairy godmother? Or maybe the older sister she'd always dreamed of, though Ruth was probably closer to her mother's age. But Ruth was nothing like her mother.

Lucy had refused her offer several times. But Ruth kept insisting that if Lucy changed her mind, she'd find the key under the mat, that is if the door was even locked. She'd handed her a map she'd sketched and directions that looked overwhelming. Then she offered to drive her to the cabin, which was on a lake about forty-five minutes away, just so she could see it. Of course Lucy said no, she couldn't waste any more of Ruth's time; she had her family brunch and all those potatoes cooling.

Lucy pulled the map from her purse now and stared at it. Maybe she should at least take a look.

* * *

THE ROAD WOUND ALONG WARWICK TURNPIKE like a roller coaster, as Lucy drove up and down mountains toward New Jersey on this golden day.

Descending on a sudden curve, she caught a slash of silver in the distance, a body of water glittering in the sun, and her breath caught. The lake was surrounded by tall trees and hills, and a moment later the road paralleled its western shore. She kept driving, the water on her left, a dark jewel set in the mountains, flashing with sunlight between the trees.

When she spotted a marina up ahead, she pulled in and opened the atlas, then looked over Ruth's directions again. This wasn't the right lake. Northern New Jersey, where it passes imperceptibly into New York State, is dotted with lakes all through its mountains and valleys. This was Greenwood Lake, apparently, which was completely different from Upper Greenwood Lake, Ruth had cautioned. You would assume from the name that it was further up north, and you'd come to it first, but now, on the map it was actually down lower to the south. But apparently the elevation was higher, hence the name. Needless to say, it was a bit confusing, as Ruth had warned.

Lucy wasn't really going out of her way much. If she didn't like the cabin, she'd simply head east toward the Jersey shore and stay in Spring Lake or even farther down on Long Beach Island, where she and David used to spend a week each summer. But the thought of staying alone in a B&B or a hotel seemed so depressing.

By early afternoon she finally passed a sign for Upper Greenwood Lake and immediately houses began to line the road. A few blocks later she spotted water ahead, and then a causeway, and stopped there a moment, getting almost a full view. The causeway separated the main lake on the right from a lagoon on the left. The lake was much smaller than the one she'd passed earlier, its mirrored surface reflecting blue sky and clouds, surrounded by a hilly shoreline that was heavily treed and littered with huge rocks. She could see houses peeking through the trees, chalets and log structures.

The lagoon on the left appeared more remote, the wide curved shoreline mostly barren of houses. Driving off the bridge, she pulled over on the side of the road, glanced at Ruth's directions, then continued around the lake. The road narrowed, and when she was nearly halfway around the houses grew fewer and glimpses of the water became impossible as the elevation rose and the trees thickened. Up ahead she spotted the rounded boulder at the foot of a driveway and put on the brakes. There was the wall of hemlocks lining both sides. She turned in. The driveway was just a rutted dirt lane that had seen better days, but it reminded Lucy of fairy tales as she traveled through the dark green tunnel.

She came out on the other side into a wide clearing, squinting at the bright sun shining off the lake at the bottom of a sloping green lawn. It was breathtakingly beautiful. Stepping out of the car, she looked around, then turned to see a cabin behind her, tucked into the trees with the land rising behind it up the mountain. It was a small log structure with a stone chimney. In the front there was an open porch and beside it a wide window.

Beyond the cabin was a small open area and then the woods began, circling around the shore. On the other side of the drive, to the left, sat another cabin, bigger and freshly painted, more like an A-frame. There was no car in its driveway. No other houses were visible. All in all, it was quite desolate, surrounded by woods and water. She leaned against the car a moment, feeling the warmth from the metal through her jeans.

She didn't like that she was afraid to stay alone. That her crazy imagination could take off at the littlest noise in the middle of the night. Something that, with David's warm body beside her, she'd toss off as a house noise, or a neighbor's cat. Here in this place she'd be spookily alone.

Walking up the two steps to the porch, she lifted the mat and found an old skeleton key, but the door was unlocked. The cabin was clean and tidy, but the furniture was decades old and there was that damp, musty smell of a house that had been closed up for too long. There was really the one rustic room, a living area with a kitchen to the rear, a tiny bedroom off to the side, and a loft above. But that one rustic room was so charming, the log walls a soft yellow, a stone fireplace rising to the roof, and a picture window overlooking the lake below.

She thought of what Ruth had said just before she left. Something that Betsy had told her when she'd first gone to work in the bookstore. "Right now your life is in crisis, but remember this, the Chinese word for crisis has two symbols. Danger, and opportunity."

And here was an opportunity, if she had the nerve.

Ten minutes later, she had opened all the windows, although the screens had seen better days, and brought in her things. Then she drove back to a small general store a few miles back and picked up some staples to get through the night and morning. Once it was dark, she knew she wouldn't be leaving.

Getting settled, she thought that the cabin had a lot of potential, and could even be fun to fix up. She loved painting and wallpapering. When she first moved into David's house in Mendham after they were married, he'd been shocked when she told him she wanted to do all the decorating herself. And cleaning, too. He couldn't fathom why she wouldn't rather hire someone. But David, who'd always had a nice home, who didn't move around as a kid, had no idea of the pleasure she took in spending Saturday mornings with music blasting, candles lit, sprucing up each and every room of her own home until it was just the way she'd envisioned it.

Although the cabin looked clean at first glance, the refrigerator needed a good scrubbing, which she did before putting away her few things. The sheets were musty, but there was an ancient washer and dryer on the back porch, and she blessed Ruth for that, imagining that with the whole family here, it had been a necessity. While the sheets washed, she wiped down the bathroom, then stood in the middle of the living room, wondering if Ruth would mind if she moved the kitchen table from the corner and set it in front of the wide window. In the morning, she could have tea there and watch the sun rise over the lake.

Dragging the wooden table across the room, she decided Ruth wouldn't care as long as she put it back later. Then Lucy walked around the cabin, looking out each window, amazed at how beautiful it was. She had one week until her signing at Ruth's store. One week in this beautiful place.

She went to the fridge and pulled out the bottle of wine she'd gotten at the store, figuring it would cure her jitters when it got dark and ensure a good night's sleep. She had resisted a pack of cigarettes, determined to stick to quitting this time for good. Walking out onto the porch, she sat down on the step and looked all around. It was late afternoon, the sun beginning to lower in the western sky to the right, casting the lake and the surrounding woods in a soft peach light. She'd probably never been so alone in her entire life.

"Here's to you, Lucinda Barrett," she said out loud, holding up her glass, "and whatever happens next."

9

O N MONDAY RUTH WENT TO HANNAH MEEKER'S small Cape Cod just a few blocks from Main Street. It was another beautiful May morning, and if not for her shoes—the low heels she'd sworn she'd never wear again—she would have walked from the store.

"Wow, Ruth, you look really nice," Hannah said as she opened her front door.

"I have an appointment later today." Before Hannah could ask questions, she continued, "Now, I can't wait to see this outfit you got."

"Pour yourself some coffee, I'll be right down," Hannah said as she headed for the stairs.

"What is that heavenly smell?"

"I just baked muffins," Hannah said, her voice fading as she climbed.

Instead of getting coffee, Ruth stood in the living room looking in a mirror over the couch. She didn't look half bad. She'd put on mascara and dabbed on pink lipstick, which was supposed to be a more youthful shade. Her hair was plaited into a French braid, something she hadn't tried in years.

Lucy had done a pretty good job. Her hair was even all the way around, no easy feat. She wondered now how Lucy had fared during her first night at the cabin. Ruth had gone into the store for a few hours after yesterday's brunch to make up for the time she wouldn't be in today, and was surprised when she got home to hear Lucy's message on her machine.

"Oh," she said aloud, her hand flying to her mouth. She should have called Colin. Someone staying in the cabin would no doubt be a shock to him. But last night there had been only one thing claiming her thoughts. That in less than twenty-four hours, she'd be seeing Thomas.

"Did you say something?" she heard Hannah call out, and a moment later she was coming downstairs.

"No, I..." but her words trailed off as Hannah reached the bottom step and twirled around.

The dress was a vivid orange, with a deep V-neck and an A-line skirt that came just above Hannah's knees. She wore a pair of black strappy heels.

"Whoa, Hannah. You have great gams, as my mother used to say. Why have you been hiding them?"

"You like it?" Hannah asked, her face like an excited child's.

"I love it, the color is gorgeous. It lights up your face."

"I know it's kind of different for me. You don't think it's too much? That I look...ridiculous?"

"In this case, different is good." Hannah almost always wore brown or gray, or some drab color that simply made her disappear into the woodwork.

"So it's a keeper?"

"Oh yes. Definitely a keeper."

"I can't wait to surprise Eddie. Be right back. Go get a muffin."

Ruth went into the tiny kitchen and sat at a round table, barely able to slide the chair out. A plate piled high with muffins sat in the middle and she couldn't resist taking one, peeling the paper off, and biting into it as Hannah came into the room.

"Umm, Hannah," she said, her mouth full, then took a moment to chew and swallow. "My God, what are these?"

"Well, I've been calling them," Hannah paused a moment, "are you ready for this? Better Than Sex Muffins."

Ruth nearly spit out her bite as she began to laugh. "Are you kidding?"

Hannah shook her head.

"They're sweet yet salty, with a bit of crunch, and cinnamon, right?"

"My secret ingredient is crushed potato chips." Hannah sat with her own coffee. "When I get bored I experiment and this one is my favorite, I think."

Ruth took another bite.

"Speaking of bored," Hannah said suddenly, "I think Eddie's bored with *me*."

"Why do you say that?"

Hannah shrugged and Ruth saw her eyes fill with tears, but she grabbed a napkin and wiped them quickly. "I've been telling him that we don't spend enough time together, and as usual he tells me he's really busy at the store, times are tough, and...that I'm too needy."

"Oh, Hannah."

"If I had a better job, he wouldn't have to work so hard. Maybe he'd be interested in what I do, you know? As much as I love Elaine, I'm tired of working there. I want—I've always wanted—something of my own. Eddie has his appliance store, you have The Book Lover, Elaine has the restaurant. I've always been kind of tagging along behind everyone. Still trying to figure out what I'm meant to do. At sixty years old, what a joke," she said, with a laugh that held no humor.

Hannah got up and brought the coffee pot over, refilling their cups.

"You love baking," Ruth said. "And you have a real knack for it, I can honestly say that." This wasn't the first time Hannah's muffins had impressed her.

Hannah set the pot back on the counter. "I do love it. When I'm in the kitchen and it smells so good, and then someone takes a bite and I can see the pleasure on their face, I'm really happy."

"So…" Ruth said, smiling, "maybe *this* is it, that thing you're meant to do."

But Hannah waved a hand in the air, dismissing the idea. "I can't afford to open a bakery or anything, and… forget it." She shook her head and sighed. "I'm sorry, Ruth. I always seem to be dumping my problems on you."

"That's what friends are for, right? To listen?"

Hannah looked up at her and smiled. "Do you ever feel like you never live a day in the day, or a moment in the moment? All these books have got me thinking about that, how I'm always worrying ahead. Do you do that, too?"

"Are you kidding? Me worry? It's my middle name."

"You'd never know it. You always seem so calm, so together."

Ruth couldn't help giggling at the absurdity of Hannah's statement.

"Well anyway, thanks for coming over. I guess I'll keep the dress."

Heading back to the store, Ruth couldn't help thinking about the last revitalization meeting, with Eddie and Dee from the salon sitting a little too close, acting awfully chummy suddenly. Dee was recently separated. She hoped to God there was nothing to that little flirtation. She couldn't imagine how Hannah would cope with *that*.

* * *

LUCY HAD WOKEN DURING THE NIGHT TO TOTAL BLACKNESS, her heart pounding in terror. She'd gotten up, stumbling to find light switches. A moment later the cabin was lit in puddles of golden light and she leaned against a wall, cursing herself for being so stupid as to lie on the couch while it was still light out, and not have the foresight to turn a lamp on.

She'd gone into the bedroom, pulled on a nightgown, then got into bed.

Ironically, then sleep wouldn't come. The earlier quiet had gone, replaced with a cacophony of crickets and tree frogs that rang through the night like an outdoor symphony. As she lay there, she'd tried to recognize the sounds outside the window. There was a swishing noise against the outer wall, no doubt a branch lifting in the wind. She'd recognized the lone honk of a goose making its way back to the flock. And then a mournful howl went on for a long moment. Her eyes opened wide. A wolf? A coyote? She began to wonder exactly what lived in the woods surrounding the house.

The earlier contentment had disappeared, replaced with a fresh surge of fury toward David, who she'd e-mailed earlier after her second glass of wine although she wasn't sure he'd even get it. But he was the reason she was there, wasn't he? She knew in that moment she'd leave first thing in the morning.

But she didn't. She sat now in front of the big window with her tea, laughing at how she'd screamed out loud when she went to the bathroom during the night, pulling the shade down as if someone out in the woods might be watching, only to have it snap up and startle her. Pulling it down more slowly, she'd noticed a light on in the cabin across the way, and a car in the driveway. Relief had flooded through her and she'd climbed back into bed, thanking God that someone was nearby.

She hated that she was afraid of being alone. That she was afraid of life without David. Sipping her tea, she stared out the window, barely believing she was really here. A ring of small mountains encircled the lake, lush and green. The water lay still and dark, a fine gray mist hovering above the glassy surface. She realized the water must be warmer than the morning air. The deep quiet had returned, the singing insects of last night silent again. There was the occasional trill of a bird, or a sudden splash of something in the distance.

As she stared at the lake, ripples began to form suddenly, concentric circles that drifted outward. She wondered if a large fish was feeding in that spot. Then she noticed a few large bubbles as the flat surface of the water broke and a head rose up suddenly, a fine-boned face looking up toward the sky.

With a gasp she jumped, spilling the tea. Was she dreaming?

His eyes were closed, his long hair slicked back from a high forehead as he emerged. Now the shoulders broke free of the water, wide, muscled, as long arms stretched high, as if in prayer, or joy, his glistening flesh steaming in the cool morning air. He was beautiful, like shining marble hovering above the mist and the water, the entire palette the pale gray of early morning. It was like a mythical god coming back from centuries asleep in the depths of the lake.

Walking around the table, she pressed her face to the window, watching as he swam toward the shore. When he had nearly reached it, he lay there with only his head above the water. She waited for several long minutes.

And then, instead of standing up and walking out of the lake, this beautiful man-god used his hands and his arms to drag himself out of the water and onto the bank. As his lower half emerged, also naked, she gasped again. His legs were thin and withered, the flesh deathly white. It was so at odds with his torso, his arms, the wide V of his chest that tapered to a taut stomach. He rolled to a sitting position and then, using his hands to propel himself, he scooted across the sandy beach, toward a tree. Under it sat a wheelchair she hadn't noticed before, and beside it a small bench. Somehow he hoisted himself up onto the bench, then into the chair and pulled a large towel around himself.

He turned the wheelchair and as Lucy watched him push it across the grass toward the cabin next door, his upper body muscled like a weight lifter, she thought there was something familiar about him.

All of a sudden the chair jolted to a stop. He kept pushing the tires, but the chair didn't move. He was obviously stuck. She waited a moment, unsure of what to do. The morning was chilly, and he was wearing nothing but a towel. She should go and help him.

But as she opened the door, the chair began to move again, ascending the slope. He turned toward her cabin and looked up. She lifted her hand to wave, but he turned away. Closing the door, she stood by the side of the window where he couldn't see her, watching as he made his way up a small ramp that she hadn't noticed yesterday, onto his deck and then through a sliding glass door. She couldn't imagine the strength it had taken to swim, and then get himself back up that long slope and into his house.

She wondered if he'd been born that way. She didn't think so. He looked more like a man who'd been fit, and then perhaps had an accident of some kind, or a degenerative disease. What a shame, she thought, turning away from the window. He was such a handsome man.

10

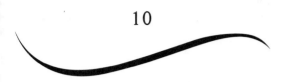

RUTH HAD THOUGHT THE HOURS WOULD DRAG until three o'clock, but it was a typical Monday and she barely had a moment to think. Book orders had to be placed, the weekend's sales tallied, shelves straightened, and boxes of new books opened. She took care of the paperwork and computer while Kris began organizing the shelves in between customers.

At noon she looked up to see Larry Porter standing on the other side of the counter. With wavy brown hair that seemed to defy combing, and a full beard, Larry was the picture of a scatterbrained professor. Larry, however, was an x-ray technician at Warwick General Hospital, and a self-professed bookaholic. He came in at least once a week, brought a stack of books to the counter, and then, as he peeled off bills and pulled coins from his pockets, famously quoted Erasmus: *When I get a little money I buy books; and if any is left I buy food and clothes.*

"I need something special. Just one book, I promise. For Angela."

"What's the occasion?"

"We met a year ago today, right here in your store, remember? I want something that..." He began to turn a furious shade of red as his words stalled.

"Something that tells her how you feel?"

"Exactly. But not too..."

"Mushy?"

"Right."

Ruth led him to the small poetry section, and pulled a slim hardcover from the shelf.

"*Sonnets From the Portuguese,*" he read aloud.

"It's a classic," she assured him.

He opened to a page at random and, to Ruth's surprise, began to read.

"How do I love thee? Let me count the ways.
I love thee to the depth and breadth and height
My soul can reach..."

He stopped and looked up at her with a shy smile. "It's perfect."

She rang up the book and after he left, she couldn't help smiling herself at Larry's passion for books, and now Angela.

BEFORE SHE KNEW IT, RUTH WAS DRIVING toward Interstate 84 and north to the prison, a route as familiar to her now as the drive home from the store. Her trembling hands clenched the steering wheel as she kept her eyes on the road. Once again she thought about Larry and Angela.

Everyone longed for love, for passion. It was part of the human condition. Hadn't she fallen hard under its spell with Bill? Wasn't it the hallmark of so many wonderful books where you could lose yourself in the longing of two characters you hoped would somehow find a way to be together by the end of the pages?

Ruth had given up on those dreams long ago. With consuming passion came consuming emotions. And risk, something she was no longer willing to take. But companionship would be lovely. The kind of passion she saw in Larry Porter's eyes was relegated to youth, she knew now. And that was okay with her.

Thomas had become a friend, a companion in a way, through their letters. If she sat and read through her five years' worth, she imagined it would read as a story of sorts. Two lonely people slowly revealing themselves, gradually becoming a bit enamored, and now...now it would probably be coming to an end. She would miss him. There would be a void she doubted she could fill again, not at this stage of her life.

She pulled into the prison parking lot, and it was as if an electric current switched on in her body. Even her hands trembled as she zipped her keys into her purse. The opportunity to talk to Thomas without a warden hovering, without the subterfuge of books, was something she'd daydreamed about for years. She'd just never imagined it would be like this.

Instead of meeting the clerk with her cartons of books, she went in alone, then filed through the various security screenings with the other visitors and finally entered the visiting room. It was noisy, filled with women and children of all ages, most dressed up for this visit with a special someone in their lives. A little girl in a pink flowered dress sat on her mother's lap turning the pages of a book, while her mother talked to a tattooed man across the plexiglass divider that separated the long tables—prisoners on one side, visitors on the other. Conversation was through a telephone-like device, and she wondered suddenly if they would be taped.

As she waited for Thomas, a toddler in denim overalls knelt on the floor in front of her, vroom vrooming a little matchbox car around the legs of his mother's chair. A very pregnant young woman sat quietly staring at the floor on Ruth's other side.

After what seemed like an eternity, a far door opened and several men in orange jumpsuits walked in with a guard. Thomas was one of them. She walked over and sat across from him, noticing that his hair had just been cut, the skin around his neck tender and raw.

His face broke into a slow smile that lit up his eyes. He picked up the phone.

"Hello, Ruth." His voice sounded different coming through a speaker.

"Hello, Thomas." She sounded out of breath. Her heart pounded.

"I can't believe you're really here." His smile broadened, and he shook his head, as if to waken from a daydream. "But you are."

She nodded. Ruth had never seen him like this, almost lighthearted. He was always so serious at their book meetings.

There was a long, awkward silence as he waited for her to speak. She looked at the wall of glass. For some reason, she'd thought it would be different. But of course there were security measures. There had to be. Around them the murmur of voices filled the room.

"You look really pretty," he said, and his look deepened.

"Thank you." The irony of it kept hitting her. She had dressed nicer to go to this prison than she had for the wedding.

"How's the store? Are things picking up at all?"

"We had a decent weekend." She paused a moment. "By the way, how is your hand?"

He held it up for her to see through the glass. There was no evidence of the bruise.

"You never told me how it happened."

"Two idiots got into it at lunch and I broke up the fight."

"Oh."

"I finished Gatsby," he said then.

"That's wonderful."

"I felt sorry for him, actually."

Had he asked her here to talk about the book?

"He was a good man, although he'd done some things that weren't so good. But...wasn't he really doing it all so he could fit in?"

"Well, yes, in a way."

"The way I see it, he did it all for Daisy. He was trying to look better in her eyes. But I think all along he knew he wasn't good enough for her."

Ruth felt her mouth go dry. "In some ways that's how Fitzgerald felt about his wife."

"Ruth, I have something important to tell you. It's good news. I didn't want to say anything until I was sure."

Her stomach churned with anticipation and something else she couldn't identify. Beside her, the pregnant young woman began to cry softly. The little boy was still making harsh engine sounds as he ran his car up and down the wooden table.

"Ruth?"

She looked up again and Thomas was looking at her, the distinct knit of worry back on his brow.

"Yes, I'm listening."

"I'm being let out on parole." A hopeful smile lit his face again. "I'm going to be free."

She let out a breath, not realizing she'd been holding it. So that was it, he would be leaving. "I'm really happy for you, Thomas. I'm going to miss you."

But he was shaking his head. "Ruth, I...I wanted to know if I might be able to see you," he said softly. "You know, outside of here."

She blinked and looked down at her hands, stunned. "But won't you be going back to Albany? Don't you have family, friends waiting for you?"

"There's nothing for me there. Besides, I don't want to go back. I want to go forward, with a new life."

"I'm not—"

"Don't," he interrupted her, holding up his palm flat on the glass separating them, as if in pleading. "Don't answer now. I know this must be a shock. So...maybe just think about it? Please?"

She said nothing, nodding.

"I think, though, you need to know the truth about me. Why I'm here."

"No, not now."

She couldn't imagine talking about it surrounded by all these people, the sobbing woman beside her and now a baby crying across the room, too. The tightness had come back, somewhere in the past few minutes, and Ruth felt as if a rubber band was wrapped around her chest.

"When will you be released?"

"There's some paperwork and a few technicalities being worked on. And I'm going through parole counseling. But it should be within a month."

She nodded. He put his hand up on the glass again and slowly she felt her own hand slide up the smooth partition, until it was right where his was on the other side. The closest they could get. His hand was large, with long thick fingers. A strong hand.

He smiled again and Ruth was startled to see tears well up in his eyes. She smiled back, her lips trembling with her own emotion.

"Can you come back again next week?" he asked. "I'll be gone before the next book meeting, obviously. I'll miss that, you know? But that's the only thing I'll miss about this place."

She hesitated a moment. "All right. I'll be back next week." She stood up.

"Wait," he said, doubt in his eyes. "What if I put it in a letter? We're good at letters, Ruth. That's another thing I'll miss. I'll write it tonight." He stared at her. "Whatever happens, I want you to understand."

As she walked out to her car, looking at the razor wire fence, the guard towers surrounding the building, Ruth knew she'd been lying to herself, about love and passion. Wasn't this what she'd dreamed about in the long lonely hours in her tub? Somehow Thomas would be free. In her imagination there was the vision of a tender kiss, long and slow, that grew into something more urgent and then...a fade to candlelight, of course. Her daydreams never went further than that, because that would be ridiculous. Ruth knew that none of it would ever be real. It was just a lonely woman's fantasy. But now, now he would be free. And he wanted to see her.

Was she really going to bring a criminal into her life?

L UCY SLEPT OFF AND ON MOST OF HER FIRST FULL DAY at the lake, not sure if she was ill, or simply catching up on months of lost sleep. She felt as if she was in an altered state, until she finally woke for good late the following morning. As she sat at the table by the window with her tea, she noticed the man next door pushing himself from bird feeder to bird feeder, using a long hook to pull them down and fill them from a heavy bag of seed that sat on his lap. She decided to get dressed and go introduce herself. By the time she did, he was gone.

She decided it was time to get back to work. She was also anxious to see if David had responded to her e-mail, though she was still unsure if he had access to a computer where he was. But fueled by the wine that first night, she'd written anyway, just one sentence: *Please tell me, is this really what you want?* Because she still couldn't believe it. Now, however, she couldn't seem to get back online.

She walked around the cabin with her laptop open, like a divining rod seeking water, hoping to see the little icon on the bottom of the toolbar turn green.

No luck.

Heading outside, she walked around front, back, and even up the driveway to the road with the laptop open in her hands. The broadband card she'd bought before leaving St. Augustine was supposed to get her online ANYWHERE. But here at the lake, which definitely qualified as the hinterlands, obviously it was hit or miss.

She went in and packed up. There had to be an internet café somewhere. She hadn't seen one in Warwick, but Warwick was too far. Maybe the little general store would have Wifi.

Although Ruth had told her it wasn't necessary, she locked the door. She realized then she hadn't heard back from Ruth after leaving her a message yesterday. Then she remembered Ruth's visit to the prison. She could tell by the look in Ruth's eyes, the way her hands moved as she spoke of Thomas, how nervous she was about it. Hopefully it had gone well. And that Ruth was as good a judge of character as she thought. Lucy would hate to think of someone trying to take advantage of her. She was such a kind woman, it probably wouldn't be hard.

Walking down the path to the driveway, Lucy noticed the man next door also leaving his cabin. She almost waved, but then his wheelchair turned away, so she went straight to her car. She turned the key, but nothing happened. Three times she tried, knowing in her gut that the click and ensuing silence probably meant one thing, a dead battery. Looking over, she saw that the man was already in his white Jeep, so she made a run for it. By the time she drew close, he was slowly backing up.

"Wait," she called. "Hello?"

The Jeep stopped and he turned, rolling down the window. She guessed he was in his late thirties, with light blonde hair nearly to his shoulders. His face was tanned and even his eyebrows, straight and thick, had golden glints. Staring at her now were the lightest blue eyes she'd ever seen. The memory of him coming out of the lake, naked, flashed before her.

"I'm sorry, but I was wondering if you might be able to give me a jump?"

He tilted his head, a slight smile curling the corners of his lips. Despite a prickle of annoyance that he'd chosen to take her words suggestively, she felt a blush crawl up her cheeks.

"I'm pretty sure it's just my battery."

"Sure, not a problem," he said. "I've got cables. I'll just drive over and meet you at the side of the car."

"Thank you."

Luckily, she knew about unreliable cars. Before David, she'd had a series of clunkers, and among other things, like changing oil and washer fluid, she'd mastered the art of jump starting a car without blowing up the battery and herself.

So when he opened his door and she saw that he was about to go through the arduous task of getting in and out of his wheelchair again, something she'd missed and wondered how he did actually accomplish, she simply said, "I've got it."

He gave her a long look. "Fine."

She opened his hood and hers, grabbed the cables and clipped them onto each battery. Then she got in her car and gave him a thumbs up. He gunned his engine as she turned the key. Nothing. They tried four times until she sat back in defeat.

He yelled over, "I'd be happy to give you a ride."

Awkward as she felt about it, she didn't have a choice. She grabbed her things and got into the passenger side of his car.

"Thank you. I'm so sorry to bother you like this."

He gave her an amused smile. "It's no bother at all. Any friend of Jenny's is a friend of mine."

"Jenny?"

"Yeah, my sister? Who's constantly calling me, worried I'll have some kind of catastrophe up here and no one will know it? That I'll lie here and mummify before it's noticed I'm missing from the world?"

"I'm sorry, I don't know Jenny. Do you know Ruth? I'm doing a signing at her store."

He began to laugh, a big, hearty, throw back your head laugh.

"You know Ruth then?" she asked, confused at his reaction.

He turned and looked at her again, shaking his head. "She's my mother."

"Your mother? Well...why didn't she..."

Then she remembered the pictures in the bedroom where she'd slept. No wonder he seemed familiar. And she recalled Ruth mentioning her son who'd been hurt in Iraq. How he lived alone on a lake, but her attention had drifted many times.

"I'm Colin, by the way," he said, extending a hand.

"Lucy," she said, shaking. "I'm doing a book signing at Ruth's store next week and, well, I got the dates confused. Anyway, she was kind enough to offer me the cabin for a few days, since I'd have to come all the way back."

"How convenient for her."

"Your mother doesn't really seem like the type to orchestrate something like this, without saying something about the circumstances."

He let out a breath. "She isn't. But with enough prodding from Jenny, she probably had no choice. My sister thinks she has to take care of everyone, and knows how to yank my mother's chain."

She didn't know what to say. He obviously could have been angry or resentful. Yes, he was handicapped, but it was apparent he knew how to survive out there. Now that she knew the circumstances, though, she could only imagine the worries Ruth and her daughter might have. Especially with him swimming in the lake alone.

"They're good women. But having a little distance from family, it's a good thing." He began backing up, using his hands to accelerate and brake, the car modified for his needs. "So where is it I'm taking you?"

"Actually, I'm not sure. First I need a garage. I also was hoping the general store has internet access."

"I doubt it. But I've got an errand to do in Vernon. I'm sure there's someplace there."

"I'm really sorry, you can just drop me off wherever and I'll figure it out."

"I can give you a ride back to the lake, it's not a problem. Otherwise you might be stuck in Vernon all day."

"That's very kind of you."

They drove in silence for a while. She really didn't know what to say to him. All the normal questions seemed awkward, because of his handicap.

"So you're a writer," he said, finally breaking the silence.

"Well, trying to be," she laughed.

"You're doing a signing, so you have a book, right? Wait, now I remember my mother talking about your book. *A Quiet Wanting*, right?"

"Yes."

"She was suggesting it to a customer. I work at the store part-time," he said, slowing as they approached a stop sign. "So if you've written a book, you *are* a writer."

"Sometimes I feel like I'm just trying to convince myself along with everyone else."

He gave her another amused look. "I'll just have to read that book of yours."

"I'd be happy to give you a copy. As a thank you."

Ten minutes later they pulled into a garage. Lucy gave the mechanic the details and address, as well as her keys. He wasn't sure he could tow it in until later that day, or perhaps the next. But she had no choice. A few miles later they began a long descent down a steep mountain road, and houses grew more frequent. A few blocks later, Colin slowed and turned into a parking lot. The sign read: *Pond View Café*, and in the window another advertised free Wifi.

"Do you want to come in?" It would be an ordeal, but she thought it rude not to ask.

"Go do your thing, I'll just wait."

"I'll be quick."

He pulled a pair of binoculars from between the seats. "I'll be happily occupied."

"Looking at what?"

He held up a battered copy of *The North American Field Guide to Birds*.

"Oh, you're a bird watcher."

He nodded and smiled. "I'll be parked on the other side of the pond," he said and pointed.

"Would you like me to get you a coffee or something in the meantime?"

"No, I'm good."

She got out and stood there. "Thank you so much. I'm sorry to be such a pest."

"Do you always apologize so much?"

She blinked. "Yeah, I think I do."

"You don't have to."

"Okay," she said, smiling.

* * *

JUST AFTER TEN O'CLOCK RUTH LOOKED UP AS KRIS came in wearing big sunglasses.

"Uh oh, not another headache, I hope."

Kris grimaced. "I took a Tylenol and an Advil which is supposed to do the trick, but so far nothing. But I've got two customers coming in for my suggestions on their next books."

Kris was passionate about books, which was why Ruth had hired her long ago when she couldn't really afford to add another person onto the payroll. When Kris liked a book, it was hard for anyone to resist her fervent recommendations.

"Well, it's still quiet, so why don't you—"

Just then something fell in the back of the store. They looked at each other. There was no one else in the store yet. Slowly they turned, walking past the front shelves, stopping in the back corner. A book lay on the scuffed wood floor, face up. Ruth picked it up, reading the title out loud: *Natural Cures for Head and Neck Pain*.

"Jesus, Ruth, I've got goose bumps up my arms. There's no way that book just fell. It was shelved sideways, wedged between those other books."

Ruth looked at Kris with raised eyebrows. "Hazel?"

"Well, I don't know what else could explain it."

"I guess she's trying to tell you something," Ruth chuckled, handing her the book.

"I don't usually go in for that kind of stuff, but..."

When she'd bought the business years ago, Ruth had no idea she'd inherited a ghost. An old woman who tended to lurk in the back corner near the clearance books. This wasn't the first time Hazel had recommended a read in her own particular way.

In the beginning, Ruth had chalked the little oddities up to coincidences, trucks rumbling by, or someone's poor shelving. Then a psychic came for a signing and the minute she walked through the door her eyes widened, and she veered right for that corner.

"You have a spirit here," she announced.

Ruth had shivered. She shouldn't have been surprised, though. How many dogs walked in and also headed for that corner, barking or whining for no apparent reason.

"She's friendly, don't worry," the psychic had assured her. "But she's been here a long time. Was this always a bookstore?"

"Well, the building is old, and before me another woman, Betsy, ran the bookstore, but before that I'm not sure."

"I'm seeing something else, flowers, colored...fabrics? Was this once a dry goods store?"

Ruth shrugged.

At the time someone had been reading a book with a ghost named Hazel in it, and so she'd been christened. Ruth forgot about her most of the time. Now she stood there, looking at the back corner, where the shelves were a little too crowded. There were some wonderful books there, just waiting for the right person to pick them up and feel that joy of discovering an unknown treasure. But these books weren't really making her any money, and they were taking up valuable space. Still, Ruth hated to part with them.

But like the bathroom, this part of the store was in need of some sprucing up. She took a few steps back and tried to envision the space differently. Before she'd canceled her cable, she used to watch HGTV at night when her eyes were too tired to read, marveling at the transformations to spaces on *Design on a Dime* and *Weekend Warrior*. As she stood there, something occurred to her out of the blue and she began to visualize...

"Ruth," Kris called. "Mail's here, and one you need to sign for."

Ruth gave the space a final glance, then walked up front.

"How's it going?" Lizzie, their mail carrier, asked.

"The usual," Ruth said.

Lizzie handed her a legal-size envelope. "Sign right there on the front of the card, and then the back."

Ruth glanced at the sender: her landlord, Jeff. Not good, she knew. She signed, handing Lizzie back the pen.

"See you tomorrow," Lizzie said.

Kris began sorting through the pile of mail, while Ruth considered the envelope in her hand. Something told her she should probably leave it until later. She hesitated, then tore the top open and pulled out a notarized letter.

"Oh, shit!" she said, closing her eyes.

"What's wrong?" she heard Kris say. "Are you all right?"

Ruth shook her head and handed Kris the letter.

"What! He can't raise the rent that much, can he? Doesn't the lease say—"

"We don't have a lease, remember? I've been asking him to renew it and he's been putting me off for months now. I was afraid maybe he was going to sell."

She sat on the stool and sighed. Five hundred dollars a month was more than she could handle. She was barely squeaking by now. And she'd just cut hours. What more could she cut? Or sell?

* * *

LUCY GOT ONLINE WITHIN SECONDS and there amidst an inbox full of junk was a message from David. She took a deep breath and opened it.

Lucy,

I know you still think I'm an addict, but I'm not. I stopped. It's over. I tried to tell you when we were sitting on the beach, but you didn't want to hear it. It was just an escape. I honestly didn't care anymore about anything in my life.

She stared out the café window, remembering that day on the beach, the only time she had seen him after his arrest. When she'd arrived, he was standing at the water's edge, looking far out into the distance, dark smudges of sleeplessness beneath his hazel eyes, looking ten years older. A flicker of compassion had tugged at her heart. She'd opened her arms and pulled him in and he held her so tightly she could feel him trembling.

Then he told her he'd cut a deal so he'd only have to serve thirty days in a minimum security prison, another month of house arrest, then six months parole with community service and mandatory counseling.

"I don't need counseling," he said, when they sat up by the dunes. "I don't have an addiction."

"How can you say that? Obviously you couldn't stop gambling."

"I could have. But I liked it, feeling like I'd stepped into somebody else's life for a while. It was exciting, and...it just made everything else bearable." He'd closed his eyes. "Like nothing else in the world existed. And when you win, it's the best feeling in the world. "

"They call it a high, and that's why it becomes an addiction. You're acting just like my brother Charlie did—"

"It wasn't like that."

"What was it you were escaping? What was so terrible about our life to make you do something so awful? And why didn't you tell me any of this?"

"What's the difference between an addiction and an obsession? Because it wasn't like you were really there to talk to, Lucy. Haven't you been escaping, too? When was the last time you really paid any attention to what's been going on with us?"

She remembered being stunned by how he was acting. He'd stolen from his clients, and then took everything they had. Where was the guilt? The begging? Where was the plea for forgiveness? It wasn't the scene she'd imagined. He shook his head as if *he didn't get it.*

"What about that horrible man on your answering machine who threatened you?"

"I paid him off the next day, and I put everything back in the trust account."

"But you took everything we had, David. I don't even—"

"I'll pay you back. Don't worry."

"You think this is just about the money? I feel like I don't even know who you are."

He gave her a long look. "Well, I guess we each found our own way of coping with what we didn't want to face. You had your book, and I had this."

"Jesus, David, are you saying this is because of Ben?"

His eyes suddenly filled with tears.

"David, I've moved on, I..." she'd felt her own tears come without warning.

"Look, you and I both know nothing's been the same since he died. We changed houses, changed states, tried on a new life, but guess what? It's still there, and every time I look at his picture that you insist on hanging, Christ, every time I look at—" He stopped abruptly and looked away.

"Every time you look at...me? Is that what you were about to say?"

He hadn't answered, but he didn't have to. She turned back to the computer now and read the last lines of his message.

I didn't really want to move here after we lost Ben. What I really wanted then was to separate. But how could I do that to you? I hoped that maybe things would change once we got away, that I would feel differently, so I gave it a go. And now, I'm almost relieved. I don't have to live this lie anymore. But for me to feel like I could have any kind of a future, I have to let go of the past, completely. You need to do that, too. Hate me if you must, but let's move on.

David

She forced herself to read it once more, her mind reeling. He'd wanted to separate after Ben died? How was that possible? She'd had absolutely no inkling, but then again, she was barely functioning then. Barely able to open her eyes each morning and get out of bed. What did that say about the past five years?

With trembling fingers she typed: *I won't be bothering you anymore*. She hit send.

She sat there for ten long minutes, trying to calm down, longing for a cigarette and a big glass of wine. Finally she packed up and left. As she crossed the parking lot and headed up the road, lined with woods but for the pond surrounded by reeds, she saw Colin sitting in his Jeep, looking through the binoculars. You would never know he was a paraplegic from the way he appeared in the driver's side window. He simply looked like any man watching for birds.

She wondered if his loss still hit him at times the way her own grief over Ben used to suddenly bludgeon her in the middle of the night. Or in the first flush of consciousness after sleep. That thing that devastated your life and would define the rest of your days.

Now that thing would be losing David.

12

THE DAY AFTER RUTH GOT JEFF'S LETTER RAISING THE RENT, Kris was still venting about it when once again Lizzie the mail carrier walked in and slapped her stack on the counter. Ruth spotted the blue envelope and immediately pulled it from the pile. Her employees all thought these letters had to do with the prison book orders which no one was allowed to touch, she told them, for security reasons. But of course it was the letter from Thomas. The one that was going to tell her exactly why he was in prison. How had he gotten it here so quickly?

"I just don't see how he has the gall to raise the rent like that. It's not like he's going to use the money to fix this place up," Kris said, giving Ruth's shoulder a squeeze. "You'll think of something, Ruth. You always do."

"Think of something for what?" she heard Colin ask.

She looked up and saw him sitting in front of the door. She hadn't even heard the bell. He pushed his chair around the counter and she noticed Lucy's book on his lap.

"Oh, nothing. Kris, why don't you go shelve those books? I'll take care of the register." Then she turned to her son again, intent on changing the subject. "I see you've got Lucy's book."

"I met her yesterday when I gave her a ride to a garage to fix her car."

"Oh dear." Colin had never returned her call about Lucy staying in the cabin next door.

"Anyway, she gave me a copy to thank me, although I told her it wasn't necessary. So how long will she be staying?"

"I'm sure she'll be leaving after her signing, but I wouldn't mind if she stayed on longer if you wouldn't. She's going through a rough time."

"I sensed that." He tilted his head, the way he'd done since he was a little boy, whenever considering something carefully. "Whatever she decides is fine with me."

"Thanks, honey."

He smiled now. "Your hair looks nice today. Again."

"Your sister keeps telling me I'm too old for a braid, so I'm putting a little more effort into it."

His smile grew. "Are you sure that's all it is? Because I get the feeling there's something going on, Mom. You seem awfully distracted lately and you keep staring off into space."

"Don't be silly," she said, with a wave of her hand. "And what about you? Gloryanne's been in several times in the past few weeks, I noticed."

He shook his head, and the teasing look disappeared. "Nothing going on."

And then he turned his wheelchair and headed toward the back of the store.

* * *

AN HOUR LATER RUTH MANAGED TO SLIP BACK into the restroom, the blue envelope tucked in her purse. She sank on the couch with a sigh. There was no saving this letter, no thrill of anticipation. Suddenly she had to know the truth. She hadn't realized how frayed her nerves were until she saw that envelope in Kris's hand. She took it from her purse and tore it open.

Dear Ruth,

I need you to know that I am not a Gatsby, or a Tom Buchanan. I've never mistreated a woman, as Tom did with Daisy, and Myrtle. And I'm never going to make up who I am or what I've done, as Gatsby did. I've had ten years in here, lots of hours to reflect on every mistake I made in my life. And every regret. The one thing keeping me going was knowing in my heart that once I got out of here, I would never come back, no matter what the statistics say.

You're a special woman, Ruth. You are smart and funny, kind and beautiful...

She put the letter down and closed her eyes. The only time in her life she'd actually felt beautiful was early on with Bill. In that first blush of love her eyes sparkled, her skin glowed, and how he'd loved her wild hair, which back then shimmered with highlights. He would bury his face and breathe it in and she would feel like the most seductive creature in the world.

She stood, facing the mirror over the sink, and stared at herself. A long, plain face looked back, nose a little too pointed, wild hair escaping a barrette. The skin around her eyes was crinkled, her neck beginning to pouch. She imagined Thomas looking back at her and smiled. In the mirror she saw her eyes light up, her entire face transform. That was what he saw.

She picked up the second page of the letter.

I know I don't really have the right to ask if I could be part of your life. If it could even be a possibility. For five years we've had a wonderful friendship, although I think we both feel more than that. But there's always been something keeping things safe. Bars. There's a bit of irony, don't you think? Because of these bars, we've never tried to go to the next step, as we would have in the outside world. But now is our chance.

I was wrong about putting what I did in a letter. It's just that you looked so frightened, and I never want you to be frightened. I need to say it to your face, Ruth, I need to see your eyes. I want to do this right. Please, when you come back next Saturday let me do that so you'll understand. Then whatever you decide, I'll agree. But I would never want you to be afraid of me.

Yours, Thomas

Of course she would go. She wasn't afraid of him and never felt the least bit nervous when she was with him.

"I'll be right out, Kris," she called then at the sudden knock on the door.

"It's me," she heard her daughter say. "Can I come in?"

Ruth shoved the letter into her purse and opened the door. There stood Jenny with a worried look on her face.

"What's wrong? Why aren't you at school?"

Jenny shut the door, sat on the couch and pulled Ruth down beside her. "What's going on with you, Mom?"

"What..." And then she remembered Colin just moments ago asking the same thing. Had he called Jenny? He wouldn't have, he never interfered in her life. Even if he had, Jenny could never have left school and gotten here so quickly.

"Nothing's going on. Why?"

"Mom..." Jenny hesitated, and Ruth felt her breath catch. "I had a meeting with the rest of the English faculty this morning. Remember Andrea? Her husband Carl is the one who got you the foot in the door to sell books at the prison?"

A wave of heat rushed up her neck, until her face began to burn with embarrassment. "Mom, why did you go visit that prisoner last week?"

13

I T WAS PAST NOON. LUCY LAY IN BED, STARING AT THE CEILING. What was she doing in this battered old cabin? How was it possible this was her life? Her fingers drew light circles across her middle as she'd practiced in Lamaze years ago, trying to calm herself. She looked at the unlit cigarette on the nightstand. After tossing the last pack, she'd discovered that the general store sold single cigarettes. She grabbed it and pulled in a long drag, letting out a slow breath, over and over until she felt her body begin to relax. Squeezing her eyes closed, she felt wetness slide down her cheeks.

In the weeks after they lost Ben, when she told her therapist she wasn't sure how she could get through an entire day, he told her to just think about getting through the next hour. And if that was too much, the next minute. She did that now, trying to envision something happy, as he'd also suggested. Something that would make her smile, because just the physical act of smiling could actually elevate your mood. It was no longer the beach at St. Augustine.

She pictured their old house in Mendham, with David and Ben, who would have been five now. She could see herself pushing him on a swing in the yard. He'd be laughing, yelling *higher, push me higher*. The yellow roses would be blooming on the arbor, a stew simmering in the kitchen, and she would be the happiest woman in that safe little world. In the house she'd thought they'd grow old in. That David hadn't wanted to leave. Because now she knew the truth, he'd just wanted to leave her. And now he had.

She threw off the covers suddenly. She'd been wallowing in bed for hours, rehashing everything since his awful email. In the early days of grief, her therapist had also told her it was okay to wallow, to let her feelings out, and there were moments the release felt good. The sadness would somehow drain out of her. The guilt for trying to make something happen that obviously wasn't meant to be. That David had never really wanted.

She was tired now of having her thoughts consumed with David and everything that had gone wrong. She couldn't make David want her. She couldn't change any of it. This was her life, and it was time to get a grip. Get back to work. Because it wasn't time that healed the deepest wounds, it was staying busy, keeping yourself distracted.

She pulled on her robe and went into the living room and stood at the table in front of the big window, looking at the stack of her books beside her laptop. David's accusation came flooding back. Was this book an obsession? She remembered him saying the same thing about having a child, after the third miscarriage. *One more try*, she'd begged. *Please*. Of course he gave in. He always gave her everything she wanted; he was so loving, so caring. And now he was someone else entirely.

She picked up a book and held it to her chest, shaking her head. This book was another dream of hers, and you didn't give up on dreams until you'd tried everything possible. Besides, wasn't this book proof that if you focused hard enough on something else, you could somehow swim out of grief that threatened to drown you? She could do it again. She was doing it, in fact. She thought of Ruth, and all of the wonderful things she'd said about the novel. A real book signing in just four days. There were other booksellers in a bunch of states now who had copies, who might actually be reading it at that moment. It was time to finally shower and get dressed and start this day, because she wasn't turning back. It wasn't as if she had anything else to lose, she thought with a laugh, because she actually had nothing left. And she'd never been a quitter.

* * *

BY TWO O'CLOCK LUCY WAS AT HER COMPUTER and miracle of miracles, she was able to get online. Maybe smacking the broadband card the way her mother used to hit the TV when it was on the blink had done the trick. Or maybe the trees were swaying just the right way. Now she stared at an e-mail from *The Midwest Book Review* and her stomach clenched in anticipation. It could be terrible. It might be the nail in the coffin of this escapade. She clicked open and gasped at the first line: *In this well-written debut novel, Lucinda Barrett mines the heart and soul of a woman dealing with love, loss and betrayal.*

Well-written! She paused, savoring the first words from this respected reviewer. She continued: *In A QUIET WANTING, Barrett writes with a sure touch, weaving an intricate plot—part romance, part mystery—that will have readers racing to the end to find out Matthew's secret, and Hope's final decision.*

Her eyes went back to the word *romance*, wondering if the reviewer was considering this a romance novel, because it wasn't. Or did they mean *romance* as in the literature vein? As in the romances of the early years of writing? Still, *intricate plot* was great, and *readers racing to the end* absolutely wonderful!

She laughed out loud! Her first official review and it was excellent. She forwarded it to Ruth along with a note: *I just want to thank you again for the use of the cabin. It's just what I need right now. I'll see you Saturday for the signing!* Just as she was opening her bookseller file, because she was sending this review to every store she'd visited, she heard the crunch of tires in her driveway and jumped up, wondering who it could be.

Colin's jeep was coming to a stop just beside the cabin. Before he went through the difficulty of getting his wheelchair out, she raced down the porch to meet him.

"You mentioned your car was going to be ready this afternoon. I can give you a lift, since I'll be going that way anyway."

"Yes, he said about three, but I don't want to bother you again."

He looked at her quizzically, then laughed. "What are you planning to do, take a cab? I don't think you'll find one around here."

She shrugged. "I…I didn't really think it through. I was kind of caught up working. I just got my first official review, and it was a really good one."

"Congratulations. You seem better than the other day."

After David's e-mail, she'd barely spoken on the ride back. "I'm sorry, I—"

He held his hand up. "There's no need to explain."

"Okay."

"So why don't you go get your things and we'll head out."

"Are you sure?"

He nodded and smiled. "You really have a hard time letting people do things for you, don't you?"

She couldn't help but smile. "Yeah, I guess I do."

* * *

WHEN SHE GOT TO THE GARAGE AND FOUND HER car wouldn't be ready for another few hours, Lucy agreed to go with Colin to "a place she might find interesting." Then he'd drop her off at the garage on the way back to the lake. He didn't talk much this time, and she looked out her window, intrigued by the mystery of their destination, moved once again by the stunning scenery as they drove south through Sussex County.

"The Appalachian Trail runs through those mountains," he said, pointing to the ridge to the west that paralleled the road. "My Dad and I used to hike there when I was a little kid. It's a gorgeous trail."

"I've been away from New Jersey for a long time. I'd forgotten how beautiful it is here. Northern New Jersey looks more like Vermont than what most people expect."

"Yeah, most people think of Newark Airport or the turnpike. And that's okay with me. Keeps it pristine."

Twenty minutes later they passed into Warren County.

"We're not far from the Delaware River," Colin said, breaking another long silence, as they drove through the tiny village of Blairstown. "Have you ever been to the Delaware Water Gap National Park?"

"No, I've driven through the Gap on Route 80, but I've never been in the park."

"It's spectacular, some of the most beautiful land in the country."

They headed west toward the river, the road rising steeply, the woods even more dense, until they veered off onto a gravel road. Up ahead she saw several buildings, and then Colin slowed the Jeep and pulled into a parking lot near a sign that said: THE RAPTOR CENTER.

"What is this place?"

He parked beside a low shingled building to the left of the lot. "It's a rehab for birds. They come here injured or orphaned and we do everything we can to rehabilitate them and send them back out into the wild."

"I don't recall, which ones are raptors?"

"Raptors are birds of prey. But we also take starlings and finches, anything wild."

Before she could ask why, he was lifting his wheelchair from behind, over his shoulders, and somehow managed in a quick, fluid motion to deposit it on the ground outside his door, where it unfolded. She turned, not wanting to look too curious, but watching from the corner of her eye as he pushed himself up with his hands, then swung his lower body out the car door and into the chair.

"I'll be about ten minutes," he said, nodding toward the long building to the left, with a sign that read Educational Center. "Feel free to walk around."

She headed in the opposite direction down a gravel path into the woods. The canopy of trees shaded everything and it took a moment for her eyes to adjust. Up ahead a path branched off to the left. She took that route and soon came upon a series of cages. Approaching the first one, she realized that of course they were aviaries.

She stopped in front of the first one, with a little placard beside it: Great Horned Owl. The wooden frame stretched about fifteen or twenty feet high, about fifteen feet wide, and was completely covered with wire fencing. Her eyes scanned several large branches stretched across the inside of the aviary, mimicking a tree and somehow attached to the structure. After nearly a minute she spotted a great horned owl on top of the higher branch, with its eyes closed. Owls, she remembered, are nocturnal creatures. Its brown feathers looked soft as down; its horns and sleeping face gave it an endearing look. She couldn't help but smile.

In the next aviary she almost gave up looking until she made out the peregrine falcon hidden in the branches of an artificial Christmas tree standing in the middle of the cage. Another falcon sat watching her. She continued past one aviary after another, losing track of time. There were ravens and a snowy owl, white and unearthly in its beauty, as well as red tail and Cooper's hawks, more birds than she'd ever remember.

Just before the path branched off again, her eyes roamed a much larger cage and her breath caught as she looked all the way up. Near the top sat a bald eagle, which she recognized instantly, sitting on a smaller limb of the main branch. It was magnificent. A fierce intelligence seemed to emanate from its startling yellow eyes, which were staring at her. She stood there, watching, but it never moved. She'd never seen an eagle in person before and was awed by its size. She wondered if it was awaiting release into the wild.

Looking ahead, she saw a man raking the gravel path about twenty yards away and began heading toward him to ask about the eagle, when she heard her name. Turning, she was surprised to see Colin pushing himself toward her.

"I just saw the eagle, it was—"

"Time to go," he interrupted, and turned without waiting for her response.

"Of course," she said, startled by his abrupt manner.

She hurried to catch up, but he was pushing himself faster than she could walk. By the time she reached the car, he was behind the wheel, his chair folded and stowed in the backseat.

"Are you all right?" she asked, noticing the gray pallor of his face.

He nodded.

"This place is absolutely incredible," she said, hoping to break the sudden tension as they pulled away. "I'd love to come back some time."

"Of course as a writer this screams cliché, doesn't it? The crippled man trying to fix crippled birds?"

She looked at him, unsure if he was joking. It was the first time he'd mentioned his handicap. By the fierce set of his mouth she could see that he wasn't. She didn't know what to say, so she said nothing.

She spent the ride back looking out the window, thinking about the beauty of the northern woods, the lake, and even The Raptor Center. What a beautiful setting this whole area could be for another book. She hadn't written in a long time. Her efforts these days were simply marketing *A Quiet Wanting*, and that took a lot of energy. She really missed writing, though, creating characters, playing with words, wondering what she could make happen next. Maybe she could begin something new during her remaining few days at the cabin. That would certainly keep her mind busy, and off the things she didn't want to dwell on.

Glancing at Colin, she felt almost guilty at the flicker of excitement this idea sparked. She realized suddenly that he might be in pain. He was clearly distressed about something.

"Thank you again," she said when he pulled into the garage. "For rescuing me."

He turned to her. "No problem."

"Anytime I can repay the favor, let me know, okay?" Although she couldn't imagine what he might let her do for him.

When she got back to the cabin, she was surprised to see a white convertible pulling into Colin's driveway. A pretty redhead got out and stood looking up at his house. When Lucy glanced over, she saw Colin, sitting on his deck, looking down at the woman.

He didn't look happy.

14

RUTH'S EYES DRIFTED AGAIN TO THE CLOCK behind the counter. It was hard not watching as the minutes ticked toward Lucy's signing. Then Thomas's visiting hours. She imagined him pacing his cell in anticipation and nervousness, having no reason to think that when he walked into the visiting room she wouldn't be there as promised. A hot wave of guilt washed over her.

She closed her mind as she'd close a book and luckily, a few minutes after they opened, customers came in one after another and it was the kind of busy Saturday she usually enjoyed. With one eye on the register and her ear tuned to the floor, she overheard a conversation Megan was having with a mother who lamented that her son didn't like to read.

"How old is he?" Megan asked, and Ruth heard that the boy was ten. "What does he like to do?"

The mother hesitated, then said softly, "He doesn't seem to know. I think he's at that age where he's trying to figure out where he fits in. School can be so…"

"Cruel?" Megan asked.

"Yes," the mother said with a grateful nod.

Megan handed her *The Diary of a Wimpy Kid.* "I guarantee he'll read this, or I'll give you your money back. And luckily, it's one of a series, so when he finishes, come back for the rest. It's one of the biggest Young Adult hits in the past few years."

Harry began pushing bookshelves to the back to make room for the signing table as well as another table of refreshments. The shelves with casters hadn't been cheap, but Harry had been right when he suggested them awhile back. They opened up the space for events, something she knew she needed to do more of.

A few more customers trickled in, one of them being the mystery woman who perused the bestsellers every so often, then walked out in a huff. Ruth wondered if the busy morning was due to such a gorgeous May day, or could it be the radio ad? She'd pulled out all the stops, knowing it was Lucy's first bookstore signing, even springing for the radio ad, something she missed now. It had taken her days to write it, a process she enjoyed—creating something with her words. She loved writing, but knew it wasn't her calling, not writing books anyway. She also got a kick out of feeling a bit like an actress as she sat in the studio, reading the script, hoping to convince someone that THIS was a must read. She knew the commercial for Lucy's book by heart:

Hello, this is Ruth from The Book Lover, and we'd like to invite you to a special event this Saturday at our store. Lucinda Barrett, an author all the way from Florida, is in town to read and share with us from her debut novel, A Quiet Wanting. *Rarely has a book touched me so deeply as this story of love and lies, dreams and loss. Does anyone ever really know what goes on inside a marriage? Come and meet Lucinda so that one day soon, you'll be able to say "I knew her when..."* A Quiet Wanting. *You'll find it at The Book Lover in downtown Warwick Village, where undiscovered gems are right at our fingertips.*

She hoped that ad would be worth the price, not just for Lucy, but for herself.

She looked up now as Colin came in with a small bouquet of sunflowers she assumed were for Gloryanne. Until he set them on the signing table, next to a stack of Lucy's books.

"Well, that's a nice touch," she said, coming over.

"I owe her an apology."

Before she could respond, Jenny walked in with a bag full of sandwiches, and Colin wheeled away. Jenny looked at her for a long moment. Ruth hesitated, searching her daughter's face. They hadn't talked since Jenny had confronted her about her visit to Thomas. Now Jenny held out the bag and gave her a big smile.

"Egg salad, fresh made this morning."

Ruth felt a rush of relief. Their conversation a few days ago was a thing of the past.

"Loralee and her sister will be here in a little while," Jenny said. "Just in case."

Ruth gave her a hug. Jenny always came to events, and usually rustled up a few friends. That was the tough thing about signings, there was no guarantee how many people would show up. She could advertise, run a radio ad, and put a sign out on the sidewalk with balloons. But sometimes a beautiful day meant people would rather be outside doing something else. And a rainy day might keep them from venturing out altogether, especially with the downtown parking situation. There were always excuses, but she hated when an author left disappointed.

Some authors, though, were seasoned and knew the drill, sending out their own newsletters and posting their events on websites and other online venues, which helped to bring in their fans. Others arrived with a haughty attitude and then left in a huff, although they'd made no effort whatsoever to reach out to anyone. They simply thought "if I show, they will come." They had no clue, Ruth realized, that these days, writing a book was only half the job. Smart authors spent an equal amount of time promoting themselves.

Ruth knew there wasn't much Lucy could do. She wasn't from the area, which meant bringing friends and family wasn't an option. And she was unknown, so luring fans wasn't going to happen. But they'd already sold some of her books. Ruth had also targeted the local book clubs, sending each an e-mail, and her fingers were crossed that a few would show up. She hoped so, for Lucy's sake. Everything in her life, it seemed, was riding on this book.

It struck her in that moment that Lucy's passion for her book, putting everything in her life behind it, wasn't so different from her own for her store. She'd done the very same thing after her own world had fallen apart, hadn't she? With no guarantees.

But it was just that way in the book world. No one did it for the money. You risked everything because you loved books.

AN HOUR BEFORE THE EVENT, Ruth looked out the window and saw Lucy across the street, pacing back and forth.

"I'll be back in a little bit," she said to Megan, grabbing her purse.

Lucy was startled to see her. "Oh, Ruth, I didn't want to be too early. Again."

They both laughed.

"Don't be silly, it's fine," she said.

"I'm so nervous, I could throw up. I'm so afraid I'm going to stumble or freeze while I read."

Wasn't it the number one fear, even before dying—speaking in public? "You don't have to read if you don't feel up to it. You can just say a few words, or even just sign books."

"I want to. I'll just take it one moment at a time."

"Why don't we go for a little walk," Ruth suggested. "We have plenty of time."

Lucy looked pretty in white capris and a peach sweater set. Her short, dirty blonde hair was tucked behind her ears, and her green eyes looked luminous with just a bit of make-up, the dark circles and lines of fatigue beginning to fade.

They walked down Main Street in silence for a few moments, then Lucy stopped as they crossed the small bridge and looked down.

"Is this a river?"

"That's the Waywayanda Creek."

"It's lovely. In fact, the whole Village of Warwick is just so charming."

Ruth smiled. "Yes, it is, but don't let this creek fool you. It flooded a few years back and caused some devastation." Which she was still paying for.

Lucy looked up at her then. "I can't believe I've been here a week already."

"Well, you look rested. So tell me, how are things going at the lake?"

"It's so beautiful, and peaceful. I've really enjoyed it, although I did have a run-in with a few spiders. Oh, and I'm going to pick up some new shades while I'm here in town, because a few times they just snapped up and scared the daylights out of me."

"No, no, don't be silly—"

"If I'd stayed in a hotel, Ruth, it would have cost me a fortune. It's the least I can do."

"It's just sitting there empty anyway."

"It's such a lovely spot. Why don't you use it?"

"Oh, you know how it is, just too busy, really."

They turned and began walking again. A moment later they were in front of Elaine's.

"How about a cup of tea?"

"Sure," Lucy said.

They went inside and although Elaine wasn't in sight, Hannah came right over.

"Hey, Ruth, how about a table by the window?"

"How'd you guess?"

"So I hear your next big revitalization meeting is coming up," Hannah said, as she led them to the front of the restaurant.

"Yes, later in the week."

"Odd it's at night, don't you think?" Hannah went on without looking at her.

Ruth caught herself before the word *What?* escaped her lips. She hesitated a moment, then said in what she hoped sounded like a natural voice, "Well, it's hard to get everyone to leave their stores during working hours."

"Oh, right," Hannah nodded, as Ruth and Lucy sat.

"We'll just have tea, Hannah. And by the way, this is Lucinda Barrett, she's doing a signing at the store in a little while."

"Wow, an author. I'll try to stop in when I'm done here. I love readings."

Ruth watched Hannah walk back to the kitchen, her insides vibrating with anger at the lie she'd just uttered. She wanted to smack Eddie.

"Is she a friend?"

Ruth turned to Lucy, who was looking at her curiously. "Yes, she is. But listen, let's catch up on you. I understand you've met my son, Colin?"

"Yes, he was kind enough to help me when I had car trouble."

"Colin's a good man, very self-sufficient. But still, it's nice to have someone nearby."

Lucy hesitated. "Would you mind if I asked what happened to him?"

Ruth closed her eyes and sighed.

"I'm sorry, Ruth, I shouldn't have asked."

"No, it's not like it happened yesterday. It's been over two years, but there's still the odd moment when...I somehow forget. Then I'll look at him, in that chair for the rest of his life, so handsome, so young, it just breaks my heart all over again."

Lucy reached across the table and squeezed her hand. "I can only imagine."

"Do you remember I mentioned the creek flooding while we were standing on the bridge? That's really when it all started. Colin was home on leave. He had one more tour left and then he and Gloryanne were going to get married. She and I were in the city shopping for a wedding dress when the flash flood came. They got sandbags and everything they could get their hands on to keep the water back, but eventually it just roared up the street and through the doors and into the store."

She and Gloryanne had gotten home that night to find the mud and debris halfway up the bookshelves, she went on, everything coated with brown sludge. Colin, Harry, Megan, Kris, and so many others had come to help. Ironically it was just the bookstore and another shop that were hit hard. But Jeff, her landlord, didn't have flood insurance on the building. She had a tenant's policy, which didn't cover floods, either.

"I thought I was going to lose the store. A week later we were nearly done cleaning up, and Colin was deployed back to Iraq. A few days later his tank was hit with an IED, you know those roadside bombs the insurgents hide in garbage cans or book bags, anywhere, really. Suddenly the flood, the store, every problem...it all paled."

"Oh, Ruth, how awful."

"Colin went into the Army just a few years out of high school. He'd been a bit of a wild child. Alex and Jenny both went to college, but he couldn't quite figure out where he belonged. He started going out to bars every night with other young guys." She looked out the window a moment. "I always wondered if Bill had lived...well, if it would have been different. I blamed myself for working so much when he was younger, after I bought the store."

"I'm sure that wasn't the case, Ruth."

"A moment later his tank would have passed and he would have been spared. Everything about his life would be different right now."

"I'm so sorry. I have to say, though, your son seems to be a survivor."

Ruth couldn't help smiling. "It took a while. Colin was always so strong and independent, but in the beginning, in the rehab, I was afraid. I knew he didn't want to be a burden to anyone. I worried about what was going through his mind. And then he asked me not to come anymore." She sighed. "I didn't want to agree, of course, but I could tell how hard it was for him when I was there. I wanted to make things better, that's what a mother does. But I agreed."

"He didn't want you to see his pain. I understand that. It's hard for a child when your parent is hurting, and there's nothing you can do."

"He did the same thing to his fiancée, Gloryanne, pushed her away. Those were awful days. After about four months, though, he finally called and asked me to come. I was a wreck, not knowing really what to expect. But he was all right. He was still Colin. He had a mentor and began to play wheelchair basketball and made friends with other paralyzed veterans and things started to change for the better. Except for Gloryanne."

"Is she the red-haired woman I've seen with him?"

Ruth nodded. "They've known each other since high school, and have had this on-again off-again relationship. When he enlisted all those years ago, she refused to have anything to do with him for a long time. Then he'd come home on leave and they'd see each other and it would be good for awhile. They were so young, and she just didn't want the Army life. After about five years, she married someone else, but it didn't last long. The next thing I know, they're back again. But she refused to get married until he was out of the service at the end of 2001. But then of course 9/11 happened, and he reenlisted. She was crushed."

Ruth took a sip of her tea and thought for a moment. "I think she still loves him. I just don't think she can commit to the kind of life she'd have with him now. Ironic, isn't it, now that he's finally out of the Army? But I don't want Colin to be alone for the rest of his life."

Just then Hannah appeared.

"Is everything okay? Would you like a refill?"

Ruth glanced at her watch. "We'd better get going, your signing is in ten minutes."

As they walked back, she asked Lucy about her book efforts.

"Well, I got that great write up from *The Midwest Book Review.*"

"Yes, that was wonderful, you must be thrilled."

"But there's been no word from anyone. And I just read in *The New York Times* there are now officially more self-published books than real published books."

"But Lucy, it hasn't been long. This is going to take some time. Your book might be next on many of their 'to-be-read' piles. I mean, you saw the stacks of books at my house."

"I feel like a lunatic," Lucy said with a laugh. "One minute I'm like *I'm going to do this! I'm not giving up!* And the next it seems indulgent and silly, and I think I should really pack it in and get back to the real world. Tell me honestly, do you think I'm nuts for doing this?"

"No, I don't. You're on a roller coaster ride, but I honestly don't think you have just another self-published book. Yours is a standout."

Lucy gave her such a grateful look.

"Keep plugging away. And I'm going to give your book to one of my publisher's sales reps. If he likes it, maybe he'll pass it to an editor."

"You know, Ruth, sometimes I can't believe a chance encounter brought me to you. I don't really have any friends anymore. After Ben died, it just…it was awkward for people, they didn't know what to say, and we kind of withdrew. Then we moved. We didn't make an effort to socialize in St. Augustine. I had Kate and Tia, a writing buddy, but I didn't talk about personal things with them. Anyway, it's nice to have a friend again. Someone I can really talk to."

Ruth had to smile at that. When she thought about it, she didn't really have a best friend. Oh, there was Hannah, but that was different. And of course Harry and Kris and Megan, but that was mostly about work. "Truth be told, books have really been my best friends all these years, so this is nice for me, too."

Although their circumstances were so different, in a way they were kindred spirits. She looked at Lucy for a long moment.

"Why don't you stay a while longer at the cabin?"

"Oh, Ruth, I couldn't..."

"We can give this a real fighting chance." Because more than anything she wanted to see Lucy succeed. She saw so much of herself in the brief glances filled with pain, or longing. The simple need to grasp onto something to survive. And Jenny was right about having someone nearby.

"You'd also be doing me a favor, by keeping an eye on Colin while you're there. We all get nervous about him swimming, you know?"

Lucy hesitated, then smiled. "I'd do anything for you, Ruth. Thank you."

As they crossed the bridge again Lucy stopped suddenly. "Oh my God, Ruth, I'm so self-consumed I almost forgot. What happened when you went to see your friend at the prison?"

Ruth stopped, too, and stared down at the water rushing by. She tried to make her voice sound normal, but even she could hear the tremble of emotion. "Actually, he told me that he's getting out on parole soon."

"Oh, Ruth, wow."

"I'm supposed to go back again later this afternoon, so that he can explain why he's there. I wasn't ready for that last week."

"Are you nervous?"

"I was," she said, "but not anymore."

"Why not?"

"Because I'm not going."

"But I thought—"

"Jenny found out about my visit, and obviously a little bit more. She left school in the middle of teaching to tell me that there was absolutely no way I should have anything to do with this man. I had to admit to her I didn't know what he'd done, which she thought was insane."

"What did he do, Ruth?"

She took a deep breath, hating to even say it out loud. "He was convicted of kidnapping. And terroristic threats."

They each said nothing for a long moment.

"Well…maybe there's a chance he's innocent. It does happen."

"I know. And I can't picture the Thomas I know doing something so awful. Taking someone, a child perhaps, holding them against their will. Terrorizing a person," she told Lucy, shaking her head, because it was all so unbelievable. "But he pled guilty."

Which meant he was guilty, she could hear Jenny saying again, along with the fact that she was being a complete and total fool.

15

WHEN LUCY WALKED INTO THE BOOK LOVER WITH RUTH, there were nearly twenty-five people sipping wine and munching appetizers in a space in the front of the store that had been cleared of bookshelves. Her legs turned to liquid. She was terrified, and thrilled.

Most were women, from twenties to probably seventies, but there were several men, as well. She recognized Ruth's daughter Jenny from the pictures in her house. Colin sat quietly to the side, a book in his lap, reading.

A moment later, Ruth was leading her to the table where stacks of her book were lined up, and they turned to face the crowd. The room fell silent. Lucy wondered if anyone could hear her heart thudding wildly in her chest. Ruth reached for her hand, gave it a quick squeeze.

"Most of you know how many books come across that door, and how many I read in the course of a month. When I picked up *A Quiet Wanting*, I had no idea what it was about, or who Lucinda Barrett was. But within just a few pages I was riveted and could not put the book down. When I finished, I invited Lucy for a signing, and I was delighted when she accepted. I would like to introduce to you one of my favorite new authors, who I hope will soon become a favorite of yours. Lucinda Barrett."

All eyes turned to her. Lucy felt her stomach pitch, as if she'd plummeted twenty floors in an elevator. A dozen things suddenly ran through her mind, and she was afraid somehow she'd blurt them out—that her life was in chaos, and she was a fraud, an imposter, with a book that was rejected over and over again. And yet here she was, trying to make it known.

Someone coughed, another person cleared her throat. She caught Ruth's eye, and Ruth smiled and nodded with encouragement. Lucy took a step forward and began to speak.

"Ever since I was a little girl, I've wanted to be a writer. I did everything I could, hoping to achieve that dream, until I was an adult. Most of you probably know how it is when you hit a certain age. You need to settle down, get a real job, and soon you're so busy those childhood dreams begin to fade away until they're simply gone. But..." she hesitated, wondering if this was too personal, but needing them to understand, "...a few years back, I rediscovered that dream to be a writer, and *A Quiet Wanting* was born. At the same time, I felt as if a part of me was reborn as well." She swallowed, pushing down a sudden lump of emotion swelling in her throat. "I'm so honored to be here. And I cannot tell you how touched I am by Ruth's support, and everyone else here at The Book Lover. I don't think a writer could ask for a better start than this."

She opened *A Quiet Wanting* and began to read, slowly, as she'd rehearsed, praying a cough or tickle wouldn't break the flow.

"*She embraced her sadness like a secret lover she met once each evening on her solitary drive home...*"

When she finished the prologue, just three pages, she looked up and she saw something magical—the looks on their faces. And then they began to clap.

Ruth came forward. "Lucy will be right here to sign books, or answer any questions."

The next hour was a blur as she signed books, chatted with people, and was amazed when a woman showed her passages highlighted in her copy, which she'd already read. Several others brought copies they'd gotten earlier in the week and one invited her to join their book club meeting next month. She hesitated, then realized she could say yes, thanks to Ruth's generous offer. This bought her much-needed time, because she really wasn't ready to face her mother yet, nor go back to Florida. In that moment, something seemed to lift within her.

She looked at the next woman in line, who exclaimed, "I felt as if you were looking over my shoulder and writing my life. I can't wait for your next book."

The last woman was an angry-looking brunette, who'd been waiting a while.

"Is this book self-published?" she blurted out.

Up until that moment, no one had mentioned that fact.

"Well...yes, it is," Lucy admitted.

The woman blinked twice and Lucy thought she might leave in a huff. But she handed over a book to be signed. When it was over, Lucy felt as if the wind had literally blown out of her sails—exhausted and exhilarated. Ruth asked about the "mystery woman," who apparently came in sporadically. This was the first time she'd ever bought a book.

"She's a frustrated writer, with two unpublished novels."

"I guess that explains it," Ruth said. "Now, about you. That was beautifully done."

"Really? I was afraid it was a bit too much."

"No, your passion came through. It was inspiring. And we sold twenty-three copies of your book!"

"Really?"

"Sometimes we get well-known authors who don't sell that many in a signing," Harry piped up suddenly, as he came over to begin clearing the table. "But Ruth and Kris have really been pushing your book."

"Keep going, Lucy," Ruth said quietly.

"I will. I feel so hopeful, I can't tell you. I'm through second-guessing myself."

"Now come over to the counter. I have a stack of books I want you to sign so we can put them on the shelves this week. Oh, and I put together a list of some booksellers not too far away you might want to contact while you're here."

"I owe you so much, Ruth," Lucy said, and gave her a quick hug. She was glad she could keep an eye on Colin for Ruth, but she'd have to think of something more.

"Don't be silly. Discovering a new writer, satisfying readers with undiscovered works, that's what I live for," Ruth said, then reached for the extra books.

Over Ruth's shoulder, she saw Colin near the door in an intense conversation with the pretty redhead. Suddenly Gloryanne turned and left. Colin looked up and caught Lucy's eye. A moment later he wheeled himself out the door, before she could even thank him for the flowers.

* * *

FINALLY, THE STORE WAS ALMOST EMPTY. Ruth looked at the clock, her stomach in knots, picturing Thomas sitting in that awful visiting room, his face lit with hope, waiting for her.

"That clock's not gonna move any faster just because you want it to," she heard Harry joke.

She turned and looked at him in surprise.

"You put in a long day, Ruth. Go home. I'll close up."

She hesitated, remembering her promise to Jenny. Yet knowing she could still make it in time if she left right now. "If you're sure you don't mind," she said, grabbing her purse.

"Go, and put your feet up."

But she didn't go home, nor did she put her feet up. She jumped into her car, heading to the thruway, with air conditioning blasting. It was hot as July. Or was it her nerves, rushing to make it? She turned the radio to the local NPR station, and let the relaxing classical music fill the car, trying to make her mind stop racing. But she couldn't.

She thought about the first time she'd met Thomas. After she'd approached the warden through Andrea's husband, Carl, the prison authorities had authorized her to hold a book fair in the prison library, to kind of test the waters. Several guards had carried extra tables in and she'd brought as many books as she could for the inmates to choose from. The event lasted four hours as one prisoner after another came in accompanied by a guard, and was given ten minutes to make a purchase.

Thomas had been in the first eight or so, when her nerves were still on high alert, and from the moment she saw him she'd felt...something. He'd come in the open doorway in that orange jumpsuit, a big, barrel-chested man back then, and stood across the room, looking all around at the tables full of books. Then his brown eyes landed on her and she watched him actually blush, then give her a shy smile.

"I haven't felt this excited since I was a kid at Christmas," he said softly.

"When I was a little girl books were always my favorite presents," she finally responded, surprised at his gentle manner. The other prisoners up until then had spoken little, their comments and questions terse.

"Well, I can tell you there's nothing as amazing as a 26-inch bicycle, or an air rifle, for a little boy. But in here, losing yourself in a good book is about as good as it gets."

She watched him pick up one book after another, his big hands holding them carefully as he turned pages and scanned, asking her opinion on each and every one. At the end of his ten minutes, he had a teetering pile of books and she sat and made out his bill.

"Thanks for doing this. I imagine it can't be easy," he said, his voice low, so that the guard at the door couldn't hear him. "You know, a nice lady like you coming to a place like this."

She nearly said it was all fine. But then she looked up at him again, and his eyes were searching hers. "Actually, I was pretty nervous at first. When I arrived I bit my lip so hard, I think it bled. But I'm really glad to be here."

"Me, too." He gave her another warm smile. "This means a lot to us.

I hope they let you come back."

The feedback from the book fair was so overwhelming, the warden had called and proposed she come back every few months so that the prisoners could order books on a regular basis. Over those next five years, she'd grown so comfortable with Thomas that there were actually moments she had a hard time believing he was really a prisoner. Or that he could possibly have done something horrible.

But he did do something horrible, she knew that for certain. Jenny had even brought a copy of an article she'd downloaded from *The Albany Times* to prove it. Now, Ruth turned into the prison complex, guard towers on all perimeters, and before the first security checkpoint, she suddenly pulled over.

"Mom, these kind of men prey on women like you," Jenny had practically yelled at her. "They know just what to say and do. And let's face it, you're always trying to help people, of course you're going to fall for it. You're too damn nice."

She'd felt like such a fool getting lectured by her daughter. Barely able to get a word in edgewise as she tried to explain that Thomas was different.

"Promise me, Mom, please. Tell me you're not going to meet this man again. I already asked Andrea's husband to take him off as your book liaison."

She didn't bother to tell Jenny it didn't matter. That he wouldn't be there anymore. But she couldn't possibly let her daughter know he was getting out. That he wanted to see her.

She sat there, just yards away from the building where the visiting room was housed. Unable to move. Was she being a fool? Could it be possible that this man she'd grown so fond of, who brought something back to life inside her after decades, who made her feel like a woman again, could he really be dangerous? Would he really hurt her in some way?

"You've got a house and a business, Mom. An entire life it's taken years to build. He could destroy that. Is that what you really want?"

What could she really say to that? That she'd bet it all Thomas wasn't like that? That she was a good judge of people, if nothing else? But of course she'd felt that way about her husband, Bill, in the beginning. Who proved her to be completely wrong.

And suddenly it was as clear as the razor wire glinting in the setting sun, as she tried to imagine Thomas somehow becoming a part of her life. How would she introduce him to people? How could he possibly fit in with the store, her family, the tiny village of Warwick where people never locked their doors?

Of course there was no way Thomas could fit into her life. How could she possibly have thought otherwise?

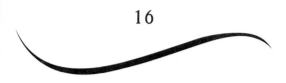

16

L UCY ARRIVED BACK AT THE LAKE WITH A BAG OF GOODIES, from a gourmet shop in town and a bottle of sangria. The threatened heat wave had arrived, and she felt as if she were walking through a steam bath as she climbed the cabin steps. Once inside, she stripped off her clammy things and slipped on nothing but an old cotton shift. There was no air conditioning and the cabin was sweltering, the mustiness of the old furniture permeating the air.

The grass was soft and cool as she walked down to the dock in bare feet. Colin's car wasn't back and she wondered if he was out with Gloryanne. She sat on the wooden dock, her feet dangling in the cold lake. Reaching down, she brought a scoop of water up and released it on her neck, enjoying the delicious feeling of droplets running down her chest and back.

She took a sip of the chilled sangria and it slid down like an ice pop melting in her throat. Then she leaned back on her hands and looked up at the mountains, barely visible through the building haze. She was so proud of herself, having faced every doubt, every fear. Despite the tumultuous events of the past few months and her crazy trip north, today was a big achievement.

She felt a new surge of energy for the upcoming days and another round of bookstore visits. There was lots to share now, best of all the review from the Warwick paper, thanks again to Ruth, which she'd forgotten in the busyness of the afternoon. *A stunning debut*, it said in the first paragraph. *Readers will be rooting for Hope as she navigates the heartbreaking terrain of a marriage falling apart, and the eventual discovery of a new future for herself.* Now she had two fabulous reviews and she was going to send them everywhere.

She kicked her foot and a spray of water splashed across the still surface of the lake. People even wanted to know when her next book was coming out!

"I'm an author!" she shouted out loud, laughing a moment later at the insanity of sitting at the edge of this lake in the middle of nowhere, having a party for one and talking to herself.

She decided it was time to start writing again. The urge had been with her since her trip to The Raptor Center. Besides, it would keep her mind distracted.

She sat there contented, enjoying that brief moment of utter stillness before the nocturnal creatures came alive again as night descended. Hearing a splash, Lucy turned to see a turtle surface, peek at her, then dive again. It was funny, but as much as she loved the ocean, and the feel of the sand and all the things that came with it, there was a unique beauty here, too. The peaceful lake surrounded by woods, ringed by mountains, the high-pitched call of a hawk or the cacophony of tree frogs and cicadas. It was a place that could transform a character if she were there long enough. That might, perhaps, begin to heal a broken heart.

She drained the last of her glass and opened the contents of the basket, when suddenly it felt as if her cheeks were on fire, no doubt from the wine and humidity. Scooting to the edge of the dock, she hesitated, then plunged into the lake, yelping as she surfaced from the shockingly cold water. Within moments, though, it felt like heaven as she swam back and forth.

Her shift rode up, the wet fabric wrapping around her waist, the cool water intensely sensual as it flowed through all her private places. Was she drunk? She wondered suddenly in the black water, half naked, feeling such a sense of abandon. Maybe a little buzzed, but what she was doing seemed perfectly natural. It was the kind of thing kids would do, and she did feel giddy as a child.

The light began to disappear quickly and she hoisted herself up on the dock, refreshed and exhausted. She sat there a moment, dripping, ravenous, ready to dig into her feast. But suddenly she was cold, and there were no lights out there at all. She grabbed everything and ran up to the cabin, shivering by the time she reached the door. Flipping the lights on, she stood on the little scatter rug inside the door, pulling off the wet shift.

She poured another sangria and drank it as she pulled on dry clothes, then sat at the table, eating the bread and cheese, polishing off the almonds and an apple as the moon ascended in the haze, a fuzzy white pearl just above the far mountain. It amazed Lucy that there was no television, no stereo, in this single, rustic room. She was stripped of all of the comforts of her former existence. She didn't miss any of it.

Once again she imagined her beautiful home. She would never live there again. But had it ever really felt like home? As she watched the moon rise through the mist, she poured a third glass of wine. And that's when the good feelings of the day, the exhilaration of the evening, somehow collided with the emotions of the house in St. Augustine and the promise of that new life which never really came to fruition.

* * *

A STRANGE NOISE WOKE LUCY THE NEXT MORNING. She opened her eyes to bright sunlight and instantly her head began to throb. The pinging noise came again. It sounded like something hitting a window.

She got up and went into the main room, wobbly and lightheaded, and there it was again. She reached the big window as a pebble hit the glass. Looking down, she saw Colin in his wheelchair, in khaki pants and a sleeveless t-shirt.

She went out onto the deck. "What are you doing?"

"I'm calling in that favor you owe me. Did I wake you?" he said, and then she saw him looking her up and down. She was standing there in nothing but an old nightie.

She backed into the doorway, then peeked out. The lake sparkled in the late morning sunshine. Everything was wet, even the trees dripping, and she realized it had rained during the night.

"Yes, I slept in I guess."

"Come on over later—I could use your help with something, if you don't mind."

"All right."

She made a cup of strong tea. The humidity and drenching heat were gone, no doubt swept away by the rain. She was regretting that third glass of sangria last night, and the second. Then she stood under the shower as long as she dared. The water never stayed warm for more than a few minutes, but as it cooled, she forced herself to endure it, hoping to sweep away the cobwebs and the hangover. Then she fought with a comb to untangle her hair, which had been matted to her head in damp clumps when she went to bed. Finally she made another mug of tea and sipped it as she walked over to Colin's.

It was gorgeous out, everything damp and glistening, the air so fresh and clean-smelling she immediately felt better. Looking down at the dock, she remembered how much she'd enjoyed herself, all alone. Suddenly, she didn't regret anything about last night.

Colin's deck was about ten feet above the ground and she walked up a long ramp, through a wide opening in the railing, marveling at the strength it must take him each time he pushed himself up the incline.

"Welcome to my humble abode," Colin said, opening the sliding screen door.

Whereas the cabin next door was shabby and cluttered, Colin's was furnished sparely, and everything appeared to be nearly new. It was bigger, but with the same basic great room layout. The walls were sheetrocked and painted a light beige. In the kitchen area she noticed there were no upper cabinets; they were all under the counters, of course, where he could access them. The counters, too, were low enough so that he could reach into the sink, and there was a peg board on the wall, with utensils hung for easy reaching.

A navy couch and recliner were grouped to the left, with a flat-screen TV hung on the opposite wall. There wasn't a coffee table, which would no doubt block the wheelchair. In the dining area, which took up the far corner of the great room, an oval table surrounded by just three chairs sat a far distance from the wall, which she realized gave easy access to the wheelchair. Aside from a few other odds and ends that was it. The walls were bare of décor, and the wood floors had no rugs at all, which would just get in the way. What enormous thought and planning must've gone into every detail, including the wide doorways that went into what she knew were the bedroom and bathroom. The windows were all open and you could hear the swish of last night's raindrops that still clung to the trees as a light breeze came through.

"It's lovely."

"It wasn't in great shape when I bought it, and it took about eight months to get it adapted to suit me. It's still a bit of a work in progress, as I realize things that could work better." He nodded to a ladder that obviously went to a loft above, the same as in her cabin. "Needless to say, I don't get up there much," he added with a laugh.

She smiled, surprised this time that she didn't feel uncomfortable at his references to his disability. After spending time with him at the store yesterday during the signing—especially when a customer backed up with a book in hand and ended up falling into his lap, only to hear Colin laugh and offer a ride—she'd realized the discomfort was all hers.

Turning, she noticed a bamboo screen blocking the front right corner of the room and wondered if he had an office there. He must have followed her eyes because he went over and pulled one panel back. Behind it was a large whirlpool tub, with windows all around it.

"This is one luxury I wouldn't want to live without. It makes swimming in the lake possible. I can't feel my body chilling like a normal person would, so a long soak in this afterward is a necessity."

She remembered seeing him emerge from the lake that first morning, naked, and felt her cheeks turn pink. Since then, he always wore shorts.

"Well, it's certainly a great house."

"Thanks. Now, about that favor." He turned and wheeled himself to the dining area, nodding at four framed prints on the table. "I never was very good at hanging pictures," he said, turning to her with a smile, "but now it's impossible."

"Oh," she said, realizing that unless he wanted the prints hung at a child's level, someone would have to place them on the walls, then pound the nails in.

"So, how good are you with a hammer and nail?"

"Well, I'd say this is your lucky day, because I'm pretty darn handy." And then she realized how that must have sounded—of course how could this be his lucky day? He was unable to do this most basic thing for himself. She looked at him, mortified.

But Colin simply gave her an amused smile.

FIFTEEN MINUTES LATER THEY STOOD LOOKING AT PRINTS of one gorgeous bird after another, lined up in a row on the dining room wall.

"These are just beautiful, especially the red one."

"That's a scarlet tanager. They're actually all through the woods here. A photographer at The Raptor Center donates the photos to help raise money." He turned to her. "So tell me, how'd you get so handy?"

She looked down at him. His blond hair was damp, pulled back in a small ponytail at the nape of his neck. His light blue eyes under those thick blond brows looked at her with interest.

"My father left when I was a kid, and my mother was just helpless. We were always moving, too, so pictures went up and pictures came down, and if you didn't want to get docked from your security deposit, you had to fill in the holes and touch up with paint." She shrugged, then smiled, noticing the prints were slightly off. "You know, we should have used a level."

"Forget it. There's nothing perfect in this world. Once you learn that, life gets a lot easier."

She was surprised at the sudden seriousness of his tone.

"Besides," he added with a grin, "I don't have a level."

He gestured toward the table, rolling his chair to the empty space where there was a chair conspicuously absent. She took a seat across from him, picking up her tea cup to take a sip.

"Here, let me warm that up for you."

She nearly said she'd get it, but caught herself. "Thanks. I really enjoyed seeing all those birds at The Raptor Center. It's an amazing place. Have you been going there for a long time?"

"I brought a bird in last fall and wound up staying all day. Then I joined the volunteers."

He wheeled to the kitchen, opening the microwave, which was chest height for him, then pressed buttons. "Actually, it took a while for them to figure out where I could help without causing the kind of problem like you saw in the bookstore yesterday. I wanted to work hands-on with the birds, but there's a lot of lifting and turning and," he waved a hand at the wall where the pictures now hung, "height issues, shall we say?"

She couldn't help smiling. He had that way of making self-deprecating remarks that made light of a situation, when it could have been so different. She recalled Ruth talking about him pushing everyone away in the first months after the accident.

"Anyway," he said, wheeling back to the table with one hand, her mug in the other, "I could have managed, but I didn't want to make waves. I'm involved in the educational programs now, which seems to cause no problems for anyone."

"What kinds of programs do they do?"

"It varies. We do a lot of school programs for kids, plus quite a few senior events, teaching them about the bird behavior, and of course, why particular birds are at the Center. There are also special programs for the developmentally disabled, or those with emotional problems. Connecting with the birds, with their injuries, and how they're still serving a purpose, really seems to work wonders."

"And what programs do you do?"

"Well…I'm actually putting together something new, for wounded vets."

"Really? What a great idea."

"We'll see." He shrugged, and she sensed he didn't want to share anything further.

"And your bird? The one you brought in?"

"A female cardinal. The contractor working on this cabin last spring took a tree down and with it came her nest, and her hatchlings."

"Oh no." She pictured it all too clearly.

"None of the hatchlings survived. The Raptor Center fixed her up and she was released a month later. I realized how careless we are. You never take a tree down during nesting season."

"How awful about the babies."

"Well, there are plenty that come to us and heal and live a good long life then die of old age. That's all any of us can really ask for."

"That's true." She wondered suddenly what impact his paralysis would have on his own life. Ironically, Colin was one of the most vital, and virile, men she'd ever met, but she imagined there were all sorts of complications that could occur.

"I'm going back this week. You're welcome to come with me."

She'd been planning to call her mother today and finally arrange a visit, plus stop at as many bookstores along the ride to Pennsylvania as she could. But she decided to put it off a little longer. Because everything about this place, from the lake and the woods to Colin and The Raptor Center, was intriguing her in ways she hadn't imagined. Bits and pieces of a story were coming already at odd moments when her mind was still, or even thinking of something else. It was part of the magic of writing and she began to recognize it now as a familiar and necessary part of the process of creating a novel. Besides, if she was really serious about this, she was going to need a next book.

"Sure," she said to Colin. "I'd love to, if you don't mind."

He looked at her. "Listen, about the last time we were there, I want to apologize—"

Just then a horn blared several times. He wheeled himself over to the door, and she got up to leave. As she followed him onto the deck, she heard someone yell, "Hey, super gimp!"

"Well, speak of the devil," Colin said softly.

She looked down at a black SUV as its door opened, wondering who on earth would say something so rude. A wheelchair was suddenly thrust onto the lawn, and a moment later, a young man with a shaved head and arms lined with tattoos swung himself into the seat.

She turned to Colin, who was smiling broadly. "Super gimp is actually a compliment," he explained.

"Oh," she said, relieved.

"Danny's the one I'm mentoring. And the reason I got all weird that day at The Raptor Center. He's going through a rough time. I've been trying to convince him to be my relay buddy for next summer's Paralyzed Veterans of America's games. They're kind of like the Olympics for guys like us."

A moment later, the man came gliding smoothly up the ramp, his upper body thick and powerful like something out of a muscle magazine.

"Lucy, this is Danny, fastest man in a chair I've ever seen," Colin said when he stopped beside them. "Danny, Lucy, my new neighbor."

Danny eyed her up and down. "Sweet," he said with a smile.

17

MEGAN OFFERED TO GO TO THE REVITALIZATION MEETING that morning after Ruth made the mistake of grumbling that she hoped they'd actually get something accomplished this time. Megan had tons of ideas, most of which involved spending money, and Ruth was tired of having that argument and catching Megan's eye rolls when she thought Ruth wasn't looking. But she listened to a few of the young woman's ideas, amazed once again that someone fresh out of college, with a mountain of loans and opportunities to make real money, would choose to stay in her store.

Then she headed up Main Street to the Darress Theatre, one of the few remaining vaudeville theaters in the country where you had to walk under the stage to take a seat in the audience. It was a crumbling gem that Lloyd Barnes had been working on for more than twenty years while running his photography business out of the lobby.

Ruth walked under the old marquee and through the lobby photo shop, then into the theater. In the first few rows she saw Lloyd, Elaine, Hannah's husband, Eddie, who had an appliance store, Dee from Shades & Shapes Salon, and assorted others. She was irked to see that Eddie and Dee were seated together and seemed to be deep in conversation.

"Okay, we're all here now," Lloyd said, standing just below the stage. "I guess I'll go first. I've got some good news and some bad news."

"So what else is new?" Eddie called out and everyone chuckled. Ruth noticed Dee watching him, laughing, with a look that caused her antennae to go up. She hadn't forgotten Hannah asking if this meeting was being held in the evening.

"As you all know, I've been struggling with the camera shop. Well...I'm going to pack it in."

Murmurs of surprise rippled through the group. Lloyd held his hands up.

"I can't compete with the drugstores anymore, and everyplace else you can get your pictures made. Not to mention online. Look, we all know this has been coming."

"I'm really sorry, Lloyd," Ruth said.

"So what's the good news?" Elaine asked.

"I'm going to put all my effort into making the theater viable again. My son just finished college and he's going to help me. We're going to offer concerts, plays, anything we can."

"Well, I don't have a Plan B to fall back on," Eddie chimed in. "Foot traffic is down, which isn't surprising since the morons on town council decided we needed parking meters on Main Street. I mean why come here and pay to park when you can go to the mall and park free?"

"But then you're paying for gas, so that's a wash," someone in the back called out.

"It's not parking, it's the fact that we can't compete with those big box store prices," said Gloria, who had the office supply store.

"I think we need to make Main Street more of a destination, you know?" Elaine suggested. "People need a reason to come here. Look at Applefest, that's everyone's best weekend every year."

"Yeah, we need people to *want* to shop local, not drive all the way out to the malls."

"Well good luck, because now it's not gonna be such a long ride," someone else said. "Did you know that new mall they're building just outside of town is designed like a downtown? I was at one in New Jersey, and it was beautiful. And mobbed."

"That's a low blow, building a mall but making it feel like a Main Street."

Ruth could see this was going to dissolve into another pity party and she didn't have two hours to waste.

"Look, I've got a few ideas. As my youngest employee, Megan, keeps telling me, we've got to get with the times. There's a book that came out a few years back, *Who Moved My Cheese*, that hits the nail on the head. We're mice, or rats, take your pick." She got a few hoped-for chuckles. "For years we knew exactly what we needed to do to find that cheese so we could eat and survive. Okay, someone moved it. We have to figure out how to find it again. If we don't—"

"We're going to starve," Elaine finished for her.

"Exactly. We have to change with the times and figure out how to get our cheese. I don't like it any better than the rest of you. I want people to keep reading real books, not scrolling lines on a cell phone, but some things are out of our control. We can't stop progress."

"So what are you suggesting?"

"According to Megan, we're overlooking some good opportunities. We should take our buy local idea and brand it with a catchy phrase or slogan, then get it on social networking sites like Facebook and Twitter and..." She stopped amidst a chorus of groans.

"Look, I don't even text," Dee called out. "And I don't wanna spend half my day putzing around on the computer. The kids have time to waste like that, but we don't."

Dee was always throwing out objections without solutions and Ruth felt like pinching her. Instead she said with false calmness, "I understand, but kids go to malls, their parents take them to malls. So all the money is going to the malls. We need to give them a reason to come to town. Plant the seed."

"My son was saying something similar," Lloyd said. "I think we're acting like old farts if we don't at least give it some consideration. My son is already working on the web and networking to attract bands and theater groups."

"I have one other idea," Ruth said, trying to keep her eyes off Eddie, who was now squeezing Dee's thigh, probably thinking no one could see because the old seats were so high. "One of my visiting authors mentioned her town does a First Friday Art Walk, where shops stay open on the first Friday of each month. They throw the doors open, play music, serve wine and cheese, and even get some vendors or music in the street or on the sidewalk."

"We only have one gallery, and it's really more of a frame shop," someone said. "And if you notice, they're not even here."

"I like that idea," Elaine said. "Who says we have to call it an art walk?"

"Exactly," Ruth said.

"And do people actually spend money?" someone else asked.

"What about when it's cold out?" Dee threw out, paying attention again.

"I think we can figure things out for the winter months. And maybe they don't spend a lot of money at first, but if we get them to come to Main Street, hopefully that's just a matter of time," she said. "Listen, my store is having a big anniversary celebration in the fall, marking thirty years that I've owned The Book Lover. Maybe we can kick off the first one then? Lloyd, that should give you enough time to put something together for later in the evening, right?"

He nodded. "I love it. I think it's a great idea."

An hour later, they had formed committees and Ruth felt a glimmer of hope that this time, perhaps, they'd really get something going. On the way out, Sandy from Scrub-a-Dub-Doggie pulled Ruth aside.

"Hey, I wanted to tell you that my grandmother's house sold finally." Sandy's grandmother had been nearly one hundred when she passed away peacefully in her sleep. A local teacher, her funeral was attended by more than half the town. "Anyway, we were cleaning out the attic and found a bunch of old newspapers and memorabilia. Turns out Gram's father once worked at The Book Lover. Isn't that amazing?"

"Your great-grandfather? Are you sure? That would be…" Ruth tried to think how long ago it might have been.

"Well, my grandmother was born in 1909, and he was in his thirties," Sandy said.

Ruth shook her head. "The store couldn't be that old."

"There's a picture in there somewhere, but hey, I'll give you all the junk, you can sort through it. We were just gonna throw it out, it's all kind of mildewed and falling apart."

"Oh, don't do that," Ruth said. "I'll take it, all of it."

Walking back to the store, Ruth glanced over her shoulder to see Eddie and Dee heading slowly the other way. A coil of anger began to burn in her belly, thinking of Hannah hauling trays with her knees aching and saving her tips for a pretty orange dress. Doing everything to try and please him, only to hear that she was too needy. Ruth thought about that morning she'd stood in the corner of the store where Hazel lurked, and the idea she'd tucked away. Maybe it was time to put some real thought into it.

Crossing the street, she suddenly felt lightheaded and stopped on the other side, her hand resting on one of the parking meters. She stood there a moment, catching her breath. She hadn't slept well last night. Again. Guilt over what she'd done to Thomas was torturing her. A few feet away, the Waywayanda Creek rushed over rocks, swollen from the past few days' rains. Listening to the soothing sound, Ruth wondered—when was the last time she'd taken vitamins? When the feeling passed, she turned and walked in the other direction to Aiken's Drugstore. Maybe she'd get those new silver Centrums, the ones specially designed for women her age.

* * *

ON FRIDAY, RUTH ARRIVED AT THE STORE an hour before opening to meet with Harry. He came in a few minutes later and she called to him from the back corner, where she was surveying the bookshelves and floor space.

"Whatcha doin' Ruth, looking for dust bunnies?"

"Oh, I know where they are, Harry," she laughed. "They're hiding under the shelves, where we can't ever quite reach them. That's why I call them dust fairies. They always seem to fly away and disappear just when I'm about to capture them."

Harry smiled. "Maybe Hazel likes to clean 'em up for you."

"Hopefully Hazel won't mind if we make a few changes back here." She took a deep breath. "I know I'm not a big one for change, but I'd like you to take this entire shelf of old hardcovers and put them on a table out front for a sidewalk sale. Mark them way down, let's just get rid of them."

She saw Harry's eyebrows lift.

"And then we're going to push these other shelves around and see how much space we can open up."

"For?"

"A little idea I'm mulling over. Hopefully by the end of the day, I'll be able to tell you."

The phone began to ring and Ruth went up front while Harry played with the shelves and books. When she hung up, she looked up to see Lynn Anderson standing on the other side of the counter, a small smile on her face. Lynn was vice-president at the local bank and today she wore a navy suit with matching heels, her blonde hair stylishly short.

"Hey, Lynn," Ruth said with a smile. "This is a surprise. It must be a good book to tear you away from the bank."

Although Lynn referred to her bank as "the money mill," Ruth knew she loved her job. She got mortgages for most everyone Ruth knew, and had managed to get her a hefty second mortgage a few years back that saved her after the flood, and months later when she'd adapted her house and store for Colin.

Ruth saw her smile fade now, and couldn't help noticing the worry in her eyes.

"What can I help you with?" Ruth asked.

"I need..." Lynn began, took a deep breath, and then continued, "I need a book on Alzheimer's. The stages. What to expect."

"Oh, Lynn. Your mom was in here just a few weeks ago and seemed sharp as a tack."

Lynn was silent a moment and Ruth put a hand on her arm.

"My mother," she said, then bit her lip and Ruth waited for her to recover. "My mother's just fine." Then she looked Ruth right in the eyes. "It's me, Ruth. Early onset."

Ruth felt the breath sucked out of her lungs. Lynn handed her a piece of paper.

"The doctor recommended this, but I figured you know what's best."

She looked at the title. "Lynn, this book is, well..." she was going to say kind of negative, but that didn't sound good. "Let me show you something more positive." She guided Lynn to the far bookshelf. "I know, you're probably thinking, what's positive about this?"

She handed Lynn *Still Alice*. "I think this will help. It's a wonderful book. In fact, the author got rejected by everyone because publishers didn't think anyone would want to read about Alzheimer's. Guess what? She published it herself and it did so well, a big publisher scooped it up and it went on to become a huge bestseller." She made a mental note to tell Lucy about the book. She'd totally forgotten about it.

"Okay then." Lynn held the book, nodding.

"Oh, Lynn. I'm so sorry."

"I know. It's just..." she didn't finish.

Ruth wouldn't let her pay for the book, although Lynn was insistent. "Absolutely not." She slipped it into Lynn's oversized purse. "Now, when you finish, let's talk about it, okay?"

Lynn nodded, gave her a hug, and left. Ruth went and sat on the little table in the children's corner, sick at heart. Lynn was in her early fifties. She had been hoping to be the first woman president of her bank. Soon she wouldn't be working at all.

Life. It always seemed to throw curve balls when you least expected it.

* * *

AT THREE O'CLOCK HANNAH WALKED INTO THE STORE, her gray-blonde hair slipping from her ponytail, and with a decided limp.

"I don't how much longer I can work there," she sighed. "Guess I'm gettin' old."

Ruth came around the counter and gave Hannah a sudden hug. "I know what you mean."

Hannah looked at her curiously. They'd been friends for years, but they also had a history few in town would probably remember.

"So, do you have a new book for me?" Hannah asked.

"No, actually I have an idea," she said, then took Hannah's arm and led her toward the back of the store.

"Did Hazel empty out this corner last night while the store was closed?" Hannah asked with a laugh.

"No, Harry did earlier today because I've had something brewing in my mind for a while and I wanted to see if it's possible. In fact, it all started that morning I came to your house."

"To see the dress?" Hannah looked at her skeptically.

"Yes, but it wasn't the dress. It was the muffins."

"Oh, right, my Better Than Sex Muffins," Hannah said with a little laugh. Then she looked at the empty corner again. "I don't understand, Ruth, what are you saying?"

"Well, I need to diversify, to get more people into the store and I thought maybe you could open a little café in this corner and have your own business here, selling muffins and coffees and teas."

Hannah looked at her and blinked.

"No one I know bakes like you, Hannah. And you said it makes you happy, so maybe that's the thing you should be doing."

"Oh, Ruth!" Hannah's hand flew to her mouth as she began to laugh, her eyes filling with tears at the same time. "It's...it's so..."

"Brilliant?"

"Yes! Oh yes."

As they stood there, as the idea began to really sink in, Ruth felt such pleasure at the look on Hannah's face as she began tossing out ideas. There was still a lot to discuss, and Ruth hoped that Hannah wouldn't get excited and change her mind in a few days, as she'd done so many times before about things she was going to try.

"It'll be fun trying to come up with a clever name," Hannah said.

"Why not just Hannah's Café?"

"I don't want to use my name."

A book fell behind them and they both turned.

"Wow, that's weird," Hannah said picking it up. "Oh my God, Ruth, this is *Starting a Small Business for Dummies*. Is Hazel calling me a dummy?" she giggled.

"Maybe we should call it Hazel's Café."

"I love it! I love it all! I can't wait to tell Eddie."

That was the real worry, Eddie. Hopefully he would be happy for Hannah, and not put roadblocks in her way.

"Ruth, I think you found it." Hannah turned and gave her a hug.

And then she heard someone clearing his throat and turned, her heart nearly stopping. Here was her own curveball, standing not ten feet away, thrown right at her heart. Thomas stood there smiling.

"I was wondering if you could recommend a good book for someone starting over."

18

THE DAYS AFTER THE BOOK SIGNING DISAPPEARED IN A BLUR. Each day Lucy hit the road with a trunk filled with books. Each time she pulled up to a store, she sat in the car, rehearsed her words, then walked inside with a book and a stack of bookmarks with Ruth's quote in bold italics, and printouts of her two wonderful reviews. Like on the long trip north, she felt like nothing more than a traveling salesperson.

She kept reminding herself that sales was a numbers game, and as Kate once laughingly said after a few glasses of wine: "Throw enough shit on the wall, and something's bound to stick." Maybe if she hit fifty stores, ten might read or carry her book. At the end of the week, her trunk was emptying and her hopes were up, despite the ups and downs of these visits.

At a store in Lafayette, which seemed to carry mostly used books, she went into her spiel once again, telling the friendly young man at the register about her signing at The Book Lover, and that *A Quiet Wanting* was now a book club pick. He was so nice at first that her enthusiasm took over and she even confessed her secret dream to get picked up by a publisher. His eyes widened and then he actually laughed and said her chances were better of getting struck by lightning. She left without giving him a book.

Walking into these bookstores, having no idea if she'd be welcome or just another pain in the ass, was one of the toughest things she'd ever done, and that included telling someone they owed more than they earned in a year in back taxes when she was still an accountant.

Her faith was rekindled at a lovely store in Sparta. The manager liked that she was originally from New Jersey, and was impressed with her passion and drive. She e-mailed Lucy just two days later that she had already read and loved the book, and agreed to carry three copies on consignment. And yet Lucy wondered how many of the books she'd left at stores up and down the east coast now would end up in the trash. Or on ebay.

On another round of bookstore visits one morning, her cell rang and when she saw it was her attorney, she pulled over quickly. Carter was calling to go over some financial information. David, apparently, still had some income, as payments for past services rendered were coming in. He was also due a third of an accident settlement he'd argued successfully.

"David's agreed to give you half of everything, although it's not going to be much, given the debts and fines," Carter explained. "I want you to ask for alimony. Even if David never practices law again, he'll have to get some kind of job."

Lucy sat there thinking. He was paying off all the debts. Thanks to him, her mother had her own place, and a decent car. Did she really want anything more from him?

"No, I don't want alimony. Just what he stole from me."

"What about the furniture and other possessions once the house is sold?"

She thought about the battered old cabin. How much did a person really need, she was beginning to wonder. Because there was something about stripping your life down to the barest essentials that somehow felt gratifying. That if you had to, you could survive. Thoreau would be proud of her.

"I'll take a few personal things. Let David keep the rest, or sell it and pay me half."

"All right. David's attorney called me this morning to tell me he'll be out in a few weeks, although he still has a period of house arrest. He'd like to stay at your house until the divorce is final, then put it on the market. He'll continue to pay the mortgage. You don't have to agree to this, though. I think it's really pushing things."

At some point, she'd have to go back. She had to get the rest of her clothes and her old writing files, as well as mementos of Ben, which obviously David wouldn't want. And, as the petitioner, she was mandated to appear in court for the divorce hearing, when things were ready to be finalized. David wasn't required to attend, but was permitted to.

"He can stay," she told Carter, "under one condition. That he not come to the divorce hearing when the time comes."

"Fair enough."

When she hung up, the irony hit her—here she sat a few blocks from yet another bookstore, about to pitch her book again: the story of a woman who discovers that her husband has been lying to her for years; that the very foundation of their marriage was a sham. When she'd spent all those months confined to her bed, waiting for Ben to be born, it had taken her weeks to decide how Hope would handle her betrayal by her husband. Ultimately, she decided that Hope loved him, didn't want to lose him. But what about her? Did she still love David? Would she still want to be married to him if he hadn't insisted on this divorce? The numbness at what he'd done was wearing off. Even the intense bursts of anger were less frequent, now replaced by a simmering resentment. He had lied to her and stolen from her. And he had committed the most egregious crime an attorney could—stealing from his own clients. It was hard to imagine they could go back to a normal relationship after all this, even if he wanted to. Still, people did. Books were filled with such stories. But this wasn't a book, where she could make a character do as she wanted him to. This was her life. Her marriage. And soon it would be over.

* * *

WHEN SHE GOT BACK TO THE CABIN THAT AFTERNOON, Colin was sitting near his bird feeders in his wheelchair. She watched, recognizing the bright yellow flash of a goldfinch as it flitted from one to the other. Birds were obviously a passion for him.

She walked over, just as he began writing in a book on his lap. He seemed as unpredictable a person as a writer could dream of for a character. She'd expect someone with his handicap, cut down in the prime of life, to be resentful. Cranky perhaps. But he seemed none of that, except for the brief moment when they were leaving The Raptor Center that first time. Apparently his friend Danny had gotten drunk that day and called Colin's cell, he'd finally explained to her after Danny left his house that day.

"Anyway, I was just frustrated, and I had no business taking it out on you."

"It's no big deal," she'd said.

"It was rude."

"It must be hard. I can't even imagine."

"In the beginning, your life is in the crapper, and you make everyone's lives hell. I did it, too."

"Well, I can identify with the crapper part. But I'm sure you didn't mean to."

"I wasn't thinking of anyone else. I was just thinking of the rest of my life, without the use of my legs. I thought I wasn't a man anymore, which isn't easy for a soldier to swallow."

"You seem pretty good now."

"Swimming saved me. But Danny found out that day that his ex-wife's getting remarried and he was in a pretty bad way. They've only been divorced about six months."

"He seems to be doing better."

Colin had nodded then. "I'm hoping racing can give him some focus, you know? That he can start feeling good about himself again. He puts on a good act with the ladies, as you noticed, but he's still pretty raw inside."

"You're a good man to help him like that."

He shrugged. "Just doing what someone else did for me."

Now he looked up as she came closer, then glanced past her and put a finger to his lips. Slowly she turned and saw a gorgeous bird about the size of a robin, black and white with a crimson patch on its breast. They watched for several minutes as the bird fed, then finally flew off. She turned back to Colin, who was writing again.

"That was a rose-breasted grosbeak." He looked up then. "Beautiful, isn't it?"

"Yes, I've never seen one before."

"Look at this."

He handed her the book. It was the field guide, and on a page with a picture of that same bird, she saw rows of dates. "I don't understand."

"Every year the grosbeak comes back to these feeders within the same three days."

"The same bird?"

"No, they don't live that long. But generations of them. These feeders are on their migratory path back north. My dad started recording it back in the sixties, and then…after a while I took over."

"That's incredible."

"Nature's an amazing thing. When we don't screw it up."

"I agree."

"So are you still up for another visit to The Raptor Center tomorrow?"

"Sure. I'm really looking forward to it."

"All right, see you then."

He wheeled himself back to his cabin, with seemingly effortless ease. She pictured him again at The Raptor Center. The huge wild birds, beautiful and haunting in their cages, awaiting freedom. Colin had said it was a cliché, a cripple helping to heal wounded birds. She didn't think so. It was poignant, even sad. They might be healed and fly to freedom again, but barring some sort of miracle, she imagined he would be confined to his chair for life. Once again she felt the pieces of an incredible story swimming in her head. She'd actually written a few pages already. But she needed more research, on the birds, and on paraplegic soldiers like Colin and Danny.

Of course she could just tell him about all this, even do a formal interview or two, which might help answer some of the questions she had. But that would change the dynamic of their friendship. And they were definitely becoming real friends.

For now, Lucy decided that was more important.

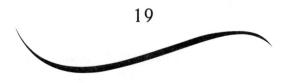

19

R UTH'S MOUTH OPENED, BUT THE WORDS STALLED in her throat. Thomas's smile began to fade.

He looked so nice in a white oxford shirt and pressed jeans—fresh-scrubbed, as if he'd just showered. She'd never seen him in anything but the drab prison jumpsuit.

She heard Hannah say goodbye and leave. Then the bell tinkled and in the corner of her mind that was hyperaware, she realized it was Megan arriving for the late shift. But then she heard Harry say hi to Jenny and the girls. Oh shit! Quickly she wrote her address on a slip of paper and whispered, "This isn't a good time. Come see me tonight, and we'll talk."

A moment later, Jenny came into the back with her daughters: Emma, eleven, and Olivia, thirteen. "And who was that?" she asked, with a big curious smile, as the girls gave Ruth a kiss, then wandered off to poke through the young adult novels.

"Oh, no one, just a customer asking for a recommendation." She could feel the heat rise from her chest up her neck and across her cheeks.

But Jenny's raised eyebrows said she wasn't buying it. "I don't know, he looks like a professor from the college maybe? He certainly left looking happy. And he didn't buy a book."

"No, he's not from around here, just passing through, and I don't have the book in stock." Her face felt as if it were on fire, so she turned and straightened a few books, her back to Jenny, while adding, "It was *The Sun Also Rises*, which I'm out of at the moment."

The rest of the day was torture. Sandy from Scrub-a-Dub Doggie brought in the promised box of papers from her grandmother's attic, which was so moldy Ruth began sneezing immediately. Megan was nearly beside herself with excitement that the store could possibly be older than they thought. As she began to dive into the box, babbling away, Ruth could barely focus, between thoughts of Thomas and sneezes. She finally told Megan she could take it home with her as long as she put it out in her car right now. Megan skipped out with it a moment later. At five, Ruth grabbed her purse and left early, pleading a headache.

Now, as she puttered in her house, having no idea what time Thomas might arrive, Ruth was excited and terrified. She changed into a long floral skirt and a blue top that gave her much-needed color. Although her skin was in pretty good condition from not spending much time in the sun, she was also pale because of it. She pulled her hair back and braided it because with the humidity it was impossible to tame. Then she put on a bit of makeup, slipped earrings on, and suddenly stopped. "What are you doing?" she muttered out loud. This wasn't a date. A convicted felon was coming to her house. Sam cocked her head. "I'm not talking to you," she told the dog.

Jenny would go insane if she knew, and no doubt call Alex and Colin and stage an intervention. They thought she was an innocent, that the roles had somehow reversed as she aged and now they needed to protect *her* from the world. Then she heard a knock at the door and her stomach lurched. She ran downstairs, Sam still at her heels, not wanting to leave Thomas standing on the porch for her curious neighbors to see. She opened the door and there he stood, holding a bouquet of yellow roses.

"Hello, Ruth." He gave her a shy smile and his face flushed. "I remember once you said these were your favorite flowers."

She took them, opening the door wider. "Please, come in."

They stood in the foyer a moment, neither speaking. Sam, who always barked at strange men, was silent, watching. "I'm sorry," they said then at the same time, uttering the same words. They both laughed, but the awkwardness grew.

"How about a cup of coffee?" she asked. "Or tea?"

He nodded. "Coffee would be nice."

He followed her to the kitchen. She stuck the flowers in a cup of water in the sink to arrange later on. As she made coffee, she was aware of him behind her, standing in the middle of her kitchen as she'd once fantasized, looking around.

"Your house is just as I imagined it would be."

"What, tired and dumpy?" she asked with a nervous laugh.

"No, Ruth. Comfortable, cheerful. Warm." He sat then at the kitchen table, watching her while she continued to putter around. "I started to say I'm sorry for showing up with no warning. I can see that it threw you. I just, well, I was just so excited. You have no idea what these past few days have been like."

She set cups on the table. "When did you get out?"

"Three days ago. I'm living in a studio apartment about a half hour away in Pine Island. I have a job at a gas station for now. They help you with all that before you get out. A place to live and a job are part of the conditions of parole."

"I see."

He took a deep breath. "God that smells good. A kitchen filled with the aroma of fresh brewed coffee. It's just...so normal."

She sat across from him, but neither of them touched the sugar or milk. His eyes shone.

"You know, don't you?"

She nodded.

"I thought so."

She could see him hesitating. Then he asked, "Is that why you didn't come back?"

"Partly."

He looked down at the table, then up at her again. "But you don't know everything. And that's why I came."

She spooned sugar into her cup, poured milk, stirred. Waiting.

"Whatever happens, Ruth, I want you to know the truth. I need that."

"All right."

"I've been trying for weeks to find the right words to tell you this, hoping for a way to, well, to lessen the impact. But," he shrugged and shook his head, "it was hopeless. I should have just told you that day you came to visit."

She said nothing, simply gave him a small, encouraging smile, and waited.

"I knew that once I told you, everything would change. I'd hoped somehow we'd be able to get past it, that somehow you'll be able to remember who I really am. Because you know me better than anyone, Ruth. And if you believe nothing else, I hope you'll believe that."

She was suddenly aware of her heart, fluttering wildly in her chest, the same as it did when she sat in the dentist's chair and opened her mouth. The anticipation of something awful.

"Just tell me everything," she said softly.

He nodded. "You know the charges, I guess, and that I pleaded guilty. Kidnapping and terroristic threats."

Hearing it out loud, in his voice, made what did not seem like it could be real, suddenly too real. He ran a hand through his hair, and she could feel her entire body begin to pulse, as if she'd had too much caffeine. He sat a moment, shaking his head with a sad smile.

"I did do it, but there was a reason. My parents were very old school, my mother an old-fashioned Italian mother, my father Polish, and they had their own little version of the American dream in Albany, a dry cleaning business. I was an only child and it was always understood I'd take over the business. I didn't mind. They made decent money and truthfully, I didn't have grandiose visions of anything else. I was a simple guy."

He picked up his coffee with a trembling hand and took a sip.

"My father died just after I got out of high school and even though I thought about going to college, I jumped right into the business then. After a while I moved out and got my own place, and my mother stayed in the apartment over the store. And life was pretty decent for a long time. Years. My mother was getting older and I began to talk to her about retiring. She had a sister who'd moved to Florida and truthfully, the cold Albany winters were killing her arthritis. Someday, she'd say, but I always wondered. I knew she'd been saving money all those years. I just didn't realize she was putting it under her mattress."

"She didn't trust banks?" Ruth asked, surprised, although she remembered her parents finding her grandfather's life savings stashed in the barrels of several rifles after he'd died. Her parents had explained it had to do with the Depression.

He shrugged. "They were old school. It was probably my father who started it and, you know, rather than drive the money to the bank, she just hid it where she thought it was safe. One day, though, I'm pressing shirts and she comes in and I think she's going to die on the spot, her face is so white and she can't seem to speak. Then she told me the money was gone."

There was only one person who could have done it, he told Ruth, a cleaning lady his mother had had for years. Who complained time and again about her worthless boyfriend. But his mother had loved her, trusted her, and wouldn't believe it. They called the cops, but there was simply no proof. His mother wanted him to let it go, but something had gone out of her with that loss. He felt her slipping away.

"I showed up at the cleaning girl's house one day and when she opened the door, I walked right in before she could even stop me. There was a big new flat screen TV, a nice new pickup truck out front, and she had on some flashy jewelry. I asked her where she got the money for all of it and she said her boyfriend got a new job. Anyway," he sighed and closed his eyes and Ruth felt a pang of sympathy for him, "I waited. Because I knew. The boyfriend, I found out after doing some more digging, was out partying the rest of my mother's money away."

"You're certain of that."

He nodded. "I went back one night. With a...gun. I wouldn't let them leave until they confessed, which they finally did. I told them I wouldn't go to the police if they gave me what was left, sold the TV and the car and gave me that, too. My parents worked their entire lives for that money and here they were just pissing it away. Even if it wasn't all of it, I wanted it."

Thomas was perspiring now, his face ashen as he stared at the table. After a long time, he looked up at her, his eyes glittering. "I told my mother I was getting her money back and she was so happy."

"I'm sorry, Thomas."

He shook his head. "I was stupid, Ruth. So stupid. The cleaning girl didn't come back, the police did. She told them the confession was a lie, that they'd been afraid I was going to kill them. And...there was no proof of the money being taken."

"What happened then?"

"I went to prison. My mother died a year later." He shrugged. "I know what I did was wrong, but...they were lowlifes. My mother was a hardworking, honorable woman. We had a lot of pride. It just didn't seem right."

"Your poor mother." She couldn't imagine the anguish, being robbed of everything she'd saved her entire life, and then losing her only child to prison.

"I got fifteen years and now...after serving ten, I'm free." He gave her such a sad smile, she felt her heart breaking.

She pulled a tissue from the holder on the table and wiped her own eyes. "Thomas, I..." but before she could finish, he put a hand up.

"I want to show you something." He pulled a new brown wallet from his back pocket, opened it and took something out, handing it to her.

Ruth looked at it. It was a photograph, a mug shot of a very large man, almost obese. "I don't understand. Who is this?"

"It's a different man, Ruth. The man I was when I went to prison."

She looked at him and at the picture again, and there were his kind brown eyes, buried in the heavy face, a grim look as the picture was snapped.

"I carry it with me everywhere, Ruth, to remind me. I'll never be that man again."

She handed him back the picture.

"I don't know what to say, Thomas." There were no words to describe how she felt.

"Just remember the me you've come to know, Ruth, okay? That's the real me."

Slowly his hand slid to the middle of the table, and paused. She closed her eyes, but try as she might, her own hand wouldn't move. A moment later she heard the scrape of his chair. And then the front door closing.

RUTH POURED HERSELF A GLASS OF WINE, her entire body trembling. She sat again, staring at the chair where he'd been, her mind reeling. As awful as it was, his story made sense. There was even a certain honor to what he'd tried to accomplish, righting a horrific wrong. Easing the pain of someone you loved. She had only to think back on the awful, gut-wrenching days after Colin was first paralyzed to know the desperate feeling of wanting to do something.

But there was one thing she couldn't seem to grasp. One question she realized she should have asked: Why on earth would he have had a gun?

The first glass went down quickly and she got up, puttered through the house, poured water into Sam's empty bowl. The dog didn't eat, though, just sat there staring at her. She poured a second glass of wine, then went out and sat on the back porch. It was after nine, but there was still light in the sky, although a dampness had settled and the air was chilly for late June.

She stared across the yard at the patch of garden she'd once tried so hard to nurture. Over the years she'd planted tomatoes and peas and even leaf lettuce, but something or other always wore down her efforts. The hunger of the rabbit that lived under her shed. The slugs that seemed to gnaw everything in sight, even her marigolds, the simplest of flowers that anyone could grow.

No, Ruth had never been much of a gardener. Sipping her wine, she thought, she hadn't been much of a cook, either. Or a wife. She was a decent mother. Or a lucky one. Her kids had turned out fine, although Colin was still a worry. And probably would be for the rest of her days. Or his. No, she wouldn't think that way.

There was just one thing she was good at, or so she told herself. Books.

She took the last sip, went into the house, grabbed her purse and car keys and drove to Main Street, where now, late at night, there was plenty of parking. She got out and stood in front of her store. The Book Lover.

She unlocked the front door and turned on just the counter light, so that the store was dimly illuminated, with the glow of the window display and just that small fixture. She looked around and inhaled deeply. This was her world, her passion. This store had been the crux of her life for so many years, that not having it would be like saying tomorrow the earth would revolve around something entirely different. Mars, perhaps. This had replaced all of the love she'd had to lock inside herself because there was no man to give it to.

Slowly she walked past the shelves, the children's section, her favorite, with the colorful covers, and the old classics. *Alice Through the Looking Glass*, *Where The Wild Things Are*, and Colin's favorite, *Drummer Hoff*. There was Plath, and Faulkner, Shreve and Hoffman, Hemingway, and Fitzgerald, her favorite. The magic of all these worlds, of Gatsby and Santiago and all of the people who'd spurred the imaginations of countless readers who walked through her door. And she'd been part of that world. Sharing her books. Living through her books.

Maybe her husband had been right. Maybe she couldn't love him because he was real. Maybe what she really wanted couldn't ever exist. Like her fantasy with Thomas.

In the back of the store, she sank to the floor, her back resting against the section of *The Hobbit* and *Narnia* and the new fantasies, all of the worlds she'd longed for once as a girl. But what was wrong with the real world? Why had she chosen to shut herself away here? What was she afraid of?

She closed her eyes, the room spinning, her body not used to two full glasses of wine. She felt the wetness on her cheeks. She wasn't afraid of Thomas, no matter what he'd done. Maybe she was a fool, but she believed him. She could have asked him to stay longer. This night could have ended differently. But she knew, too, that too many years had gone by. The fantasies she'd allowed herself to visit again and again were just that. Fantasies, like in those books.

She was a widow who'd not been with a man in decades. Maybe in books such things were possible, but this was real life. And for Ruth Hardaway, such romantic notions were simply too late. There was only one love for her. One thing she was capable of sharing.

Books.

20

DRIVING TO THE RAPTOR CENTER THAT AFTERNOON was different from the last time, when Lucy had felt so awkward with Colin. This time they chatted the whole way, partly because she kept asking so many questions.

"A raptor is any bird of prey," he explained as he drove. "Hawks, eagles, owls, falcons, anything with a hooked beak and taloned feet."

"But they also rescue regular birds at the Center, right?"

"Yes, any bird will be cared for, and hopefully rehabilitated and sent back out into the wild."

The cool morning rain had stopped, but low clouds still obscured the mountains as they headed southwest through Sussex County into Warren County.

"What about the birds I saw in the aviaries?"

"Those are birds that are either unreleasable, which means they're used for display to educate, or they're still awaiting release. Right now it's our busy season, spring through summer, what with mating and feeding and so many fledglings leaving the nest."

He pulled over suddenly and turned to her. "Hey, since you've never actually been in the Delaware Water Gap National Park, how about a quick side trip? It's one of the best places on the east coast to see birds in the wild."

"I'd love to. But don't you have to be at the Center?"

"Not any particular time today."

A few miles ahead he turned right toward the Delaware river, driving for another twenty minutes until she saw a sign that read Worthington State Forest, which he explained was part of the National Park. They followed a blacktop road that narrowed to one lane, and soon they were sitting for a very long time at a stop light in a most unlikely place. They were in the middle of nowhere, surrounded by woods. Not a car came through from the other side, but Colin explained that this was where they entered the heart of the forest and had to go through a tricky stretch that was one car wide. Sure enough, they finally went through the light and the road became gravel as the woods to the right rose sharply.

"This is Old Mine Road, which believe it or not is the oldest road in the country," he said, as they kept driving and she spotted the river again on their left.

"Are you serious?"

He nodded. "This area was rife with copper mines, still is in fact, although they're no longer mined. The Dutch built this road back in the 1600s and it went all the way up to Kingston, New York. But now it's part of the park."

"How do you know all this stuff?"

"This is one of my favorite places. I've been coming here since I was a boy."

A few minutes later he pulled into a small clearing on the side of the road and she realized they were getting out. As soon as she opened her door, he began reaching for his wheelchair. In less than a minute, as she stood there looking across the road at the wide river, muddy from the earlier rains, he was in his chair and nodding for her to follow. They headed across the road to a grassy path on the embankment about fifteen feet above the river.

It was like stepping into a primeval forest. They walked past the deep woods along the river, with no hint of another human anywhere. The wind kicked up suddenly and the low clouds began to lift and swirl. Another cool front was moving in, and within minutes she could see the high mountains on the Pennsylvania side of the river. The path was worn and rutted in places, but didn't seem difficult for Colin and she wondered if his was a specific kind of wheelchair to navigate outdoors, although it didn't look much different than others she'd seen. She made a mental note to ask him another time. Right now, the silence, save for the rush of the river and swish of the wet leaves, was simply beautiful.

After a while, Colin stopped abruptly, pulling his binoculars to his eyes. Without a word, he pointed to a tree on the other side of the river, a huge sycamore, then handed her the binoculars. It took a minute to adjust, then she scanned the tree, branch by branch, spotting nothing, and finally getting dizzy from the magnified leaves rushing by. Then suddenly she saw it, a light spot in the midst of thick green leaves.

"It's an osprey," he said softly.

She watched, hoping to see it leave the branch and dive into the river for fish. Just as her arms began to grow trembly from holding up the heavy binoculars, she felt a tap on her shoulder and turned to see Colin looking above.

Barely fifty feet overhead, a huge bird soared slowly, its wings stretched wide, riding an air current.

"Oh my God!" she whispered.

"Yup, it's a bald eagle."

"I've never seen one in the wild before. It's enormous, and so graceful."

"They're one of the largest birds of prey. Its wings can span up to eight feet. In fact, an eagle nest can top a ton or more."

She held up the binoculars to get a better look, but it was too difficult.

"This place has quite an eagle population."

"I can see why, it's so remote. But I thought eagles were rare?"

"They were, bordering on extinction. But tougher conservation guidelines in the seventies really helped them make a comeback."

A moment later the eagle veered east, over the high treetops and out of sight. Lucy was surprised by the surge of emotion she felt at what she'd just witnessed.

"It's funny, but seeing the eagle at The Raptor Center was amazing. Seeing it in the wild, soaring so majestically like that...this might sound corny, but thinking about how that creature is the symbol of us, our freedom, it's really moving, you know?"

He didn't answer and she looked down at him sitting in his chair. He gave her a little smile and nodded.

"Back in the 1700s, congress wanted the founding fathers to come up with a symbol for the fledgiing United States. It took a while, but I think they made the right choice. The bald eagle can be found nowhere else but in North America."

They stood there in silence.

"Thanks for bringing me here. That alone was worth it," she said, handing Colin his binoculars again. "I thought it was remote at the lake, but I don't think I've ever been anyplace this isolated. I have to keep reminding myself I'm actually still in New Jersey."

"Let's go a little farther."

It was so still, the only sounds again the occasional splash of rain from the trees as a breeze blew, and of course the different birds in the surrounding forest. Colin whispered their identities each time they heard something new, from the high-pitched scream of a red-tailed hawk to the sharp *jay-jay* screech of a blue jay. Suddenly she heard the most beautiful birdsong coming from the woods, a repetitive warble, long and lilting. Colin stopped.

"That's a scarlet tanager," he whispered, and she remembered the gorgeous red bird print.

He cupped his hand and she watched, amazed, as he mimicked the bird's cry. A few seconds later, the bird in the woods sang again. They did this for several minutes, Colin and the bird echoing each other, the bird sounding closer and closer, until she saw the red flash as the bird flew out of the trees and then back in again.

"How did you know that?"

"My father taught me. Scarlet tanagers are actually pretty easy to imitate and lure out of the woods."

She laughed. "If you know what you're doing."

"It's not that hard, really. There are other—"

"Colin, look!" She put a hand on his chair, halting him. Just ahead, down the steep slope of the riverbank, she spotted a huge bird, close enough to recognize the white cap and dark body.

Colin pulled his binoculars to his eyes. The bird must have sensed them, because it turned and began to open its wings, then stopped, staring at them.

"You don't usually see an eagle on the ground unless it's eating. Otherwise it's perching, diving, or flying. That bird clearly isn't eating." He turned to her. "I don't have my cell, do you?"

She unzipped the maroon backpack she'd found in the cabin and handed it to him, wondering if it was really possible to get reception there. A moment later, she saw you could.

"Hey Randy, it's Colin Hardaway. I was on my way in and stopped at Worthington and I'm watching an eagle that I think might be in distress." He paused a moment, listening, then said, "It's on the riverbank, close to the water. I think you'd better bring a kayak."

He handed her the phone then.

"What can we do?"

"Nothing. Just be quiet so we don't stress it any further, and hopefully the bird stays right where it is and doesn't venture into the water. If it does it might drown."

She had so many questions to ask him. She felt helpless just standing there. In the endless minutes waiting for help, she prayed the bird wouldn't move. Beside her, she imagined Colin was doing the same thing as he sat there in silence.

A SMALL GROUP FROM THE RAPTOR CENTER, led by Randy, one of their medics, and Susan, who was in charge of the education programs, arrived on the scene about forty minutes later, a kayak strapped to the top of their van.

The situation grew tense as they first tried to scale down the river bank, with heavy gloves to their elbows, carrying several large blankets to retrieve the bird. Lucy and Colin inched closer. Her heart broke for the wounded eagle as it backed away and began to thrash once it hit the water, desperately trying to get away from them, its fight or flight instinct in high gear. But it was helpless. After a few minutes, the current caught the bird and it was carried into the river. They could see it struggling, its wings flailing, one horribly crooked. Randy and another man jumped into the kayak and paddled furiously toward the eagle.

"Oh, Colin, I hope they get it before it drowns."

"It's not just drowning we have to worry about. Being touched by a human is a major stress on a healthy bird. That alone can kill it," Colin said softly.

They watched as the kayak closed in on the bird and suddenly Randy tossed the blanket, covering the eagle. He grabbed the ends and they began pulling it back to shore. It was a dangerous mission, for both the men and the eagle, but within minutes the bird was carried to the van by both men, their gloves still on, and they drove off.

When Lucy and Colin arrived at The Raptor Center, Randy informed them that the bird had been examined and had blood drawn.

"It's got a broken wing, and probably lead poisoning, but we won't know for sure until we get the lab results." He then explained that the eagle was safely ensconced in the Quiet Zone, an ICU for birds, on the floor above the infirmary. "As soon as we get a bird assessed, our first course of action is to get it in a warm, dark, quiet place where there's minimal human contact, so it can begin to calm down," he explained to Lucy.

"Do you think this bird will make it?"

"I'm not sure. He's pretty weak, that's why I'm guessing lead poisoning. He was probably diving for fish and just didn't make it. The wing break seems pretty fresh."

"So it's a he?" Lucy asked.

Randy smiled. "Yes, a he."

He excused himself then and she and Colin left the infirmary.

"If I hadn't been with you, I would have had no idea that bird was injured," she said, as they headed back on the gravel path. "I would have just been thrilled to see an eagle up close."

"Well, it was a good spot on your part. We might've just walked past and not even noticed him in the brush there."

"I'd like to volunteer, too. Do you think they'd let me?"

"They might just have you wash dishes, or clean cages," he said with a smile.

"I don't care," she said, smiling right back.

"Well, I've got to stop in the office. You can ask Susan yourself."

Susan was delighted at her request, but turned her down, explaining that they needed volunteers who could make long-term commitments, sometimes a year in advance. That was something she just couldn't do.

She had no idea where she might be a year from now.

21

AS SHE WAITED FOR THE PAGE TURNERS TO ARRIVE, Ruth stared out the store window at the pots of purple petunias and red geraniums that sat on each corner of Main Street, beneath the gas lanterns. It was June already, with the longest day of the year just a few weeks away. It would be the 4th of July before you knew it, and then Labor Day and Halloween, and on and on. Life seemed to speed up each year, and when you were nearly sixty-five, it was hard to imagine how many might actually be left.

She looked back at the registration form for the Independent Bookseller's Convention in September. She knew she shouldn't spend the money, an argument she had with herself every year. It was her one big splurge and now she gazed at pictures of Philadelphia's historic district, with horse-drawn carriage rides. Not that she'd do much sightseeing. She loved just talking books with the other booksellers, getting reenergized and full of ideas. And coming home with bags of galleys and signed copies from some of the biggest authors in the country.

What else did she really have to look forward to? The seasons of her life had been established long ago: work, family, duty. Right now she needed something else to get her through the long days that loomed ahead. Of course Thomas's face flashed before her.

Just then the bell tinkled and in walked Larry Porter, a welcome interruption to her thoughts.

"And how did she like *Sonnets From The Portuguese?*"

"She loved it. We read to each other over dinner."

"I'm so glad. Where's Angela been, anyway? She hasn't come in with you in a while."

"She's working a lot of overtime at the hospital. I'm here to find something for both of us. We're going away for the weekend."

"Well, save some money for food," she joked.

He chuckled, then headed to the romance shelf, which she knew was Angela's passion. Ruth turned back to the convention form. Things were tighter than ever since the rent increase, but she hoped that after August, she might be able to pay off some debts. The past three years, August had always been her best month, thanks to Stephanie Meyer's vampire series. And Megan's idea to hold midnight release parties, which grew each year.

Maybe she'd call her friend Deb from Chapter One Books to share a room again; that would cut the cost in half. She was going, she decided, no matter what it took. She filled in the registration form, wrote out a check and put a stamp on the envelope.

Larry came up with a stack of books and after she rang them up, she asked him to drop the envelope in the mailbox out front, before she changed her mind.

AT SEVEN O'CLOCK THE PAGE TURNERS TRICKLED in for their monthly book club meeting. They were ten women, give or take, and brought wine and snacks. For Ruth it was nice to hear the chatter in the back corner of the store, which typically got louder as the evening wore on. By eight, she'd sit with them as they picked her brain about new books, favorite authors, and her recommendations. Last month she'd suggested Lucy's book, but they'd passed because someone already had a book picked. Ruth hoped they'd order it tonight for their next meeting.

As they settled down in the back of the store, she turned to the day's mail. Bills and more bills. She shoved them in her purse to agonize over later. There was no blue envelope, of course. There wouldn't be any more. Again and again she'd picked up the phone to call the cell number he'd left on the table, but never made the call. She wondered for the thousandth time how Thomas was doing in Pine Island, pumping gas at the garage, living in a few rooms above it. She knew the world wouldn't be an easy place for him to navigate. Perhaps he wasn't even there anymore. Perhaps he'd gone back to Albany, finally giving up on her. He must still have a few friends there, some family. But what if there was no one?

All she had to do was drive out to Pine Island to see if he was still there. That he was doing okay. To explain that it wasn't really him or what he did. It was her. It was simply too late.

A loud voice brought her back to the moment. The Page Turners were chatting up a storm now. Then Ruth overheard a name that made her stop and listen more carefully.

"It's true, I heard it when I was at town hall." She recognized Vicki Hoffman's voice. "Won't that be great?"

Vicki had just told them that BookWorld was coming to Warwick, in that new mall that had the revitalization committee up in arms, just a few miles from downtown.

"I love BookWorld," Nancy Beasley chimed in. "Whenever I go to my sister's in Virginia, we spend hours at hers."

Ruth wanted to go smack Nancy. Last month, before Ruth even got back to the register to ring up the books for this meeting, Nancy had whispered in that gravelly voice that she was going to order hers online and save money. That they didn't have to get all of their books from Ruth, even if they did meet in her store and she took the time to sit with them and give them her personal recommendations. Someone had shushed her, and more than half had ordered the book that night, a few others saying they were going to share, which was fine with Ruth. She understood economizing. No one understood that better than her.

But Ruth knew Nancy wasn't in the minority. For every customer who came into The Book Lover and paid for the privilege of her staff's hand selling, knowing their tastes, catering to their idiosyncrasies, giving them a warm and comfortable place to linger with books, there were probably a few dozen others who bargain-shopped online, or at discount box chains. Then they lamented when another store in town went out of business, Ruth thought.

She said nothing now, as she hadn't last month. She just gritted her teeth and told herself once again you couldn't win them all. But who was she kidding? A megabookstore was coming to town. E-books were taking off, and you didn't need a bricks and mortar store for that, you just had to go online, as they'd been lamenting at the past few conventions. They would laugh about being dinosaurs, worrying that phones and handheld gadgets would wipe out books as they knew them one day. Ruth loved a real book, with a beautiful cover and bound pages, a carefully chosen find.

She looked around at her shelves and shelves of books. The creative labor of someone's mind and hands for months or even years. Once, the most precious thing someone might own.

Ruth couldn't imagine giving up the pleasure of a real book.

But little by little the world was changing, the book business was changing and as much as she kept trying to keep up with it, somehow she felt things slipping from her grasp.

22

LUCY CONTINUED TO RISE EARLY EACH MORNING, at first dabbling in poetry, and now creating snippets of scenes for a new book. The first thing she always did, though, as she opened her laptop and sipped her first cup of tea, was check her e-mail, in hopes of hearing something good about her book. But every time she got even a shred of good news, it always seemed to be followed by something bad. She was starting to feel like a yo-yo, constantly up and down.

She had a handful of bookstores on board now, and gladly sent copies on consignment. Some even suggested *A Quiet Wanting* to their book clubs, as Ruth had done, but…Ruth's store club, The Page Turners, had decided to pass on her book, after all.

A reader e-mailed to say she loved Lucy's novel, and gave it a five-star review online. When Lucy checked the website, she was floored to see a one-star review just below it. *Been there, done that*, was all it said. She tried to stay upbeat, reminding herself that five stars was incredible. But her confidence was a fragile thing, and it was that one star that haunted her.

This morning her eyes were riveted to two e-mails, one from Clinton Books in New Jersey, with a subject line: *We'd love to do a signing with you*. The other was from David, and the subject line was blank. She opted for the good news first. Yes, they wanted her for a signing! She'd sent them a book on Ruth's recommendation, and the owner's mother—*We consider her the Oprah of Clinton*, they wrote—screened all their women's fiction and loved it. They were going to invite all their book clubs and make it a "Girls' Night Out." She just had to send them a press release for the media. Yes! She squealed, pumping her fists. She would gladly put together a new press release. She'd become an expert while working at Serendipity.

Then she looked at David's e-mail, knowing that this was probably the down to her current up.

She clicked it open:

Dear Lucy,

As you no doubt know, I'm home now, and have begun my house arrest. I've had a lot of time to think, as I'm sure you have, too. My attorney told me that you're somewhere up north, traveling around for your book. I hope it's working out for you.

Lucy, I need you to understand what's been going on with me.

She stopped, shaking her head. He needed her to understand? Was he kidding? As if she hadn't been willing to listen? To understand? Hadn't she been trying since this nightmare unfolded to get him to open up?

Ever since Ben died, I've felt like someone who is just going through the motions. I'm not using that as an excuse for what I did. I take full blame for that. No matter how much turmoil I was in, that was horribly wrong. I'm sorry.

The two words she'd waited and waited for and here they were, nearly three months later. She shook her head, running her hands through her hair.

Do you remember when we started talking about the future after our mothers met? We both said we didn't want children. You'd spent most of your childhood being the caretaker for your brothers and it made sense you didn't want to do it again. I told you I didn't think I was father material. I had no siblings, no other family besides my parents. And to be honest, I thought I was probably a little too selfish to be a good father.

After a while, you changed your mind. Despite my own feelings, I agreed.

When we couldn't get pregnant, I went along with all the fertility treatments. When the first pregnancy ended in miscarriage, I was upset as much as you were. Then it happened again. The third time it was so early, and I was almost relieved. Don't hate me for saying that, I just want to be honest. It was barely real, and I was scared. It was wearing us both down, the constant sadness. Then you got pregnant with Ben, ironically without even trying. You said it was a miracle. I was holding my breath. In the beginning I told myself that if it happened again, that would be it. I would tell you I wasn't going to go through it again.

The feelings I had consumed me with guilt, not that you knew any of this. But none of it compared to the guilt I felt when Ben died. I knew it was my fault. That God was punishing me for not really wanting a child. If you knew all of this you would hate me. While you retreated from me and the rest of the world in your grief, I said nothing. Because Lucy you have to believe me, from the moment I held him, when his gray eyes looked up at me and his tiny hand grasped my finger, I was a goner. I wanted him more than anything in this world. Suddenly it was real. We had a son.

Why was he doing this? Bringing all this up now? And then she remembered the rest of his sentence. He must have started his mandatory counseling. So the gambling, the stealing, the betrayal was all because of Ben?

When we lost our son I was consumed with guilt. But I was also filled with anger. Toward you, for putting me through it all. But even while I was angry, I was grieving for you because you were suffering so much. Moving south seemed like a good solution and after a while, things started to fade. I thought I'd gotten over it all, that time really could heal all wounds. But I guess it didn't, because somewhere deep inside it's been simmering away and I didn't even realize it. I was just trying to escape it. I can't begin to understand it all yet, and I'm not using it as an excuse. I just need to tell you this. It's been eating away at me for a long time.

David.

She sat there, her head reeling. So it wasn't because of Ben. It was because of her. All of it, because of her. A sob bubbled up in her chest and she closed her eyes, pressing them with the heels of her hands. She jumped up and ran to the door, throwing it open, heading toward the lake, sparkling in the morning sun. She needed to walk, but there was nowhere to go with woods stretching along the shore past Colin's cabin.

Then she remembered Ruth mentioning a trail. She went back up the hill and rounded the cabin. Just beyond the small patch of grass she saw an opening in the woods that might be a path. If she recalled correctly, Ruth also said it led to a state park that covered the ridge on this side of the lake and continued down to the other side, where the park entrance was. The trail was narrow, barely enough for one person, and cut straight though a thicket of hardwoods. She moved quickly, breathing hard as she climbed, inhaling the woodsy scent of dirt and decaying leaves and the fresh, almost sweet smell of ferns and skunk cabbage that grew in the wet spots.

At the top of the trail she looked up at the roof of the forest, a patchwork of trees and leaves, with sunlight pouring through the gaps. She sat a moment on a fallen branch, pausing to catch her breath. A sudden breeze shifted the air and the trees began to move, long branches swaying, leaves lifting, their undersides a silvery green. She stared for a long time, watching them move, change colors, amazed at how many greens there could be: the freshly minted green of new buds just coming into leaf, the deep velvety green of the pines, and the soft, lacy green of the hemlocks, always her favorite. She remembered hearing that the native Alaskans had nearly a hundred different words for snow, and thought that was how it probably should be for green in the northeast.

As she sat there in a patch of sunlight, she could feel its warmth begin to calm her shaking limbs. It was so beautiful, the glory of spring unfolding after the long gray winter in the northern woods. She stood finally and continued walking down the other side of the ridge, watching her footing now because of the slope and loose rocks. Climbing over a downed tree, she halted on the other side as a startled deer leapt away from her. Twin fawns, their tan coats spotted with white, froze for a moment, then followed their mother, white tails flashing.

All around nature was bursting with life. There had been baby rabbits flittering across the grass the past two mornings. Squirrels and chipmunks scampering from tree to tree, and of course the birds nesting all around the cabins. Somehow it all looked so easy. So simple.

A sob escaped her, reverberating in the silent forest. She'd been doing so well with the loss of Ben. But now it was coming back in fresh waves of sorrow thanks to David, and their marriage ending. Because it was all somehow connected, she didn't really need him to tell her that.

She slipped off her sweatshirt, tied it around her waist and kept walking, coming out eventually into a clearing flooded with early morning sunlight. Puffy white seeds of dandelions drifted in the air like dust motes. Purple phlox bloomed in the brush and she lifted her nose, detecting something sweet and fragrant. Wild roses? It seemed too early for that.

Here in the midst of such beauty she was certain God resided, just as she'd felt it on the beach. In all of her churchgoing years as a child, sitting in the hard pews beside her mother and brothers, she'd never felt God's presence as she did now. The only other time was when Ben was moving inside her.

Somehow she had to let go of David and her anger. Sitting on the grass, she leaned back on her hands, looking up at the sky. *Please God, help me find the strength to do that*, she prayed. She didn't like being bitter. She'd spent too many years watching her mother poison herself with it after her father left. She wanted to be better than that.

She wanted to feel hope again.

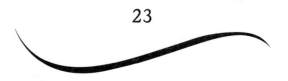

23

WHEN RUTH FINALLY CALLED DEBORA at Chapter One Books in Belvidere a week later to suggest sharing a room at the convention, she was stunned at Debora's news. With a calm resignation that Ruth couldn't quite fathom, Debora told her she was closing her store the following week.

"Oh, Deb, isn't there something—"

"Ruth, I'm done," she interrupted. "I've spent the years like a college kid with an addiction, living hand to mouth and putting every cent I own into the store. No wonder my husband almost left me. It's time to let go."

"What will you do?"

She heard a big sigh. "I don't know. Take a few weeks off. Go visit my daughter in Atlanta. They'd love for us to move there. But I also have to get a real job."

"Deb, this is—"

"I know it's a real job. It's three jobs. But to the outside world, it just looks like an obsession, throwing these little book events, reading in our spare time between customers..."

"Come on, not everyone feels that way."

"Sorry, I'm just cranky."

"No, I'm sorry. If there's anything I can do—"

"Just listen to what they've been saying at the conventions the past few years. Everything has been about diversifying and I just kept ignoring it. I didn't want to be a barista or a post office or a gift shop. I just wanted to sell books."

"Actually, I have been thinking about it."

"Good. And you need to do more events, too. That was my downfall—I just found them exhausting and it's so hard sometimes trying to convince the publicists why their big authors should come way out here where you never know how many people will show up."

Deb's store was in a sleepy town with little traffic. Ruth wasn't sure how Deb had lasted this long, but wanted to say something on a positive note. "They need to remember that after their author leaves, we hand sell those signed copies. A signed copy is a sold copy."

"I'm going to miss it, though. There's something magical about this business, that I think people on the outside will never understand. I thought I'd grow old and die in this store."

"Well, I've gotten to the growing old part," Ruth joked, trying to lighten Deb's mood.

"Oh, come on, Ruth. They call it 'vintage' now, don't they? It makes you more valuable."

"Well, this vintage bookseller is about to have another milestone. In fact, our downtown revitalization project is finally getting proactive. We're planning to start First Friday Walks and the first one is going to coordinate with my store's anniversary celebration coming up in the fall."

"That's right, what is it—twenty years?"

"Would you believe thirty?"

"Jesus, Ruth, you are a legend. That is a milestone, especially in our business. I wish you all the luck in the world. I've had my husband all these years. You've done it alone."

"Well, I'm hanging on by my fingernails here, though after August I can relax a bit. Megan's made the Stephanie Meyer vampire releases our biggest event of the year, a midnight costume party, and of course a prepaid book purchase is your ticket in. Each year, they've gotten bigger."

"Maybe I should've found me a Megan, but…it's too late."

Hanging up, Ruth stood there, looking out the front window as the morning sun began to hit the buildings across the street, wondering how different her life might have been if she hadn't been widowed at such a young age. Yes, Debora had her husband, and Ruth had her store. Maybe it was an obsession for her. In a way, hadn't she let it take the place of a husband, a lover? And the intimacy she might have had if she'd made different choices?

She couldn't say she had regrets, though. She'd married the wrong man, blinded by desire to what was probably staring her in the face all along: it could never have worked. Out of that mistake she had three wonderful children, and four grandchildren.

And she still had her store.

24

I N THE BEGINNING, LUCY HAD THOUGHT SHE'D BE GOING stir crazy at the cabin as the days passed, but she wasn't. There were long stretches of nothing where she simply couldn't work or focus, and she'd stare out the window, or from the porch, at the lake and mountains on the other side as summer exploded with a profusion of color. Everything was lush and green, the woods littered with pink and white petals of flowering dogwood, like confetti after a parade. Each day she now walked there, even just for a little while, and felt peace descend as if she'd swallowed a pill.

There were sleepless hours, too, when she'd lie in bed, eyes fixed on the ceiling in the darkness, but unafraid now. She thought a lot about the past and it seemed as if her exhausted mind and body were finally processing the surreal turn of events in her life. One day soon, yes, she'd have to think about a future. But for now, she was here.

And she was becoming better friends with Colin.

Last week he'd told her his goal was to swim to the island and back by the end of summer, something he'd done with ease before the accident. She'd nearly yelped in alarm. What if something were to go wrong, who would know? Even if he called for help, what if she was out? The other houses were too far away for anyone to hear him, if anyone was even home. He must have seen her worry, because he reminded her that he was training for next summer's competition and the months he'd be able to practice in the lake, which he preferred over a public pool for obvious reasons, were short.

She didn't want to insult him by questioning his ability, or tell him that his mother and sister would go ballistic. So she offered to time him. Each morning now began with this ritual. She would untie the canoe from the dock and paddle alongside him, as he ventured a little farther across the lake each time. It was a glorious way to start the day, before the world was fully awake, watching the birds slowly come to life, the sun ascending over the far mountain, the rhythmic splash as Colin's arms sliced through the water. It was now her favorite part of the day.

When they finished, he'd sit drying off for a few moments—wearing trunks, of course. Neither of them ever mentioned that first morning, and she wondered if he'd really seen her. Colin then went to sit in his whirlpool for a while, to warm his body.

"I won't be here tomorrow morning," she told him now, as they headed to their own cabins. "I'm going to see my mother, remember?"

"I remembered."

"And?"

He tilted his head and studied her a moment. "I'll be fine."

"You promised." Although he swam effortlessly, she knew that was no guarantee. And she couldn't tell Ruth, because she had promised she wouldn't. He wanted to surprise her.

"Please," she said and saw a slow smile curl his lips.

"All right, I did promise. Just this once."

"Thank you."

Two hours later her car was packed and Lucy was off.

* * *

HER MOTHER LIVED IN A LITTLE CONDO IN Bethlehem, Pennsylvania, which David had insisted they buy for her after she was forced to retire due to carpal tunnel syndrome that had been plaguing her for years. The prices and taxes were much cheaper than New Jersey and she was all about getting "the most bang for our buck," although it had been Lucy and David putting up the bucks. Still, it made Lucy happy to see her mother finally settled someplace where she'd never have to move again.

When she crossed the Delaware River from New Jersey into Pennsylvania, Lucy couldn't help glancing north, thinking about the eagle they'd rescued up the river in the Water Gap. She'd gone back to The Raptor Center with Colin once again, anxious to see it, but the bird was still sequestered in the Quiet Zone. Randy wasn't holding out much hope it would be going back out into the wild. He told them it definitely had lead poisoning, but they'd done chelation therapy and the bird was finally improving. Its wing was another story, however. The break was near the joint, probably too close for it to ever be able to fly again. Her heart broke at the news, thinking of the huge, powerful bird confined to a cage for life. Beside her, Colin had said nothing.

"Well, I'm going to stay optimistic," she'd said. "You never know, right?"

At what point, she thought now as she drove, did you give up? At what instant did Colin resign himself to never walking again? Maybe it was that moment you needed to stop grieving, and start healing, as she had that day in the woods. When you needed hope again.

Still, she wasn't ready to give up on this bird. Because somehow, she knew what it would mean to Colin to see it fly again, to watch it soar above the tree-tops as it was meant to do.

A half-hour later she exited off Route 78 into Bethlehem. Pulling into her mother's driveway, she saw that her mother's car was running and there was a suitcase in the backseat. Then the front door flew open and out she came, followed by a short man with thinning brown hair and a big smile, just as she'd pictured him.

Artie gave her a big hug. "Your mother's a great lady. I'll take good care of her. Now, I'm off to see the grandkids."

Lucy was stunned then when her mother looked at her and her eyes filled with tears. Then she pulled Lucy into a tight embrace—they were not huggers, so this should have been a red flag—but Lucy squeezed back.

"I've got a fresh pot of coffee brewing," her mother said as they went inside.

Lucy got the cups while her mother lit a cigarette. Her mother poured, then sat across from her.

"I talked to David last week. He told me everything."

Lucy's stomach seized. Then she reached for a cigarette and lit it.

"I called the house, worried. I knew something was going on. Jesus, Lucy, why do you always have to hold everything in? Just like—"

"I know, just like my father."

Not sixty seconds had gone by and already the old patterns were back in play.

Lucy stood up. "You know what? How about I get settled and we talk about this a little later, okay? I'm really tired from the drive."

Her mother watched Oprah as Lucy unpacked, and from the spare room she could hear Oprah's guest spilling her guts and tears about being obese all her life, while Oprah kept asking, *What is it you're really hungry for?*

A few minutes later, Lucy was surprised when her mother poked her head in.

"Why don't you take a nap and then we go out for a nice dinner?"

"Okay, Mom, that would be nice."

"I don't mind missing my Bonco game tonight."

"Well, why don't we go out for lunch tomorrow instead?"

"I already told Lydia I probably wouldn't be coming. I'm sure she doesn't mind."

"Are you sure?"

"Positive, although her desserts are to die for."

"Mom, you knew I was coming, why didn't you tell her before?"

"Lucy, you've been telling me you're coming for weeks now. How was I supposed to know if you really were this time?"

"I...I'm sorry."

"And who's been doing your hair?"

Her fingers automatically went to her head. "I have."

Her mother shook her head. "You know better than that. You never cut your own hair, no matter how good you are."

The day after Ben died, she'd cut her long blonde hair to within an inch of her scalp. She'd looked like a chemo patient, but she didn't care. She just couldn't bear to see herself looking so normal. David had never said a word. Her mother had just stared at her at the cemetery and Lucy knew what she'd been thinking, because she remembered the salon sagas of how women always took their frustrations out on their hair.

"Your layers are at an awkward stage," her mother said softly.

"I don't care if they're awkward," she said, making the decision just that moment. "I'm letting it grow."

Her mother nodded and closed the door.

* * *

HANNAH BURST INTO THE STORE AFTER HER SHIFT AT ELAINE'S with a basket dangling from her hand. "Look, my first prototype," she said, practically dancing as she held up her wares. "A Book Lover Basket, what do you think?"

Ruth examined the small picnic-type basket with a red paisley liner. Inside, artfully arranged, were a book, bookmark, muffins, gourmet tea bags, and a cut glass mug, all wrapped up with sparkling cellophane and a bright red ribbon.

"I love it!"

"Me too. And I've been reading up on business plans, Ruth, you know in that book that Hazel suggested?" They both laughed. "Anyway, I'm going to stop and see Lynn at the bank, and try to get a small business loan."

Ruth couldn't say anything about Lynn, who was still working, although

Ruth was certain she wouldn't be much longer.

"I saw these great bistro tables online, very country French, but not cheap," Hannah went on.

"Well, don't get too carried away. It may take a while until you're in the black."

"Eddie thinks I'm nuts. That there's no way this is going to work."

Ruth bit her tongue, then said, "Your gift baskets are brilliant."

"I'm beyond excited, Ruth. And I'm going to make this work."

Just then Megan came in for the evening shift, and she, too, loved the gift basket idea. Before Hannah left, they decided to coordinate the grand opening of Hazel's Café with the anniversary celebration at the inaugural First Friday Walk. Both would be promoted during Applefest in October, which was downtown Warwick's biggest event each year.

After Hannah left, Megan looked at Ruth. "The café was really a great idea of yours, by the way."

"Thanks, Megan." It was rare that Megan ever gave her a pat on the back. "By the way, I nearly forgot, whatever happened with all that stuff from Sandy's grandmother and the age of the store?"

"Oh, right," Megan said, opening a big Tupperware bowl to eat her dinner before Ruth left. "I did some research and came up with nothing."

"Well, that's too bad."

"Mmm," Megan said, digging into her salad, "have you tried that new farm stand out in Pine Island? It's a little drive, but their organic produce is to die for."

Ruth stared at the plump red tomato slices and famous Pine Island onions. How many days had she held herself back from taking that drive? Needing to know: Was he still there?

"You know, Megan, I think a big summer salad might be perfect for this Sunday's brunch."

Twenty minutes later Ruth was in her car, her heart pounding. There were only two gas stations in Pine Island that she could recall, so if Thomas was still there, he'd have to be at one or the other.

25

THE OLD BETHLEHEM STEEL COMPLEX, ABANDONED YEARS AGO, was now a casino, complete with glitz and glamour, and that's where her mother chose to go. They ate at Emeril's and Lucy nearly choked at the prices, knowing her mother would expect her to pay.

As her mother feasted on surf and turf, and Lucy picked at her flounder and rice, her mother began to talk about the book club she now belonged to. It was the perfect time to tell her about Lucy's own novel, but she couldn't quite bring herself to do it. Her mother had always thought her writing aspirations unrealistic. And after the first few years of rejection after college, she'd told her mother she'd simply packed it in.

"You know, we all want to improve ourselves, but most of Oprah's picks are depressing as hell," her mother went on.

Lucy thought her mother was doing a great job at improving herself. Her short curls were now a burnished auburn, her face dewy from the new Mary Kay night cream her neighbor sold to all the women in the complex.

As soon as they finished their entrees, her mother brought up David again. Apparently she'd just been biding her time. Lucy was surprised to find out that he'd told her everything.

"He was very quiet, very...somber. I'd never heard David like that before, except..."

Except after Ben died, of course.

"Mom, he's a criminal, of course he's somber."

"You should go back to Florida and try to make it work."

"Mom, I will be going back, but to finalize the divorce and get the rest of my things. David's made it clear he wants a new life, without me. Besides..."

"Besides?"

She knew her mother wouldn't like this. "Besides, I think that would be a mistake, even if he did."

"That's ridiculous, you two have a wonderful life."

"Had a wonderful life. It's over."

"He's a good man, Lucy. He made some mistakes."

"Are you kidding?"

"Listen, I wasn't the best wife in the world. And your father wasn't so horrible, really. You think I didn't have regrets?"

"But he left you."

"Maybe I could have done some things differently."

If her mother had stood on her head in the middle of the restaurant, Lucy couldn't have been more stunned. In her entire life, this was the first time she could recall her mother taking blame for anything.

"We were just..." her mother hesitated a moment, "too young? Too selfish? No one tells you how hard it's going to be, you know? That first blush of passion doesn't last, but no one tells you that. And then you have to try to hang on somehow, with money problems and kids, and..." She waved her hand, as if the rest didn't need to be said. And it didn't.

The waitress came back with their coffees and her mother's cheesecake. Lucy kept her mouth shut, afraid that whatever she said would be the wrong thing. She wanted her mother to continue. When the waitress left, Lucy looked at her mother, surprised to see her eyes glistening.

"Look, Lucy, I know you got a raw deal as a kid. I heaped too much responsibility on you when you were so young. I couldn't keep your father here, and I wasn't the best mother, either."

"Oh come on, Mom. You raised three good kids on your own."

"I didn't do such a hot job with Charlie. It was awful what we went through for a while there."

"Charlie's fine now. Lots of kids get mixed up in drugs, and he's over it. He's got a wonderful life in Australia."

"Except no one has seen him in ten years."

"Maybe you should go with Artie."

"Do you know what that would cost?"

This was when Lucy would usually offer to help, or say *let me talk to David*. But she said nothing now, because she couldn't.

"Look, we're getting off the subject. What I was trying to say was that what you and David had was worlds different than what your father and I had. That's the kind of love that lasts. You're going through a rough patch now and I think that's not surprising after what the two of you went through, all those miscarriages, then losing a baby. I'm amazed it didn't happen sooner."

"I know, Mom."

"Sometimes I think I should've tried harder. Don't make that mistake.

You two have respect, common interests, shared values. And you had security. That's way more important than the fireworks."

"Is that what you have now with Artie?"

"Yes. And you know what? We don't fight. There's none of that constant struggle like I had with your father."

"Mom, it doesn't matter anymore, it's over."

"He's ashamed, Lucy. I could barely get him to talk at first. But you know David. He's too polite to just tell me to go away."

"Well, he wasn't too polite to tell me he wants me out of his life."

"That's what he thinks. You need to convince him otherwise."

"You're not listening to me, Mom. Maybe this is all for the best. It's been months. I'm stronger now, and I'm healing. I'm starting to see things about not just David and our marriage, but even about myself, a lot more clearly." The problem was, she wasn't sure they were things she really wanted to face.

When they got back to the condo, Lucy went in her room, got a copy of her book and brought it into the kitchen, where her mother was on the phone with Artie, smoking a cigarette. She set the book on the counter then went to bed.

* * *

IT WAS LESS THAN A TWENTY MINUTE DRIVE from Warwick to Pine Island. As Ruth pulled onto the county road, her cell phone rang. She saw it was Jenny. Her daughter, she was convinced, had some kind of radar. She opened the window for noise, then turned on her favorite classical station to drown out the ring.

The smells of summer drifted in as Ruth's mind wandered over the years and visits she'd had with Thomas. One in particular came to her now, probably not more than a year ago at most. Thomas was sitting across from her and they'd just finished going over the final numbers due from each prisoner for that day's book orders. There were still a few moments left before the guard realized their time was up, and Thomas began discussing a book he'd just finished that she'd recommended, *Outlander*, a story in which a nurse from 20th century England travels back in time to 18th century Scotland, and falls in love. She began telling him about *Time and Again*, which she had discovered back in the seventies after Bill died. It was still one of her top five favorite books, and the most realistic version of time travel she'd ever read.

Thomas glanced over his shoulder then to check on the guard. The guard was engrossed in conversation with another guard a few feet out in the hall.

"So, this author really had you believing that time travel was possible?" he asked in a playful tone.

"It's hard to explain how he did it, but yes, he made it seem so real. I wanted to somehow get myself into the Dakota, a very famous residence overlooking Central Park where his character traveled back to Victorian New York, and try it myself."

"Imagine if you could really do that?" he said, shaking his head in wonder. "Would you try it? I'd do it in a heartbeat, because I could undo every mistake I ever made."

She'd sat there a moment because it was exactly what she'd always thought, that if she could, she'd undo all her past mistakes. But she realized suddenly that if she did, she wouldn't have married Bill, which meant she wouldn't have her children, or grandchildren. It was unthinkable, really.

"Would you really undo it all?" she asked him then. Because if he did, he wouldn't be sitting across the table from her in that prison. They never would have met.

The scent of the black dirt, or muck as locals called it, suddenly filled the car and brought her back to the present. Sure enough, within a few moments the rich residue of an old glacial lake that had long ago made Pine Island famous for its onions stretched on both sides of the county road. Rows of produce seemed to go on forever, bathed in the late day haze of a hot summer sun.

Her cell rang again. It was Jenny. She reached over and put her purse on top of it, to muffle the sound. The speed limit dropped as she neared the village limits and up ahead she saw the sign for the first gas station on her right. She slowed her car, glancing over as she came abreast of the gas pumps. There were cars at each one, and a few waiting. Quickly her eyes scanned the pumps, but she didn't see anyone. She nearly came to a halt when she saw a large man coming out of the mini-mart, wondering if it was Thomas. A horn blasted behind her and she hit the gas, her face flaming in embarrassment.

She pulled into a restaurant parking lot a minute later to get a grip, realizing suddenly how ridiculous she was being. Even if she saw him, he had no idea what her car looked like, so it was unlikely he'd notice her. Unless he'd been waiting, watching.

She drove a few more miles and there was the other gas station, much smaller, with a two bay garage for repairs and windows above it, which might be where Thomas was living. On the other side of the road, slightly past, was a driveway that led to a farm set way back. Ruth put her blinker on and pulled in on an angle, so she could look across the road.

There was only one car at the pump. As she watched, the door to the garage opened and there he was. Her breath caught. She watched him come around the car and hand the driver change. Her entire body seemed to be vibrating with anticipation. She hadn't really thought further than just seeing if he was still here. She could drive over and get gas, as if she had no idea this was where he worked. As if she'd somehow forgotten. It was the kind of silly subterfuge she'd overheard popular girls whisper about a million years ago when she was in high school lunch, her head buried in a book.

And that's exactly how she felt right now, like a teenager who sneaked out without her parents' permission, driving by the house of the boy she had a crush on. As if in response, her cell began to ring under her purse again. It was weeks since he'd come to her house. She owed him an answer, if nothing else.

But he probably knew her answer by her silence. Perhaps he was no longer interested. Maybe he'd already found someone else.

She put the car back in drive. A car was coming from the left, so she waited. Then another on the right. Her cell rang again, then stopped. She pulled it from under her purse and saw four missed calls from Jenny. Something, she suddenly realized, must be wrong.

She threw the car back in park and pressed call. Jenny answered on the first ring.

"Mom?" It was a pitiful wail. "Where are you? I've been trying—"

"Just tell me what's wrong!"

"I didn't want to worry you, Mom, so I never said anything but..." Jenny was crying now. "Emma had some tests last week, and I've been a wreck waiting for the doctor—"

"What did the tests say?" A surge of dread roared up her chest, making it impossible to breathe. Sweet Jesus! Her little granddaughter!

"I couldn't stand the waiting, I thought I was losing my mind, that's when I started calling you, but I just found out it's all good. She's fine." And then Jenny began to sob.

"Oh, honey..." Ruth closed her eyes as hot tears slid down her cheeks. "What a relief."

"What's wrong with me, Mom? The doctor kept telling me it was probably nothing, not to worry. But I couldn't help it, I just worry about *everything*. I think there's something wrong with me, that's all I do."

"Honey, there's nothing wrong with you. I'm the same way. That's what mothers do."

Jenny started to laugh, too. "So I'm not insane? Because Olivia's starting to look at me like I am."

"Well she's right about that age where you started doing that to me. Adolescence, it goes with the territory." And Jenny had two daughters to get through it with, so she'd get paid back in spades.

A pickup truck caught her eye as it pulled into the gas station and stopped at the pump. The garage door opened. It wasn't Thomas.

"So where are you, Mom? They said you'd left the store."

"Oh...I just went to get some produce," she said as she glanced at the clock on her dashboard. It was after seven. "Do you want me to come by?"

"No, it's okay. And I promised the girls we'd watch a movie. But thanks, Mom."

She hung up and sighed, suddenly exhausted from the adrenaline crash. Her daughter had gone through hell, but Emma was just fine. And now Thomas was gone, his shift obviously over. The timing of it all seemed uncanny. Or maybe not.

She put her blinker on and pulled out, heading back to Warwick.

* * *

IT WAS LATE MORNING WHEN LUCY'S MOTHER finally came into the kitchen. Lucy was at the table with a cup of tea, her laptop opened, working on a poem she'd been tinkering with for days now. She heard a sniffle and turned.

"You made me cry," her mother said, standing in the doorway in her pink robe, a tissue in her hand.

"I'm sorry, Mom, I don't—"

"No, not you," her mother said, waving her hand, "your book. I started it last night because I couldn't sleep. I just finished it."

"You read the entire book? You never slept?"

"I couldn't stop. It's wonderful, Lucy, the ending just beautiful, but so sad. Why didn't you tell me you had a book published? I thought you stopped writing a long time ago."

"I did stop writing for a while. And I didn't really get my book published."

Her mother held the book up. "Then what do you call this?"

Lucy sighed. "Why don't you start your coffee and sit down. It's a long story."

Thirty minutes later her mother sat across from her shaking her head. "I can't believe you couldn't get it taken. And who knew what you were going through? David?"

"Most of it. I skipped a few rejections here and there. And when I decided to self-publish I didn't tell him until it was in the works. But a few friends aside from that."

"And was any of this based on truth? Things in your own life? Because Hope's mother, who was never home, seemed a bit familiar, if you know what I mean. And how Hope couldn't wait to get out of the house, so she married Matthew despite her doubts."

"Mom, the mother isn't you, Hope isn't me. It's just what writers do, take bits and pieces of their lives, and those around them and mix it all up like a cake. The end result is something entirely different."

"And what about Matthew, who turns out to be gay after twenty years of marriage. Did you just think that one up?"

"It's not so uncommon, you know."

"Of course I know. I have some lovely gay friends here in the complex, both men and women."

Her mother got up and poured another cup of coffee. "He reminded me a little of that boy you dated when we lived in Dover, the one who broke your heart. Jamie?"

She stared at her mother, stunned. "I can't believe you even remembered him. The book was just a 'what if.' You know, what if we had gotten married." Because for a while there, she thought they would.

"I knew how devastated you were. My heart was breaking for you but you would never let me in. Never let me even try to help you."

He was her first love, her first kiss. He also introduced her to her first cigarette, and her first drink. Then he gave it all up to hang out with the Jesus freaks. When he broke up with her a few years later, telling her he was really gay, she'd hoped it was just another lifestyle he was trying on. Ten years later she heard he died of AIDS.

"I guess I was just a bitchy teenager, but I really hated that high school, too. And I'm sorry I didn't let you in."

Her mother reached over and tucked a stray hair behind her ear. "How could you let me in? I was a train wreck then. And you were always just trying to make things easier for me." Her mother hesitated a moment. "That scene when she's a kid, when her father comes up to the attic to say he's leaving? That was real, wasn't it?"

Slowly she nodded.

"I've changed, Lucy, and if your father had lived longer, maybe he'd have too. I wish I could go back and live those years over because I'm a helluva lot smarter now. And you don't have to protect me anymore."

Lucy smiled. "I can see that, Mom."

"I know we haven't seen a lot of each other in years. Part of that was because I knew you needed time and distance after Ben. But the other part was, well, I finally saw that I needed to make some adjustments to me. And I think that's how Artie happened into my life. The universe realized I was ready for him."

"He seems like a great guy."

"Anyway, enough about me. Let's get back to your book. I have an idea. Do you remember Adele Gray? She's my favorite author and she's doing a signing downtown at Moravian Books today. I was going to surprise you and take you there. Let's give her your book! Maybe she'll love it, too, and give it to her agent."

"Oh, Mom, she probably has people giving her their books all the time. I don't think I have the stomach for that today."

"Why not? Your book is just as good as any of hers, Lucy, and that's the truth."

"I think so too, but she's got hundreds of thousands of readers, and...I'm nobody. I just got an email from a publisher's sales rep this morning that I'd been really counting on. He read my book, but thought it was a bit too quiet to fit in commercial women's fiction." Another bullet hole. She wondered if Ruth knew.

"Then just leave me a book. I'll take it to the store tomorrow and tell them that our book club is going to read it—and we will. That will hopefully get you some attention."

"Thanks, Mom, I really appreciate that." She stood up and closed her laptop. "Now I'm going to start getting ready, I've got a signing at Clinton Books later on my way back." Which she felt like bagging now but didn't have the nerve.

"Listen, Lucy, before you go, just think about what I said about David yesterday, okay?"

"Mom..." she started to protest.

"But do what you think is best."

She drove away that afternoon thinking about the last twenty-four hours with her mother. Feeling lighter, happier, as if some burden had been lifted from her. Looking in the rear view mirror, she had to laugh, her writer's mind envisioning the baggage of their past littering the highway behind her.

26

LUCY SMELLED THE LAKE BEFORE SHE SAW IT. Pulling down the long drive, the dank earthy dampness rose up to her, and with it, a sense of coming home. It was nearly ten o'clock when she got out of the car, still hot and sultry with cicadas and tree frogs echoing from the woods. For a moment, she toyed with a jump in the water.

As she pulled out her small suitcase, she noticed Colin's house all lit up. There were no other cars in the driveway, which meant he was alone. Leaving her bag on the porch step, she walked over, longing to tell someone about her success. She climbed the ramp to his deck, then knocked on the screen door. He was sitting at the dining room table and waved her in.

Walking across the room, she knew immediately something was horribly wrong. He didn't say a word, just stared down at the table where a bottle of Jack Daniel's sat in front of him, and beside it a small tumbler.

"Grab yourself a glass," he said.

She hesitated, then went to the kitchen and got a small juice glass from a cabinet. His light blue eyes were bright and his jaw kept moving, as if he were grinding his teeth back and forth. She sat across the table and he opened the bottle, pouring a small amount into each of their glasses. He lifted his, then waited for her to pick up hers.

"*Salud,*" he said softly, then threw his head back and drank.

She did the same, but a second later was coughing, trying to catch her breath as the fiery liquid slid down. Neither of them said anything for a long moment. She'd never seen him like this and wasn't sure whether to wait or break the silence. Before she could decide, he poured another finger in each glass. She almost protested, but something in his eyes stopped her. Again they drank, and again he poured. Already she was feeling warm and fuzzy and knew this could get dangerous.

"How many of these have you had?"

His lips curled into a smile. "Not enough."

"Colin, what happened?"

They stared at each other and she was stunned to see his eyes fill with tears. He wiped them quickly with his hand, then picked up his glass and threw it across the room. It shattered and she stood up, suddenly frightened.

"Wait," he said, pushing himself around the table to block her path. "I'm sorry. Don't go."

She hesitated. He took her hand, holding her there. "Please, Lucy, I didn't mean to scare you like that."

"All right."

He let go. "Let's sit outside."

The long day, the signing, the late drive back, and what must've amounted to about two shots of whiskey suddenly sloshing around an empty stomach all made her a bit woozy. He turned off most of the lights as she followed him out to the deck.

There was no moon, so they sat in near darkness, her eyes slowly adjusting to the night. Here, she realized, she wouldn't be able to see the pain, the grief, that was all too apparent on his face inside.

"How was your trip?" he asked.

"It went well. My mother and I didn't argue once," she said with a chuckle, trying to instill some levity into the atmosphere.

"And your signing at Clinton Books?"

"I didn't want to go because I was feeling really down about the whole book thing, but it turned out wonderful. Harvey and Rob were so welcoming and supportive, just like your mom. So we had a great turnout, and I got a few more book club invitations. They all seem so excited to have me come and discuss the book with them."

"That's great."

"Oh, and Harvey's mother is considered the Oprah of Clinton and it turned out she loves my book! So it's a 'Mom Pick,' which is about the highest praise you can get there. I signed more than twenty copies."

"You've worked hard. You deserve it."

"Thank you, I appreciate that." When he said nothing she finally worked up the nerve to ask, "So do you want to tell me now what happened?"

She could hear him sigh, and it was a long moment before he spoke again. "Do you remember that first time you came with me to The Raptor Center? I told you I was upset about Danny calling me all drunked up, that's why we left so abruptly?"

"Yes."

"I didn't tell you the rest of it. He overdosed on pain pills that day, said it was accidental."

"Oh, Colin." That day she'd met Danny he seemed so...together, so friendly and nice. But what did she know?

"Danny was paralyzed about a year after me. It's a tough thing for a man to swallow, that you'll never walk again. Never make love to a woman, perhaps. Never have the rest of your life the way you thought the rest of your life would be..."

He looked up at the sky, scanning the stars as if there might be some answer up there. In the ambient light she could see that his face was filled with such sadness, and she reached over, took his hand, and squeezed. He squeezed back, but didn't let go.

"Danny was twenty-four years old, and maybe that's what made the difference. To him, I'm an old man at forty. Isn't that middle-aged?" he asked with a little laugh.

"Not by my accounting. And I used to be an accountant. I don't think middle-aged starts until fifty."

"And you are?"

"Still thirty-nine."

"Hmm. I'd have sworn not a day over thirty."

She smiled, but his disappeared and he turned away, quiet again for a while. She waited.

"They give you lots of painkillers in the early days. It's kind of a paradox, you know, you're paralyzed, but there's still pain. And after a while, if you're not careful it's hard to live without the stuff. Danny was a good soldier, but he was always a hard drinker and after that, well, he began having addiction issues."

"Is that common?"

He shrugged. "It's not uncommon. When I came to in the middle of that road in Iraq, everyone screaming, blood and smoke everywhere, and I couldn't move, I knew in that instant that I was never going to walk again. But even so, in those early weeks there's such denial, you think if you just find the right thing, acupuncture, or Reiki, or maybe when the swelling finally starts to subside, you'll start to feel something. Because you can't imagine things otherwise. It took me a long time to swallow what I knew in that first moment. But Danny spent months and months trying anything he could find, even experimental crap down in Mexico. He just couldn't face it. And now...he doesn't have to anymore."

"Oh, Colin, he died?" He squeezed her hand so hard she nearly cried out.

"Early on I told him that if he focused on what he still had then—a wife, a family that loved him, a lot of good years ahead of him—that he could still do something worthwhile with his life. But...he couldn't be a soldier anymore. His personal life just fell apart, his wife couldn't take the drinking, the anger..." He sat there, shaking his head.

Although weeks ago Colin had told her the same abbreviated version of what had happened to him as Ruth had, this was the first time he ever really talked about how difficult it had been. Because of his outward strength and confidence, she never really put much thought to the hell he'd gone through. The difficult moments that must still come at him when he least expected it.

"I understood everything Danny went through, the anger, the frustration. The waste. I was about to retire from the military, get married, have the life I'd waited a long time for. It would have been so easy to lose myself in some altered state. But I just kept thinking of my dad, dead so young. I would have taken him paralyzed, over not having him at all. And I thought of my mom, losing a husband, then a son. I decided if I was going to live, I wasn't going to make everyone else around me miserable. I was going to do something worthwhile with my life."

He gave a long, ragged sigh. "Danny was a good soldier. I thought when I persuaded him to be my relay buddy for the games, that might do the trick, you know—give him a goal, a purpose each day. And damn, he was good. He could push that chair like no one else I ever saw. Yesterday he apparently found out his ex is pregnant."

"Do you think that was the catalyst?"

He shrugged. "It couldn't have helped. That's my one regret, too. I'd have liked kids."

"I understand. I'll never have them either."

He turned to her. "But you're still young enough, there's probably still time."

"It just wasn't meant to be. And I've learned to live with it."

"I'm sorry. And I'm sorry to dump so much on you."

"I'm glad you did."

"Maybe it's because you didn't know me...before. I find myself telling you things I haven't shared with anyone."

"Me too."

She knew what it was. They were friends, pure and simple. There was no need for pretense, because there also wasn't that delicate mating dance between a man and a woman. But as she stood to leave, he took her hand again and gently pulled her onto his lap, wrapping his arms around her. Without hesitation she laid her head on his shoulder.

After a moment he whispered, "Thanks for listening. I have to admit, I was a bit put out when you moved in next door, but I'm glad you're here."

She stood up then and smiled. "So you wouldn't mind it if I stayed on a few more months while I figure out my big picture?"

He shook his head. "You're a tough lady. I have to give you credit, that cabin's pretty rustic and I don't know a lot of women who would've stuck it out."

"Well, I didn't have much choice at first, but now, I'm kind of shocked to admit it, but it's starting to feel like home. And I don't mind the cabin, or the fact that I wear the same clothes all the time, have just a handful of toiletries, a few pair of shoes..." She laughed suddenly. "It's kind of liberating to do without and realize you can do just fine. Maybe even focus on the things that are way more important than the *stuff*."

He was smiling at her, his head tilted.

"But you know all that, of course."

"I do, but the average person doesn't."

"It's funny, I grew up pretty poor, always moving around, always wanting the things I thought would make me happy, but...I realize now that real contentment comes from within, not from other people or..."

"*Stuff?*"

"Right," she said, and they both laughed. "Sometimes I feel like I'm living a novel, or maybe a Lifetime Movie, you know? This woman who was somehow sleepwalking through her own life until she loses everything and goes after this dream of being an author one last time. I just hope I can be the plucky heroine who somehow pulls it together for a happy ending."

"I'll be rooting for you."

"Thanks."

"I almost forgot," he said. "I won't be swimming in the morning. A few of us are going to visit Danny's family."

"All right." She turned to go, then turned back to him. "That reminds me, I do have to leave soon to go back to St. Augustine to finalize my divorce. It'll just be a few days, but you promise you won't swim alone while I'm gone again?"

"I'll miss you," he said after a moment.

"I'll miss you, too." She smiled. "And?"

"And I promise."

* * *

SHE SLEPT LATE THE NEXT MORNING, and it was after ten when Lucy sat down at her laptop with her first cup of tea. She couldn't stop thinking about her conversation with Colin the night before, Danny's tragic story, and the scene she was now writing. What was war to the average person? To her, and millions of others, it was something far away, removed from your daily life. You forgot about it after you put away the morning paper. Or you avoided it altogether by refusing to read gruesome articles. But men like Colin and Danny, and women, were just like characters in a novel, living with the consequences of their choices. Enduring the scorching after effects for the rest of their lives.

It was powerful stuff, and she wanted to do it justice as she worked it into her story somehow. She'd tried last night, just putting down thoughts and snippets of their talk when she got in. But it just wasn't coming. Erasing the last few lines now, she swallowed the last of her tea and decided to let it go and take a walk in the woods. If she let her mind relax, it would hopefully come to her.

She put on shorts, laced up her sneakers, and headed out the door. Rounding the cabin toward the path, she noticed a man in a soldier's uniform pushing himself in a wheelchair from Colin's house. She realized it must be another friend going with him to see Danny's family. But when the soldier reached the grass and turned the chair, coming toward the driveway, she was stunned to see that it wasn't a stranger. It was Colin.

His long blond hair was shaved to a stubble, barely visible beneath the beret. He sat there a moment looking at her, in the green jacket with brass buttons and gold braid, with a crisp white shirt and black tie, so formal and handsome in his dress greens. There were emblems and badges, but she had no idea what they were for. He was a soldier, going to pay his respects for another soldier.

She watched him, realizing that the Colin she knew, the Colin she'd become friends with, was just a small part of who this man really was.

27

TWO THINGS KEPT RUTH FOCUSED, and able to ignore the things she simply didn't want to think about—the midnight release party for the new vampire novel, and the plans for Hazel's café. It was time, too, to start putting some real thought into the anniversary celebration for the store. Although it was still a few months off, Ruth knew it would be here before she knew it.

That morning she'd held a staff meeting to bounce around ideas. Everyone had great suggestions, especially Megan, who looked as if she'd combust from excitement, guaranteeing it would "blow their feckin' doors off." But when she wouldn't share yet, Ruth was afraid it was going to be another money drain, and she'd have to say no.

But Ruth, too, had a surprise she wasn't able to share. Larry Porter was going to propose to Angela right there in the store on the day of the anniversary party. So there was no chance of her finding out, Ruth promised she wouldn't let her staff in on it until right before the event. It was utterly romantic and brought a smile to her face every time she thought of it.

She wished Colin had been able to share in the planning, but he had an appointment with the V.A. doctor. It was just routine, he assured her. She hoped so. Colin, she knew, kept a lot to himself, reluctant to worry her. But she was worried. When he'd come in the other morning with his head shaved, her eyes had filled with tears and she had to turn away. He hadn't looked like that since before his accident. In that moment a rush of emotion hit her like a tidal wave. After what he'd gone through, he deserved every good thing that was possible in life. And yet there he was, still alone. Gloryanne's visits to the store had come to a sudden halt.

And then she realized, Lucy was right there keeping an eye on things. If anything was wrong, maybe she'd know about it. Besides, except for a few e-mails, they hadn't talked in weeks, so they could catch up, as well.

Lucy answered her cell on the first ring.

"Oh, Ruth, you must have ESP, I've been thinking about you all morning!"

"Well, it's been a while, and I remembered you had your first book club meeting this week, right? How'd it go?"

"Actually...it was weird at first," Lucy said with a little laugh. "I mean I was with all these lovely women who all knew each other and chatted about kids, and little league and cheerleading, and I felt so, I don't know, out of place I guess. I mean I had nothing in common with them, so I grabbed some wine and nibbled on appetizers and kind of watched from a quiet corner. Then we went and sat in the family room to discuss the book and I have to tell you, that was intense."

"I should have warned you. Some book clubs, and some women, can be difficult. We did a role-playing seminar at our last convention about The Perils & Pitfalls of Book Clubs. It was a hoot."

"I felt like I was getting the third degree as they questioned my character's motives and decisions, which obviously were my decisions as the author. I guess I was assuming they were questioning the validity of some of what I wrote, but they were really trying to understand why I did what I did as the author."

"So they liked they book."

"We had quite a heated discussion, and a few women didn't quite buy some parts of it—like how could Hope really not have known he was gay—but they told me it was the first time they unanimously agreed they liked a book. So I felt better when I left. I know I need book clubs, Ruth, but that's going to be a huge investment in nervous energy."

"You'll handle it. And I hear from Rob at Clinton Books that you've got a few of theirs on board, too."

"Actually, Ruth, I've got more than fifteen book club requests now, from eight different states. I'll be doing some via Skype. Can you believe it?"

"Word's getting out, as I knew it would, because it's a wonderful book."

"And yet your sales rep didn't think so."

"He told me he'd e-mailed you directly. I'm sorry, but it's just one opinion. Don't let it get you down."

"I know, I'm trying. But then there are some pretty bad reviews online. I have to tell you, some days I'm up and down more times than a yo-yo."

"Well, I have to be honest, Lucy, there are no certainties in this business. I know I'm encouraging you to go for it, but I can't guarantee anything."

"Oh, Ruth, of course I know that. And if nothing happens, well, it's getting me through one of the toughest times in my life. And, I've got the pleasure of getting some wonderful e-mails from readers. My words, my characters, are moving them."

"That must be a great feeling."

"It's the best. But it's not just the book, Ruth. I want to thank you for everything else you've done for me, especially my staying at the cabin. It's giving me the time to start making peace with the past, and to really start thinking about the future. If it's all right with you, I'd like to stay until fall."

"Well, that's not far away at all. You can stay longer if you want, it's only going to sit there empty. But please, no more rent. What you've paid me so far is more than enough."

"Sorry, Ruth, I can't make any promises there," Lucy giggled.

Just then four teenage girls came in the door, no doubt to sign up for the midnight release party in a few weeks.

"Listen, Lucy, before we hang up, I just wanted to check. Does everything seem all right next door? You know, with Colin?"

"Oh...yes, everything's fine. He was a bit shaken by his friend's death, but he seems better now. I think his volunteer work at The Raptor Center is helping."

"Have you seen Gloryanne visiting him?"

"Just that one time, right after I first moved in. Why? Is something wrong?" The girls were huddled at the counter now, waiting for her to get off the phone.

"No, nothing at all. I have to run, Lucy, but keep me posted on all your book news."

"Will do, Ruth. Bye."

Ruth pulled out Megan's sign-up sheet for the party and gasped out loud. They already had one hundred and fifty kids registered, an all-time high. That must be the news she was holding back. Ruth thought of the backlog of unpaid bills, her ridiculous new rent, and the cost of the convention. And the dreaded meeting with her accountant coming up.

Suddenly it all didn't seem so disastrous. And maybe she wouldn't have to find someone to share a room with at the convention after all.

* * *

LUCY COULDN'T STOP THINKING ABOUT RUTH. In their last few talks there was something missing in her voice. She wondered if it had to do with Thomas. Ruth hadn't mentioned him since the day of the book signing, when she told Lucy he was getting out on parole. And what he'd done.

As she waited for Colin, Lucy went outside and sat on the porch, watching the lightning flicker above the mountains. Everything was so still and steamy, so green and incredibly lush. Orange tiger lilies lined the roads now and Jersey sweet corn and tomatoes were for sale at farm stands and pickups all over the countryside. It was summer at its best, and how she'd grown to love it here. Ruth, she knew, would probably let her stay on indefinitely, but she would never take advantage of her kindness. She was still trying to find a way to thank Ruth for all she'd already done. Once again, her thoughts drifted to Ruth and this cabin and the nagging feeling that there was something besides being too busy that was keeping her away.

When she had mentioned it to Colin the other morning after his swim, he told her he thought it just seemed too painful. "This place embodied my Dad. A few times Jenny talked about making some changes, you know, redecorating a bit so it wasn't so hard for her to be here, and it looks exactly like it did back then, but…it never happened."

As she thought about his words now, it suddenly hit her! She couldn't believe it hadn't come to her sooner. As Colin's jeep pulled in the driveway and he honked the horn, Lucy knew exactly what she was going to do to thank Ruth. And she wanted it to be a huge surprise. So she kept her mouth shut on their way to The Raptor Center, despite the fact her mind was humming with ideas.

They were going to check the progress of their wounded eagle. He had a name now, Kit, since he was found near the Kittatiny Range. Colin barely said a word, either. She knew he was still reeling from Danny's death.

She sat there looking at him for a long moment. With his hair shaved he looked so much younger. It was easy to picture the towheaded little boy jumping off the dock in freezing April water, the "runt" as his father had called him, trying to impress them all with his feats of daring.

When they pulled into the lot Colin told her to go ahead while he checked in at the education building. He was going to be helping with a program on Lady, the great horned owl, that weekend. As she headed into the wooded path, she stopped at the plaque she'd only glanced at before.

The Raptor Center's philosophy is a belief that all living things are important and if, because of humans and human activities, injuries and injustices befall wild creatures, then humans have a responsibility to help heal the injuries and attempt to correct the injustices. And if, through education and understanding, many of the injuries and injustices can be prevented, so much the better for us all. And by living in this manner, The Raptor Center tries to provide a humane example for others.

What a beautiful philosophy, she thought. She was so excited to be writing about it. She'd learned a lot about the center from her research on their website. It began as one man's passion to rehabilitate wild birds, in the laundry room of his home on the far side of these twenty-five acres where he still lived. Now there were seventy aviaries and exterior cages, and a complex of buildings that contained a medical infirmary, education classrooms, offices and a gift shop.

She heard Colin approaching and turned.

"Susan's going to be a few minutes, so how about we go see Lady and I'll practice my spiel on you."

"I'll try not to throw tomatoes if you flub up."

It was nice to see him laugh.

"So how many birds are here anyway?"

"Right now there are about sixty hawks, a handful of eagles, including a few golden, as well as the two bald eagles, which includes Kit. And there are about twenty different owl species. But if you count all the songbirds and nestlings, this time of year there could be several thousand birds."

"That's incredible," she said, thinking of that original laundry room and how it had become this amazing place.

They stopped in front of Lady's cage. Lucy looked at the beautiful owl sitting there so quietly amidst the branches—its soft brown feathers, the horned ears that gave it its distinct look.

"So, let me begin," Colin said, clearing his throat with a hint of drama. "Besides using these birds for education programs and public viewing, the unreleasable raptors are used for captive breeding, or like Lady here, foster parenting. A huge part of our work here is in raising young birds that were separated from their parents during nesting season, or orphaned."

"You mean Lady will take another owl's young to raise?"

He nodded. "Every winter she lays two eggs. Obviously they're infertile because she doesn't have a mate. But her hormones trigger a mothering instinct. Of course her own eggs won't hatch, but when the time is right, we swap those eggs for healthy babies who need a mother. She'll begin caring for them and keeping them warm. As soon as those babies begin to beg for food,

Lady will gently begin to feed them, as if they're her own. Not only that, they learn essential owl behavior from her that'll help them survive in the wild even though she can't."

"Oh Colin, that is so touching."

"Lady's been fostering baby owls here for nearly twenty years, over three hundred of them. The woods of New Jersey are filled with Lady's chicks."

She looked at Lady, asleep on the branch, nearly thirty years old now, and felt her eyes fill, imagining her feeding and caring for one baby after another, year after year, as if they were her own. It was an incredible story.

"No wonder she's so tired," she joked, turning to Colin. "I think that was a great spiel."

"I'm getting there. It rambled a bit, but I guess you got the gist."

They headed toward the infirmary, a red barnlike building where Susan was waiting.

"Susan, I had a question," Lucy said, since they had a few moments. "I read that lead shot was banned. So how did Kit get lead poisoning?"

"But it's cheap, and some hunters still manage to get their hands on it. So when they shoot and can't find their kill, it makes its way into the food chain. Your eagle no doubt feasted on a felled deer or duck. They don't just fish, eagles are scavengers, too."

"How awful. Don't they—"

But just then the infirmary door opened and they turned. Out came Randy, walking very slowly, his arms covered in heavy leather gloves that went past his elbows. Kit was perched on one outstretched arm. A leather leash, attached to one of the bird's feet, tethered him to the glove in case he tried to take off, which was highly unlikely. Kit hadn't flown for weeks now, and they doubted he ever would. The fact that he'd been named meant the odds were he was going to be a display bird.

She was stunned again at the size of the bird next to the man, realizing once more what a dangerous job this was. Kit was huge and his fierce yellow eyes darted everywhere as his head bobbed from side to side, making it easy to see how nervous it was. He hadn't been outside the Quiet Zone since he was first brought in.

She thought about how human contact was such a stress on a bird, and imagined Kit must be terrified, being carried by a man, having no idea where he was going, or what was about to happen next. Perhaps he was even still in pain. Despite what they knew, there was so much they never would.

Slowly Randy carried the bird into the opened cage, then gently set Kit on a low branch, untethered him and carefully backed into the antechamber. Kit sat there, his head still bobbing as he turned from side to side, his bright yellow eyes surveying his new surroundings. Lucy stood beside Colin and Susan, waiting, praying. Kit's lead levels, so high that it almost killed him, were back to normal, thanks to the chelation therapy, which essentially washed his blood of the toxic metal. He looked strong again, but until today, he'd had no chance to try out his healed wing. Lucy's heart was in her throat, hoping he'd be able to fly. For some reason, as she stood beside Colin, she didn't want to see Kit become a display bird.

As they waited in silence, she couldn't help thinking of Colin and his wounded vets, and even David and herself. In life, everyone got hurt, suffered loss, but in the end, hopefully they could heal and find new purpose. Perhaps that's what was really drawing her there.

Just then Kit lifted his shoulders, as if shrugging. He did it again, and again. Then he stretched his wings ever so slightly, no doubt testing their strength after his long recuperation. She imagined not moving her legs or arms for weeks, the loss of muscle that would result. Beside her she knew Colin had similar thoughts. After a few moments, Kit spread his wings to a nearly seven foot span and it was easy to see the difference between the two, the right wing slightly bent. His talons released their grip on the branch and they waited for him to lift in the air, but he wobbled, seeming to lose his balance, then latched on tightly again with those strong feet.

Kit closed his wings and didn't open them again.

28

I T WAS BRUTALLY HOT TODAY, BUT RUTH PROPPED THE DOOR OPEN, hoping to lure in anyone who might be passing by. Of course that made it ridiculous to put the air conditioning on. Not that other stores didn't, but she wasn't about to throw money out the door like that.

A bead of perspiration trickled down her back as she thought about the busy day ahead of her: a huge shipment of books to be unpacked, a pile of paperwork only she could take care of, and Hannah coming to talk about more plans for the café. She reminded herself that after work she absolutely had to stop at the grocery store. Oh, and start getting ready for the meeting with her accountant next week. She wasn't looking forward to that. But she was looking forward to seeing Hannah, who was like a new woman now, determined, focused, and happier than Ruth could ever recall. She kept thanking Ruth for helping her to find that "thing" she was meant to do.

Since Kris was out to lunch and the store quiet, Ruth opened the folder for the Catholic grade school fund raiser. She was putting together a presentation on fifteen books for children and young adults and needed to write a one paragraph "teaser" synopsis of each book that ended with a cliffhanger—so they'd simply *have* to buy it to find out what happens. Although the public high school had been ordering from her for years, this was her first time dealing with St. Mary's. Of course she'd had to cut her already dismal profit to the bone to agree to their request. But hopefully she'd get some of their kids and parents to start coming into the store, too. Every reader was precious to her. Besides, she knew the school was operating on the same kind of budget as hers—a wing and a prayer. Literally.

She looked at the first book on her list, *The Diary of a Young Girl*. She'd been stunned to learn neither of her granddaughters had even heard of this classic. Trying to think up a great opening line, she stared out the window, letting her mind go, hoping it would suddenly float into focus. A jagged flash of lightning cut the sky and she hoped the coming storm would usher in cooler air. She closed the folder and put it back on the pile of paperwork, realizing she just didn't have the mental energy for a big project right now. Maybe she could start working on the essay contest for the convention. That deadline was fast approaching.

She couldn't wait to go to the convention and get away. When was the last time she'd been out of Warwick? Ruth loved those weekend getaways every year, a chance to come away with a shopping bag full of galleys of upcoming books, and also to share ideas about running things more efficiently. And, of course, the old standby: getting more business and bringing in more revenue.

Over cocktails at night, most of them commiserated about the inability to ever get ahead, although that was usually followed by lively discussions about everyone's latest or favorite new read. God how she loved that part, dissecting characters and plots, and even someone's style of writing. That's why they did it, they'd all agree by the end of the evening, cheeks flushed with alcohol, eyes bright with excitement over their shared ideas. Booksellers didn't go into the business for the money.

The title of this year's essay seemed a bit redundant: *Why I'm a Bookseller*. Without a doubt each and every one of them could answer: *Because I love books*. It was going to be a challenge, finding another way of saying it. Or another reason. She sat back on the stool, knowing she didn't have the creative focus for this project either. She'd just have to get up extra early tomorrow and tackle it while her brain was fresh.

She walked around the counter to go dig out the old oscillating fan, buried somewhere in the storage room, when she heard a noise and turned, expecting to see Hannah.

"Eddie," she said, the surprise evident in her voice as Hannah's husband strolled in.

"Hey, Ruth. Hannah's a bit under the weather and probably won't be over. I thought I'd stop by and check things out."

Ruth couldn't imagine anything keeping Hannah from their meeting. She'd been foraging garage sales and thrift shops for the contents of her café. She told Ruth she was painting a few old mirrors with flowers and panes to make them look like windows, to brighten up the back corner. She was supposed to bring one in today to show her, as well as another new recipe for her to sample.

Ruth led Eddie to the back of the store. "I hope it isn't anything serious."

"Nah, just a headache."

She stopped and turned to him. Eddie was a short man, powerfully built, and back in high school, a million years ago, when he and Hannah first began dating, she'd thought him good-looking. Now he was losing his hair, his muscles had softened, and he wore his pants dangerously low under a hefty paunch.

"This whole back corner of the store is where she'll be setting up her café," Ruth said, waving her arm to show the area she meant. "We'll be clearing out those bookshelves soon, and she'll have about three hundred square feet to work with, which I think—"

"Are you serious?" Eddie interrupted with a laugh.

Ruth looked at him, not sure what he was getting at.

"She'll be able to fit what? Maybe two or three tables there?" he asked with great sarcasm.

"She's hoping for five, actually. Which I think is very doable. She's getting bistro tables at garage sales and consignment shops."

"And she thinks she's going to serve a few tables coffee and muffins and make what she's making at Elaine's?" He turned to her, his hands on his hips now. "She gave her notice, you know, just like that. On a whim. You know my wife and her whims."

"This isn't a whim, Eddie. I think it's perfect for her. But it'll take a while, like any business. And she's got great ideas, like gift baskets and—"

"Come on, Ruth," he said, with a sly smile. "Isn't this more about you? Getting some revenue? Don't you think $500 a month is a little ridiculous for this?"

She could feel her mouth fall open. "What are you getting at?"

He was shaking his head, as if he couldn't believe her question. "It's no secret your rent went up. And that you're hanging on here by your fingernails. We both know my wife is a sucker for—"

"Maybe you don't know your wife as well as you think you do," she interrupted, her chest tightening with anger. "Maybe you've been a little too... distracted. With your own business affairs?"

Eddie's look sharpened. "The only thing I'm distracted with, Ruth, is trying to eke out a living to support us."

"I hope that's true, because you know how it is in a small town, how word gets around. I wouldn't want Hannah to get hurt."

Slowly he smiled. "Speaking from experience, Ruth? Because I'd say that's about thirty years too late."

God, how she wanted to smack him.

"So back to the point, I don't want my wife getting hurt either. There's no way she's going to be paying $500 a month for a corner of your shop."

Ruth's breath was coming in short bursts now. She could almost see Hannah's shattered look when her ideas went sliding down the tubes.

"But Eddie," she said, forcing a sweet tone into her voice. "Didn't Hannah tell you?"

"Tell me what?"

"I'm not charging her any rent at all. Not until she begins making a profit."

He blinked.

"I want her to succeed. I've never seen her so excited. Or happy. Why would I want to put something in the way of that, like rent?" Her heart was galloping now, her anger turning to satisfaction as she watched his face change. "And if people come in for her muffins and coffee, then hopefully they'll buy a book, too. It'll be a win-win for us both. Think Starbucks. There's big money in lattes and muffins." Ha! Starbucks, that was feckin' brilliant.

"We'll see," Eddie said.

Ruth watched him leave, her momentary satisfaction deflating like a punctured balloon. She leaned against a bookshelf to steady herself, her knees suddenly wobbly.

God, how she hated confrontations like this. Where you could feel that sickening grip of anger squeezing, threatening to unbalance you. When you'd say or do something you'd regret later on. The kind of confrontation she'd had with Bill one too many times, and that usually cost her in the long run. As it would now.

No matter how much of an ass Eddie was, she knew that righteousness was a dangerous thing. It had just cost her $500 a month.

*   *   *

HANNAH NEVER DID SHOW UP. The moment Kris came back from lunch, Ruth left, needing to get away from the store, from the maddening scene with Eddie, and reminders of the anger that was once so much a part of her life. She decided to walk for a while. She could certainly use the exercise, although it was so hot.

She walked slowly, looking in the store windows, thinking of how many had changed over the years. So much of her life was spent on these streets, from the time she got her first job at fifteen at Aiken's Pharmacy, which still looked the way it did way back when she spent her after school hours tidying the greeting cards, arranging prescriptions alphabetically, and ringing up her first sale of Trojans, having no idea what a condom even was and wondering why Mr. Taylor had blushed so profusely when she couldn't find them and had to ask out loud. They'd been tucked out of sight, in a little drawer under the counter.

She passed Tynan's Butcher Shop, where her father had supplied beef a million years ago. Now it was a women's boutique, although locals still referred to the building as Tynan's when giving directions, which was obviously confusing to newcomers.

Mama's Pizza, the big hangout when she was still in school, had been gone for years, relocated to a strip mall on the outskirts of town decades ago. A few years ago, Sandy became the latest tenant when she opened Scrub-a-Dub Doggie. She seemed to be doing well. Ruth stood a moment at the bridge, looking down at the Waywayanda Creek, enjoying the cool damp shade of the huge sycamore that had stood on its banks for as long as she could remember. As a kid, she'd thrown pennies into the rushing water, making wishes. How silly.

She could almost picture herself all those years ago, a big, gawky girl who got up at dawn to milk cows with her father. She'd loved watching the sunrise, the smell of the barn, the early quiet. It was a simple life, and she'd been unaware of how her parents had struggled. They always had food and books, and so she never realized how much they'd lived without. Until she became an adolescent and the competition for nice clothes, boys, and popularity began.

Then her tossed pennies began to wish for different things. Someone to love her. A husband, one day children. A simple dream, as old as time. Back then it was all so different for girls. The late fifties and early sixties were still a man's world. A time when women's roles were so traditional—when most women got married, had children, and stayed home to take care of the family. Like her mother, and her grandmother before her. It all seemed so quaint now. So hard to fathom that back in those days she'd needed a man to sign for a credit card, or she couldn't get one. That without a husband, she couldn't get a loan. Ruth hadn't questioned any of it at the time. It was simply the way the world worked.

Then suddenly it all began to change. But she was having one baby after another, barely keeping up with what was going on in the outside world—civil rights, women's lib, birth control, free love, the British invasion, Viet Nam, all of it a kind of blur between bottles and diapers, cleaning and cooking, ear infections, measles, and sleepless nights. What a turbulent time for the world, and her. Because marriage had turned out to be nothing like she expected.

She leaned on the bridge now and closed her eyes.

Oh stop it, Ruth. Why are you doing this now?

She knew it wasn't just the scene with Eddie, the flash of sudden anger at him that evoked those other scenes. Memories she'd managed to keep tucked away for years were popping up everywhere she turned lately, throwing her neat, orderly world—her safe world—off balance.

She knew it was because of Thomas.

29

T HE DOG DAYS OF AUGUST ARRIVED AND LUCY'S BOOKSTORE runs were now interspersed with little shopping expeditions, spending more than she'd planned, of course, but having so much fun. It had been months since she'd bought anything other than food or essentials for living. As she emptied her trunk, she realized her last big shopping trip had been for the red dress for her book launch. Which seemed a lifetime ago.

Each time she arrived back at the cabin, she double checked that Colin wasn't home before carrying bags in. There were blue and white striped curtains and a coordinating floral slipcover for the couch. She planned to spray paint the old kitchen table and chairs black, which would make a great contrast with the bright yellow seat cushions she'd found. She'd even thought of painting the walls, but the soft yellow was so cheerful she decided not to take a chance screwing it up.

The major job was going to be painting. The old knotty pine was definitely retro, but also masculine, with that hunting lodge feel. She wanted the cabin to have a happy, feminine air. She wanted Ruth to walk in and *want* to stay.

It was such a pleasure to do something fun. She'd program music on her laptop, turn on a floor fan to blow fumes out the window, start painting, and the hours would fly by. Her mind would also settle into a quiet rhythm and the next thing she knew, ideas for her story came popping up and she'd stop and jot them down. She couldn't remember the last time she'd felt so content. After months of doing nothing but marketing *A Quiet Wanting*, or researching or writing the new book, she began to see now that her life was out of balance. And that it was time she stop escaping in her work, as she'd been doing for years.

Late afternoons she'd fix a sandwich or salad, then sit at the table by the window and check e-mails. She read one now that left her in awe. It came from a woman in the U.K., who'd gotten the book as a birthday gift from a cousin here in the states:

"After reading your fine novel I think I have the courage to finally do what I've been putting off for years. I love my husband, he's a good man. But we've never had a real marriage and now I think I know why. Thank you for writing this book."

She pictured this woman she didn't even know turning her pages, reading her words, and being so affected. Ruth was right, if things never went any further than this, she'd already achieved the ultimate success as a writer. Hope and Matthew were as real to readers as they'd become to her.

Word of mouth was spreading from book club to book club and more requests came in, and more book signings. Of course she was still haunted by the rejection from Ruth's sales rep, and some of the one and two star reviews she found online from time to time. And there were still quite a few bookstores that never got back to her at all. But she kept hanging onto the fact that the book was selling, readers were enjoying it and best of all, she was writing a new novel.

It was amazing how quickly this new story was falling into place. Of course setting the book right where she was living at that moment helped immensely. She was surrounded by nature and beauty and felt their transformative powers healing her a little at a time, as she would have them heal Catherine, her main character, as well.

She was like a real author, except for the fact that she didn't have a real publisher. But she felt a new surge of hope that perhaps there was a chance after all. Ruth would be going to her convention in September and was going to talk up *A Quiet Wanting* whenever she could. And it was becoming obvious that there was an audience for this book, which was proven by each new reader, and each new bookseller who came on board. This was more than the story of a woman who still loved her husband, despite the fact that he was gay. And that he loved her, despite his sexuality. It was a moving story of a marriage built on a lie. It was obvious women *did* want to read about that, no matter what agents had said.

Of course as she answered questions about the lies and betrayals with book clubs now, a little voice began to whisper in her head, asking the same questions about her own marriage. *Was it really possible she'd had no idea what was going on? Or did she choose to turn a blind eye to certain truths that were staring her right in the face? And wasn't she, in a way, guilty, too?*

In the midst of that afternoon's flurry of e-mails, was another one from David.

Lucy,

The last e-mail I sent you was a mistake. I shouldn't have done it because it makes it sound like I'm still angry with you and I'm really not, not anymore. I've learned that anger is a part of the grief process and I'm finally letting go of it, even the anger at myself. I regret not going for counseling years ago, because I'm discovering a lot about myself, things that actually have nothing to do with you, or Ben. But truthfully, having all of this time alone, to think, and pretty much do nothing else, has been a large part of it. Sometimes it's easier to just escape, like I did with poker, rather than face what we don't want to see. I used to think that's what you were doing with your writing. I still wonder about that.

You've probably heard by now through your attorney that the office building sold to the upstairs tenant. My house arrest will be over in a few weeks and then I begin my stint of community service. An appraiser came to the house yesterday to give us an evaluation and it sounds like we won't lose money, although we won't make any either. So the financials are just about settled and the final divorce hearing should be soon after that.

I have a favor to ask you, although I know I don't have the right to ask it. I've already agreed not to go to the divorce hearing, as your attorney said you requested. But I'd like to see you one more time, when you come down here.

David.

She sat there, staring at his words, then sent back a one word reply: *Why?* Within minutes he responded: *Because I don't want you to hate me for the rest of your life.*

Obviously David needed to unburden himself, although she found herself going for longer and longer stretches without even thinking about him. Did she really want to do this? Open this dialogue, examine all the past hurts and finger pointing? Because in the end, she'd begun to realize that the blame wasn't all his. She thought about it for several long minutes, then sent her reply: *Agreed.*

The following afternoon her attorney called to tell her the final divorce hearing had indeed been scheduled.

* * *

THE STORE ALWAYS GREW QUIET BY THE MIDDLE OF AUGUST. People were either on vacation or already in the throes of back-to-school shopping. Jenny was busy with lesson plans and taking Olivia and Emma to the mall, and Ruth realized she hadn't talked to her in several days, which was rare.

Megan was away, and although Harry was on vacation from his custodial job, he offered to come in and help unload the shipment of vampire books. It was the largest order she'd ever placed. She'd scheduled the task for today because she knew Colin wouldn't be in. He'd want to help somehow, but it was such an awkward job for him.

It wasn't until Danny's death that she realized she'd become complacent about Colin and his situation, because he seemed to have settled into a comfortable life. But, she reminded herself once again, it would never be an easy life. And her worries would never disappear completely. After her phone call to Lucy a few weeks ago, which had ended abruptly, Lucy had followed up with an e-mail.

Don't worry, Ruth, Colin seems a little better each time I see him. The project he's working on at The Raptor Center is really keeping him occupied and I've been going with him as well because I'm doing some research there for my new novel. Yes, Ruth, I've started a new book!

She wrote back:

Thank you, Lucy. I feel better knowing someone is there. And I can't wait to see the new book.

It's not in any shape to be read yet, Lucy responded. *But I promise, when it's ready, you'll be the first to read it.*

She was so thankful Lucy was there, and that they'd become friends. It amazed her how much Lucy had changed since they first met. Gone were the worry lines around her eyes, the pinched mouth. She smiled more easily and grew prettier each time Ruth saw her. The Audrey Hepburn pixie was becoming a chin-length bob that suited her heart-shaped face, the big green eyes.

Lucy would be leaving tomorrow for Florida to finalize her divorce. When they'd first met, Lucy told her that it seemed barbaric that she had to be there, in person, when she'd been the injured party. Sometimes there's nothing fair about life, Ruth had wanted to say, but didn't. She'd been hurting enough already. But in her latest e-mail, she sensed a shift in Lucy's emotions.

David wants to see me one more time, she wrote. *Part of me is dreading it. The other part is almost glad because there are things I need to say to him, too. Is anyone ever blameless in a marriage gone bad?*

That was an easy one for Ruth to answer—of course not. She had to wonder if this softening, on both Lucy's part and her husband's, might be the bridge to a new beginning. She hoped so. Lucy had become a true friend. And yet, at moments like this, she seemed more like a daughter Ruth wanted to protect.

Lucy had also told Ruth about a few horrible events during the past weekend.

I did two signings, Ruth, where not a soul showed up. It was awful. At one, the store manager barely even spoke to me, spent all her time glued to her computer, and when people walked in, they wouldn't even make eye contact with me because there I was right by the front door. It was so uncomfortable. They didn't keep a single book to put on their shelves afterward.

Of course you couldn't guarantee people were going to show up, but at least you had to make the author feel welcome, and talk about the book!

"Okay, the books are all unloaded and stacked in the back," Harry said, coming up to the counter and breaking her thoughts. "Two hundred copies of teenage vampires running around a high school. Would you ever have bet money ten years ago that something like this would be our biggest seller?"

"The kids love it. And lots of adults, too." She shook her head, laughing. "Let's hope she doesn't end the series, like J.K. Rowling did."

"Well, I guess I'll shove off now, Ruth, unless you need anything else."

"No, Harry, but thank you. Enjoy the rest of your vacation. I'll see you at the midnight release party next week. Do you have your vampire fangs?"

"No, but I'm sure Megan will be bringing fangs and capes and buckets of blood for the lot of us."

By early afternoon, Ruth was surprised to get a number of calls cancelling the RSVPs for the midnight release party. Each cancellation was also a cancelled book order, which was disturbing. She hoped Megan hadn't somehow made a mistake, but she couldn't imagine what it could be. She decided not to worry about it, since Megan would be back in tomorrow.

Then she went back to the essay for the bookseller's convention which she'd put off again and again. It had to be mailed in tomorrow.

"Guess what?" she heard then and looked up to see Hannah in the open doorway, dragging in a small round table. "I found the last bistro table!"

After Eddie's visit, Hannah had come in only once, seeming subdued, and Ruth wondered if the café was going to go down the tubes. Then she asked if Ruth was absolutely sure she wanted to waive the rent until she turned a profit? And Ruth realized the future of the café was hanging on her answer.

"Absolutely, I meant every word I said." Not that Hannah had to know every word of that conversation.

Hannah had smiled and nodded, but still seemed uncertain. Now she set the wrought iron table down and went out and brought in a matching chair.

"What do you think? I'm going to spray paint them black and have red gingham tablecloths. Red is a power color, you know, and I want kind of a country French look. I'm just about done painting the mirrors to look like windows. One overlooks a field of lavender, the other some rolling green hills."

"It sounds very picturesque."

The excited Hannah was back and Ruth felt relieved.

"Are you okay, Ruth? You look tired," she said with a sudden frown.

"I'm fine, it's just that time of year, back to school, half my staff on vacation."

There was a long, quiet moment. "You don't think about them? You know, this time of year and all?"

Ruth shook her head.

"I do. I still miss her. Sometimes it's hard—"

The door opened and Ruth could have kissed Lizzie, her mail carrier, who nudged Hannah aside and slapped the mail on the counter.

"Thanks for bringing that in, Hannah," Ruth said.

Hannah looked perplexed at her dismissal, and left a moment later.

After Lizzie left, Ruth stared out the big front window at the quiet sidewalk, the gray afternoon skies. Of course she thought about them. Every August, without fail, though she tried not to. Although this was the first time Hannah had brought it up in years.

She tossed aside visions of the past, and picked up the mail, sorting through it. Her heart froze as she came to a white envelope. She knew that handwriting as well as she knew each line on her face, even though the envelope wasn't blue. It was postmarked two days ago in Albany.

So, he'd finally given up on her.

30

THE DAY BEFORE HER FLIGHT BACK TO FLORIDA, Lucy couldn't concentrate on anything. Each time she'd drifted off last night, images flashed before her, and when she finally got out of bed as dawn rose over the lake, she was exhausted. Luckily she didn't have to get ready for her morning paddle beside Colin, because she doubted she had the energy. He was probably up already, too, getting ready for the memorial service for Danny, a two-hour drive from there. As she sat at the table in front of the window with a cup of tea and a pad, pieces of her dreams were still swimming in her head and she began a poem.

She kneels in her garden
in the gray light of early
morning, in a circle of pines
her tools lined up beside her.

While mourning doves sleep
wet brown stains spread
across the knees of her faded jeans
as she plunges her rusting
spade into an empty bed.

Her hair, long slivered bits
of white, caught in a comb,
curls like a weathered nest
on the white flesh of her neck.

She digs hole after hole
searching for bulbs
in earth empty as her
womb, building a mound
of dirt that swells soft

and fertile, as the sun
climbs over the pines.

Bulbs, white, dirt crusted,
clustered like grapes are
soon uncovered. She pulls
them out into the warming
air and tenderly plies them apart

It was sad but beautiful, filled with fragmented pieces of her life now: Ruth's hair, Colin's birds, the garden she once loved in Mendham, where she finally had what her father had always talked about, a little patch of earth. Although she wasn't very good at gardening, Lucy loved being outside in the early mornings while the world still slept, breathing in the smell of the earth, even marveling at the mysterious bugs crawling around her knees and hands.

It awed her that a packet of dry, hard seeds could become a green shoot, a living thing that would grow toward the sun a little more each day and create petals and flowers in the most gorgeous colors and scents. It was like a miracle.

In St. Augustine her brown thumb didn't matter, everything grew. In just one summer a bougainvillea, jasmine or hibiscus could take over a wall of house and climb through gutters, snaking underneath the roof tiles. She pictured those flowers now, in that lovely yard with the smell of the bay on the wind. And the beautiful house that she'd tried so hard to make feel like home. But even now, when she thought of home, she always thought of the house in Mendham.

She closed her eyes and saw another image that had haunted her dreams last night—David in the pouring rain cutting the grass after work. Drenched, yet pushing the lawnmower in circles around that house, again and again. Opening her eyes, she picked up the pen and wrote a title at the top of the poem: *Barren.*

Then she turned to a clean page on her legal pad and began a grocery list. She was not going to spend the rest of the day moping about the past.

* * *

RUTH WAS FIVE MINUTES EARLY FOR HER MEETING with Chuck Bradley, her accountant. She sat back in the frigid waiting room, feeling her overheated skin turn to ice. It was stupid walking six blocks in the blistering heat.

She folded her arms for warmth and stared out the window. Thomas's letter, which she had finally worked up the nerve to read last night, came back to her, word by word.

Dear Ruth,

I wanted to send you one last letter, to apologize for even suggesting that there might be a place for me in your life. You're so kind, I can only imagine the anxiety I must have caused you. That wasn't fair.

You're also a lot smarter than I am, Ruth, and you probably already knew what I'm quickly finding out. That life for a paroled felon will never be an easy road. It's not so hard for me to see now how so many end up back in prison.

The only thing I can do is to continue trying to learn. I've enrolled in a class at Warwick Community College starting next month. Isn't life really all about learning? Thank you for bringing a love of books into my life. It's made all the difference.

Take care, Ruth. I wish you all the best life can bring.

Thomas

Once again she wondered about the Albany postmark. If he was going to take a class at Warwick Community College, he certainly couldn't do it from there.

"Hey Ruth, sorry to keep you waiting."

She looked up and Chuck was standing there with his glasses halfway down his nose and his tie askew.

"That's all right, Chuck," she said, following him. "How's the family?"

His office was no doubt the most disorganized-looking place she'd ever seen. Piles of papers sat on every surface, and all over the floor. She couldn't imagine how he got anything done, or kept anything straight, but somehow he did. He'd been doing her books since she bought the business.

"We're all good. Heading to the Jersey shore in a few days," he said, as he somehow found her papers amidst the mountains.

After a few more pleasantries, Chuck sat back in his chair and gave her a smile she knew didn't hold good news.

"Just give it to me straight, Chuck, okay?"

"Your sales revenue is down more than eight percent from last summer. I know it doesn't sound like much, but..." he shrugged.

He didn't have to tell her. The profit margin on books was so miniscule that any loss of profit could be devastating. And hardcovers had taken a huge hit, with people opting for the more affordable paperbacks lately.

"Now," he said, picking up a different file, "the second mortgage you took on your house is going to adjust next month. It was interest only, but now you'll have to pay principal as well. And the rate is going up, so the payment will jump considerably, Ruth. I wish I had better news. You know I didn't want you to take that mortgage in the first place. I can't imagine why Lynn advised you to do such a thing."

Lynn at the bank really hadn't wanted her to do it, but Ruth had insisted, "Find me the lowest payment possible." There'd been the flood damage, of course, and then she'd had to modify the store for Colin, as well as a ramp to the side door of her house. She'd had no choice.

"Well, there are a few bright spots. I almost forgot to tell you, I'm getting some rent for the lake cabin," she admitted. "I'm not putting that on the books, is that okay?"

Chuck shrugged. "Don't worry about that."

"And hopefully in about three or four months I'll be pulling in some additional money in the store, renting out a corner to Hannah for a café."

Chuck nodded, listening.

"Oh, and best of all, the new Stephanie Meyer vampire book comes out soon. That's our biggest money maker every year now. We've got a record number presold and Megan's holding a midnight release party, which should bring in more sales. That's usually a lifesaver."

Chuck smiled. "Put me down for five. I'll give them as gifts."

"Thanks, Chuck. And who knows, maybe this year I'll win the Independent Bookseller's Essay Contest. I was a finalist last year. That would be a thousand bucks. Or maybe I should buy some lottery tickets, eh?"

Chuck laughed.

"How many years have we been doing this? It's always the same story, isn't it? You must think I'm crazy."

He shook his head. "Nah. You're doing what you love, how many people can say that?"

"So we should be all right for a while?"

"Somehow, Ruth, you always manage to pull through."

She got up to leave.

"You know, if you sold that cabin, you could pay off the second mortgage, maybe even have some money left over."

She stood there a moment, then sighed. "It's not that simple. Bill wanted that cabin to stay in his family. Always."

* * *

LUCY HADN'T REALLY COOKED MUCH SINCE MOVING into the cabin, living on sandwiches, omelets and salads. Suddenly, though, she wanted to make something nice, a kind of farewell dinner. In a few days she would officially be starting a new life. She was also excited by an idea she'd come up with for Colin's program for wounded vets and couldn't wait to tell him. She knew he'd be feeling low after Danny's memorial service.

As she sliced onions, peppers, and lots of garlic and chopped tomatoes, then sautéed them with butter, the cabin filled with the delicious smells. There was something so cozy about cooking inside with all the windows open and listening to the distant rumbles of thunder. She was making a primavera sauce to go with pasta and shrimp, something that suddenly made her stomach roar with hunger. She also had a bowl of fresh strawberries, washed and sliced, and a quart of vanilla ice cream.

She stopped and slammed the knife down as her absentmindedness hit her. Colin wouldn't be able to come to her cabin and eat. Not without a great amount of difficulty. There was no ramp. There were five steps up to the porch, and even if he could manage that, she doubted the door was wide enough to accommodate his chair.

It was nearly dark when she heard Colin's jeep pull in next door. She waited for him to lift his chair out of the car and push himself up and into it, and then went outside and called over to him. He turned his chair as she walked over. She suddenly felt awkward. He was still in his green uniform, but his beret was on his lap. His shaved blond hair made his blue eyes even more startling in his tan face.

"Hey," he said with a small smile, looking up at her.

"Hey. Are you hungry?"

He looked out at the lake a minute. The earlier storm hadn't panned out, and now the water and sky were just a flat grey. "Actually, I am hungry. What did you have in mind?"

"Well, I'm making some pasta primavera with shrimp. I could bring it over."

He looked at her cabin. "I really hate to make you bring everything over."

"I don't mind. I could actually toss it all in one big bowl. You can supply the rest."

He turned back to her. "I thought you'd be packing for your trip."

"I can do that tomorrow. My flight's not until late."

"Well, in that case, I'll go get changed and set the table."

"Okay, be over shortly."

31

H EADING TO THE A&P ON HER WAY HOME, Ruth drove past the new mall, which was about to have their grand opening. As she sat at the stop light, she glanced over and saw BookWorld, a wide brick building that looked to be more than 30,000 square feet, no doubt filled with more books than she could ever dream of. She thought of her own space, which was barely 2,000 square feet. And soon a portion of that was going to be Hazel's Café.

Pulling into the A&P parking lot, she was relieved that Hannah was still going through with her plans, despite the lost shelf space. It would bring more people into the store, and even if they didn't come in for a book, hopefully they'd be irresistibly drawn to buying one.

She turned off the car and gave Sam a treat while she went to shop. She should have made a list because she was out of so many things. Instead she simply wandered the aisles, slowly pushing her cart, promising herself she'd stay under the "20 Items or Less" so she wouldn't have to stand in one of the endless lines. Hannah was right, she was tired. She had to admit, this year she finally felt her age despite the new Centrum Silver vitamins she took every day now.

She ran into Bertha Piakowski, picking up the ingredients for more pierogies. Ruth wondered how she did it. At nearly eighty, Bertha seemed to have the energy of a thirty-year-old.

In the pasta aisle, Lynn Anderson's daughter, Melissa, stopped her. Melissa looked like a younger, blonder version of her mother.

"I wanted to thank you for giving my mom that book, *Still Alice*. We've all read it. At first it almost made it worse, knowing how she's going to get. But when the Alzheimer's reaches that point…at least we'll understand it better. It'll still be *her*."

"Oh, Melissa, how are you all doing?" Ruth reached over and gave her a hug.

"Okay for now." Melissa's big dark eyes filled with tears.

"Please tell Lynn I was asking for her."

As she finished the aisles, nearly forgetting dog food, the whole reason she'd come, Ruth thought to herself that whenever you thought your own problems were too much, there always seemed to be something or someone to remind you how lucky you were. Her heart broke for Lynn, and her family.

She pushed her cart to the front of the store. The "20 Items or Less" line was already seven deep and Ruth found herself behind Elaine.

"Fancy meeting you here," she called over her cart.

"Oh, hey Ruth," Elaine said, turning with a surprised smile. "We have to stop meeting like this."

"I for one would rather be home in my PJ's, with my feet up."

"Well, maybe they should just start making this a Happy Hour, you know? Serve some drinks and munchies and...Ruth? Ruth, are you all right?"

But Elaine's voice faded as Ruth stared past her, forgetting about their complaints, and Lynn Anderson, or even the snail's pace of the line. She didn't hear what Elaine was saying because her head was suddenly filled with a roaring noise. There on the shelves in front of the register, where everyone was destined to spend a few bored moments, sat stacks and stacks of the new Stephanie Meyer vampire book, due out next week.

Ruth's jaw dropped. The on sale date was sacrosanct to booksellers. Didn't she have two hundred copies sitting in the back of the store, waiting for the midnight release party? When she could in good conscience sell them at one minute after twelve? What the hell was the A&P doing selling it? And a week early? Then she saw the sign above it, and a surge of hot anger bubbled up in her chest. They were charging less than Ruth paid for the book wholesale. They would actually *lose* money on it.

But Ruth knew what this game was all about. It was a "loss leader"—even though they'd lose money selling the book, it would bring customers in the door. And that explained why the reservations for the midnight release party were suddenly shrinking.

She picked up her purse, pushed her cart aside, and walked out of the A&P.

By the time she put her copies on the shelf in front of her store, half the town would no doubt already have theirs—from the A&P. Her biggest money maker of the year had just gone out the window, thanks to a grocery store.

She didn't even remember the drive home. But when she opened and closed the freezer, then stood in front of the near-empty fridge, it hit her that she'd cut off her nose to spite her face, leaving her cart. She needed the food more than A&P needed her money. She didn't even have eggs. She opened the freezer again and took out a pack of leftover hot dogs, defrosted them in the microwave, then browned them on the stove, her stomach growling with hunger. She'd forgotten to eat lunch again. She sliced two up and slid them into Sam's bowl. Sam looked up at her in happy astonishment. Then suspicion. This was forbidden fruit.

"Eat your heart out," Ruth grumbled.

She tossed hers on a plate then dove into the depths of the fridge for a jar of pickles. She knew they were there, she remembered seeing them...oh... oh sweet Jesus, she couldn't breathe. She straightened up and her heart began to race, thudding so violently beneath her ribcage it seemed to vibrate in her ears. Clutching the handle of the refrigerator door, she forced a slow, deep breath. On her second slow breath, something heavy seemed to push on her chest. She let out a little groan. Sam stopped eating and turned to look up at her.

"Eat," she said, but her voice was a shaky whisper. "I'm fine."

Sam turned and continued eating just as a tiny twinge went up her neck. She walked to the phone and dialed Jenny. The answering machine came on in the same instant her entire body seemed to lose all strength.

There was no hesitation this time. Ruth grabbed her car keys and left without a backward glance at Sam.

32

AS LUCY WALKED OVER TO COLIN'S, fireflies began magically lifting from the grass while flickers of heat lightning lit up the mountains. She stood a moment in the soft night air and thought: *is there anything more beautiful than this*? Then she climbed the ramp, the bowl in her hands, a bottle of wine and the strawberries and ice cream in a bag hanging from her wrist. She knocked on his screen and heard him yell come in.

Both the bedroom and bathroom doors were closed, and the room was so quiet she got busy, turning the oven on warm and sliding the bowl of pasta inside. Then she set the table and opened the bottle of wine. She tried to make noise, wanting to give him some privacy. Finally, she poured a glass of wine and went out on the deck. It was close to nine and the sky was dark, swirling with heavy gray clouds. Above the distant mountains the heat lightning continued, illuminating the lake, the island far out in the cove, and even the distant shore and the peaks of houses nestled in the trees.

She thought about the trip tomorrow. It would be strange to see David after all this time. She knew it would be a deeply emotional meeting. They'd been living separate lives for months now, something that once seemed unfathomable. She wasn't sure exactly what he wanted to say. And of course, he had no idea what she was about to tell him. It would be the supreme irony if it turned out that she could forgive him, and he wouldn't be able to forgive her.

But she didn't want to think about that right now. Here in this beautiful place she felt herself becoming stronger than she'd been in years. Certainly since the loss of Ben. She was living her dream of being a writer—even if it was only on her terms. Was it odd that she'd been in this place only four months yet felt so at home here? She remembered that first terrified night in the cabin, and couldn't help smiling. But part of her also wondered if she wasn't existing in a sort of limbo, a place apart from the real world. And maybe that's what she really liked. Because there were times it felt as though it was a fairy tale, living in this enchanted place.

A sudden crack of thunder broke the quiet, louder and closer than before. Even the insects and night creatures were silent now, as if waiting for the rain to finally arrive. Her thoughts turned to Colin and their unlikely friendship. He was like no man she'd ever met. Despite his handicap, he oozed a quiet confidence and strength. He also had a wonderful, often self-deprecating, sense of humor. Perhaps the most unexpected thing about him was that he was sexy. The realization startled her. Was she crazy? Lonely? No, it was his confidence and easy manner. And of course his looks, despite the wheelchair.

Just then the screen slid open and she turned to see Colin in the doorway, sitting in his wheelchair, wearing a pair of soft, faded jeans and a black t-shirt.

"Sorry to keep you waiting so long. It's probably the biggest frustration of...this." He waved a hand at his legs and the chair. "Everything takes so long."

"It's no big deal. I was standing here enjoying the view."

He came out onto the deck and stopped, looking up at her for a long moment, without smiling. "The other thing that's frustrating is when I'm with someone for a while and have to keep looking up at them. Imagine staring at the ceiling for more than five minutes. Your neck starts to ache."

"Oh...I'm sorry," she said, realizing what he was getting at. How had that never occurred to her? She grabbed a chair and sat, turning to him. They were now at eye level.

"Shit," he whispered, rubbing his face with his hands. "I'm sorry, Lucy. I'm being a cranky pain in the ass."

"No, you're not. I've been thoughtless."

He took her wrist and held it tightly, looking right in her eyes. "Yes, I am. I have no business taking my frustrations out on you."

"Well...I guess that makes us good friends, then. Because who else can you do that to and get away with it, huh?"

"You can do that with another soldier." After a moment he finally smiled. "Come on, let's get that dinner. Hopefully it isn't petrified by now."

He seemed tired from the memorial and the gathering afterward, so she talked a lot while they ate, filling the silences with chatter about The Raptor Center and Kit.

"I still haven't figured out what I'm doing there. I just...I find the place amazing. The birds are beautiful and...innocent. Does that sound silly? I mean most of them are predators."

He nodded, then sipped his wine. "That's kind of what happened to me in the beginning. I had no idea what I was looking for. Something about the place, though, was calling out to me." He tilted his head and stared at the table. "After all my time in Iraq, all that devastation day in and day out, I think it was what I needed."

"I can imagine." She hesitated, then asked, "Is it hard for you to talk about?"

He shrugged. "Yes and no. Being so far away from it now, for so long, it's sometimes hard to believe it all really happened. But I like to remember, to talk about it sometimes, because it was such a part of who I was."

"I'd be happy to listen."

He smiled, then looked across the room for a moment, as if gathering his thoughts.

"I loved being a soldier. And I loved my men." And then he gave a little laugh. "And women, although I only had a handful of female soldiers over the years. I was a sergeant and my men trusted me. Losing one was always the hardest thing...." He shook his head, with a sad smile.

She didn't know what to say, so remained silent.

"I was ordered back to Baghdad for the surge. Our unit's job was to clear neighborhoods of any kind of threats, making things secure so that one day the Iraqi people could live in peace. We lived behind blast walls. Ate, slept, peed, played cards, whatever, we did it all behind those blast walls because once you went outside you had no idea where a bomb might be hidden—in a tree, under some garbage, strapped to a person, or the trunk of a car. Anyway, once the surge began, the IEDs just got worse. I saw men and women lose arms, legs, even faces, the explosions destroying their lives without killing them. And everywhere we went there was always this burning, bitter smell that never seemed to go away. And sand...fucking sand everywhere." He sat there shaking his head. "We were trying to make it safe, but...things were getting worse and they just wanted us gone, you know? Day after day little kids would just watch all this violence and screaming and blood. Or get killed themselves. It was a fucking nightmare. But we did our job, because that's what soldiers do."

Of course she'd seen coverage on the news and in the papers, things she often glanced at but might not read because it was so awful. What she saw in Colin's eyes now made it so much more real.

"Danny's wife...I mean his ex-wife, she cried her heart out today. I kept thinking that if only he could see how she still loved him."

"That's just so sad."

"I knew how Danny felt. It's not easy, having a relationship with a woman."

He looked directly at her then. "Take the usual struggles that exist between a couple and throw in a barrel full of frustrations and complications and...you can just imagine. But worst of all is feeling like the woman has to take care of you, in a way."

Colin was so strong and independent she couldn't imagine anyone taking care of him. But then again, everything she knew was surface.

"Still," he went on, "I think it's something you just have to learn to deal with if you want to be with someone. And you have to find a woman who can handle it. For the long run."

She couldn't help thinking of the beautiful redhead in that moment, Gloryanne. She wondered what had happened with them. Gloryanne hadn't been around in a long time.

He put his fork down and she saw that his plate was empty.

"How about some more?"

He shook his head. "I'm saving room for dessert."

She got the strawberries and ice cream while he scraped and stacked the dishes at the table.

"I have an idea for your project," she said, scooping the ice cream into bowls and covering it with the sliced strawberries. "What if you use the bald eagle?"

He shook his head and started laughing.

"What?"

"You're a mind reader. I've actually been thinking about it, too. One minute it seems perfect, then the next I wonder if the cliché is so obvious it screams at you."

"No, Colin, the symbolism is gorgeous. The eagle stands for strength, freedom, honor. Everything your wounded vets put their lives on the line for. Isn't that something you're hoping they'll remember? And hopefully bond with?"

He nodded.

"But I wasn't thinking about using them in one of your typical programs. This would have to be something special, something really powerful."

"I'm listening."

"From what you've told me, your educational programs, like the story of Lady, take place in one of the classrooms, right, and they bring the bird in?"

"Yes, and it'll be tethered, just in case it gets nervous."

"Well, what if you started out in the classroom, but followed up in the field? Releasing the rehabilitated eagle back into the wild?"

Colin looked at her, his head tilted.

"What a powerful metaphor this could be, you know?" She could just picture it, how moving it would be.

"But Kit probably isn't going to be released. It's been a few weeks now and he still shows no sign of flying."

"I know, I thought of that. If you have to, use another bird, but the point is the release. As the eagle, or hawk or owl, soars back into the sky, it would be like the triumph of spirit over body. Like the raptor, these soldiers were injured, then rehabbed, and now going on to a new, although different, life."

"I'll have to think about it and talk to Susan some more. Even if it isn't released, it will have a second life as a teaching bird."

"It was just a thought."

"Listen, don't be so disappointed. I think it's a great idea, actually. I think Susan told me they've only ever released a raptor with an audience once before, for some high-risk teens, so it actually hadn't even occurred to me. But I heard it made a great impact on the kids."

They talked about the possibilities until dessert was gone. Then they cleared the dishes together, Colin wheeling back and forth from the table to the sink. They were nearly done and Lucy was rinsing the sponge when she turned and suddenly smacked into him as he was bringing the last dish over.

The dish crashed to the floor and she grabbed the arms of the chair as he rolled backward, fearing he might tip. Their faces were mere inches apart. He took her wrists and held them, looking at her so fiercely she was afraid she'd offended or angered him. But then, still watching her, Colin brought both of her hands to his mouth, brushing her fingers with his lips. She froze. She could do nothing but watch as he pulled her onto his lap, let go of her hands, then turned her face toward him again.

Her heart stilled as his light blue eyes searched her own with such longing that it sent an erotic charge through her middle. Then he closed his eyes, and brought her lips to his, kissing her so softly, so tenderly, she thought she was melting. He held her head, kissing her longer, deeper, and she heard a small whimper break the quiet of the cabin.

It was hers.

33

WARWICK HOSPITAL WAS LESS THAN A MILE from Main Street. Ruth could have walked there from the store in ten minutes. Driving from her house it took just that. As she pulled into an empty spot in the Emergency Room parking lot in the dark, it all felt surreal to her. She got out of her car and the bright lights, the bustle of people behind the desks as the double glass doors slid open to the ER were suddenly so reassuring that Ruth felt silly. Maybe she had panicked. The sensation was still there but it was probably indigestion, just like that last time.

Surprisingly, there were just a few people in the waiting room. She found a chair in the corner and took a long, shaky breath, deciding she'd just sit for a bit and see how she felt. Who would know she wasn't just waiting for someone? If she really was having a heart attack—God forbid—she was already here. If she wasn't, she wouldn't have to waste time or money that she couldn't afford.

She leaned her head back and closed her eyes.

"Mrs. Hardaway?"

Ruth opened her eyes and turned. Oh no, how could she have forgotten? Coming around the information desk, her auburn hair pulled back into a clip, was Gloryanne, wearing a white hospital coat with a name tag: Gloryanne Graham, ER Receptionist.

"Are you waiting for someone?" Gloryanne asked, sitting beside her.

"Uh, yes.. no. I...I think I'm going to go now."

"You seem upset, is there anyone I can go check on for you?"

She remembered the first time Colin had brought Gloryanne home, when they were seniors in high school. Gloryanne was shy and sweet, with freckles across her nose. Ruth had liked her a lot and thought she might be a stabilizing force for Colin. She looked now at Gloryanne's wide gray eyes, filled with concern.

"Oh it's... me, actually. I wasn't feeling so great and I just thought I'd sit here a bit."

"You do look pale. What are your symptoms?"

Ruth told her about the chest discomfort and palpitations.

"Why don't we just let the triage nurse listen to your heart, okay? You don't have to stay, but this way you can go home with peace of mind. You don't want to take any chances, especially not..." her words trailed off.

"At my age. I know."

Things happened quickly after that. The triage nurse heard something she didn't like. Ruth was wheeled—they wouldn't even let her walk—into an ER exam room and quickly hooked up to an EKG monitor. A few moments later a young man with a ponytail came in and drew her blood. It seemed but a few beats after that a young woman—why did everyone look so young?—wheeled in a contraption and told Ruth she'd be doing an echocardiogram. For twenty minutes, Ruth turned from side to side as a cold gel was rubbed on her chest and the girl took pictures, none of which Ruth could discern on that monitor.

Then she was left alone in the freezing room for what seemed like forever, suddenly wishing she could just go home and sleep. It was nearly midnight now, she saw by the big clock over the door. She should probably call someone, but decided it was too late. Then the door opened and Gloryanne came in with a clipboard.

"We need to get your paperwork processed. We did things a bit backwards, you know."

Ruth reached over and unzipped her purse, pulling out her wallet, then handing Gloryanne her ID and insurance card.

"How are you feeling?" Gloryanne asked, as she wrote down the information.

Ruth shrugged. "The same. Right now, though, I just want to go to sleep. All this has been a bit much for the nerves, you know? I'm sure my blood pressure's up."

Gloryanne smiled. "You did the right thing. I know Colin would agree." And then she looked up. "He doesn't know you're here, does he? Does anyone?"

Ruth shook her head.

"Do you want me to—"

"No!" She said it louder than she'd intended. "I'm sorry, it's late and I'm sure it's nothing. I don't want to get everyone all upset."

"All right, but if you change your mind, I'm here until one. I'll be out at the desk." She handed her back Ruth's cards.

"Thanks, Gloryanne, I appreciate it."

At the door Gloryanne turned before opening it. "Can I ask you something, Mrs. Hardaway?"

"Sure."

She came back into the room, looking at the floor for a long moment.

"I know it hasn't always seemed like it, but...I love Colin. I always have."

"Things haven't been easy for you, I understand."

"I was trying to get him to trust me again, but..." she shrugged, shaking her head as if in defeat.

Ruth didn't know what to say.

"Is there someone else?" Gloryanne asked.

"You mean is he seeing someone?"

She nodded.

"Not that I know of. Why do you ask?"

"He just seems...different."

"Well, he's moving on, adjusting to his new life, thank God. And he's busy. Swimming keeps him focused, and still athletic, which we both know is a big part of who he is. I have to say, he's an asset at the store. But I think his time volunteering at the bird rehab has helped the most. I think Colin has become a much stronger person because of his injury."

"I know." Gloryanne's eyes suddenly filled with tears. "It's funny, but after he wouldn't see me, I began to think it was for the best. I wasn't sure I could be saddled with that kind of responsibility. That he would be...less of a man. Oh God, that sounds so awful."

"It's all right, I understand what you're trying to say."

"After all that time, when he was ready to try again, I wasn't. But you're right, he's become..." she paused, searching for words.

"A better man."

"Yes. And I think I'm too late."

Just then the door swung open and Gloryanne jumped up. She stepped aside to let a doctor in. Then she gave Ruth a little wave and slipped out.

"Well, Mrs. Hardaway," the doctor said, "it seems you have some fluid around your heart."

"What!"

She looked at him, stunned. No chit chat or nice nice? He just walks in, flips open her chart and drops a bomb like that?

"Fluid around your heart," he repeated. He wore wire-rimmed glasses and had shaggy hair that needed a cut. "We need to know what's causing it, so I'm going to admit you."

"Admit me?" She couldn't have heard right.

He looked up, this time with an amused grin. She sounded like a parrot.

"The good news is your blood enzymes came back fine, so it doesn't appear you've had a heart attack."

But all she could think of was her father-in-law, who died a few years after Bill of congestive heart failure. They couldn't stop the fluid from building up around his heart and it eventually destroyed the muscle. He wasn't even sixty.

An hour later she was wheeled to a room on the fourth floor. By then, Gloryanne was gone. Ruth would have to call everyone in the morning. But then she thought of Sam, alone in the house, all the lights on, no one to walk her upstairs and help her up on the bed. No one to take her out for a last pee. Luckily, Sam had the bladder of a camel.

She looked out the window. It was raining now, gray streaks running down the dark glass. There was fluid around her heart. How was that really possible? She was strong, healthy, she'd never had a serious illness in her life. But she'd also been ignoring her symptoms for months. Had she damaged her heart? Made it worse than it would have been if she'd simply done what a normal person would have and gone to the doctor?

A fist full of fear hit her in the stomach. Was this the beginning of the end? She wasn't ready for her life to be over. She wasn't ready for a debilitating illness. Why had she ignored it? What a fool she was.

Despite her exhaustion, now Ruth couldn't sleep. Doubts, regrets, anger at herself jabbed at her each time she tried to doze. She watched the town darken as she lay awake in the hospital bed, staring at the streets spread out below her, as one light after another was extinguished, feeling as if she were awake in a bad dream. Suddenly wishing for one more chance.

34

AFTER WHAT HAD HAPPENED THE NIGHT BEFORE with Colin, Lucy's head was a jumbled mess as she sat at the window, drinking tea, listening to the soft patter of rain and staring at her laptop. A movement outside caught her eye. Colin was pushing himself down to the lake.

She jumped up, remembering. Today he was going to swim all the way to the island and back. Grabbing a tattered umbrella that sat in a coat rack in the corner of the room, she ran outside and down the steps toward him.

"Wait," she called out.

He turned in his chair and called out over his shoulder, "You don't have to come. I'll be fine."

She stopped near his wheelchair at the water's edge, out of breath. He pulled his wet t-shirt over his head. She hesitated, unsure what to do. Last night something had shifted between them.

"You're getting soaked," she said as she leaned over with the umbrella to keep the rain off him.

He laughed, and she realized how ridiculous that must have sounded; he'd be in the water in a moment anyway. And then his laugh died and he gave her a long look. He wore black spandex shorts which clung to his thin, pale legs. It was a stark contrast to his naked upper half, the tanned muscles in his wide chest and shoulders slick with rainwater, like a bodybuilder's. Her eyes met his then, and her mouth went dry.

A moment later she turned and ran back to the cabin, digging in the closet until she found an old slicker, gave it a shake—in case anything was lurking inside the sleeves—and slipped it on. He was already in the water when she made it back and untied the canoe and got in.

Then he was off, swimming toward the island in sure, easy strokes, beginning with an Australian crawl as the rain fell on the lake, a lovely sound all around them. She began paddling, always a few feet behind him, falling into a rhythm as the warm rain hit her face. She didn't mind. There was something so beautiful about it, everything so quiet and still but for the patter of raindrops on the lake, the lapping of the paddle, and the small splashes each time Colin's arms sliced through the water. It was as if they were the only two people in the world.

She wondered if they were someplace else, not in this magical place that often seemed apart from the real world, if she would have responded as she had last night. A moment after she heard herself whimper, lost in a wanting she hadn't felt in years, he pulled away.

"I'm sorry, I shouldn't have done that," he'd said, as she sat there on his lap, both of them breathless.

She'd stood, turning away, suddenly uncomfortable. He took her hand and tugged, forcing her to look at him.

"It's not that I didn't mean it," he whispered. "But you're not free yet. I was trying to wait." Then he smiled. "I guess I should have tried harder."

Speechless, she'd wondered what it all meant. After a long moment, he let go.

"I should probably go pack," she'd said, and left a few moments later.

Now, rowing beside him, she had to admit there'd been a growing attraction to Colin. How could there not be? He was extremely handsome in a rugged way that ironically was so at odds with his disability it often made her forget. He was unlike any man she'd ever met. It wasn't just what he didn't have—the use of his lower body—that made him different. Watching him now, unable to take her eyes off the beauty of his form, she knew that she'd never met anyone else with his determination. But he had another kind of strength; he was so open and honest and kind.

Was she looking to get into a relationship, though? And something this complicated?

He was right, too. She wasn't free yet. She was healing, and picking up the pieces of her life, but she knew the trip to St. Augustine, facing the failure of her marriage, David's betrayal, the end of them once and for all, would take a toll, no matter how well she seemed to be doing.

As Colin reached the shallow water near the island, he dove and turned, swimming toward shore in a backstroke. Awkwardly, she began turning the canoe, something she'd never quite gotten the hang of. His arms reached back now, his hands slicing into the water, his face turned to the sky with his eyes closed. Once he'd told her that when he was in the water, he felt just like anyone else. For those brief, passionate moments last night, she'd thought the same thing.

But he wasn't, and never would be. And she never wanted to do anything to hurt this man.

Lost in thought, she didn't see the woman standing on the dock until a moment later. She was waving frantically and Lucy realized she was calling for Colin. She paddled faster, veering over and tapping him on the back with a paddle. He stopped suddenly and looked up and she pointed, then rubbed the rain from her eyes, seeing that it was Jenny.

Before they were even out of the water, Jenny began yelling at him.

"I've been calling your phone for the past ninety minutes, you ass. Mom's in the hospital and I don't have time to come running over here to make sure you're still alive because you're too inconsiderate to live in town where we wouldn't have to worry about you all the time."

Ruth in the hospital? Lucy opened her mouth then closed it, watching Colin as he swam to the dock, instead of the water's edge. He hoisted himself up, which took incredible strength, then sat there catching his breath. Jenny, too, was out of breath, and Lucy could see she'd been crying. She must have driven in a panic. He didn't shout back, didn't defend himself for not answering his phone, he simply said, "Is she all right?"

"No, she's not, she's got fluid around her heart. Just like Grandpa did." Jenny began to cry again.

He looked at Lucy, but before his words came, she was already on her way for his chair and the bench under the tree. A moment later, Colin lifted himself in his chair and began pushing toward his house. "Let's go," he said, though Lucy wasn't sure which one of them he was talking to.

Jenny turned to her. "I'm sorry, Lucy. I didn't mean to flip out in front of you."

"It's all right, but I'm so worried about your mom."

"She needs to get out of that store. That place is just wearing her down. I wish she'd be like other women her age and go to Florida or take up golf, maybe meet a nice guy. It's like she's hiding from the world in there."

"That's not true," they heard, then turned. Colin was on his deck, sliding the door shut. He came down the ramp with a slicker on, the hood up to keep him dry. He was still wearing the wet shorts, and she knew why. It would take too long to change.

Jenny met him with her hands on her hips. "Maybe she'd have a life if she ever got out of that store."

"Point of view is a funny thing, Jen. I think she sees the whole world from there."

"Jesus, you're just like her."

"I'll take that as a compliment."

"She lives like a college kid, Colin, barely scraping by each month. And you know she won't take a dime from any of us."

"Let's just go. The main thing right now is that she's okay."

"Colin," Lucy said, as Jenny went to her car and she followed him to his, "won't you get chilled? Shouldn't you change?" He didn't take his hot bath. She knew he couldn't feel the cold.

"I'll keep the heater on. The shorts'll dry by the time I get there and I'll slip sweatpants on over them." He lifted himself into the car, reached for his chair, folded it, then lifted it in and tucked it behind him. "I'll be fine. Good luck with your trip."

Before she could say a word, he shut the door and drove away.

* * *

SHE WAITED AND WAITED. She called the hospital, but didn't ask for Ruth, not knowing how serious it was. Instead she spoke with a nurse who told her—which she should have realized—that because of confidentiality guidelines, she couldn't tell her anything.

Unable to distract herself with work, she thought about painting a few more cabinets since they were only half done, but passed on that. Pacing the cabin, she stopped in a far corner of the room at a big old bookshelf that was painted brown, but now chipping. She hadn't really paid much attention to it before and decided that perhaps she should paint it the same creamy white as the cabinets.

Studying the shelves, she saw that they were filled with old games, carvings on tree branches, various colored rocks, and of course, a supply of old books. They ran the gamut from old mysteries by Agatha Christie, to dated romance novels by Kathleen Woodiwiss. There were paperbacks from James Bond thrillers to classics by Willa Cather, Edith Wharton, and of course F. Scott Fitzgerald.

Her eyes stopped on a beautiful leather-bound book. She pulled it out. It was a poetry anthology. She carried it out to the porch, hoping to find some Walt Whitman, who'd wooed her in high school and then college, his seductive, romantic verses perfect for the blooming heart of a young girl. Sitting in the rocker, she looked out at the lake. It was afternoon already, and still no word from Colin. Everything was still that platinum shade, the water, the sky, even the surrounding mountains and trees wrapped in gray gauze, like a moth's cocoon.

She opened the anthology to search for Whitman, but the book separated. Nestled against the spine was a crumbling flower, a red rose that had faded to brown, dried and brittle, bits of leaf and petal in the crease where the pages met.

She stared, wondering at the mystery behind it, her writer's imagination instantly taking off. The story of that rose, the lovers involved, and the hope that perhaps even today, that love was still alive. She loved old books for that reason, finding fossils of past readers, bits of their lives lost amidst the pages, artifacts of real stories.

How many times over the years had she gotten a book from the library, or even a used book bin, and found tiny pieces of other lives. A grocery list, a lock of hair, a card with someone's handwritten note: *Can't wait to touch you, Stephen*, which she'd never forgotten. And then there were the food smudges, the whiffs of something, perfume, rose lotion, or simply the smell of the old book, a scent she loved. All of it implying that the life of the book was part of the reader's life and had journeyed along for days, or perhaps weeks, through whatever drama was unfolding as the reader held that book, read those words, and lost him or herself for precious hours. As she'd done throughout the years with Nancy Drew and *The Secret Garden*, progressing to Dickens and Mark Twain, then copies of her mother's Ayn Rand books, and Hermann Hesse's *Siddhartha*, then Melville, Thoreau and Emerson. All of those books somehow touching her life when they seemed most needed.

Rooting through those shelves inside was like digging for treasure. Paging through the anthology, she stopped at "Song of Myself" and read. Then she found "Intimations of Immortality," and skimmed through the long stanzas until she found the one she wanted:

> *What though the radiance which was once so bright*
> *Be now for ever taken from my sight,*
> *Though nothing can bring back the hour*
> *Of splendour in the grass, of glory in the flower;*
> *We will grieve not, rather find*
> *Strength in what remains behind;*

This poem never failed to bring her to tears, especially now as she thought of Ruth in the hospital, the crumbling rose, and her husband dead so long ago. Somehow, Lucy knew it had to be from him.

By late afternoon Colin still hadn't called. It was then that Lucy called her attorney and postponed tomorrow's divorce hearing, telling him a dear friend was ill. She e-mailed David the same message, then walked out with her purse and the book of poems.

35

A T SEVEN-THIRTY, WHEN VISITING HOURS WERE nearly over and she hoped the family gone, Lucy went to the hospital. As she walked into the room and Ruth turned to see who was coming, Lucy was struck by how pale she looked, which only made the deep circles under her eyes more dramatic. And those big brown eyes held none of their usual sparkle. Suddenly, Ruth looked her age. Lucy walked over and gave her a hug.

"How are you?" Lucy asked just as Ruth said, "What on earth are you doing here?"

They both laughed.

"I thought you were already in St. Augustine."

"No, things were delayed a few days." A white lie, but Lucy didn't want Ruth to feel responsible, as she would have.

"Well, that's interesting," Ruth said with a small smile.

"No, it's nothing like that. Now, how are you?"

Ruth looked out the window a moment, shaking her head. "Scared. Relieved. Mad at myself."

"What do you mean?"

"I have mono," she said, with a little laugh. "You know the kissing disease? Except I haven't been kissed in about thirty years. How's that for irony?"

"But I thought it was your heart?"

"Yes, I do have fluid around my heart, but it's not congestive heart failure as I first feared. It's caused by the mono, no doubt because I ignored it for so long. It can happen, apparently, from any kind of virus. I kept thinking I was so tired because," she paused and gave another little laugh, "well, I am nearly sixty-five years old."

Lucy smiled, relieved, too. "Don't be mad at yourself. I think a lot of us keep pushing when we should probably slow down."

"I have to get out of here, though. This is putting me into an even bigger financial mess. "

"Wait, slow down."

"I have a horrible policy, with an outrageous deductible, and still the premiums are ridiculously high. But it was the best I could manage. I figured I never get sick, so why bother, right?"

And yet here she was.

"The doctor wants me to stay a few more days. Of course Jenny is pushing me, too. I had to swear that when I get out of here I won't set foot in the store for weeks. I don't know that I could if I wanted to. Now that I've stopped pushing myself, I'm totally exhausted. I *feel* like I have mono."

"Ruth, listen, I used to run a gift shop in Florida. I was the manager for two years. Before that I was an accountant. Let me help you, okay? It's the least I can do."

"Oh, I don't—"

There was a knock at her door and a moment later Lucy's heart went still as Gloryanne walked in. She held out a to-go cup and straw to Ruth.

"A strawberry milkshake from Bellvale Farms," she said with a smile. "Remember how we used to bring you one every time we went there for ice cream?" And then Gloryanne noticed her. "Oh, I'm sorry, I didn't realize you had company."

Ruth introduced them and Gloryanne gave her a little smile. She was truly beautiful, with porcelain skin, huge gray eyes, and that gorgeous red hair falling all around her shoulders.

"I was just about to leave," Lucy said, feeling horribly uncomfortable, wondering if Gloryanne knew Colin had feelings for her. Afraid she might say something in front of Ruth.

"No, stay. I have to get to work downstairs. Anyway, enjoy your shake, Mrs. Hardaway. It was nice meeting you, Lucy."

When the door closed, Lucy hesitated a moment, then said, "That was sweet of her. She's Colin's...girlfriend?"

Ruth pulled the straw from its sleeve. "She was. But that's a tough question to answer. She works downstairs in the ER, which I'd forgotten, so we've had a few...talks since I got here. I think maybe we were all a little hard on her, you know? She's ready, she says, to make a commitment to Colin."

"Really?" Lucy felt a little jolt of alarm. "What does Colin think?"

"I don't know. He's a very private person with things like that. But maybe it would be the best thing for him. I don't want him alone for the rest of his life. I know he'll never be like other men, but that doesn't mean he doesn't deserve to be loved. If it weren't for his accident, they'd have been married by now." She paused. "She thinks he's punishing her."

"Do you think that's true?"

"No. That's not something he would do. At least not intentionally." And then she hesitated. "You two have become pretty close. Has he mentioned anything about her?"

"Oh...we don't really talk about personal things, either." That wasn't the truth, but she didn't feel comfortable telling Ruth about Colin, especially now, on the heels of Gloryanne's visit, and what had happened last night. So she changed the subject.

"I almost forgot," Lucy said, reaching into her bag. "I brought you something. I found it at the cabin and thought you might enjoy it."

As she handed Ruth the book of poetry, her eyes widened and her face went white, looking, Lucy thought, just like the old cliché: as if she'd seen a ghost.

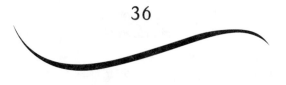

36

R UTH STARED AT THE BROWN LEATHER COVER IN DISBELIEF. How ironic to see this book again, today of all days, after she'd sat up most of the night thinking over the years of her life; how nothing ever quite turns out the way you expect it to.

She'd gazed out the window for hours at the town below, picturing herself going back and forth from her house to the store, day after day for the past thirty years. Or years ago, driving the kids to school each morning. And even before that, leaving her parents' farm on a school bus into town. Nearly her entire life had existed within a few miles' radius of where she sat in this hospital.

And yet she'd never felt confined or deprived. The world came to her through her books, or the stories her customers brought to her of their lives and travels. She had her children and grandchildren so she'd never been lonely, really. Until lately. Because lately she'd had a taste of possibility—of a different kind of life she could have if only she dared.

Now, here in her hands was proof of why she shouldn't. This book she'd once loved, a symbolic reminder of her failure as a woman, her guilt as a wife.

"Ruth, are you all right?"

She looked up. Lucy's face was filled with concern.

"I'm sorry, Ruth. It's such a beautiful book, and I thought Whitman might be a good diversion while you're here. And I found—"

"No, it's fine," Ruth interrupted. "I love Whitman, too. And this book, well, I haven't actually seen it in decades. It's just such a surprise." She pulled it to her nose and a mixture of scents rose up to her—rich leather, musty pages, the tang of old ink. "My mother gave me this book for my sixteenth birthday. I knew it was expensive by the soft leather and the gold leaf on the cover. She must have saved for it a long time. To me it was a treasure. It made me think of what it must've been like when books were a rare thing, and people cherished them. I imagined it would become an heirloom in my family one day."

Lucy smiled. "I figured it had happy memories for you. Especially when I saw the rose pressed in the pages. I could almost see you all dressed up for the prom with a beautiful corsage pinned on your gown."

"I never went to a prom. I never got asked." She opened the cover and the pages parted to the crumbling flower. She remembered the moment she had pressed it so carefully into this book. Her two most precious possessions at the time. "Bill gave me this rose. It was one of our first dates. We were just going out to dinner for my birthday, but he was always so romantic."

"You've never really told me about your husband."

Ruth looked out the window, hesitating. It was nearly dark again, rain still trickling down the glass. "I know I never really spoke about my husband. That was deliberate, to you and to everyone else. The truth is I couldn't stand to. Because to talk about it would be to think about it and...oh, Lucy, I feel like a liar of grand proportions." She shook her head. Why was she doing this now? Why didn't she just keep her mouth shut?

She pulled the book to her nose again, inhaling deeply, wondering at the power of a scent, the visceral feeling of a moment in time it could evoke.

"I gave this book to Bill on our fifth anniversary. When I still had a bit of hope that we could make things work. When I was still...trying."

"Listen, Ruth, you don't have to go into this now, maybe it's not—"

"No, I want to. I think it's time." Then she added with a little laugh, "And after all, Lucy, haven't we told each other pretty much everything?"

Lucy looked uncomfortable for a moment and Ruth hesitated, wondering if perhaps she was taking their honesty too far. Maybe Lucy didn't really want to hear all this. But then Lucy gave her a kind smile, pulled her chair closer and put a comforting hand on her arm. And Ruth continued.

"It wasn't until months after Bill and I were married that I realized he didn't read. At all. I couldn't believe it, you know? To be honest, when we were dating, I hadn't even noticed, we were always so busy doing things. But at night, I was always buried in a book, especially if he was working late. And he worked all sorts of odd hours on the railroad.

"Saying it out loud, it doesn't seem so awful. Big deal, he didn't read, except maybe the sports pages. I kept telling myself that no other woman would care about such a thing. I was a lucky girl to have him. But I began to realize more and more as time went by and then children came, that we had nothing in common, really. That without the excitement of dating, in the day to day reality of marriage, we were horribly mismatched. And Bill was bored. Bill needed a lot of fun, a lot of stimulation. Once I was his, I guess I wasn't so much of that anymore. So he would go out at night when he was off, to see his friends at the bars, play pool, who knew what else. Pretty soon, he didn't come home much. It wasn't long before I started hearing the rumors."

The hurt, the shame, she could feel it even now, roiling inside of her, turning her stomach.

"We started to argue, terrible fights. He'd promise to stop. He'd say that if I gave him half the attention I did to my books..." She closed her eyes, leaning back against the pillow at the force of those cruel memories.

You're frigid, he'd yell when she wouldn't respond to him. And if she couldn't give him what he needed, he'd just keep getting it elsewhere. Frigid, a word from another era. A label that had scarred her. Who ever heard it now? Looking back at herself, so young, navigating the difficult waters of motherhood, betrayed and exhausted, she thought now: of course you couldn't respond, he was cheating on you. Of course you began to hate him, who wouldn't?

But she couldn't say those things out loud, even now, not even to Lucy. For so long she'd been afraid he was right. That she wasn't enough of a woman and failed him somehow.

She lifted the rose from the book and bits of petal disintegrated onto her lap. "Today it would be so easy to walk away from a marriage like that, you know? People would think you were crazy if you stayed. But back then, I didn't work. I was a mother, with young children. There weren't many jobs for women anyway, it was all so different. Besides, I kept thinking if I tried harder, somehow I could get it to work. Because I just felt like I wasn't enough for him."

"Please, Ruth, don't..."

"One night I was so distraught, I couldn't take it anymore. It was this time of year, and he was supposed to be getting everything ready for a big bonfire up at the lake before the kids went back to school. He didn't come home and I finally got my neighbor to come over and sit with the kids. I drove up to the lake, shaking all the way, knowing in my gut what I would find. And I did. It was awful, the worst moment of my life. She ran out in a hurry, half dressed. I stood there and I swear I thought my heart would explode with rage. I screamed at him over and over, that I wished...he was dead." There, she'd said it out loud. She looked up at Lucy, who was looking at her not with horror, but with a look of such sadness.

"Stop, Ruth, please."

"He actually started to cry," she went on, unable to stop now. "And it threw me. I expected him to defend himself, like he usually did. To yell and make excuses. But he knelt at my feet, wrapped his arms around my legs and told me he never deserved me. Then he got up and left."

"Look, Ruth, I know what it's like to be cheated on, maybe not in this same way, but I was so full of rage at times it scared me."

"But he did die." She saw Lucy's eyes widen. "I went home and three hours later the police were at my door. His car hit a tree and he died instantly. So did she. She was Hannah's older sister."

She could hear Lucy's soft gasp. Ruth's body shook now as it had when she'd opened the door, the kids asleep upstairs, their world changed forever. Her knees had buckled and she'd slid to the floor, unable to get up.

"The police knew us. This is a small town, you know, and everyone loved Bill, he was so full of life. They stood in my house with tears in their eyes. The condolences over the coming days were heart wrenching. The worst, though, was the children."

Lucy took both of her hands and held them tightly.

"He wasn't all bad, of course. He loved the children and was always doing fun things with them when he was home. They had lots of campouts at the lake. I began to realize he was so much like them, always wanting to play, to find the fun in life and I...I was so serious."

Lucy handed her a tissue. Silent tears were spilling from Ruth's eyes and she hadn't even felt them. She wiped her face then blew her nose.

"Afterward, I thought I would die of the guilt, every time I tucked my kids in bed at night. Every time they cried. I felt like I was to blame."

"But you don't still think that, do you?"

She shrugged. "After a while, I just refused to think about it. It was easier that way. I buried my memories with him. Now over these past months, it seems like everything's been coming to a head. Maybe it's my age. Maybe it's sitting here wondering just how many days I have left on earth. None of us knows, really. And I keep thinking about what Jenny says, that I've been hiding in the store. I wonder if she isn't right."

"You know what I think? I think you held this in for too long and it had to come out. Come on, Ruth, you're not a hateful or vindictive person. Anyone who knows you knows that. You didn't mean what you said."

"But do we ever really know another person? I thought I knew Bill. You thought you knew your husband. I never imagined I was capable of the things

I said to Bill. How do we ever trust again?"

"Are you talking about Thomas?"

She turned and looked out the window again. One by one the houses and stores and street lights came on, as they had last night. Already there was a rhythm to this, and she wondered if a new phase of her life had begun.

"I never told you, but a while back Thomas came to see me at my house."

"He's out of prison?"

"Yes. And he told me why he was in there. He was trying to get back money that was stolen from his mother. What he did was stupid, crazy and...I think I believe him. But could you imagine Jenny finding out I'm seeing an ex-convict? And who knows what my sons would say?"

"Ruth, I don't think this is about your kids or anyone else. This is about what you want."

"I've thought about almost nothing else since I've been in here. I'm not sure I have the courage to try again. Maybe it's been too long. Lucy, I haven't been kissed, much less intimate with another man since I was married to Bill. As much as I want to...I'm not sure I can. It's not just that. This sounds so shallow, but what if...I'm ashamed of him in public, you know? Oh yes, this is my new boyfriend, who spent the last ten years in prison. I'm not sure I can completely get beyond that. And the funny thing is that it made me realize some of what Gloryanne went through. The stigma of being with a man who people will always look at differently."

She paused a moment, exhausted suddenly.

"But Ruth, didn't you say yourself a little while ago that just because Colin is different doesn't mean he doesn't deserve to be loved? Maybe the same could be said for Thomas."

She looked at Lucy for a long moment. Then she held out the leather bound book of poetry.

"Here, put this back on the shelf in the cabin. That's where it belongs."

JUST BEFORE MIDNIGHT THERE WAS A HUGE COMMOTION as a drug addict was admitted in the bed next to hers. When the night nurse came in, Ruth was surprised to see it was Larry Porter's girlfriend, Angela, who apologized, explaining it was the last bed and they had no choice. While the woman moaned and thrashed, Angela sat in the room, and she and Ruth chatted for a while about books, reminiscing about how she and Larry had met in the store by chance. Ruth lamented the shift change, when Angela said goodbye.

She alternately slept and wrote until the sun rose over Warwick and by then, as her breakfast tray was wheeled in, she'd come to two decisions. She was going to sell the store. If she couldn't—which was highly possible—she'd shut it down after the anniversary.

And as soon as she got home, she was going to call Thomas.

She left the tray untouched, got dressed, and then signed herself out of the hospital, stopping to mail her essay, "Why I'm a Bookseller," on her way home. She couldn't come up with just one explanation, so instead she'd spent the night listing all of the reasons she had loved what she did for the past thirty-five years. It seemed like a fitting farewell.

37

MUCH TO MEGAN'S CHAGRIN, LUCY PITCHED IN at the bookstore, organizing the bills and paperwork that Ruth had apparently never let Megan touch. She also spruced up the bathroom/storeroom where she'd fallen apart all those months ago.

Before she knew it, she was locking the door of the cabin and heading to LaGuardia Airport. Driving around the lake, she took one final look in her rearview mirror, and felt a shiver run up her spine, though she wasn't sure why. Colin had promised he wouldn't try to swim to the island and back alone. Yesterday, when she was at the store, she'd reminded him of that promise. He nodded, then handed her a CD. "I thought this might help with your research on eagles."

"Thanks, I'll watch it on the plane."

"When you come back you can tell me what you think."

She'd looked at him, realizing what he was asking. "I'll even take notes," she'd joked.

But for once he didn't smile. Since that kiss a few nights ago, he'd been looking at her differently. The wanting was right there, in his eyes. How had she not noticed it before, or her own growing attraction to him? She'd responded to him instantly when he'd pulled her onto his lap, and since then it was hard to get him, or that moment, out of her mind.

"I'll see you in two days," he finally said and she nodded.

In two days, she would be free and he'd want to take things to the next level. She had to be very careful. She did not want to hurt him. Or Ruth.

On the plane her anxiety grew and she began to laugh. It was her old fear of flying, of course, and nothing more, that's what was unnerving her. And this was the first time since she'd met David all those years ago that she was flying alone.

Lucy hoisted her bag into the overhead compartment and took her seat. She bit a Xanax in half, enough to relax but not make her loopy. Then she closed her eyes and waited, saying a small prayer. It was funny how it came automatically when she was in fearful situations. The last time she'd really prayed was when Ben was born. And that night in front of David's office, when she'd thought he was dead.

As the plane backed out of the gate, then bounced across the tarmac, her heart began to race, despite the Xanax. Gripping the seat rests, she closed her eyes and thought of David, that first time she'd done this very same thing, but grabbed his warm hand instead. How he'd always made her feel safe.

The plane turned, the engines firing up to full throttle, and then they were hurtling down the runway. She waited for that moment they left the earth, praying they wouldn't fall, as it seemed they should from the sheer weight of the jet. Her stomach dropped as the plane lifted and she counted Lamaze breaths over and over until finally they were at cruising altitude and everyone began to chat and relax. She immediately opened her tote bag and pulled out the research material she'd printed over the past week from the internet, enough pages to distract herself for three flights.

As she leafed through the enormous file, she remembered the CD from Colin. She got out her laptop, opened it on the tray and slid the disc in, pressing earphones into her ears. A moment later, the screen filled with a panoramic shot high above a glittering blue lake and in the distance, mountains dotted with snow. Classical music began, a gorgeous piece that tugged at her emotions immediately, and a woman began telling the story of the struggle for independence that led to the newly formed United States. How the founding fathers searched for a majestic symbol of their hard-won freedom, finally choosing the bald eagle.

Lucy watched as a distant object on the screen slowly came into focus and she recognized an eagle, which then spread its wings and took flight above forests and woodlands, skimming treetops, gliding across frozen, snow-covered fields, as if surveying his world in all of its magnificent glory. It was a stirring opening and a sudden lump of tears grew in her throat. She couldn't help but think of Colin and his wounded veterans who had all fought, just as those men fought centuries ago, to reinforce the freedom this bird represented. Something like this, she thought, might be a perfect opening for Colin's program.

The bald eagle is one of the largest birds of prey, the narrator went on. *Its startling white head and penetrating yellow eyes make it the most recognizable raptor, but most people know very little about its difficult and inspiring life in the wild.*

The music changed and as the eagle flew back to its nest, another eagle soared into view. It was a female, checking out his home. Noticing her, he suddenly took off from the nest, following her across the sky for a long distance, growing ever closer until they began to circle each other over and over at a leisurely pace, the male just above the female. Lucy marveled at this intricate aerial ballet until suddenly he dove toward the female. Lucy thought he was going to attack her, but with just seconds to contact, the female suddenly turned upside down, thrusting her feet toward him. He grasped her talons with his own. They were locked together, unable to fly. She watched in horror as the two eagles plummeted toward the earth, bodies twirling as they held onto each other. This was the dance of courtship, although it seemed to Lucy as though they were destined for death. At the very last second the birds suddenly broke free, soaring off in opposite directions. But the bond was established. Hopefully, they would now mate.

She paused the video and sat there, moved beyond words by what she'd just witnessed. The trust it would take for the female to be held like that, it was beyond comprehension. She pressed play, and watched as the male, back in his nest which he'd been tending all winter, began filling it with huge twigs, fish carcasses, and other goodies that had attracted her at first glance. Her arrival soon afterward was proof, the narrator continued, that mating had indeed occurred.

It was a tentative beginning as they worked to improve the nest together. Eagles, like many birds, have "site fidelity," meaning that each bird is drawn to the area in which it was born to build its own nest, sometimes flying back from several hundred miles away. She imagined Kit, working tirelessly in a nest, readying it for his own mate's arrival, no doubt somewhere near the Water Gap. Had Kit left a mate behind, or even worse, babies which she was then forced to care for alone?

Once the female eagle laid her eggs, they took turns keeping them warm. He would bring her food, then sit on the eggs while she flew off, fishing with amazing accuracy, diving from great heights into a river, despite her blindness in one eye, then swooping up with a fish dangling from her talons as she flew it back to the nest to be shared. Then it was his turn to hunt again. It was grueling work. Lucy was amazed at the hardships these wild creatures endured to bring their young into the world. They were fierce predators, yet gentle parents. Their diligence and sensitivity touched her heart, especially as he carefully maneuvered his powerful talons over the eggs so he didn't crack them when he sat to warm them. The eggs could freeze in a minute if exposed.

It went on for weeks, as early spring turned cold again and suddenly a late blizzard blew in. The nest swayed and pitched as each eagle took turns sitting on the eggs, their feathers rippling in the cruel, gale force winds and blinding snow, yellow eyes ever alert. Soon they were all but covered in snow. And yet they never moved, never wavered, mother and father guarding their young with all their might. How difficult their lives are, she thought; how easily the nest could have blown away, or one of them freeze to death. But there they sat.

She stopped the video suddenly, and closed her eyes. Thoughts of Colin and his program, or her book, had evaporated long minutes ago. Because as she watched this pair of eagles struggling to make something happen that seemed so against the odds, ironically even against nature, it was impossible not to think of her and David. All they'd endured, for nothing.

* * *

FROM THE MOMENT SHE GOT IN THE RENTAL CAR and headed toward St. Augustine, the familiarity of the roads came back instantly. For almost five years, this was coming home.

With each mile closer, her nerves began to tick harder. In a little while, she'd be at the house on Charlotte Street, which David had agreed to vacate. She'd taken very little when she left months ago. Now she had to sort through the rest, though it wouldn't take long.

Exiting Route 95, she drove east toward the coast, past houses and churches and soon there it was ahead, the beautiful little city. She passed Flagler College, and the beautiful Casa Monica, which looked more like a castle than a hotel. The green on her left was filled with vendors, and in that moment the cathedral bells began to ring, as if in welcome. When she came to the Bridge of Lions, she made a sudden decision and drove straight, instead of turning toward the house. Over the harbor she soared, onto Anastasia Island. A few minutes later she drove through the gate for the state park beach.

Wind surfers and fishermen filled the lagoon as she passed, continuing to the parking lot by the beach. Late summer in Florida is intense, with blistering humidity and strong sun, but at the moment she didn't mind. Standing beside the car, she could hear the roar of the ocean just beyond the dunes, the crash of waves, and the lone cry of a gull.

She crossed the boardwalk and a moment later stood there, her heart catching at the wide swath of pure white sand, the glittering sea stretched out before her. She walked toward the water and there, where the soft wind came off the ocean and the sand was cooler, slipped off her sandals and rolled up her pants.

She walked north, forcing her mind not to dwell on the memories of all her walks here, simply wanting to enjoy this last one. But they came anyway, like the waves, one after another, starting with that first time she and David had walked here, wondering if this could be the place to start over, when suddenly that flock of white gulls lifted and hovered above them, like messengers from God.

There was the morning she finished writing *A Quiet Wanting*, when she nearly ran to the tip of the island, so filled with excitement she thought she'd explode—thinking it would soon be published. Then the long string of rejections. And of course coming here again and again after David's arrest. Now she was here for the last time, ending their marriage.

The image of David cutting the grass came to her then, spurred no doubt by the video of the bald eagle in his exhausting routine. Every single day after they lost Ben, week after week, he was out there filling the long lonely hours after work when she'd been emotionally absent to him. Punishing himself.

She turned, staring at the water, at that distant line on the horizon where the light green sea and blue sky met. David had been grieving, too, in his silent, senseless ritual. But she hadn't thought about that because she'd only had room for her own grief. She was the one who'd carried Ben for nine months. Who'd felt him moving inside her. She was the one whose engorged breasts leaked, longing for the moment when she'd be able to feed her baby the way she'd always dreamed of. But of course it had never happened.

David had brought her Xanax every six hours in the days that followed, and for a while she allowed herself to succumb to the fog of feeling half-alive. It was easier that way. Then one morning she woke up, got in the car with the manuscript she'd started while bedridden, and drove to the park and sat there, writing by hand again.

She went for therapy, but he'd refused. And she'd had this other world of Hope and Matthew she was creating, that she could bury herself in. She went to the park every day and began to think that if they could just remove themselves from that house, that life, all of it built around the dream of a child, they could somehow survive.

She'd never gone into the nursery again. David had donated everything to a women's shelter. He sold the house, pared down their belongings, and arranged for the movers. She kept writing, lost in someone else's problems, heartache, and eventual joy—Hope's. And back to her dream of being a writer. But in all the time she was escaping, David was facing the day to day realities of their loss. David, who had been honest early on that he didn't want children.

She wondered if he'd told his therapist here how she'd withdrawn, how she'd let him pick up the pieces alone. How he'd brought her cups of tea in the middle of the night when her breasts had turned to bricks, as she waited for the milk to dry up.

Now as she walked up that beautiful beach in the harsh light of midday, all of the mistakes that had been rising to the surface for so long hit her square in the face. She'd left everything up to David. She hadn't taken responsibility for any of it. First she'd lied to him; she'd always wanted children. Then she was blinded by grief and David, as usual, took care of everything. No wonder he'd hated her.

She sat on the sand suddenly, the force of guilt nearly taking her breath away.

"Oh, Lucy. You fool."

She stayed there for a long time staring at the water, seeing the bald eagle exhausting itself for its family, realizing finally that David had done the same thing for her. And Ben.

* * *

CHARLOTTE STREET WAS PERHAPS THE MOST BEAUTIFUL STREET in town. The graceful old live oaks, their arching limbs veiled in Spanish moss, charming stucco homes with tile roofs, or old Victorians with wrap-around porches, each house a little different. The feel of the past everywhere, her own included, as Lucy drove down the narrow road and pulled in the driveway.

Soon it would be autumn, her favorite season here, when the heat and humidity lifted, yet everything was still lush and blooming. The light was already a bit different. The pink climbing roses on the side of the garage were in full bloom now, and would be again in March or April. She would miss the long autumn, the early spring.

She unlocked the front door, wondering if it would all be different. Walking through the rooms, it was all as she'd left it. David hadn't moved or changed a thing. She'd tried so hard to put in all the right touches, but there was still so much unfinished. Her eyes went to the blank wall above the fireplace.

How long she'd searched for the right painting to put there. The sheers on the arched windows were a temporary solution, now hanging for five years. If she'd been able to finish, make it the perfect house she'd envisioned, would it have made any difference, really?

Walking to the kitchen, she looked out the glass doors into the courtyard, the bougainvillea also in full bloom, crimson petals covering most of the back wall. On her way to the bedroom, she stopped, surprised to see the picture still on the wall. It was Ben in his isolette, wrapped in a blue receiving blanket, his slate gray eyes wide open. A hospital snapshot blown up until it was almost grainy. A few hours later it would all change. Who knew there wouldn't be time for more? Lucy placed her lips on Ben's as she'd done every morning in this house.

Then she opened the bedroom door and gasped. David was sitting in the corner chair.

"What are you doing here?" she asked in the same moment he said, "I know I'm not supposed to be here..."

He stood up. "I'm sorry, Lucy, for everything."

She watched his eyes fill with tears as she fought her own.

"I'm sorry, too, David."

She walked into his open arms.

38

R UTH WALKED INTO THE HOUSE SHE'D LEFT forty-eight hours before, a different woman. Climbing the stairs to her bedroom, she had to stop halfway up to catch her breath, and by the top her legs were trembling. She called Jenny and told her she was home, not that she'd signed herself out. Before Jenny could launch into another lecture, Ruth told her she was selling or closing the store. Then she went to bed and slept until the following morning.

Jenny had come while she slept and stocked her refrigerator. She found a note on the counter, *I love you, Mom. You're doing the right thing. Call me when you're up for a visit. Love, Jenny. P.S. Sam is fine, I'll bring her back in a few days.* Her head felt groggy, and there was a surreal feeling to standing alone in her kitchen in the middle of the morning with nothing she had to do. Even the dog bowls were gone. She sat heavily in a kitchen chair, wondering if she had ever been this bone tired in her life. She felt like one of the kids' old wind-up toys that once stopped, simply could not be wound up again.

She microwaved a container of chicken soup Jenny had divided into individual servings. Then she swallowed two of the ginseng capsules she found on the counter next to an arsenal of vitamins and herbs. She went in the living room and lay on the couch, picking up a book from the pile on the floor, then putting it down. It was frightening not even having the strength to read, although the doctor kept assuring her that with a few weeks' rest, the virus would begin to disappear and so should the fluid around her heart. But what if it didn't?

She closed her eyes, wondering how things were going at the store without her. She knew her decision was going to make a lot of people unhappy, would no doubt send a little shock wave through the village of Warwick. Worst of all was Hannah, who would be completely shattered if someone didn't buy the store and keep her café. She couldn't think about Hannah or any of it right now because there was no turning back. Even if she had a change of heart, she was out of money. And energy.

* * *

"DID THAT REALLY JUST HAPPEN?" DAVID ASKED.

Lucy turned to his face on the pillow beside her, staring at the ceiling, his dark hair tousled.

"I can't believe it, either," she managed.

"I had everything rehearsed that I wanted to say to you, but…" He turned and looked at her with a little smile. "So I guess you don't hate me?"

She shook her head, but his smile disappeared.

"I need to talk about Ben," he said. "Is that okay?"

"Yes."

He was quiet for a long time, and she wondered if he had changed his mind when he finally said, "Do you ever wonder what our lives would have been like if he'd lived? What he'd have been like?"

"Of course." For a long time it had completely consumed her. "That entire first year I kept imagining him making his first sounds, reaching for the spoon as I fed him cereal. Sitting up at six months, then beginning to walk and terrified to let go." She knew every upcoming step, because along with writing her novel, she'd read everything she could find on what to expect the first year. "I pictured him as a chubby toddler with silky dark hair like yours, saying all the unintelligible words babies say at first, and hoping I'd know what he meant."

"The therapist made me do it," David said then. "At first I thought it would be torture because before I couldn't even let myself think about him. But in a way it made him seem more real. When we lost him, even though I saw him and held him…it was like it wasn't real."

"I know. He was there, and then he simply vanished as if he never existed at all. And we never got to bond with him." She took a deep breath, remembering her own therapist telling her the same thing. Only for her it wasn't that she was trying *not* to think of an older Ben, how he would change over the months and years. It was that she couldn't *stop*.

It amazed Lucy that they were talking like this. You'd have thought they lost their son five days, not five years ago.

"After a while, I couldn't go to the park anymore," she continued. "You know the one with the playground where I would sit and write? I'd watch the kids with their mothers, toddlers on a swing or coming down a slide for the first time, squealing. I even wrote a poem about it one day."

"What's it called?"

She hesitated a moment. "'My Son, The Autumn Dancer.'"

"I'd love to hear it."

"I don't know."

"Please, Lucy."

Neither of them spoke for a while. Then she took a deep breath. This poem was sacred to her, and she knew it by heart. It wasn't just words, it was a scene she imagined, a moment frozen in time, if she could have had just one more moment with him again.

> *"Like crimson leaves on a crisp*
> *fall day, you swirl about*
> *the rich green grass,*
> *a final burst of color, so bold*
> *it almost hurts the eye.*
>
> *A golden face sliding*
> *into a pool of sunlight,*
> *it is a joy which we*
> *drink deeply, a time*
> *never to be forgotten.*
>
> *You are an autumn dancer*
> *and for this precious moment*
> *this park is yours, this*
> *delight is yours, this*
> *earth is yours.*
>
> *Such love and beauty are*
> *almost painful as I watch*
> *you helplessly, slipping*
> *naturally into the years*
> *to come. But for just this*
> *moment, it is ours."*

"Oh, Lucy."

She turned to see David with his eyes closed, a tear rolling down the side of his face.

"I imagined we were just another mother and child there at the park, and that we had our whole lives ahead of us. What this one beautiful, golden moment might be like, and how I would savor it, knowing that he would grow up and grow away, as kids normally do."

"Have you ever gone back, since you're up there?"

"To the cemetery? No." It wasn't that she hadn't thought about it. Part of her felt guilty because it wasn't that far, really.

"I've been thinking about coming up," David said. "I think it would be good for me. Closure, finally."

"I understand."

"You're letting your hair grow," he said then and smiled tenderly, reaching for a strand and twirling it around his finger. "I'm glad you don't hate me. I wouldn't blame you if you did."

"David, you're not the only one..."

"Shhh," he said, putting a finger over her lips. "It's nearly dark, and I think I heard your stomach growling."

"I haven't really eaten since yesterday morning."

"Well, I'm famished, but there's nothing here. Do you want to go out?"

"Not really." She sat up and slipped on her shirt, pulled on her underpants.

"I'll run over to Harry's," David said, sitting up.

A few minutes later he was gone. She stood under the shower, letting the water beat on her head, wondering at what had just happened. It was as though the David she once knew had returned, after a long, strange absence. He'd never mentioned the word divorce, and neither had she.

It was as if a fragile peace had descended and for the moment, neither one of them wanted to shatter it with a touch of reality. But she knew that soon she would have to.

THEY SAT ON THE PATIO EATING RIBS AND DIRTY RICE and drinking chardonnay, like they might have any night before. But David only picked at his food, then pushed it aside. He broke the peace first.

"There are so many things I want to say to you right now. I'm sorry seems so inadequate."

"Before you do, there are some things that I need to tell you."

"Please," he said, taking her hand. "Just listen, okay?"

He took a deep breath, squeezing her hand. "It wasn't until my life was taken away from me, Lucy, that I slowly began to realize how trapped I felt. I'm not making excuses, trust me. What I did, the gambling, taking the money from you, and the trust accounts, it was beyond disgusting. But it was almost as if it was someone else doing it, not me, because I didn't think about the right or wrong, accountability, none of it. It just made getting through the days easier. And we were in debt from the move, so...I kept thinking maybe I could pay some of it off. Crazy, huh?"

He sat there a moment, staring across the patio, as if reliving it all.

"When Ben died I felt like I went into some kind of autopilot. I thought if I just kept working and taking care of things, somehow I would get through it. But I see now that doing that, moving, working like a dog here to build the practice, sneaking in poker games anytime I could, I was just avoiding the pain. And after a while, it was like I was numb inside."

"I know the feeling."

"It wasn't just losing Ben, it was everything about my life, just squeezing and squeezing me until I thought my head would explode. I didn't want to be a lawyer. It was never really what I wanted, but...you know how it is, you go for the good job, the security, you don't want to let people down."

"You mean your parents?"

He nodded.

"When I was in that prison camp, I felt...free." He actually laughed. "Ironic, isn't it? It sounds insane, I know, but having nothing was a relief. I didn't have to pretend anymore and there was nothing left to lose. I remembered my father saying when he first got sick, that every day you wake up with a hundred problems, but the day you lose your health, you wake up with just one problem. I started to think about that a lot. I still had my health, and my whole life ahead of me. Maybe I didn't have to be a lawyer anymore. I could just start over. I didn't have to try to get my license back to practice law. I started to feel...hope."

"You're not going to try to get the bar..."

But he was already shaking his head. "No."

"I can't believe it."

"I hope that doesn't disappoint you."

"No, it doesn't. It's just that I never had any idea. You never let on at all."

"You know, for as far back as I could remember, my father always told me I was going to be a lawyer and work with him. When I was little I used to go to the office with him, sit on the other side of the big partners' desk and just love being there. I never questioned my future. When I got older and began to have other thoughts, I just... I didn't want to disappoint them."

"But you've never mentioned wanting to do anything else."

"Oh, I had this fantasy of being an archeologist once," he laughed, but she could see there was something serious there. "I used to read *National Geographic* every month and dream about those kinds of adventures. But really, how many people get to have that kind of life, you know? It's like saying you want to be an astronaut."

"Why didn't you ever tell me this?"

He shrugged. "I think I did once, but you probably forgot. Anyway, after my father died, I was just about done with law school and then I took over his practice. Being a lawyer was who I was, part of the fabric of my life, and I couldn't envision anything else after a while."

"And now?"

"I'm doing some clerical work at legal aid for St. John's County for now, as part of my community service, but when that's over, I'm done with the legal profession. And also..." he hesitated, "I'm a bartender at Harry's."

"What!"

David began to laugh. "I know, it sounds shocking, but it's just for now. There's no pressure, I like meeting people, and believe it or not, the money's pretty good, so I'm getting by. And there's something else. I realize now how lucky you are, to know exactly what you want, to be a writer. And to have the guts to go after it. I never really gave you the support there that you deserved."

"That's not really true."

"It is, maybe not all the time, but still..." His words ran out and he sat there a long moment. "You know, all my life, I've done the responsible thing, the expected thing. Whatever would make someone else happy, and I see now how that was part of my undoing. But Lucy, what I did to you..." He shook his head, as if there were no words.

"David, it's over and done with. I don't hate you anymore. Obviously."

"I should have gone for counseling with you, after Ben died. I know that now. Everything I held in all that time, it was just, I don't know, like I didn't even really know myself anymore. To be honest, it wasn't until recently that I began to see how much anger I was holding in, too."

"I was angry for a long time afterward, too. It's one of the early stages of grief."

"Yeah, but you dealt with it. I didn't. And it's not like I'm done. I'm going to keep going for a while, even though it's not mandated any longer. "

"You know what? I still had a lot of baggage, too. It wasn't until I went north that I began to see it. I hurt you, David, in ways you don't even know. I wasn't there for you after Ben died. And even later on when we came here, I pretty much wasn't present at all. I was always focused on something I was working toward, the book, then the shop, then back to the book, trying to keep myself so busy I didn't stop most of the time to even think about my life, or our marriage."

"I know. And that was my excuse to myself when I was feeling guilty."

"I'm sorry for that. I know you were grieving."

He smiled. "Hindsight is an amazing thing, isn't it?"

She nodded, but couldn't smile. "David, do you remember when we started making plans for our future and you said you didn't want children?"

He nodded.

"Do you remember what I said?"

"Not exactly. Just something to the effect that you didn't either."

"That wasn't completely true. I was young and *in that moment*, I didn't want children."

He looked puzzled. "What are you saying?"

"I was afraid to be completely honest with you. I knew that I wanted them, I just wasn't ready then. I saw it all, the beautiful house in Mendham, a yard filled with swing sets and sandboxes, and you coming home for dinner every night. It was the kind of life I always wanted as a kid and...I figured when the time came, you'd hopefully change your mind."

He stared at her for a long moment.

"I should have been honest with you, David, right from the beginning. That was unfair. And I put you through hell, with all the fertility treatments and then losing Ben. I'm sorry, deeply sorry."

He got up and walked across the patio, his hand raking through his hair over and over again.

"For such a long time, David, I kept wondering which was the domino that set this all in motion and I think it was that. If I hadn't done that, you wouldn't have gone through—"

"Stop it," he said, turning back to her. "Don't do this."

"You even moved here because of me."

He came over and sat back down. "You know what I'm learning more than anything? That you can't go back. You can't undo mistakes, you just have to learn to live with them. What I did to you was horrible. What you just told me—that at twenty-three years old you maybe did or didn't want kids— hell, that isn't even in the same league. I don't regret what we went through. Because I did want a child, once I got over my fears. I wanted it just as much as you. It was the continual loss that was unbearable. But I would never undo any of it, because that would erase Ben, and I could never do that. For however little time we had him, he was ours."

She bit her lip, but the tears spilled from her eyes. David's, too, were full of tears.

"Let's just let it go, all of it," he said. "There was a lot of good in our marriage. We're here now, in the present, and I don't want to make any more mistakes that I'll regret. I'm not the same man I was when we stood on that beach and I told you I wanted a divorce."

"What are you saying?"

"That I don't think we should rush into it. When you postponed it a few days ago, I started to hope that maybe you were having the same doubts, but I didn't want to say anything until you were here. I needed to talk to you in person."

"Oh, David…"

"It doesn't matter. We're a family, Lucy, just the two of us."

She stood and walked across the patio, her mind reeling.

"Call your attorney and tell him it was a mistake. It happens all the time, people at the last minute have a change of heart."

She couldn't believe what he was saying. As she stood there, trying to absorb everything that had happened in the past twenty-four hours, she already knew what her decision had to be. She'd known it the moment she'd turned to him on the pillow beside her, both of them blindsided by the force of emotions.

Because David was right, she didn't want to make any more mistakes.

39

RUTH REMEMBERED THE CONVENTION on her fourth morning home. It was too late to get her money back, and there was no point in going even if she felt better. A moment later, she picked up her phone and dialed Lucy's cell. She answered on the first ring.

"Ruth! How are you? I sent you a few e-mails, but I didn't want to call and bother you."

"I'm okay, just tired, making up for lost sleep and all. And I'm sorry I haven't written back. I haven't gone near the computer since I got home. But listen, I'm calling because I have a brilliant idea, if you're interested."

She told Lucy about the convention, and how she could meet more booksellers in a day than she could in six months on her own.

"Oh, Ruth, what an opportunity! I think I'd be terrified, though."

"You'll be fine. Just give out books and tell them how well you've been doing. Maybe get a few of the booksellers you know to talk you up a bit. What do you say?"

"Well, I'm still in St. Augustine. Things here turned out not quite the way I expected. David doesn't want the divorce."

"Oh my, you must have been floored."

"To say the least."

"Well if you're not coming back, you don't have to—"

"No, I do have to come back, but..." her voice drifted and Ruth heard talking in the background and then Lucy was whispering, "Listen, I'll explain more when I see you because I'm in a bookstore in Fernandina Beach and the owner is heading my way. As for the convention, the thought of meeting that many booksellers is a little nerve wracking, but yes, I'd love to. Thank you."

Ruth promised to e-mail the details then hung up with a smile—Lucy's husband still loved her! From everything Lucy had told her, he sounded like a good man who'd made some bad decisions. And now, most likely the divorce wouldn't be finalized. Of course she had to come back—her car was here, as were all of her things at the cabin. She could stop at the convention in Philadelphia on her way back to Florida. Well, at least one of them was getting a happy ending, she thought as she reached over to pet Sam, disappointed to realize once again that Sam wasn't there.

BEING HOME SO MUCH, IT WAS HARD TO IGNORE the years of neglect staring her in the face. Everything needed a fresh coat of paint. The kitchen hadn't been updated in—actually, aside from replacing broken appliances, it had never been updated. But the house had good bones, a term she'd heard on HGTV. It was a project, something to look forward to, but she would have to bide her time. Right now there was just one thing she wanted above everything else—to feel like herself again.

As she sat on the porch at the end of the week, Sam barely acknowledging her existence as she curled up in the furthest corner, still miffed at her sudden banishment, Ruth rocked back and forth watching the comings and goings of her neighbors on a sunny August afternoon. Honeybees buzzed lazily across the lawns from flower to flower and the birds were beginning their late day feedings. It was peaceful, and Ruth wondered if this was what retirement was like, literally stopping to see the flowers, finally. She was feeling slightly better, able to make the stairs now in one try. Even cooking a few meals. Last night, after a long, quiet day, she'd finally called Thomas. He didn't pick up, so she left him a message to call her. He still hadn't, and she realized it was time to face facts—his letter was probably him letting go. He'd moved on, probably met someone younger and with a lot less baggage.

A familiar green Volkswagen coming up her street caught her eye, then pulled in her driveway. Megan got out, carrying a brown shopping bag. It wasn't until Ruth stood and met Megan at the porch steps that she could see the young woman had been crying.

"I know I'm not supposed to call you or bother you about work, but Ruth, I had to find out if it's true. Please tell me you're not really closing the store."

"Oh, Megan." She took Megan's hand and led her into the house, where they sat on the living room couch. "Look, do you realize how hard this is for me? But I have to do it."

"I can't believe I've held this in all week," Megan said, pulling her hand away and putting the bag on the couch between them. Then she closed her eyes and made a little humming sound, as if she were in a trance. She realized Megan was trying to calm herself.

Then Megan turned and dumped the contents of the bag on the couch between them. "I threw out that disgusting box that Sandy gave you and copied what I needed, but I kept a few originals."

"This is about Sandy's grandfather? But I thought…"

"I lied." Megan lifted a yellowed, laminated page from the pile. "Just look at this."

Ruth took the yellowed newspaper page, taped and brittle-looking but now preserved in the layer of plastic, and scanned it with her eyes, stopping at the date: July 21, 1862. She looked up at Megan.

"I did throw a lot of what was in that box out, but there were just a few things that got me curious and I started searching online. I also got into the archives of *The Warwick Gazette*. But Ruth, keep reading this page," Megan said, practically clapping her hands.

Below the 1862 date was an article about the Warwick Valley Railroad, which had just finished its maiden run. Another article speculated about the future of the dairy industry and other local trades that would now be able to transport their products to other towns in a more timely fashion. The new railroad was going to be a boon to the local economy.

Ruth thought about her father's farm, and how her own great-grandfather had begun the family dairy business, which had dwindled over the years of her own life until it disappeared. But here, right in this article, was where it had no doubt begun to boom.

There was just another small piece on the bottom, about the mayoral race heating up, and she glanced further, looking at the advertisements luring readers to try the "Quality Calicos and Fine Laces at Quincy's Dry Goods Store," or another for Rightmyers Pharmacy, the predecessor of Akin's on Main Street, advertising Doctor Tucker's Amazing Digestive Tonic: "Derangements of the Stomach or Bowels Promptly Relieved." She laughed out loud.

Then she noticed the small column ad in the bottom right corner and her breath caught. "The Book Lover. Expanding Our Inventory—Now carrying wallpaper and window shades for the modern home."

She looked up at Megan. "Wallpaper and window shades?"

"Well, think about it. How clever was that to come up with other products made of paper, and not just books?"

"And this is…" She looked at the date again, still shaking her head, "1862? But I thought Betsy was only the second owner?"

"I think that's right, but if you keep looking," Megan said, now leafing through a clipped bunch of photocopied pages, "you'll find that the former owners had the store in their family for generations. These are copies I made from some of those moldy papers."

Ruth took the pages from her and looked at the top sheet filled with the fluid ink of a fountain pen. It was a review of *The House of the Seven Gables* by an Otto Klinger. She scanned the lines, amused at the vernacular of the period, and then in the last paragraph her eyes widened.

"He's saying that Nathaniel Hawthorne originally self-published his first novel?"

"Yes, amazing, isn't it?"

"But...I had no idea. It says it was called *Fanshawe*...and...he burned the unsold copies?" She turned the page over, but there was nothing else, no date.

"I verified all of it about Hawthorne. It's all true. As for the store, I couldn't find anything at the historical society on the store going back that far, but it turns out they had a fire years ago and lost a lot of stuff. So I went to the county deed office and found out the Klingers owned this building until Betsy bought it. It's amazing, isn't it?"

Megan continued to rummage through the papers, finally handing her another. In front of her very own window stood three people, an older woman in a long dress with a lace collar, ribbon sash, and a bonnet tied under her chin. Beside her was a young man, and then a little girl who couldn't have been more than ten. The caption read: *Three Generations of Klingers Open The Book Lover.* The young man was identified as Otto Klinger. But Ruth kept looking at the date, 1860.

"Oh Lord, Megan..." she could barely breathe.

Megan was giggling. "Our store is going to be one hundred and fifty years old, Ruth."

"I can't...I simply can't believe it."

"And to think, if you hadn't come along..."

"Things were so tight. When Betsy couldn't find a buyer she nearly just closed shop." And here she was, about to do the same thing. Ruth could only afford the business, so someone else had bought the building, which had changed hands three times since.

"Ruth, I think we're the oldest bookstore in the country, do you realize that?" Megan was bouncing in her seat.

"No, that's the Moravian Bookshop in Bethlehem, Pennsylvania. They actually opened in 1745 but moved locations."

"So maybe we're the oldest in the same location. But who cares, there are bookstores that don't make ten years. This is pretty incredible."

"I still don't get the connection to Sandy's grandfather."

"Well, he did work there for a while. This is him in a photo in front of the store when they put in the first electric lights, with Alma Klinger, Otto's granddaughter."

"But how did he end up with some of this in his attic? Did he marry her?"

"No, I asked Sandy about that. She thinks maybe Alma Klinger was his girlfriend before he married her grandmother. Anyway, I've searched the area, but there don't seem to be any Klingers left."

"Maybe we'll never really know. I'm just glad Sandy didn't throw it out."

"The Book Lover is a landmark, Ruth. It's a piece of history. You can't close!"

She looked up at Megan and sighed.

"Come on, Ruth, don't tell me you don't miss the excitement already? Who's coming in today? What new book is arriving? We're part of that whole magical process. Helping people discover new reads, finding books they don't even know they want yet and then falling in love. We're not just a store, we're a haven for people. Oh, and Larry Porter came in and told me about his proposal, because I guess he also heard the rumors."

"Oh, Megan..."

"Look, I know you work like a dog, so let me help. Stop being such a control freak. I'm perfectly capable of doing payroll and bills, you don't have to get Lucy to do that. I could do so much more. You know I went to the revitalization meeting for you the other day."

Oh, she'd forgotten about that, too.

Now Megan explained to her that she'd been researching other towns just like Warwick, with struggling downtowns that were competing with malls, and that they were sharing ideas on Facebook and Twitter.

"I told them at the meeting that what we really need," Megan said, "is to find some businesses that will bring customers downtown. Things you can't get from the box stores or the internet. Of course that ass Eddie Meeker had piped up 'What can't you get from box stores or the Internet?' I told them ice cream, for starters. A Facebook friend in New Jersey told me they just got an old-fashioned ice cream parlor on their Main Street, and even though there's a Dairy Queen out by their mall, people are walking into town now and lining up for this ice cream. Maybe we can get Bellevale Farms to open a stand here in town."

"Megan, I can't tell you how impressed I am." And she hadn't uttered a single "feck" or "brilliant."

"I want to get an MBA."

Ruth looked at her. "I can truly see you running a big corporation one day. Or starting up the next Google—"

"Are you kidding? I don't want to run any big corporation. I want to run a bookstore."

"The world of books is changing, you know, more each year now than it has in probably the past five centuries," Ruth cautioned. "Sometimes it scares me. A hundred years from now, will a book as we know it, with a cover and bound paper pages, even exist?"

"It has to. I mean, I love technology, don't get me wrong, but that's one of the things I find exciting and challenging, finding ways to keep real books alive. Oh, and I almost forgot. We're going to be able to sell e-books thanks to Google! We can start going after that market, Ruth. I want to be in on this new era of bookselling." Megan paused and shrugged. "I have no idea how it's going to happen, but I'm going back to school and then I want to buy your store. So...do you think you could hang in there a few more years?"

She looked into Megan's young face, filled with excitement, and promise. Megan sat there not moving, waiting for an answer. As Ruth looked around, her mind racing, her eyes roaming from the scuffed pine floors to the old windows that rattled in the wind, she knew what her answer should be.

"I'd probably work for free if you couldn't pay me," Megan said, breaking the long silence.

Ruth stood up suddenly and turned to her. "Don't be ridiculous. You know I would never allow that."

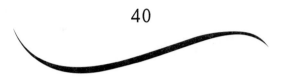

40

A WEEK AFTER SHE LEFT TO END HER MARRIAGE, Lucy flew back and headed straight to Warwick to see how Ruth was. But the moment Ruth opened the door and pulled her into a hug, a wave of panic hit her in the chest. She'd made a terrible mistake. It wasn't here she needed to begin. It was with Colin. Because if she didn't handle this right, in the long run Ruth might think badly of her. She couldn't bear that.

"I'm so glad to see you," Ruth said, leading her inside.

"You seem much better," Lucy managed, her voice sounding shaky. She cleared her throat, forcing herself to relax.

Ruth looked rested, the worry lines softened around her eyes, and even a hint of color in her cheeks.

"I got bored and sat in the sun a few afternoons. It felt heavenly. And I think I've made up for a year's worth of sleep."

"You mean you're not going stir crazy yet?"

"Of course I am," she laughed. "I can't wait for my sentence to be up."

The smile disappeared as Ruth realized what she had said. Lucy looked at her with raised eyebrows, glad to be focusing on her. Despite a prickle of guilt, she realized she needed to keep steering the conversation that way.

"I'm going to see Thomas in a few days, although no one knows about him yet."

"Really? I think that's wonderful!"

"We'll see." It seemed she didn't want to really talk about Thomas.

Lucy followed Ruth through the kitchen, where they grabbed a pitcher of iced tea and glasses, then down the back porch steps. They sat at an old wooden picnic table.

"So you've made peace with closing the store, it seems?"

Ruth put the pitcher down and looked across the yard for a moment. "I thought I had."

"I'm sorry, Ruth."

"Don't be. I think sometimes we need to lose something, or almost lose it, to realize how much we take it for granted. As your husband obviously did.

And Gloryanne with Colin."

Her unease grew at the mention of Gloryanne, who along with Ruth obviously knew nothing about Colin's feelings for her. That before she left, he'd made them clear. He was waiting for her to return, free. But before Lucy could respond, Ruth continued talking.

"I'm not ready to retire. And I don't want to give up that part of my life just yet. I thought I had to, but maybe I just need to believe a little more. You've had a lot to do with that."

"Me? I don't understand."

"I've watched you over these past months going after your dream—getting your book out there. Refusing to take no for an answer. Pounding the pavement going from store to store, fighting to get reviews on the internet and in newspapers. And by the way, the book clubs here are raving about you, telling their friends and fellow book clubs, so expect more to come."

"Really? Ruth, that is so exciting. You know I've done some meetings over my web cam, and a few by speaker phone. I'm getting better. Not so defensive when they ask questions."

"Well, there's more," Ruth said, her smile turning joyous. "As you know, we've got the anniversary coming up and Megan's been putting together some statistics. It turns out," she paused for a dramatic breath, "your novel is The Book Lover's top selling paperback this year."

"Are you serious, Ruth?"

"Of course I am. You've outsold our paperback New York Times bestsellers, in fact."

"Oh my God. I can't believe it."

"Well, when you go to the convention next week, make sure you tell every bookseller."

"Oh, Ruth. How can I ever repay you?" Suddenly her little project at the cabin didn't seem nearly enough.

Ruth held up her hand, shushing her. "I want to thank you. I was starting to tell you that when I thought of everything you're doing to make your dream come true, it inspired me. I don't want to give up the store, if it's at all possible. I've got some irons in the fire, and let's just say by the time the convention is over I hope to have things worked out."

"That's wonderful, Ruth, because honestly I can't imagine the store without you. Or you without the store."

"Me either. Anyway, enough about me, tell me about everything with your husband."

Lucy hesitated, wishing she could just tell her the truth, all of it. She couldn't stand keeping things from her, even for a few days. But until Colin knew, she had to wait because that could change everything. And then she looked at Ruth, who was pouring more tea. Why was she so afraid? Ruth was the kindest, most compassionate woman she'd ever met.

"Mom?"

They both turned to see Jenny coming out the back kitchen door with her daughters.

"We made you a cake, Grammy," they said in unison, and she saw that Jenny was holding a glass plate with an angel food cake topped with strawberries.

"We picked the strawberries ourselves at the beginning of the summer," the younger one, with dark pigtails, exclaimed, "and Mommy froze them."

Jenny then introduced Emma and Olivia.

"Mrs. Barrett writes books," she told her girls. "She's one of our favorite authors."

They gave her shy smiles and Lucy stood, realizing that this was a perfect excuse to leave. "Why don't I let you enjoy your visit with your granddaughters." Now she could make things right with Colin first.

"Don't worry, I'm not going anywhere," Ruth said with a chuckle. "But you are and you've just returned, so I'm sure you're exhausted. Why don't we just catch up when you get back from the convention? Then I'll hopefully have news for you, too."

"That's just perfect."

Pulling away, Lucy couldn't help remembering that long-ago morning after she'd slept at Ruth's, a stranger then, and driven this same route toward Main Street, the trees just budding with green leaves. She'd been a quivering mess of uncertainty. Now in the lushness of summer's end, the pots on Main Street bursting with geraniums and purple petunias, she was a different woman.

A few minutes later she pulled into the municipal parking lot, only to find it full. As she turned to search for a spot along the street, she glanced over at The Book Lover and froze. She'd come to see Colin, who she knew was working, only there was Gloryanne walking inside. Her fingers tapped the steering wheel. She needed to tell Colin the truth, as soon as possible. But obviously this wasn't the time, or place. She put her blinker on and drove away.

SHE SAT ON THE PORCH FOR HOURS, WAITING FOR COLIN to return. It was a perfect summer day, puffy white clouds scattered across a wide blue sky, all of it, including the circle of rolling green mountains, reflected in the mirrored surface of the lake. She thought about a hike to calm her nerves, but didn't want to chance missing him. Finally she heard the crunch of tires and a moment later his Jeep slowed to a halt in the driveway next door. She got up and stood there a moment, her nerves vibrating. She walked over just as he lowered himself into his wheelchair.

He looked up at her. "Hey," he said, without smiling.

"Hi."

"I'm surprised to see you here."

"I just got back a little while ago."

"Packing up again?"

"Not yet. Look, Colin, I know I said I'd be back in a few days, and maybe I should have called to explain, but—"

He put up a hand, stopping her. "Good luck with all that, I'm glad things worked out. Have a safe trip back."

"I'm leaving again to go to the convention. Where did you think I was going?"

"Back to your husband, of course. I understand he didn't want a divorce after all."

Ruth must have told him. That had never occurred to her, fool that she was.

He turned his chair and began pushing himself toward his cabin.

"Wait." She grabbed the back of his chair, but was unable to stop it and ran in front of him and knelt down, blocking his way. They were at eye level. "Colin, I'm sorry I didn't call or e-mail but—"

"You don't have to explain."

"Yes I do."

"Look, Lucy," he said, and his voice softened a bit, "this isn't a game. I know things got …close between us. But maybe this is for the best. I can never give you—"

"Shut up," she interrupted.

He gave her a startled look.

"I'm sorry, I didn't mean to say that, but I need you to listen. Obviously your mother told you what happened. And I should have called you myself, but I didn't because, well, honestly I just didn't want to involve you. It was something I had to take care of myself, without distraction. And in the end, it was clear to me." She took a deep breath. "I'm here because...I want to be with you."

He looked out at the lake, saying nothing.

"I know it will never be like other relationships, but I want to..." She paused, then took his hand. What did she really say here? How much could she promise? "I want to see if this can work."

"And your husband?"

"I love David. And I always will. We shared fifteen years, and a son. But I can tell you what I know now, and what I think I've known all along, that it's been over for a long time."

When she had fallen into bed with David, it felt as if they were drowning, clinging to each other with tears and a frenzied need to somehow connect. But minutes later, as she lay beside him catching her breath, her mind coming back into focus, she'd felt as if she'd betrayed Colin.

For days afterward, she was unable to forgive herself, and yet she wavered in her decision with David, out of guilt and obligation. It was when she popped in to visit her writing friend Tia at the assisted living complex, then spilled her guts after Tia asked what was wrong, that she finally realized that what happened wasn't so extraordinary. Tia reminded her of war stories, when perfect strangers found themselves having sex in bomb shelters, desperate to reaffirm life somehow. Then they both recalled someone in a workshop joking about her memoir, where she wrote about divorce sex, that it was even more intense than make-up sex. Tia told her to forgive herself, and she had, finally. Somehow for her it was part of the letting go.

But she wasn't going to tell all of that to Colin. It wasn't necessary, and would probably hurt him. What was important was to convince him of her true feelings.

"I married David," she said then, "for the kind of life I always wanted, the kind my mother always urged me to go for: security, a home, a stable future. And I did love him, but not the way I really should have."

Maybe it was the time and distance apart, maybe it was being with Colin, but she'd finally admitted to herself what she'd always really known—that she'd never loved David in the way she'd once loved Jamie. Nor did she feel the same passion and physical need that she now felt for Colin. But it wasn't just physical, there was some kind of bond between them that was inexplicable.

"Well, I guess I'm about as far in the opposite direction of security as you could get," he said, giving her an almost fierce look.

"I don't care. I'm ready to take that risk." But her heart thundered in her chest, thinking of Gloryanne, who was so beautiful, wondering if she'd waited too long to tell him.

"You're free?"

She looked into those light blue eyes and nodded.

He pulled her up and onto his lap, wrapping her in his arms. She buried her face in his neck, breathing him in as his own warm breath filled her ear, hushing the white lie that now hung between them.

41

THERE WAS SOMETHING BOTH THRILLING and terrifying about what she was doing. But Ruth kept telling herself this: what did she really have to lose? When you think you're dying, nothing else matters but living. Now that the fluid had all but disappeared, now that her strength was coming back, she had the rest of her life ahead of her. And with that realization—and Thomas's return phone call finally—came a giddy rush of exhilaration. It seemed that anything was possible if only she dared to reach for it.

She sat rocking on the porch now. Bolts of golden light lit the far corner of the front yard and she realized the sun had shifted recently, lower in the sky by a few degrees. Each year as she turned the calendar page to September, it was as if someone sent Mother Nature a reminder, and a sudden nip of coolness began to descend in the evenings. The light and the sporadic chill meant autumn wasn't far off.

Thomas had called her back after she'd all but given up on hearing from him again. Who could blame him? But he'd been apologetic, explaining that he'd been working as many hours as he could, and had started his class at the local community college. No one ever called him, so he never really noticed that his phone battery had died. What he didn't say, what she knew, was that he'd given up on hearing from her.

She told him she thought he'd moved back to Albany after getting that last letter, but he'd explained that it was simply a farewell trip of sorts, closing out a bank account, tying up some loose ends from his past.

"It just seemed time to wipe the slate clean and start over here. I also felt like I needed to let you off the hook. I didn't think I'd been fair after thinking about what I'd asked of you."

"Well… I'm glad you came back."

That night they'd talked for over an hour, and each day since. On the phone, as with their letters, they were able to reach beyond the barrier of what lay between them—his crime—and find that comfortable place again where they could talk openly. They discussed everything from the wonder of the night sky—which he said everyone should be required to go outside and see at least once a week—to the sometimes difficult adjustments to his new life in Pine Island. When they hung up that night, she'd gone out to the back of her yard, sat on the old bench, and gazed above for a long time at the velvety blackness glittering with millions of stars. She spotted the constellations she once knew so well from her walks to the barn in the dark—Orion's belt, Cassiopeia, the glittering jewel of Venus, and then a gorgeous half moon ascending above her house. She was filled with awe. She imagined Thomas doing the same thing at that same moment, and felt like a teenage girl.

"At night sometimes I feel like walking for miles, just because I can, you know? But that probably wouldn't be a smart thing to do," he admitted during their last call. He had to be careful, he'd explained, avoid anything that might cause him suspicion, because of his parole. One stupid thing could undo him, which made him extremely nervous. A few weeks ago, a woman accused him of shortchanging her at the pump, and as she got louder and angrier, he'd felt as if his blood was draining from his body. He knew she was wrong, or lying, but he just gave her the money. He'd had a number of "driveaways," cars that gassed up then drove off without paying. He didn't even tell the owner, just put the money in himself.

"I'm afraid word might be getting out that I'm an easy target."

"That's not fair."

"Ruth, I'm not about to take any chances. Besides, who ever said life was fair? I just think I need to find something else really soon."

"Well, you shouldn't have to live like that."

"It still beats where I spent the past ten years," he said with a chuckle.

She asked him, finally, the thing that had been bothering her for a long time. "Thomas, where did you get the gun?"

She could hear the long sigh over the phone before he answered. "I told you my parents were very old school. My father always kept a gun in the store, just in case. It was so ancient it never even occurred to me where he might've gotten it all those years ago. But it had never been registered, which of course didn't help my case."

"I see."

"Really, Ruth?"

Now she hesitated, thinking about her own parents and grandparents who, as farmers, also often lived by their own ways. "Yes, Thomas, I do."

And then she changed the subject. Of course they talked about books each night. He didn't have a TV, which he confessed he really didn't miss, and he spent his hours off reading. There was no bookstore in Pine Island, so he went to the library every few days.

"I'm reading a lot of memoirs, and classics, too. You were right about Hemingway, I really like him. His style is so simple he makes it look easy. But I know that's not the case. When I get a permanent place, I think I'm going to build myself a library, a room filled with books where I can just sit and read." And then she heard him laughing. "Who would have thought I'd ever say something like that?"

Last night he asked if she felt well enough yet for a visit. After a long pause she said yes. He told her not to do a thing, he'd bring dinner. She'd taken a long bath, spent time on her hair, which she decided to leave down with the sides swept back in antique tortoise shell combs she'd treated herself to decades ago and couldn't remember the last time she'd used. And she felt... something new. A flush of excitement.

From the corner of her eye she caught a movement and turned. He'd taken the bus and now he was coming up the street with a bag in his hand, wearing nice brown pants and a white button down shirt. He was whistling, and it struck her that he looked as if he were any man on this street returning home after a day at work. A moment later he glanced up and saw her on the porch. He stopped, then his face broke into a shy smile.

PERHAPS IT WAS TOO MUCH EXPECTATION. Perhaps it wasn't possible for anything to live up to what they'd fantasized, each of them over the long lonely nights of the past five years. From the moment they walked into her house and sat at the dining room table, with her mother's old crystal candlesticks lit, awkwardness descended upon them that seemed impossible to undo.

"I'm glad it's not so hot out," she said inanely, as he pulled cartons from the bag.

"I hope the food is good," he said, opening the fried rice, as she uncovered the Kung Pao chicken.

"Their food is usually wonderful," she said.

Then silence. They each filled their plates. He picked up his fork, waiting, while she unwrapped her chopsticks.

"Ruth," he finally said, as they both looked at their plates of food. "How many times have you read Gatsby?"

"Oh, probably a dozen or so."

"I've only read it twice. But I read it so slowly I think I've probably got it memorized."

She nodded and couldn't help thinking of when Gatsby, after waiting years to see Daisy again, finally met her for a cup of tea at Nick Carraway's cottage.

As if he were reading her mind, Thomas said, "Do you remember the scene where Nick watches Gatsby looking at Daisy, and is surprised to see the expression of bewilderment on Gatsby's face? He wonders how Daisy could ever live up to Gatsby's expectation? I'm afraid..." His words ran out, and he sat there shaking his head.

A tender laugh escaped her. "Oh, Thomas, I've thought the same thing. I'm the creation of my letters, as are you. For five years we've talked mostly of books."

"It's more than books, Ruth," he said very quietly, looking at her intensely.

"I know."

"I'm not a very educated man," he said with a worried look. "To be honest, Ruth, I'm almost embarrassed to admit this, but before prison, I didn't really read much."

"Oh?"

"I never really stopped long enough to take the time. Truthfully, I was never much of a student, and I didn't like what I *had* to read. But being in prison, there was nothing else to try to stay involved in the outside world, so I started picking up books."

"And the first one you read was *Outlander* and you couldn't believe that suddenly you felt as if you were living in 18th century Scotland."

He smiled in astonishment.

"You told me that at our very first book meeting. I couldn't forget because as you found out, it was one of my favorite books, too."

He picked up his fork and took a bite of food, as she dug in with her chopsticks. He let out a long moan of pleasure. "I haven't had good Chinese food in...well, you know. I missed out on so much when I was free. I'm almost embarrassed to admit this, but I had an easy life and I was never very ambitious. But now, I don't want to miss anything."

"I know what you mean. Now that I'm feeling better, I feel like I have this second chance at life."

"I bet you can't wait to get back to the store. You must really miss it."

"I do. I'm going back tomorrow."

"You don't look happy, though."

"The morning I left the hospital, I decided I was giving up the store."

He put his fork down. "You can't be serious. Listen, if it's money—"

But she put a hand up, stopping him. "Let's not go there right now, okay?"

He hesitated, then nodded. They ate in silence for a few moments.

"Were you ever married?" she asked, wondering why it had never occurred to her before.

He smiled slowly, then shook his head. "Engaged twice, actually. But in the end neither one felt right and we broke it off."

"What did you do for fun?" she asked.

"Running your own business—just my mom and me after a while—there's never much time off." And then he looked at her and laughed. "But I guess you know about that. Really there were just Sundays, and Saturday nights. But most Saturday nights I was pretty worn out. On Sundays I'd go watch a ball game or play cards. Nothing particularly exciting. Or intellectual. You know how it is when you're young, and you've got money in your pocket. The years begin to race by and before you know it, you're not so young anymore."

"What happened to your parents' business?"

"After my mother died it was sold, along with the building. I got a little nest egg from it I've been hanging on to, just in case. No one's particularly eager to hire an ex-con, that's why I'm all the way out in Pine Island. The owner had a kid who got in trouble years ago, and my parole officer knew him, so he was okay with it. I'm not living there anymore, though. I found a rooming house not too far away and I'm paying a bit more than everyone else, so she was willing to have me for a while. We're going month to month, so we'll see. A simple, boring life, but I'm not complaining."

"Are there things you can't do?"

"I can't leave the state. I have to report to my parole officer every few weeks. I can't move without notifying him, or change jobs. It's kind of like being a teenager again. And I need to live a squeaky clean life, which is scary, because I told you about some of the problems I've had at the garage. But I'm trying not to dwell on things that could go wrong." He let out a long sigh. "You know, it took me a long time to forgive myself. For what I did to my mother, which in the end was worse than her being robbed in the first place. For ruining my own life. I wasn't a bad person, Ruth, I hope you can believe that. I wish there was some way I could prove it to you."

"I think sometimes, Thomas, good people make bad choices."

"It's funny, but that's what my parole officer said to me." There was a long pause, then he said, *"In truth the prison, unto which we doom ourselves, no prison is..."*

"That's Whitman," she said, stunned.

"You mentioned once he was your favorite poet. I can't say I understand everything I read of his, but there were a few that hit me. That line, in particular."

"It's so true. How many of us make our own prisons, then live our lives within those walls."

She looked at him sitting across from her, the candlelight flickering across his face, his brown eyes filled with caring and expectation. Was she going to continue living in the prison of her own past? She reached across the table and he looked down at her hand, then slowly his own hand drifted across the tablecloth until their fingers touched. Then he took her hand, and held it, squeezing, smiling.

It was all there in his eyes, his affection, his kindness, the promise of a future. And with it the realization that had been swirling in her head for days now. It was time to really let go of the past.

So she began to tell him everything.

42

THE DAYS THAT LED UP TO THE CONVENTION were busy ones for Lucy. Several nights each week were usually taken up with book club meetings, either in person or via Skype. In the brochure she was crafting to take to the convention she'd excitedly added to the cover: *Now With 30 Book Clubs in 10 States!* Inside she put a brief summary of the novel, along with her growing bookseller quotes and reviews. She was going to have five hundred printed up to give out at the convention.

Each day she also surfed the web for more book bloggers and sites where she could get some publicity, if someone was willing to read her book. Every once in a while she'd Google her name or title, amazed to find it mentioned in chat rooms and online book sites she'd never heard of, wondering how they'd heard of her. It was thrilling to see that word was spreading.

She went back to The Raptor Center often with Colin to check on their wounded eagle's progress. And he was making some improvement. Just yesterday Kit again tried to spread his wings, and after releasing his talons from the branch finally lifted in the air, hovering a moment before landing awkwardly on the ground just a few feet from where he started. It wasn't much, but Colin's beaming smile was reward enough for her.

She worked furiously on the new novel, the scenes spilling from her as she stood in the shower each morning, or drove to bookstores, her recorder filling up until she could get back to the cabin and type them up. Part of it was spending so much time with Colin, and the other was that she was researching online what to expect if they decided to move forward and build a life together.

Colin wanted to read passages and hinted each morning after his swim with a teasing smile that he was ready to repay her for paddling beside him. But she kept telling him not yet, she wasn't ready. In truth, he didn't know what she was actually writing about, just that it somehow involved birds. She knew it would have to be finished before she'd feel comfortable letting him see it. Otherwise he might misconstrue everything.

* * *

THERE ARE MANY WAYS TO BE INTIMATE WITH A MAN who is paralyzed from the waist down, Lucy learned. They began slowly, hesitantly, and she was much more nervous than he was. That night, they sat on the dock watching the night sky unfold as the chorus of tree frogs, crickets and other night creatures began, a ritual she'd come to love. A glimpse of the beach on St. Augustine flashed across her mind and she knew in that moment she loved this as much. The wild, natural beauty of the northern woods, the hidden creatures of the night, even the coming winter, in which she envisioned the lake frozen over until it shone like glass, the ice-jeweled tree branches shimmering in the sun.

Earlier Colin had spent an hour loading firewood onto his deck, a task he had begun while she was away, in preparation for the coming cold weather. She watched from her cabin while he pushed himself up and down his deck, bringing logs and stacking them carefully on a wooden platform he must have had built so that no wood sat on the deck floor itself. Once again she was awed by his quiet strength, his will not to be daunted by the lowliest tasks.

Sitting beside him on a lawn chair now, she again thought he was like no one she'd ever met. Would she feel that way if she'd known him before? She wondered. Or was this strong yet tender man the result of his own loss, as she was the result of her own.

"Do you still miss the army?" she asked.

He took a long moment before answering. "Yes and no. I love living here, on the lake. But I miss my men. In the beginning I missed the structure, and the simplicity of the life. You never have much more than you can carry on your back."

She thought about all she'd gone without in the past months, and not missed at all.

"I don't miss the fear, for myself or one of them, that this day or hour might be your last. I don't miss having to aim a rifle at someone, or the God-awful sand down your neck, in your eyes. I surely don't miss the smell of garbage."

He paused and looked up for a long moment. They were watching the nearly full moon, hoping to see birds making their way across the sky in the dark. Earlier Colin had explained that once migration began, which for some birds was already starting, they would fly day and night. And if you watched the moon carefully enough, you could see their silhouettes across its bright expanse as they winged past. Lucy was enthralled, having already spotted half a dozen.

"I never intended to make the army a career," Colin continued after a while. "Not in the beginning. I just figured I'd straighten myself out and grow up. I was kind of lost when I graduated high school and to be truthful, I didn't want to be like my old man. I loved him and there were a lot of good things about him, but Warwick is a small town. I heard the stories as I got older. I knew he cheated on my mother, and I knew there was a bit of that wild streak in me. I can't imagine how that hurt her and...that's why I wanted to wait for your divorce, you know?" He turned to her and smiled, as a ripple of unease swept through her.

A wisp of cloud drifted across the moon, and they watched the stars come out, one by one, as he talked softly, the trees and houses mere shadows in the distance. She could tell him the truth now, that David thought she was being foolish. That with a little more time she'd come to her senses. But she knew in her heart it was he who would come to his senses and realize it wasn't love, but once again responsibility, and obligation, that was fueling his determination. Her attorney assured her that he could only delay things a while longer.

"I started as an Army Ranger," Colin said, hushing her thoughts, "with a three-year tour, but after serving in Desert Storm, I reenlisted twice more. I knew it was hard on my mother, but after a while I felt like I was right where I always belonged. I got to see the world. And I felt good, proud to serve my country. Then 9/11 happened, and I just couldn't leave after that. I was a soldier, it was the thing that defined me."

"You don't feel any bitterness about what happened?"

In the darkness he shook his head. "We all took risks, every time we left the blast zone. You lived in constant fear of being the next guy hit. But it could have been worse for me. I told you about the guys who got their heads blown apart. I saw too many of those, and if they make it home, somebody has to give up their life to care for you because you're little more than a vegetable. Anyway, I don't have it so bad. I can take care of myself. I have a pretty good life. The army sends me money every month, so I don't have to worry about how I'll survive financially. Not a bad life, really." He turned and ran a finger down her cheek. "But then you came along and...now it's a whole lot better."

She smiled.

"There's a lot you don't know about me, Lucy. A lot you should know."

"I realize that and...I guess I could say the same about myself."

"Why don't we take it slow, okay?"

She nodded.

He brought her hand to his mouth and opened it, kissing her palm softly, his lips brushing a path to her fingers, which he kissed one by one as her eyes closed.

"When I dream, I'm always the way I was before, as if the accident never happened," he whispered. "That's how I feel with you."

Then he tugged her hand, to make her stand, which she did, understanding his signals already. She followed him into his cabin, where he turned out the lights, one by one, and by the glow of just a few candles, they lay on his bed and he held her full length against him, as the blood rushed to her middle. A moment later, he let go and slowly unbuttoned her blouse, kissing her collar bone, the tender hollow at the base of her neck, while a finger traced the curve of breast above her bra.

He began to kiss her on the mouth, longer, deeper, with a fierce hunger that matched her own. Her hands ran up and down his back, under his shirt, not knowing what would come next, but knowing that it no longer mattered. He stopped and looked deep in her eyes, then gently turned her around, her back to his chest. As they lay there in the candlelight, he whispered her name over and over again while his hands loved her as his body couldn't.

43

HALFWAY THROUGH HER DRIVE TO THE CONVENTION in Phila-delphia, Lucy found herself missing Colin already. The past days had been magical, each pierced with the clarity and beauty of simply being alive. It was strange, but it felt as though after all the struggles in her life, she was where she was meant to be. David was right about one thing—you couldn't go back in life, you had to go forward. Once she let go of the past and stopped trying to hold back, she knew with certainty that she was in love with Colin. She had probably begun to fall in love with him in that first moment she saw him rising out of the lake, naked, beautiful, imperfect.

Last night they'd gone further in their intimacy, to a place she wasn't certain was even possible. He seemed uneasy about her leaving again, and she assured him that this time there would be no delays coming back. He cooked a beautiful candlelit dinner while she readied for the trip. Afterward, as she lay on his bed waiting for him, he came out of the bathroom with nothing but a towel across his lap. As he swung himself up and onto the bed and then turned to face her, for the first time since that morning he emerged out of the lake, she saw all of him. And she was surprised to see that he was erect as any normal man.

"The miracle of modern medicine," he whispered with a smile.

He pulled her to him, her skin igniting as it touched his, their bodies as close as it was possible to get without melting into each other. Then he slowly pulled her on top of him, their eyes locked as he held her above him, a moment more erotic than anything she'd ever experienced. Watching him as he watched her, his light blue eyes filled with wanting.

"Can you feel this, any of this?" she whispered.

"There's something, like a shiver that runs through you. But believe me, I'm enjoying this every bit as much as you are."

Then he took her hands, clasping her fingers, and she held on tightly as she moved for them both, rising, soaring, then finally tumbling back to earth.

As they lay there afterward, he asked, "Can you see a future for us?"

She opened her mouth to speak, but he put a finger to her lips.

"Don't answer that now."

She'd sat up. "Why not?"

He didn't speak, but she knew what was going on. Although she'd told him that she wanted to tell Ruth about them, because she was still uneasy about all she'd been holding back, he'd asked her not to yet. Despite her own certainty, she knew Colin still harbored doubts about her being able to commit. How could he not, after Gloryanne?

Lucy was hoping that by the time she returned from the convention, David would finally give in and she could be open about everything. Because she was also tortured by holding back about that.

Finally he said, "This time with you here, it's been like..."

"A dream?"

He nodded.

"I know. It's like this magical place apart from the rest of the world."

"But there is a real world out there. And maybe yours is going to change."

"What do you mean?"

"I hear the buzz in the store. And I've heard customers coming in and talking about how wonderful your book is." He shook his head, as if he couldn't believe she didn't get it. "Lucy, one day soon you may find a publisher knocking on your door, offering you a whole new world of possibilities."

"From your lips to God's ears," she laughed, but she could see he was serious. "If by some miracle that happened, none of this would change."

Then he said that while she was gone he was going to talk to Gloryanne one more time and hopefully convince her that she needed to finally move on. She was still calling him, he said, and he felt bad for her, but he'd been up front with her for weeks now. Again, that little dagger of guilt jabbed at her. Like Ruth, Gloryanne had no idea about her and Colin.

"I think she still loves you."

He looked at her quizzically. "You've heard that from Jenny, no doubt, or my mother. She doesn't love me. She's just confused and guilty. It's time to let go."

"Was she your first love?"

"The only one, really. Until now."

"And if you hadn't met me, do you think you'd be with her?"

He shook his head. "Why is it we always seem to be talking about me? What about you, have you let go?"

"I didn't think I could ever get over losing Ben. And truthfully, I didn't want to. As long as I was immersed in grieving, he was somehow still with me. It felt wrong to let it go. As if I were somehow letting *him* go." She felt the familiar sorrow building in her throat. "But after a while, I learned that there's a limit to how much grief you can endure. One day you wake up and you just want to be, no you *need* to be, normal, and have a day like everyone else. So you let it go for five minutes, then an hour. Gradually you let go of what you think you never could, until one day there are more normal stretches than grieving ones."

Colin's fingers had stroked her hair over and over as she talked, a soothing gesture, and she'd felt like a little girl whose bruises were fresh, as were her tears. She saw tears in his own eyes.

"Of course you understand all this," she said, knowing that's how he'd finally made peace with his own loss. "But there's still the guilt, that one day I won't think of him at all, for a day, or two days, and it'll be as if he never existed. I see now that's what held David and me together. And finally really opening up completely when I was there, about everything, enabled me to see that it was okay to let go."

"It must have been painful, all that talking about such a sad time. I understand how he could have a hard time letting go."

"It was painful, but...he's doing better."

David seemed to be making strides letting go of so many things, except for her. She'd e-mailed him several times, assuring him she wasn't going to change her mind. He thought that deep down she was still angry and hurt, that it was only natural it would take time for her to trust him again. What he couldn't understand, he kept writing, was why she was unwilling to just give it a little time.

"I think when you have a long history with someone, as you and I both had," Colin said then, breaking into her thoughts, "it's easy to just hang on. You get used to the familiar, you know? And I think that's what's going on with Gloryanne."

He'd pulled her close, holding her for a long time, and she couldn't help remembering what Ruth had said way back in the beginning when she was falling apart. That the Chinese word for crisis has two characters: danger and opportunity. Maybe you needed to face some kind of crisis to really open your eyes. If it hadn't been for losing Ben, she might not have rediscovered her love for writing. While she'd have given up everything to keep Ben, there wasn't a choice.

And if David hadn't lied and betrayed her, she wouldn't have found Colin. If he hadn't been paralyzed, Colin would no doubt have been married to Gloryanne by now.

She'd pulled away from him in that moment and looked deep into his eyes, feeling that somehow, everything had turned out as it was supposed to, despite the agonies along the way. That was life.

* * *

THE MOMENT SHE PULLED INTO THE HOTEL PARKING LOT for the convention, Lucy's nerves kicked into high gear. The lobby was crawling with people wearing name tags and she peered at them as she walked past, wheeling her huge suitcase stuffed with books. There were booksellers everywhere, but also well-known authors and publicists from some of the largest publishers in the world. They were clustered in groups, laughing and talking, and she suddenly felt like turning around and bolting.

This would be a hundred times worse than doing a book signing. She was walking into an inner sanctum of the publishing world, and to most of these people she'd be viewed as that most dreaded person—a self-published author. How was she going to go through with this? Simply walk up to people, introduce herself, and hand them her self-published book, along with her carefully crafted brochure? Suddenly that seemed like the most embarrassing thing in the world.

She checked in and headed to her room, passing the convention floor along the way. She stood there a moment, looking into the gargantuan room filled with tables and booths and stacks of books everywhere. In an hour she'd have to walk in there along with hundreds of others, and she almost laughed, picturing them all running in the other direction when they saw her. How she wished that Ruth was with her.

She went to her room on the twentieth floor, opened the drapes, then scanned the minibar. She grabbed a small bottle of Jack Daniel's because she was shaking so badly. Sitting on the edge of the bed, she took the tiniest of sips, with deep breaths in between, trying to calm down. Praying she could work up the nerve to go back down to the convention floor. When she finished the bottle, a warm buzz pulsed through her. Then her hand flew to her mouth, realizing she probably reeked like whiskey. Great, now she'd be seen as a self-published pariah AND a lush.

She went in the bathroom and washed her face with cold water, rinsed with mouth wash, then looked in the mirror. If Ruth were beside her she'd no doubt say: *You can do this, Lucy. You can. Your book is wonderful.*

And that's how she managed to get into the elevator, carrying a tote bag filled with books and brochures, with Ruth's voice echoing in her ear. *Your book is wonderful. Your book is wonderful. Your book is wonderful.*

Whatever happened next, she told herself, she'd get through it. More than anything, she longed to go back to Colin. She hoped it went smoothly when he talked to Gloryanne, that she could move on without too much pain. She seemed like a nice woman, and Ruth seemed fond of her. But more than anything, Lucy couldn't wait to go back and see Ruth again. She couldn't wait to tell her that she was in love with her son.

44

I N THE THIRTY YEARS SHE'D OWNED THE BOOK LOVER, Ruth had never been away from the store for more than a day, perhaps two. The first time she walked back through the door, she felt as if she were coming home. This had been her world for more than three decades, she thought as she opened the door and the bell tinkled cheerfully. This had been the center of her universe, the long shelves of books, readers drifting in and out over the course of a day, all the magic and discovery right here at her fingertips. It had been hers to share with the world.

Megan looked up from behind the counter and gave her a tight smile. "Welcome back, Ruth."

Before she could answer, she caught a movement in the back of the store.

"Hannah's packing up her things," Megan said.

She hadn't expected Hannah to be there, but this actually would be better. She could tell them all at once.

Ruth walked to the back and as she did, her mouth fell open in disbelief. The walls were now a bright cherry red, the black bistro tables covered with red and white checked table cloths, and of course the mirrors painted like windows overlooking the countryside. It was stunning, the entire area transformed to feel like a French café. Hannah sat at one of the tables, wrapping cups in newspaper and putting them in a box on the floor.

"Ruth, you're back," she said, standing and coming over to give her a hug. "You look better. Not so tired."

"I'm getting there," Ruth said. "What are you doing?"

Hannah said nothing for a moment. "I need to get back to the real world, as Eddie puts it. I didn't want to bother you while you were getting better, or burden you with my problems. I know you were just doing me a favor here. But I know you have to do what's right for you."

"What do you mean?"

"It's all over town, that you're going bankrupt and closing down."

Megan had been right. She'd bet money that Eddie was at the heart of it. But it didn't matter who'd started the rumors. The front door opened and she turned to see Harry walk in, then just behind him Kris. She hadn't asked Colin. She'd talk to him later.

"Wait here just a moment, Hannah," she said.

She walked to the front of the store where her three employees looked at her expectantly. How loyal they'd been all these years, working for a pittance, not just because of their love of books, but because of their devotion to her.

"How about we talk in the back, where we can sit down?"

She was startled to see Megan's lower lip begin to quiver. Kris and Harry just exchanged glances. Ruth locked the front door, and turned the open sign around.

A moment later, they sat with Hannah at two of the bistro tables.

"I missed all of you," she began, "and I can't thank you enough for pitching in even more while I was out sick. There's no way I can ever repay you for all that you've done for me, as well, over the years." She hesitated a moment. "I can tell by the looks on your faces that you know what I'm about to say."

There was a heavy silence. It reminded her of being in school years ago, after someone was severely disciplined, the pall of discomfort, and how no one could make eye contact.

"That I'm in financial ruin, that I'm closing the store, and that I'm giving up." She took a deep breath. "Well, you're wrong."

Megan looked up as if she'd heard a gunshot. Kris and Harry exchanged puzzled looks. Hannah frowned skeptically, wondering if she'd heard right.

"When Megan came to see me right after I got home from the hospital, I was exhausted, and yes, I felt defeated. But she said something else that got me to thinking—that I'm too much of a control freak. Well, she's right. As the days went on and I started feeling better, and getting really bored," they giggled at that, and she could see their faces brightening, "I realized that the one thing I never really controlled was this store. Because I didn't own it. If I want to keep going here, that has to change. So...I'm going to buy the building."

"But..." Hannah's voice faded, unable to voice what she knew they were all thinking.

"But how can I buy the building when I've barely been able to keep the store afloat?"

They all nodded.

"I'm selling my house. I'm going to live in the apartment upstairs. And I'm going to fix this place up. Maddy Akin gave me a price on my house—what it's worth if I do a little sprucing up, and I made Jeff an offer. Because the building is in such poor shape, my house, surprisingly, is worth more."

"What did he say?" Kris asked.

"Maddy convinced him to say yes, and to give me thirty days to sell my house. As we know, he's been thinking about selling, that's why he wouldn't renew our lease. And no one's going to offer him as much as I have, there are other buildings they can get for less. I'm his best bet."

"I just want to be clear, Ruth, you're not closing the store? For real?" Megan asked.

"For real. I'm making you assistant manager, Megan. I need to have some balance in my life. A little more life, a little less work. And I think you've got a good grasp on the future of bookselling."

"Oh, Ruth, I'm gobsmacked!" Megan jumped up and came over and hugged her.

"And Hannah," she said, when Megan stepped back, "please don't pack up. I know Megan will back me up on this. We can't be just a small bookstore anymore. You've got a real talent that's been untapped. And let's face it, in retail Christmas is around the corner, so let's start stockpiling Book Lover Gift Baskets. I'm hoping we have our best holiday season ever."

"Ruth," Kris said, standing and looking at her curiously. "What kind of medicine did they give you?"

Ruth looked at them all. "Nothing more than another chance at life."

* * *

WHILE SHE CLEARED THE COUNTERS IN HER KITCHEN that afternoon, Thomas began painting the cabinets. The old maple was chipped and scratched and Ruth had seen enough HGTV in the past to know Mandy was right—she'd make more by simply sprucing up a bit here and there. Thomas had jumped on board last night when she told him her plan to keep the store and buy the building. He was pretty handy with a paintbrush, he'd insisted, after painting everything that didn't move in prison during his time. Besides, she'd done so much for him over the years he wanted to do something for her. The old Ruth, the control freak, would have refused. She'd simply said "Thank you. I appreciate it."

Now as she packed up boxes of clutter, making her counters appear more spacious, Thomas stood on a ladder, brushing a soft antique white on the cabinet frames. It was going to transform the room, and she lamented that she hadn't done things like this sooner, so that she could enjoy them. But it didn't matter. She was more than ready to move on.

"Thomas, I've been meaning to ask you," she said casually, as she tucked her old blender into a cardboard box, "how old are you?"

All along, she'd assumed he was close to her age, but last night she'd really studied him, his hair not so severely short anymore, his face somehow softened since he left prison. He suddenly looked much younger.

"I'm fifty-seven."

She waited for him to ask her the same question, but he didn't. The radio played on in the background as she thought about this new information. He was nearly eight years younger.

"Do you really think age matters, Ruth?" She heard him coming down the ladder and turned to face him.

"I'm older than you. Not by a little bit."

"I don't care. We're both somewhere in late middle age. Isn't that close enough?"

She had to smile. "I could argue with that, but I won't. I like to fool myself that I'm still in that category."

"I remember when my grandmother turned eighty, she told me she still felt eighteen inside."

"I think my mother said something like that."

"I don't think we should argue with them."

The music changed suddenly on the radio, to an old Righteous Brothers song, "Unchained Melody," one of her favorites. Thomas reached over and turned up the volume. Then he turned to her and opened his arms.

"May I have this dance?"

"Oh..."

A beat later, she slowly walked into his arms. One hand took hers, his other circled her waist, pulling her toward him, then stopping at a respectable distance so their bodies weren't touching. Last night they'd held hands, but nothing more. Now as they swayed from side to side he drew her closer and she looked up to see him staring down at her.

"I've been wanting to kiss you, Ruth Hardaway, for years."

"Oh," she said again, her heart kicking into high gear as he lowered his mouth and touched her lips.

"Mom?"

They broke apart as the front door slammed, and she pushed Thomas back toward the ladder. A moment later Jenny was standing in the kitchen doorway.

Ruth turned to the box on the table, hiding her crimson face as she spoke. "Oh, honey, hi. I'm packing up some clutter, and this is Thomas. He's doing some painting for me."

A pause. "I see."

She heard Thomas climb down the ladder again—how had he gotten back up there so quickly? Just as she turned, he and Jenny were shaking hands.

"Mom, could I talk to you?" Jenny said then, and nudged her head toward the dining room.

Oh no. She hadn't wanted them to meet like this.

Once they were in the dining room, Jenny's smile disappeared and she looked at her mother with blazing eyes. Before Ruth could say a word, Jenny launched into a tirade about Lucy. And Colin. And the conversation she'd just had with Gloryanne.

Lucy, apparently, had been playing them all for fools.

* * *

ON THE SEAT BESIDE RUTH WAS THE BOOK she'd told Lucy about long ago, *Max Perkins, Editor of Genius*, that she'd finally ordered last week and had been anxiously waiting to give her. It was a valid excuse to drive out to the lake. She insisted to Jenny that there had to be a mistake. She was quite certain Lucy was reconciling with her husband. Even so, Lucy would never be so devious. She tried to calm herself as she drove the winding roads, remembering the last time she'd made this drive back in the spring for Bill's birthday. So much had changed in her life since then.

The wind kicked up suddenly and a few leaves fluttered to the road from the woods on either side of her. Already there was the occasional tree turning red or yellow. Soon Applefest would be arriving again, and then the anniversary celebration. And she'd be sharing all of it with Thomas.

Before she knew it she saw the flash of water sparkling through the trees and the road narrowed as she wound around the lake. Minutes later she pulled into the gravel drive, coming through the tunnel of pines, which swayed in the wind. She was relieved to see Lucy's car, having taken a chance she'd be back by now. She hadn't called ahead. She wanted to catch Lucy completely unawares.

Luckily Colin's car was gone. He spent Mondays at the VA.

She walked up the porch steps and knocked on the screen door. The inside door was wide open.

"Hello?" she called in, but could see that no one was inside. She turned and scanned the shoreline, but there was no sign of Lucy.

"Anybody home?" she called again as she pulled the screen open and poked her head inside. As her eyes adjusted to the darker room she saw pages all over the floor, obviously blown about by the wind coming through the open windows and door. She went inside and gasped out loud.

Everything was different—new curtains and slipcovers, the cabinets nearly all painted white, rugs and...she was flabbergasted. It was a horribly bold and thoughtless act. Lucy had apparently made herself quite at home without asking permission for anything.

"Lucy?" she called again and then bent down, gathering up pages into a messy pile and taking them to the kitchen table, which Lucy had moved to the front window. Setting them down, she realized this must be the manuscript for Lucy's new novel, which she'd also been secretive about. She began sorting through the pages then. When she put the first page on top, she couldn't help glancing at a paragraph.

Catherine looked up from her laptop and across the short stretch of sloping green lawn to the water's edge. A ripple caught her eye and she stared for a moment with a frown. Then, as if in a dream, a head surfaced through the dark lake, eyes closed, high cheekbones glistening, long hair slicked back as the man held his face to the sky. The shoulders broke through, followed by strong, muscled arms and Catherine wondered if this was in fact a god of nature emerging before her in the lake.

She imagined next a wide chest, shimmering with crystal beads of water, and she wasn't disappointed. As he continued to rise up out of the water, Catherine wondered if she hadn't crossed a dimension as she watched this man-god swim to the lake's edge. Instead of walking out of the water, he began to push himself with his hands and a moment later his withered lower half emerged and the beautiful man became...a beast. And damn her, she couldn't turn away. She sat there and stared, wondering what life was like for this man who was like a creature from a fairy tale.

The page fluttered to the floor. She'd kept insisting to Jenny that she had to be wrong, but now Jenny's angry insistence roared in her head. "Mom, she's going to leave one day soon. Gloryanne loves him and wants to marry him. They belong together. But he won't listen to her."

She leafed through more pages, skimming lines, stopping suddenly.

He came out of the bathroom with nothing but a towel across his lap. A moment later, he pushed himself onto the bed and gathered her into his arms. They began to kiss and then he took both her hands, clasping them tightly, lifting her above him, and she couldn't help but think of the eagles for a brief instant, clasping talons in their aerial ballet as they plunged to earth, and she felt him filling her, miraculously, their own fingers entwined as they soared and circled, then tumbled, falling, falling toward the earth.

Dear God, Jenny was right. Lucy was having an affair with Colin, right under her nose. She'd been too stupid to see a thing. Even worse, Lucy was using him to write this modern day fable of two lost souls, which thank God Jenny knew nothing about. And Colin, what was he thinking? Was he so flattered by the attention that he turned his back on someone who truly cared for him? She looked around the cabin, the scene of her own betrayal, and a familiar flash of anger raged up in her throat.

She was trembling so badly she had to sit. She stared out the window, determined to wait for Lucy for as long as it took.

45

COMING DOWN THE MOUNTAIN BEHIND THE CABIN after a long hike, Lucy stopped where the trees began to thin and looked at the world below. Above her branches swayed, the wind swishing through the leaves and blowing her hair in front of her face again. She held it back with both hands as she sat on a rock, catching her breath. At the bottom of the hill, on the far side of these woods, was her cabin, and to the right of it across the grass, Colin's. Just beyond that stretched the lake, looking like a shimmering blue jewel ringed by mountains, as it reflected the sky and hills around it. Closing her eyes, she sighed as the wind seemed to caress her face. She'd only been gone for a few days, but truly missed this place. And Colin.

She was completely wrung out from the convention, feeling like David pitted against the Goliaths of the publishing world. Although she came away with some sense of accomplishment, overall she was completely overwhelmed. Yes, little by little she was getting more bookstores on board, and readers, but there wasn't anyone in the publishing industry paying any attention to her book. And maybe they never would.

But as she sat there now, surrounded by such beauty, she consoled herself with this—if it never happened, if she completely gave up on the books, because she was nearly finished with a draft of the second—she would still have this. She could sit here and feel her soul soothed by the sounds of the trees in the wind, the smells of the ferns, the wild roses, and the earth itself. She could lay back and let the sun warm her face. Continue to dabble in poetry and write stories, for her own pleasure and no one else's. She was a writer, and always would be. Maybe she'd just continue in anonymity, like so many thousands of others. And that would be enough. Here, with Colin, she believed it could be.

Ironically, the best moment at the convention had to do with Ruth, who wasn't even there. And she couldn't wait to tell her about it. Heading back down the trail, finally, she spotted a car in her driveway, then realized it was Ruth's. What an amazing coincidence! She began to run.

When she rounded the cabin, she found Ruth sitting on the porch and stooped to give her a quick hug. "What a surprise! Come on in, I'll make tea."

"No, please don't go to the trouble. I can't stay long. I needed to get out and so I brought you something I promised you long ago," Ruth said, following her inside.

The moment Lucy walked in, her hand flew to her mouth. She hadn't finished painting, but everything else was in place. She turned, and saw Ruth looking at her.

"Oh, Ruth, I wanted to surprise you. It's not finished."

Ruth looked around, but her face barely changed. There was no look of appreciation, or joy, and Lucy realized in that moment perhaps she'd been presumptuous, and gone too far. Maybe Ruth wanted to keep the cabin just the way it was. The way the family remembered it.

"It's lovely," she said then, almost as an afterthought. "Now here, open this."

They sat on the couch and she opened the bag. *Max Perkins: Editor of Genius*. Thank you so much, Ruth. I remember you telling me how he helped some of the greatest writers of the last century. I'll start it tonight."

"I think you'll find it very enlightening," she said, and then smiled.

Lucy looked at her for a moment. Her face was flushed and Ruth seemed as if she was waiting for her to say something else.

"I also want to thank you for giving me your ticket and your room for the convention. I actually have some surprising news for you."

"Well, so do I, but you go first."

She had to stand so she could pace, suddenly filled with nervous energy again as she relayed everything. "Oh, Ruth, I was just terrified at first. But after a while, after I went in and just walked around, I realized everyone was doing the same thing, all the big publishers and authors—they were just hawking their books, like me. Of course the booksellers waited in long lines to meet the big authors and get signed copies of their books, and that's when it really hit me—I was way over my head. There was no way I could compete with that. I mean, the big publishers must've given away hundreds and hundreds of books."

"Yes, they do, because if the booksellers read them, they'll hopefully order them."

"So, I just kept walking around, right by the big displays, introducing myself to every bookseller that passed me, asking if they'd like to read my book, and showing them my brochure, with all of my quotes and statistics, especially that it was a book club pick in ten states and that I was the top selling paperback at your store."

Ruth was sitting there listening intently, her fingers twisting the straps of her purse, as if she were full of nerves herself.

"Don't get me wrong, it wasn't easy," Lucy went on. "There were booksellers that barely acknowledged me and others who thought I was gutsy. Then I met one of my mother's favorite authors, Adele Gray, and finally got up the courage to give her a book, figuring maybe she'd actually read it, or even give it to her agent—you know, that I'd finally make that connection I was hoping for. But after she took it, I actually saw her hand it off to someone else, laughing, and I felt kind of sick for a while. But then I saw the bookseller from Mendham, where David and I used to live, and who I'd e-mailed a handful of times with no response. He remembered me coming in and buying books years ago and invited me for a signing. I think I'll get others, but again, at least a handful asked me to send them copies and they'll put them out."

Ruth nodded. "That's wonderful."

She didn't tell the rest of it, how she'd been so down a few times she nearly left. How she imagined her book lost in the sea of tote bags, buried under bestsellers and the latest new works. She was too grateful to Ruth for the opportunity to sound like sour grapes.

"When I was alone in my room at night, I finally sat down and figured out how many books I've sold so far. Ruth, I've sold more than two thousand books already."

Ruth blinked, clearly surprised.

"That's a lot, isn't it?"

"Yes, considering that's not far from what the average literary novel does in a lifetime."

"But still, I couldn't get one publisher to take a copy there. They all kept saying to get an agent first. I keep thinking maybe I should try to find an agent again, but I can't bear the thought of another rejection. Although now I've got proof that my book has an audience. Plus all of these readers are waiting for my next book. I get e-mails all the time asking me when my next book is coming out."

"So tell me, what is your next book about?"

She stopped pacing then and turned to Ruth. She had a funny look on her face, and it occurred to her suddenly that Ruth was hurt. They'd shared so much and talked about all the books they read and loved, but Lucy hadn't told her a word about the new one; the book she'd been writing right here in the cabin that Ruth had been kind enough to let her use. If it weren't for Ruth, she knew there wouldn't be a new book.

"Well, the new book is very different from *A Quiet Wanting*," she began, suddenly really nervous, because she needed Ruth to know her relationship with Colin first, for her to understand the story. And she'd been planning to tell Colin as soon as he came home that night that it was time. She didn't want to hold back anymore, especially with Ruth. But in the excitement of seeing her, and of the big news she was about to tell her, she'd simply forgotten all of that. "Anyway, it's kind of a modern day fairy tale. I don't have a title yet, although I've been thinking about *Confessions of a Poet*, because my main character dabbles in poetry. And I want you to read it, Ruth, but not until it's done, okay?"

Ruth sat there, staring at her, her head tilted the way Colin always did, yet it was the first time she'd noticed.

"I've been running on and on about me, but Ruth, the really amazing part of the convention was you." She went over to her purse and pulled out an envelope. "This is your prize. You won the essay contest."

Ruth's mouth opened, but no words came out, and Lucy could see was floored. She handed her the envelope and Ruth held it in her trembling fingers, her face full of emotion.

"Because I went in your place, they let me bring it back. I think they thought I worked at the store, too. It's not a huge prize, but I know you've been trying to figure out a way to hang onto the store, and I hope it helps."

Ruth swallowed, and seemed to compose herself. "Well, this is amazing, but yes, it is just a drop in the bucket."

"Oh, Ruth, I'm so sorry." She must be closing the store, after all. How ironic to win now.

Ruth stood and walked over to the big window overlooking the lake. "It doesn't matter, really, because I figured out a way to make it all work. I've decided not to sell the store. I'm selling my house. And this cabin."

"Wow...I'm really glad, Ruth. I can't imagine the store without you, I..."

"There's more good news," she said, turning back now, a bright smile on her face. "Jenny and I are ecstatic because Gloryanne wants to marry Colin. Isn't it wonderful? We're all so relieved this is finally happening, because he shouldn't be alone. And they've loved each other since they were in high school."

She thought her legs might go out from under her. Lucy sat again on the couch, trying to maintain her composure. And her eyes landed on the manuscript for the new book, sitting next to her laptop. On the left of it, not the right, where she always set it.

"Ruth," she said, going to the table and picking up the manuscript. "This isn't what you think. Oh God, you can't believe—"

But Ruth was shaking her head, her eyes narrowed with disappointment. "What I believe, Lucy, is that I trusted you, with my most intimate thoughts and feelings. I opened my home and my life to you. And my family. When I asked you to keep an eye on Colin, this wasn't what I had in mind. But I think you know that."

A sickening dread overcame her as she stood there facing Ruth, her voice full of hurt and anger, this woman she loved like an older sister, or a best friend. Or even, at times, like a mother.

"Ruth, I wanted—"

"You deliberately kept it from me that you were having an affair with Colin."

"Ruth, I love him."

"But your husband, he still wants you back, doesn't he?"

"I...yes, he does, but—"

"And now it's clear to me why we conveniently never finished talking about your trip back to St. Augustine." There was a long pause. "You're not divorced, are you?"

And there it was, not quite a lie, but another sin of omission. It had seemed inconsequential, a technicality, because emotionally she was as good as divorced from David.

"We will be, very soon. I have to go back one more time...David...he knows I don't want to reconcile, and it's taking time for him to accept."

Her words died as Ruth picked up her purse. "Colin is at the VA and he won't be back until late tonight. I'd really appreciate it if you'd leave before he gets back here."

"But Ruth, I do love him, and I wanted to tell you. Colin didn't want us to tell anyone yet."

"Of course he didn't, Lucy, because it's a fling."

"Oh, Ruth, it's not like that, you have to believe me."

For a moment her face softened. "Look, Lucy, what you're doing here with my son isn't real. You haven't even been separated that long. You think I don't know what betrayal does to your heart? One moment you hate his guts and the next you'd do anything to have him want you again. How do you know you're over your husband so soon?"

She knew how painful this was for Ruth as her eyes filled with tears and she had to bite her lip to hold back hers.

"I was so foolish letting you stay here when you were nothing more than another wounded bird. How could he resist you? But Gloryanne has loved him for years, and he's loved her. Maybe they've had some rough patches, but who wouldn't under the circumstances? And here you come, an attractive stranger, someone who didn't have to deal with the trauma of his life changing, or the realities of what his future now meant, and suddenly life is exciting for him again. It's not that long since Colin's accident. I don't think he's thinking all that clearly."

"I was going to tell you everything, I swear."

"Does he know what this book you're writing is about?"

"I was waiting...until it was finished." Another sin of omission.

"You're not even divorced, you just admitted it. You're in no shape to make a commitment to Colin. Gloryanne is ready to give him a future. Do you want to destroy that chance? Are you that selfish?"

Hot tears slid down her cheeks as she shook her head.

"Please Lucy, he doesn't even know you're back yet. Just leave. I'll tell him that you're sorry, that things changed. Don't ruin this for him. He has the chance to be with the woman he's always wanted. She'll care for him. Your life is in turmoil right now. What if you change your mind next week, or next month? Gloryanne has been through it all and she's making this commitment with the full knowledge of what it entails. And if it weren't for you, they'd no doubt be planning a wedding right now."

"I would never do anything to hurt him, Ruth."

"But Lucy, you already have."

And then she was gone. Lucy sat on the couch, her breath coming in spurts, tears dripping onto the manuscript that lay on her lap, the words blurring until they were unrecognizable.

46

L UCY HAD KNOWN WHEN SHE MOVED INTO THE CABIN all those months ago that her stay there would be temporary. A stopping over on the uncharted road to her new future alone. How could she have had any idea how much would change during those months on this beautiful lake? Despite her initial anguish when she arrived, and all of the creature comforts she'd lived without, she couldn't remember a time she was happier.

Driving away, she knew she could return to Florida and pick up the frayed thread of her old life with David. It would have been so easy, because it's what he wanted. But she didn't. She drove to her mother's, surprising herself, and was in turn surprised to find them packing once again. Charlie, her mother told her with shining eyes, had invited them to come to Australia for six weeks. He even sent plane tickets. It was the trip of a lifetime, Artie chirped in. Two days later they were gone and she had the place, blessedly, to herself.

She tried to bury herself in work, as in the past, but it was impossible. The guilt over Ruth's accusations ate away at her at night when she lay in bed unable to sleep, imagining Colin's face when Ruth told him she'd gone. All she could remember was the look on his face when he said that their time together seemed like a dream. The more Lucy thought about it, the more she realized there was some truth in what Ruth said. With her, there was nothing for Colin to lose. With her, he discovered that intimacy could exist again. Perhaps he hadn't been able to take that step with Gloryanne, and now he could.

Then she remembered him asking, "Can you see a future for us?" Maybe he wanted her to say no. Perhaps that was the real reason he didn't want anyone to know about them.

In the long moments after Ruth walked out, she'd debated what to do. Wondering if she had the nerve to defy her and wait for Colin. It began to occur to her that perhaps she had been selfish, as Ruth accused. Colin filled the empty places inside of her, and she had come alive again at the lake. She'd been selfish in marrying David, knowing in the beginning she didn't really love him as she should have. But she'd wanted and needed him, and grew to love him. What if she'd done the same thing with Colin, without regard to his own future?

Images of him haunted her all hours of the day and night, the muscles in his arms and shoulders as they sliced through the water, wheeling himself up and down the ramp stacking wood or filling his bird feeders, those light blue eyes blazing at her as they made love. And most haunting of all, Colin sitting quietly in his wheelchair, staring at the wounded eagle in his cage.

Ruth's accusations had punched holes in every certainty she'd had. She was riddled with doubts, and her dishonesty to Ruth tortured her. There was so much she needed to say to her that she didn't have a chance to. She had a million excuses for everything she'd kept from her, but she was beginning to realize her own justification was beside the point. The fact that Ruth thought so badly of her was gut wrenching. A week after leaving, Lucy sent her an e-mail in the middle of another sleepless night.

Dear Ruth,

I had to write and tell you once again how sorry I am. I am sick at heart that I've hurt you, and that despite my best intentions, I was less than honest with you. I'm spending every waking moment, it seems, reliving my life, examining why I do such things. I now recognize a pattern of avoiding the truth. I came back from Florida so determined not to make any more mistakes, because as much as David was in the wrong, I wasn't blameless.

I made the worst mistake of all with you, Ruth, and with Colin. I hope one day I can earn your forgiveness. I realize there's a lot of truth in what you said. I haven't been separated all that long. And I wasn't there for the really bad times with Colin. But one thing I can tell you with complete honesty, and certainty: I will never forget your kindness, or everything you've done for me. I love you, Ruth. And I love Colin.

I hope everything works out for you with the store. You deserve only the best.

Lucy

Once she sent the letter, it wasn't as hard to get back to writing because she needed to finish the new book. She needed to someday have Ruth see the entire story, not just the bits and pieces she must have scanned that day. Her hope was that she would understand what this was: a love story, a tribute to a man who others might see as someone different—like the beast in the fairy tale—but who inside was tender, caring and strong. A beautiful man she'd come to love, and whose loss she now grieved. Once she read it, hopefully Ruth might forgive her.

When her brain was too fried to write, she continued promoting *A Quiet Wanting*. Slowly she began to fill the hours, always checking to see if there might be some reply from Ruth. But there wasn't. At night, she lay in bed exhausted, her mind continuing to go over the past, the puzzle still trying to work itself in her brain. Why did she seem to avoid the truth in some of the most important moments of her life?

* * *

ONE DAY SHE WALKED TO MORAVIAN BOOKS and introduced herself. They all knew her mother, and true to her word, she'd given them a book. It was a pleasure to stand there and hear how much they all loved it. They even asked her to do a signing, and she hesitated, then realized she had more than a month until her mother returned, so they set a date.

She was surprised when she got back to find an e-mail from her former workshop buddy, acid-tongued Regan, who'd come to her launch party.

Hey Lucy,

Just wondering how the book is doing. We talked about it in the workshop. It's really a good book, although a few of us thought the husband could have been more sympathetic. Anyway, I'm writing because I'm thinking of doing it, too. I swore I'd never give in if I couldn't get a real deal, but I'm at my wit's end. Let me know as soon as you can.

Regan

P.S. Have you sent any more queries out since you self-published?

As she sat there staring at her *P.S.*, Ruth's words from weeks ago came back once more, that maybe it was time to try again. "What do you have to lose?" she'd asked, her brown eyes so full of caring then. "If you get rejected, then you just keep plugging away, as you have been. But if you get a good agent who can sell it to a publisher, you'll be able to get your novel into every bookstore in the country."

That night while the TV droned, her mind numb and not even hearing the show, she grabbed her laptop and began typing up a query letter to agents about *A Quiet Wanting*. As much as she wanted to be "the real deal," an author with a legitimate publisher, she wasn't sure she had the stomach to face rejection again, especially now. But Ruth had a point. One by one she was adding stores, but it was tedious. After six months she had more than thirty stores on board, but there was no way to get the entire country by herself. And she was beyond exhausted, the months of effort suddenly catching up with her. But maybe it was time to give it one more try, and if it didn't happen, then so be it. There was more to life than getting published, she'd realized that afternoon as she sat on the rock overlooking the lake. Maybe it was time to get back to that life.

A query was supposed to be just one page, a succinct sales pitch about your story to hopefully entice an agent to say *send me a chapter*, or better yet, *send me the entire manuscript*. Her query letter turned into two and a half pages, because she couldn't resist throwing in everything—blurbs from reviews online and in newspapers, that her self-published novel was a book club pick in twelve states now, and she'd sold more than 2,200 books in mere months, what most literary novels did in a lifetime. Then she added her best reader and bookseller quotes.

Most of all, she wrote, all of this proved that her book had an audience, and now there were more than a few thousand readers waiting for her next novel, which was nearly done. When she finished the letter, she searched online for agents, copying and pasting their addresses, until there were ten query letters ready in her outbox. But then she closed the laptop, still uncertain she was ready to face this again. Just as she began to fall asleep on the couch, the house phone rang. Her brother Charlie's name showed on the caller ID and she felt an instant jolt of alarm.

"Are you asleep?" her mother asked, when she picked up.

"I was just dozing on the couch. Is everything all right?"

"Yes, it's great. But I'm worried about you."

"I'm okay, Mom, keeping busy."

"Did you stop in the bookstore yet?"

"Yes, I did, you were right, they're lovely, and we're doing a signing."

"Then why do you sound so depressed?"

She sighed. "I'm just so tired. I've been doing this for how many months now? Plus, I've been working on a query letter for hours. I think my brain may have overheated."

Then she had to explain what a query letter was.

"Oh, Lucy, just send the damn letters out. And picture it happening. You have to *feel* it. If you do the universe will feel it, too."

"Okay, Mom," she said, with a little laugh.

"I'm serious."

"I can tell."

Then her mother explained—no surprise here—that Artie had given her a copy of *The Secret* awhile back, and she'd been living by that philosophy. Lucy had to admit, after their last visit, that something good was definitely working on her mother.

"Besides, I've read six books since yours and none was as good."

"Well...Mom, thanks, that really means a lot to me."

"I'm going to light a candle and say a prayer right now. You go find a candle and I'll hold on while you do."

She knew better than to argue. It wasn't hard to find one, her mother had candles everywhere, and a lighter in her kitchen drawer next to a pack of cigarettes. Lucy grabbed them both, then got back on the phone.

"Okay, Mom, my candle is lit."

"Now go send the letters."

She put the laptop on the dining room table beside the candle and opened her outbox, paused a moment, then clicked Send, watching the queries disappear as she whispered, "Please...please let it happen this time."

Then she got back on the phone and assured her mother it was done.

"Good. Now believe it is already happening."

"Okay, Mom," she said, although this part was a stretch for her. It wasn't that she didn't believe it should, she just knew what the odds were.

She stood there watching the candlelight flickering on her laptop and her chaos all over that table, and wondered about her mother. Maybe it wasn't ever too late for someone to change. Maybe it was just a matter of surrounding yourself with the right people. With her father, her mother had always been depressed. With her three children, she'd been...overwhelmed. But with Artie, her mother had finally become someone she really liked.

Then Lucy said something she couldn't ever remember saying. "I love you, Mom."

She threw the cigarettes back in the drawer.

47

RUTH WOKE EARLY, WENT DOWNSTAIRS TO MAKE COFFEE, and let Sam outside. She stood on the back porch a moment, waiting for Sam to do her business. Sam was still showing signs of separation anxiety. Even going out in the yard caused her to glance at Ruth with long, anxious looks, as if asking, *you'll be here when I come back in, right?*

She wrapped her robe tighter and looked out at the yard, a fine glaze of ice crystals coating the still green grass, and lamented the regular frosts already. The sugar maple, always the first to blaze red in early fall, was now bare, although the oaks clung to their withered brown leaves.

Sam trotted back up the steps and Ruth opened the door, both of them entering the warm kitchen with a shiver. She set Sam's breakfast on the floor, then poured her coffee and sat at the table, but she just looked at her food. The store's 150th anniversary celebration was just weeks away now, as was the inaugural First Friday Downtown Walk, and she would finally be going out in public with Thomas.

She stared out the back window and told herself to cheer up. Two months ago she'd been sitting in the hospital worried about her life, her store, and Thomas. Sick with dread. Now it seemed as though she had worried for nothing. Her heart was fine, her energy was back. And the store was still open, and would be until she was really ready to retire.

Telling the children about Thomas hadn't gone well, at first. When she had them all for Sunday brunch a few weeks ago and Jenny walked in, it took her daughter a moment to notice that most of the clutter was gone, furniture strategically rearranged, and the kitchen "refreshed," as her realtor so aptly put it. Everything was neutral and airy and already it felt like someone else's house to Ruth, which made the sudden emotional tugs as she walked through the rooms a bit easier to handle.

After brunch, while her grandchildren were playing in the yard, she'd sat Colin, Jenny and Alex down and told them her plans.

"My God, Mom, it's about time. I don't know why you held onto this old house for so long," Jenny had said. "You should get a nice little ranch, or better yet, a condo."

"Actually, I'm buying The Book Lover building, and I'm going to live upstairs for a while. It's a beautiful apartment, very spacious."

As Jenny's mouth opened to protest, Alex and Colin both piped up that it was a great idea.

She looked at Jenny. "Listen, I know you worry about me, and I love you for that. But I'm not ready to retire, honey. I promise I'm going to scale back my hours. I promoted Megan to assistant manager. One day she'll hopefully buy the store from me. Until then, I'm not only going to keep it going, I'm planning to expand, open the wall to the vacant space next door and bring in a used book section. And if Hazel's Café takes off, that'll allow me to give Hannah more space, too. I have a feeling her Book Lover Baskets are going to be a hit."

"It's a great idea," Colin said.

"Now, there's one more thing I have to tell you," she said then, and had to stand because she was too nervous to sit still. "I've been seeing someone."

Their faces said it all—shock, raised eyebrows, a smile from Colin.

"Would he happen to be the man who was conveniently painting your cabinets that day?" Jenny asked, with a teasing lilt in her voice.

"Yes." She could feel her heart thudding in her throat.

"Now *I'll* say it," Alex said, laughing. "It's about time, Mom."

She took a deep breath, looking at their smiling faces, their happiness for her palpable. "Well, there's something you need to know about him. I met him five years ago." She paused suddenly, praying this ended well. "When I began selling books at the prison."

Jenny jumped up. "Oh my God, Mom, don't tell me—"

She put her hand up, stopping her daughter. "Yes, he was in prison, but now he's out. I've thought about this long and hard. He's a good man who made a bad choice, one he's paid for. We all make mistakes, and hopefully we grow from them. Now, I'm giving this a chance. I'd like your support."

"Jesus," Jenny said softly, shaking her head.

Alex gave her a long look. "You really care for him?"

"I do."

"You don't need anyone's permission, Mom." Colin said, looking straight at Jenny. "We're not going to stand in your way."

A few days afterward Jenny had come back, looking so glum that Ruth waited for something awful as they sat in the kitchen.

"I checked up on Thomas, and did some digging. I even called my friend Andrea's husband, Carl. Remember he's the one who got you into the prison to sell books?"

"Of course I remember him."

Jenny began shaking her head. "I couldn't find one person to say a negative thing about your Thomas."

Ruth let the breath she'd been holding out of her lungs.

"You're a big girl, Mom, and it looks like you know what you're doing."

"So I've got your blessing on this?"

Jenny nodded.

"Thank you for caring about me, but I have to tell you, I'd already made up my mind to see him, whether you kids agreed or not."

"Okay, Mom. I'm glad you're finally making some changes in your life. You seem...different. Happier, I guess. And I'm sorry to be such a pain in the ass." Jenny flashed her a rueful smile. "The girls keep telling me I should change my middle name to 'worry.'"

Ruth got up and gave her a hug. "It's nice to be cared about, honey. And I hate to tell you, I think I passed that middle name down to you."

She was blessed to have children who worried about her. She felt blessed by everything in her life these days, right down to the books on her shelves.

Now the house was under contract, as was the cabin. She'd said she was selling the cabin that day out of anger, but afterward, she realized she was being a fool for not selling the cabin as her accountant had often suggested. It was that final piece of the past she needed to let go, once and for all. She told herself she would do it, no matter what the kids thought, but in the end, they didn't seem to mind that, either. And it had made all the difference for her financially.

She'd gotten a decent price, not for the cabin really, although it showed much better thanks to Lucy's redecorating, but because of the land, that wide swath of lakefront on the private cove. A young couple just starting out put an offer on it within days. Her hope now was that they'd be good neighbors, and hopefully become friends with Colin when they moved in after closing.

At the thought of Colin, she put her cup down. He'd been so quiet since Lucy left. And then there was another jab of guilt when she got Lucy's e-mail, apologizing. But Jenny kept assuring her that he'd get over it, and that Gloryanne was willing to wait.

The day she confronted Lucy, she'd driven away shaking so badly she had to pull over on the other side of the lake. Sitting there, she looked across the water, thinking of the months that Lucy and Colin were lovers, and how Lucy said absolutely nothing. Because of Colin's handicap it had never even occurred to her that something like that could happen. But looking back, she'd thrown two wounded souls together. Naturally they'd tried to comfort each other. She'd been such a fool. And then, of course, there was the secret manuscript.

She was very careful in telling him afterward. She wasn't supposed to know about the affair, so she tried to be casual. When he came into The Book Lover the next afternoon, when it was just the two of them, she'd simply said, "By the way, I heard from Lucy. It seems she packed up her things and left."

He didn't even look at her, he'd simply sat in his wheelchair staring out the front window, his face not revealing a thing.

"Apparently her husband won't give up."

A muscle in his cheek quivered, as if he were grinding his teeth. "I hope it works out for her," he'd said, then wheeled his chair to the back of the store.

In the following weeks it was so easy to think she'd done the right thing. Neither of them brought up Lucy again, and then Colin and Gloryanne began spending more time together. When Gloryanne stopped in last night, Ruth was certain it was with news, and she was right. But the news wasn't at all what she expected.

"I came to say goodbye," Gloryanne said, standing in the doorway with a bright smile. "I'm moving to Colorado."

Ruth was stunned. Instead of planning a future, as they'd all thought, she told Ruth as they sat in her kitchen that she and Colin had spent the last weeks rehashing their past.

"He made me realize that it was over a long time ago. With him being in the service and gone so much, it was so easy to ignore our problems because when he came home, we were just so happy to see each other. It was like a continual honeymoon, but..." and then Ruth saw a glitter of tears fill her eyes, "sometimes it's just hard to let go."

"I know, honey."

"I think if that writer hadn't come, I wouldn't have gotten so confused. I have to admit it, I got really jealous. But that's not a reason to marry someone, just because you can't bear the thought of him being with someone else. Anyway, we'll always care deeply for each other—how couldn't we, after all our history? But it's time for me to move on."

"Are you going to be okay?"

Gloryanne nodded. "I'm going to live with my cousin in Denver for a few months and try to start over. Actually, I'm kind of excited."

Ruth gave her a long hug, and a short while later Gloryanne was gone.

After that, the uneasy feeling she'd been trying to ignore began to plague her night and day. She'd been wrong to meddle in Colin's life. Even if he was having an affair with Lucy, even if Lucy was writing about him, it was Colin's business, not hers. Of course she'd always want to protect her children, but she knew now that if she'd given herself some time to digest what she'd learned, she probably wouldn't have acted as she had. But Jenny had planted the seed, and she'd let her anger take off, once again causing her to do something she regretted.

And that, really, was why she felt sick to her stomach this morning. Because much as she dreaded it, she needed to tell Colin the truth.

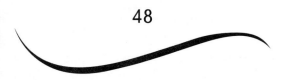

48

THE DAY AFTER SHE SENT THE QUERY LETTERS, Lucy received four rejections. Two more came over the following days. A week later, walking through her mother's condo complex, she began to think that perhaps all these fast rejections, and being unable to write an ending to her new book, were simply the universe—oh how her mother would loathe this—telling her to give up. That the writing was literally on the wall and it was time to pack it in.

A heated debate ensued in her head as she walked, watching the gray autumn clouds skittering away, unveiling bright blue skies. There was still hope for the remaining few queries, wasn't there? And if she could just let the doubts go for a while, and let her mind relax and allow her creative juices to flow, as they usually did when she walked, the ending would come to her.

Coming to the gravel path that meandered through the complex's small wooded border, she stopped a moment and couldn't help thinking about the similar path at the Raptor Center and her final visit there. She continued walking, her mind drifting to that afternoon she'd left the cabin for good. It wasn't far off the drive to her mother's, and she knew she wouldn't chance returning another time when Colin might be there. As she'd pulled into the parking area and walked into the shaded path, she couldn't help remembering that first day Colin brought her there months ago, when he was just a stranger, a handicapped man she had no clue how to relate to. Never imagining she'd return one day grieving not for her husband, as she'd been then, but for him.

She'd walked past one aviary after another, familiar now with the occupants: Lady, the great horned owl and foster mother to so many, the red-tailed hawk, peregrine falcon, snowy owls, and even the albino starling. As she got closer to the aviary where she knew she'd find the bald eagle, she noticed a small group of people. And then one turned and smiled.

"Lucy, how did you know?" Susan asked, walking over.

"Know what?"

"Well, then I guess this is a happy coincidence. We're about to introduce Kit to Scarlett."

She looked at her, confused. Scarlett, it turned out, was the female eagle she'd seen that first day in the cage. For some reason, she'd never known her name.

Just then Randy came up the path, carrying Kit on his gloved hand. They all watched as he opened the cage door and stepped inside. A moment later he set Kit, who as a male was smaller than Scarlett, on a long branch at the other side of where she sat, higher in the cage, watching what was happening with those alert yellow eyes. Randy slowly walked to the alcove of the aviary and stood there, waiting.

Scarlett looked from side to side, and did nothing for long minutes. Kit opened his broad wings and she could still see the slightly crooked angle to the one. Somehow, in one quick move, he made a flying lurch to the other branch where he landed beside Scarlett.

"He's flying!"

"Just a bit," Susan whispered, and she realized she'd spoken too loud.

Kit began sidling up to Scarlett, but she lunged at him. Again he tried, and again she pounced, more fiercely this time, spreading her wings in a posturing display. It was easy to see her own injury in her deformed left wing. Then Kit charged at her and she pushed him with her beak, as if trying to topple him off the branch.

"They're really solitary creatures, you know," Susan said softly. "They have very large territories and typically only get together during mating season."

"Do you think they will?"

"Oh, no, they won't mate in captivity. That was never a possibility."

She couldn't help thinking of the eagles in the CD Colin had given her. Their incredible aerial ballet in which they bonded—a sort of foreplay before mating. Then their diligence in preparing the nest for their young, the constant search for food. None of that was possible here, she realized with a jolt of pity.

"It doesn't appear his wing will improve much more, so he'll stay here for display and educational purposes. And there's nothing wrong with that," Susan said.

"What if you didn't have room for him, what would have happened?"

"His choices were either pair him, or euthanize him. Fortunately, we had a spot here. They're doing okay so far, but this 'getting to know you' will go on for days. Their first time together, two bald eagles could actually kill each other trying to take control. Hopefully after a while, Scarlett will give it up."

"How old is she?"

"About twenty. She's been here since she was four. They found her down south, near an old flooded rice plantation, hence her name."

After a while, Randy removed Kit. Susan told her that tomorrow they'd do it again. It was hard not to look up, above the aviary and the treetops, where hawks circled in the warming air. It seemed almost cruel that just above these caged eagles, among the most powerful birds in the world, others soared freely. She'd left, regretting deeply that she wouldn't get to see the rest of Kit's future unfold.

Now as she continued walking, thinking about the eagles and her own first notion that they would somehow fall in love, or at least mate, images of those wounded birds in their cage, and then of Colin and her at the lake, began to blur. She remembered what Ruth had said—that as strong as he seemed Colin was still just a few years from his accident, from the devastating changes in his life. She'd seen the occasional mood shifts. Yes, he did have a long road ahead of him. But it was one that she would have been willing to share.

And in that magical, mysterious way that things brewed in her head, it suddenly came as she stopped there on the gravel path—the conclusion she'd been struggling with for the new book. The ending to Catherine's own story. Quickly she pulled her recorder from her pocket so she wouldn't forget the words that were already writing themselves in her mind. As she began talking into the microphone, her cell began to ring in the other pocket and she hesitated, not wanting to lose the train of thought. But she grabbed the phone anyway and recognized a New York area code. She answered immediately.

"Is this Lucinda Barrett?" a pleasant woman's voice asked.

"Yes it is."

"This is Renee Wilson from The Valerie Sampson Agency in New York. I'm Valerie's assistant. We received your query letter and we'd like to take a look at your novel, *A Quiet Wanting*."

"Oh...yes, of course." She'd prayed for one lousy response to her ten e-mails, but a phone call?

"We'd like a two week exclusive, would that be all right?"

"Yes, of course."

The assistant asked for a copy of the book to be sent right away, and a moment later they hung up. Lucy closed her eyes, clenched her fists and nearly sank to the sidewalk before reminding herself not to get excited. This could end up just one more rejection. But they called! They wanted to read the entire thing! That was something.

Two weeks came and went. Then three. As the trees began to flame with color, and autumn took firm hold, she began to worry that Renee Wilson at The Valerie Sampson Agency had forgotten about her. She'd finally heard from one other agent who'd sent a tepid e-mail asking for the first three chapters, but was honoring the exclusive she'd agreed to, despite the temptation.

She was actually quite proud of that decision, because the old Lucy would have sent those chapters. The old Lucy would have rationalized that no one would know, really, and she would be fearful of missing an opportunity. What if she got rejected by the first agency, after all, and the second one lost interest waiting?

Because as the weeks wore on and she kept digging into her past mistakes, it became more and more clear that her sins of omission, her little white lies, all of it was the result of one thing, really. Fear. She was afraid if David knew that she wanted children, he wouldn't marry her; she was afraid if Colin learned she wasn't divorced yet, he would turn back to Gloryanne. She was afraid if Ruth found out that she was in a relationship with Colin, and wasn't yet free, that she would turn on her. She'd deliberately led people to believe *A Quiet Wanting* was with a real publisher because she was afraid they wouldn't read it. It was so easy to make excuses for all of it, because she'd been doing it since she was a kid, when her father would give her a wink and say time after time, "Let's not worry your mother with this."

Now here she was, thirty-nine years old and all alone, because she'd been too afraid to be honest with anyone she loved. She didn't trust them to love her enough back to hear the truth, and not turn away.

* * *

SHE CALLED DAVID AGAIN, to tell him it was time for him to let go, and he should acquiesce gracefully or Carter would take him back to court. David told her that he was coming up for Ben's anniversary, and wanted to see her, too. She agreed, but told him nothing was going to change because she was in love with someone else. He seemed surprised, but after all, they'd been separated a long time. She then explained that even though it hadn't worked out with this other person, it made her realize a lot of things. She needed to start over.

She wasn't holding back anything anymore. Suddenly, she wanted nothing more than to right every wrong. It had already started, she realized, with her mother. When she told her "I love you."

A week later, she was halfway to the grocery store, famished and tired of canned soup and cheese and crackers, when her cell phone rang. She recognized the New York number immediately and pulled over as a horn honked behind her.

"Hello?"

"Hello, Lucinda, this is Renee Wilson from The Valerie Sampson Agency," she said, as if Lucy wouldn't remember her.

"Yes, hello." Her heart was racing.

"Valerie asked me to call and see if you could come in to sign."

Sign? SIGN????

"You mean you want to represent me?" And then the phone began to ping, warning that it was about to die.

"Yes. Can you come in Friday, say ten in the morning?"

"Yes, of course, I'm not far at all."

She hung up just before the phone died, and before going to the grocery store, pulled into the liquor store to pick up a bottle of champagne. How she longed to tell Ruth and Colin. This was a huge moment. Even if she didn't get as far as a publisher, at least she had an agent who now believed in her book.

Tonight she would celebrate, even if it was all alone, and hopefully after a few glasses of bubbly, finally be able to get some sleep.

But as she got out of the car, a wave of nausea rolled through her stomach, followed by a scorching taste of bile in her throat. She sat back down in the driver's seat and took a few deep breaths, as it gradually dawned on her—she'd felt this hollowness in her middle before. This need to eat, and yet the inability to swallow a thing. It wasn't nerves these past few weeks, but something very different taking hold of her body.

Another miracle she'd all but given up on.

49

RUTH OPENED HER FRONT DOOR AND THERE STOOD THOMAS IN a navy blue suit with a striped tie, and she felt her breath catch. She'd never seen him dressed up before and she noticed now that his hair was growing in and that his sideburns were flecked with gray. He looked distinguished, and downright handsome.

"Don't you look beautiful," he said softly, and reached a hand to her face, his finger tracing the curve of her cheek.

She took his hand and held it there a moment. She felt beautiful, too. Not because she'd had her hair done yesterday, finally. Not because she was wearing a new red dress that lit up her face, as the saleswoman had proclaimed, and she had to agree. But because of the way Thomas made her feel.

"Come in, let me just get my coat. Are you going to be warm enough in your suit?"

It was cold out, and they were going to walk. And then she realized he probably didn't have a dress coat.

"I'm fine, Ruth. Don't worry about it." Then he took his other hand, which had been behind his back, and held out a small white box. She opened it to find a perfect gardenia corsage.

"Oh, Thomas." She pulled it to her nose and closed her eyes, inhaling the sweet, tropical fragrance.

"They were my mother's favorite flower. My father always gave them to her."

She stood there as he pinned it to her coat.

As they walked down the steps and turned toward Main Street, Thomas took her hand, and a thrill of anticipation ran through her. Here she was, Ruth Hardaway, turning sixty-five in a few months, who for all intents and purposes should have been thinking of retirement; whose chance at romance should have been long over. Maybe, Ruth thought then, you had to live without something for a very long time to really know how precious it was.

"This is a beautiful town," Thomas said as they strolled through her neighborhood, past the stately old colonials with wide porches and colorful mums in bloom. When they were nearly to Main Street, she stopped on the small bridge over the Waywayanda Creek and pulled two pennies from her pocket.

"Make a wish," she said, handing one to Thomas.

Closing her eyes, she tossed hers in the small stream, then looked down as Thomas's hit the water. They looked at each other, smiled, and turned toward the store.

When they reached The Book Lover, Thomas took her arm, holding her there on the sidewalk a moment as he looked at the wide window filled with books, and a sign announcing today's events.

"This is a huge day for you, Ruth."

She nodded, emotion suddenly rising in her throat.

"And you did it, all on your own."

"Yes, I did it all on my own."

When she opened the door, and the little bell tinkled, Thomas was right behind her. She watched his eyes scanning the shelves and shelves of books.

"Welcome to my world," she said.

"SURPRISE!"

Ruth turned with a start, then saw the small crowd beyond the counter, a small blonde in the middle, smiling broadly. It took her a moment to realize it was Megan, sans the black hair and blue tips. "National Public Radio is here, Ruth, to tape our historic event!"

"Oh Megan," she said, walking over and giving her a hug. "NPR? How did you ever...and what happened to your hair?"

"I went back to my real color," she whispered in Ruth's ear.

It reminded her of her children's weddings, a day you plan months for and want to savor every second of, but seems to fly by in a rush all too quickly.

Megan and Harry had stayed late last night, pushing some of the shelves back, and setting up a table in the front, which would hold a series of local author signings all throughout the day. She lamented for a moment how much this would have helped Lucy, if she were still there. Kris arrived a few minutes later with two fists full of balloons, and then Harry, who shyly handed Ruth a large bouquet of daisies.

"Congratulations, Ruth. You made it."

"*We* made it," she said, taking the bouquet and bringing it to her nose. "Oh, Harry, this was so sweet."

"It's just a little thank you for giving me a place that I love to come to all these years. I can't even call it work, because it's not."

She leaned over and kissed his cheek. "I know."

She introduced them all to Thomas and he quickly threw himself into helping out however he could. Then Hannah arrived in a tizzy, with boxes and boxes of muffins, all different kinds, and exotic coffees and teas, afraid she might run out of what she already had on hand.

Ruth and Thomas helped her carry it all back to Hazel's Café, then sat at one of the bistro tables as Hannah fluttered around getting ready. The café was so charming and colorful. In addition to the painted mirrors, Hannah had also hand painted a sign: *HAZEL'S CAFÉ, Out of this world baked goods.*

"Eddie thinks I'm crazy, giving away free stuff today, but I think it's smart marketing. Once they taste my muffins..."

"They'll be dying to buy them," Ruth finished for her.

Hannah turned to her, laughing at the pun. "I think Hazel would approve."

"I think you're right."

They both looked at Thomas, who was devouring a muffin, a look of pleasure on his face.

"Are those the *Better than...*" she asked.

"*Better Than Sex* muffins? Yes, and no. Same muffin, different name, because I figure our audience is now PG. So I renamed them *Sinfully Delicious*. There's a new one, *Hazel's Nut*, which of course has hazelnuts."

"If you're selling stock in your business, I'll buy some," Thomas said, wiping his mouth with a napkin.

Hannah laughed.

"I'm serious," Thomas said, and Ruth and Hannah looked at him. Apparently, he was.

Then the bell began to ring endlessly, and Ruth headed back to the front of the store as the family of regular customers poured in, followed a few moments later by Lauren Greene and her crew from NPR, who'd gone to Elaine's for a bite before launching into work for the next six hours. Lauren was a tall woman, who Ruth judged to be in her mid-thirties, and who reminded her, ironically, of herself back then, with her long peasant skirt, high black boots, and dark, wild hair caught back with a clip.

Ruth was thankful the show wasn't running live. They would be taping throughout the day then edit the material and put together what was to be a thirty-minute segment to be aired in a few weeks. She gave Lauren free reign to interview staff and customers alike, with the exception of Larry Porter's surprise proposal. When the time came, Ruth asked that the crew take a break, or perhaps just go outside for a few minutes. Ruth didn't want anything ruining the big moment.

She stood in front of the store as the crew set up then, happy to see Main Street alive with pedestrians for this First Friday Downtown Walk, which didn't officially kick off until later in the afternoon. They'd advertised like crazy during Applefest, hoping the crowds would come back, and here they were.

"We're here today in the Village of Warwick," Lauren Greene began, "to celebrate the 150th anniversary of The Book Lover, an independent bookstore that's been owned and managed by Ruth Hardaway for the past thirty years. As is often the case with properties that change hands, the history of The Book Lover was a mystery to Ruth, until the store's assistant manager Megan Crockett began doing a little snooping..."

Against the background noise of the door opening, the bell tinkling and people chatting and browsing, Lauren Greene finished taping her introduction. Then they moved inside, where she interviewed Megan, asking her what her thoughts were for surviving in a future where megastores and online shopping seemed to be closing one independent after another.

"The way of the future is educating the buying public," Megan began. "Here in Warwick, our downtown revitalization committee has begun a 'Buy Warwick' campaign that we hope will help people who live here realize finally that if they spend their money here, it helps everyone."

Megan showed her copies of store receipts and newsletters, as well as e-mail printouts as she read out loud what they were now handing out. "If you spend $25 in your town at an independent store, $13.75 stays in your community. If it's a big box or chain store, it would be $3.90. If you spend that same $25 on the internet, you're giving $0 to your community. People have to think beyond saving a few cents, or even a few bucks. This is where we live. No one wants boarded-up shops on Main Street, but in some places, that's what you have."

Just then Lynn Anderson came in with her daughter Melissa. Ruth hadn't seen her in a few months, and she was dressed as nicely as ever. Melissa went to pick out some children's books and Lynn came over to Ruth with a gift bag in her hand.

"This is just a small token of my thanks for giving me so much pleasure over the years. It was like having my own personal book shopper. You always knew exactly what I wanted. And sometimes needed."

"Thanks, Lynn." She opened the bag and pulled out a tiny gold music box. As she lifted the cover, she recognized the tune immediately: *When you wish upon a star*... "Oh, it's just lovely, Lynn."

"I'm glad you got to keep the store open. I just couldn't imagine Warwick without The Book Lover. Or The Book Lover without you."

Lynn gave her a quick hug and went to join her daughter, who was sitting at a bistro table sampling some of Hannah's muffins. Lauren was there, interviewing several others. In fact, Hannah's corner of the store was packed. Ruth turned away, an ache in her heart. There was something missing in Lynn's eyes already, as if a bit of the light had already begun to fade.

As she walked toward the front of the store, where Thomas was sampling some of Bertha Piakowski's pierogies—she'd arrived with two platters of them while Ruth was being interviewed—she saw Colin finally arrive. She'd been wondering where he was. He kept insisting he wasn't angry with her, but she had her doubts.

When she went to the lake last week and knocked on his cabin door, he didn't seem surprised to see her. He was sitting at his dining room table, which was covered with papers. She sat across from him as he explained that he was finalizing a program at The Raptor Center for wounded vets.

"But you're not here about this," he said with a little smile, his head tilted to the side, which she'd always found so endearing. For a moment he looked like the Colin who used to wow his father, that mischievous twinkle in his eye before he'd jump into the freezing lake.

He thought she'd come because of Gloryanne.

"She's doing the right thing," he said then. "It's been over a long time. She was just too sweet to admit it."

"I'm not here to talk about her, Colin. I'm here to talk about Lucy."

He'd looked startled. For a long moment she said nothing, praying he wouldn't hate her. She told him then that she knew about the affair. "To be honest, I felt betrayed."

"She wanted to tell you, Mom. I asked her not to."

"When she came back from Florida, you assumed she was divorced, but she wasn't. Her husband was fighting it."

"So that part was true."

"Yes."

"What else?"

"Did you know she was writing a book about you?"

"What do you mean?"

"The character was a paraplegic, obviously modeled after you. There was some very intimate detail. And of course the birds."

She was surprised to see him smile then, shaking his head. "And that upset you?"

"I felt like she was using you."

"She wasn't using me. If she writes about a paraplegic, it can only raise awareness."

"So you don't care?"

He shook his head. "I love her."

And she sat there, remembering Lucy saying the same thing, "I love him, Ruth."

"But you're right, she did lie about being divorced. I never wanted to do what Dad did. I know how much he must have hurt you. I swore I'd never do something like that to anyone, whether I knew them or not."

She felt her face flush with embarrassment. Although it was a small town, she often wondered how much her kids had heard over the years. None of them had ever brought it up, though. Until now.

"I've made peace with it, Colin, finally, after all these years, so let's not talk about that."

"I loved Dad, nothing will change that. Maybe he was like Thomas, a good man who made some bad choices. Maybe if he'd lived long enough he would have learned to appreciate what he had."

She reached across the table and squeezed his hand. "Thanks for saying that, honey. I think maybe you're right."

"And I'm not mad at you. Lucy knows where I am. If this is right, she'll come back, no matter what you've done."

Now Colin pushed himself through the store, which took a while because it was getting crowded, the counter and register hopping as browsers took advantage of the anniversary sale. She waited, and when he finally reached her he sat there a moment, unable to get up and hug her. So he took her hand, brought it to his lips, and kissed it.

"You're an incredible woman, Mom."

Dammit, she started to cry.

* * *

SOON THEY WERE ALL CAUGHT UP WORKING. She lost track of Lauren, looking up occasionally to see her interviewing a customer as Kris recommended particular reads, and Harry talked about his sci-fi expertise. She went back to the café to check on Hannah, who was thrilled to report she had more than twenty orders for Book Lover Gift Baskets, each of which included a hardcover book.

"Eddie called to tell me that it's really hopping there. I guess advertising this during Applefest was a great idea. He knocked twenty percent off all his appliances and he's moving a lot of inventory."

"Did you tell him how well it's going here?"

Hannah nodded and gave her a huge smile. "Believe it or not, he told me he's proud of me."

"Good. He should be."

When Ruth had her hair done yesterday, she was prepared to say something to Dee about being a little too friendly with Eddie. But before she could, Dee began to gush about running into an old boyfriend she hadn't seen in years, and they were now dating. So apparently whatever had gone on with Eddie was over.

"Oh my God, here comes Larry Porter," Hannah whispered loudly.

Ruth turned to see Larry coming through the front door with a dozen red roses, which Kris stashed behind the counter.

"Okay, I'm going to clear this place out. I don't want them to be part of the show."

"Isn't it romantic? Proposing to her here?"

"Do you know almost every Friday since they met they've come here before going out for dinner? I can't tell you how many times they had to get take-out instead, because they bought too many books."

The NPR crew went back to Elaine's for a half hour, since she was open late for the festivities, and Ruth had the staff ring up the rest of the customers as quickly as possible, telling them they were closing for a short dinner break. Larry paced nervously and Ruth saw the square bulge of a ring box in his blazer pocket.

"She's a lucky woman," Ruth told him.

But he shook his head. "No, I'm the lucky guy."

"She's here!" Megan whispered, and as Larry nonchalantly walked back to the history section, the door opened and Angela came in, wearing a red coat and a long black skirt. She waved to them all, blissfully clueless, then headed back to the fiction section, stopping along the way to give Larry a kiss. A moment later, he glanced at Megan and nodded. She slipped his CD into the stereo, which normally played light classical music during store hours. Megan turned up the volume and Sam Cooke's "You Send Me," Larry and Angela's favorite song, filled the store.

Ruth saw that none of her staff could look at each other, afraid they might smile, giving it away. Surprisingly, Thomas and Jenny were chatting quietly near the counter. She peeked over and saw Angela glancing around with a look of surprise, then turning to Larry, who pretended to be riveted to a huge volume of history. Angela went back to perusing a novel. Then Larry quietly came to the counter and got the red roses. A moment later he tapped Angela's shoulder and they all heard her gasp. Now they all watched as he gave her the roses, and as she stood there holding them with a look of astonishment, he dropped to one knee.

"Oh my God," Angela whispered, loud enough for them to hear.

"I thought it only fitting to ask right here where we had our first date, if you would do me the honor of being my wife?"

"Oh my God. Yes!" she said and burst into tears.

Ruth's eyes filled, and she saw they were all smiling and laughing with tears in their eyes, even Thomas and Harry.

"We'll never be rich," Larry said, slipping the ring on her finger. "But we'll have lots of books."

Ruth suddenly noticed that Colin was missing. She turned, just as Larry and Angela began to kiss, and scanned the store, realizing in that moment that of course this would be difficult for him to watch. How thoughtless of her. She spotted him then, sitting in his wheelchair in the front corner opposite the door, and was relieved to see that he wasn't watching Larry and Angela at all. He was staring out the big front window across the street, where a group of people were clustered in front of the municipal parking lot.

A moment later, they walked away and it was then that she noticed the small woman with the shoulder length hair, still standing there alone. Staring across at the store.

It was Lucy.

50

IT OCCURRED TO LUCY WHEN SHE'D READ RUTH'S E-MAIL, that she couldn't possibly have scripted things more ironically in a work of fiction than they were unfolding in her life. Once again she imagined an editor saying, "This isn't realistic. No one will believe it." And yet, it was true.

The morning she opened her laptop to find Ruth's letter, apologizing for telling her to leave, she'd been waiting for David to arrive. They were going to the cemetery to put flowers on Ben's grave, where neither of them had been since the funeral. And then she was going to tell him her news.

It was bittersweet, reading Ruth's words that Colin and Gloryanne weren't planning a future, after all. That he was free and told her he loved Lucy. Because she was pregnant by David, something that felt at once wondrous, and cruel.

Maybe how you felt didn't matter at all in the grand scheme of things. Maybe some things simply were meant to be, as David had often insisted.

Now, as she stood across the street from The Book Lover, the afternoon sun was setting, hitting the front window with a golden glare so she couldn't see what was going on inside. She'd watched the NPR crew leave a short while ago—which she imagined must have thrilled Ruth— and then a steady stream of customers. Lucy wondered if the store was closing early, which seemed silly given the throngs of people walking through town. Even the weather, mild for early November, seemed to have cooperated for this First Friday.

Despite Ruth's e-mail, she hadn't quite worked up the nerve to write back. Now she found herself glued to the sidewalk, despite her intention to cross the street and go into the store. She'd been standing there for nearly half an hour and was growing chilled. As she made up her mind to just do it and not think further, the door suddenly opened and Ruth came out. She stood in front of the store, folded her arms, and stared straight at her. Lucy's stomach began to vibrate, her knees turning to Jello.

Ruth brushed her hair from her face, a familiar gesture Lucy had seen her make countless times, and then began to cross the street. Lucy nearly turned around because she was terrified, despite Ruth's apology. Whatever Ruth may have done wrong, Lucy was still ashamed of her dishonesty. She needed to make it right.

A moment later Ruth was there, right in front of her. "Hello, Lucy."

"Hi, Ruth." Her voice was barely a whisper.

They stood there, looking at each other for a long moment, as Lucy's heart thudded wildly. Then Ruth smiled and it reached her beautiful brown eyes.

"I'm so glad you're here." She pulled Lucy into a warm embrace.

"Oh, Ruth." Suddenly she was crying, then laughing because it reminded her of the first time they met, when she began to cry as Ruth pulled her into the bathroom. "I'm so sorry for everything."

"It's water over the bridge. Or under the dam. I never could quite get that straight."

They looked at each other and laughed.

"You remembered the anniversary. I'm so glad."

But Lucy shook her head. "Actually I realized when I got here what was happening. With everything going on, I guess I forgot."

"Well, let's go inside, it's too cold to stand out here," she said, taking Lucy's arm and leading her across the street.

"Is Colin there?"

Ruth stopped and looked at her. "Yes, he is."

Lucy hesitated, not sure how this was going to unfold. But she had to. This was the real reason she'd come. "All right. Let's go."

She was so anxious as they walked in the store it felt as if her already thudding heart was now ricocheting off her rib cage. The little bell tinkled cheerfully, just as she remembered, and Megan, who she didn't recognize at first, was the first person she saw and greeted her warmly.

"This is just perfect," Megan said, though Lucy had no idea what she meant.

As her eyes scoured the store for Colin, and she said quick hellos to Harry and Kris, she noticed Ruth walking toward the back, then waving her over. She walked slowly past shelves of books and in the corner of the store opposite the new café, Colin sat with his back to her, a book on his lap. Ruth nodded, and Lucy walked toward him alone.

He looked up at her, unsurprised.

"Good book?" she asked, unable to hide the tremble of nerves in her voice.

He held it up. It was *The Good Soldier*. "Yes, but not an easy read."

She nodded. He was still looking up at her and she knelt down then, so they were eye level. "I'm sorry I left without saying anything to you."

"From what I understand, my mother asked you to."

"That's no excuse." She hesitated. "I was ashamed. And confused."

"I can imagine. Although I'm sure the choice between me and your husband was an easy one, after all," he said, and gestured toward his lower half.

"Oh, Colin, it wasn't that at all. When Ruth began telling me that what I was doing was selfish, that I was going to ruin your future, I...I never meant to hurt you."

He looked at her, but didn't say a word.

"I know I wasn't legally free, but I felt emotionally free, and the other just seemed like... a minor technicality. Something I was planning to rectify as soon as David gave up."

"It wasn't a minor technicality to me," he said, looking away, anger in his eyes now. She couldn't blame him. "But it's a moot point, Lucy, isn't it?"

"I love you."

He blinked, startled.

"And yes, now it is a moot point."

"I don't understand."

"Do you love me?"

He tilted his head then, a gesture she loved, that meant he was thinking about something hard, all the while looking at her.

"Yes, I love you."

She took a deep breath. "Enough to marry me?"

"Is this a joke?"

"I've never been more serious in my life," she said. "The reason it's all a moot point is because I am free now, legally and emotionally. And I want to spend the rest of my life with you."

He closed his eyes and sat there for a long moment without saying anything. She couldn't even move. Then he took her hand, pulling her up and onto his lap, wrapping her in his arms and holding so tightly she could feel his heart, pounding as hard as her own.

"You should know what you're getting into," he whispered in her ear. "It's not pretty sometimes."

"I know," she said, because she'd done weeks of research, finding out everything she could about what her future with a paraplegic man would entail. "I know exactly what I'm getting into."

He squeezed her so hard, she squealed. "Is that a yes?"

"That's a yes," he said.

Pulling back from him, she looked into those light blue eyes she loved. "Good, because we're going to have a baby."

His mouth opened, but no words came out.

"I'm pregnant. But I didn't want that to influence your decision. I want you to marry me because you want to. Not because you have to, although that doesn't really happen anymore, does it?"

"Shut up, Lucy," he whispered, then kissed her long and hard.

She pulled away again. "There's something else I need to tell you. That I probably wouldn't have before but...I can't be afraid of the truth anymore. And this is the truth, Colin. I slept with David when I went back for the divorce. It was nothing more than a goodbye, something that happened in the heat of so much emotion. But I knew in an instant it was wrong, and I felt as if I'd betrayed you."

He said nothing at first, and she waited.

"How do you know it's not his child?"

She got up from his lap, then knelt again so they were at eye level. "I did think it was his at first, because I wasn't sure it was even possible with...your injuries. David came up and we went to the cemetery for our son's anniversary and when we left, we sat in my car and I told him that he was going to be a father again. He looked at me, not shocked, as I'd expected, but bewildered. What he told me next shocked *me*—that after Ben died, he'd had a vasectomy, because he was unwilling to take a chance on another pregnancy, no matter how unlikely it was. As horrible as that felt, I insisted that a vasectomy could fail, I'd read about it. But no, with further embarrassment he told me he was going to start dating, and he'd gotten tested recently, just to be sure."

Still Colin said nothing, just staring at her.

"I sat in my car reeling, as it slowly dawned on me that this baby is yours, Colin. Which is truly a miracle. I came to the store today straight from the airport. My divorce was finalized yesterday."

He let out a long sigh. "Thank you for telling me all that. I know you didn't have to."

"Yes, I did. I'll never be anything but up front with you, I promise."

He pulled her onto his lap again, his eyes never leaving hers. "Where do you want to live?"

"With you, at the lake, of course."

"It's not exactly the lap of luxury."

"It's everything I've ever wanted. And so are you."

He sat there and put a palm on her abdomen, looking at her in wonder. "In my wildest dreams I never thought something like this could happen."

"Me either." She buried her face in his neck as he held her, breathing him in.

Suddenly there was a commotion at the front of the store. She stood up and followed Colin there to find that the NPR crew was back and Megan was talking animatedly to a woman with a microphone.

"Would you mind if I interviewed you for a few moments?" the woman, who Megan introduced as Lauren, asked Lucy then. She looked at Colin and he nodded, wheeling himself to the side.

"No, not at all," she said, "as long as we can have everyone's attention."

But Ruth was already there, apparently waiting for her and Colin to emerge from the back. Within seconds the rest of them gathered around and she saw Thomas take Ruth's hand.

"I'm talking now to Lucinda Barrett, the author of *A Quiet Wanting*, a self-published novel that's become The Book Lover's top selling paperback this year," Lauren began. "Were you surprised, Lucinda, when they told you how well your book was doing?"

"Yes… and no," she said, not nervous but trembling with excitement because it seemed she'd been waiting her whole life for this moment. "I mean, I believed in the book enough to publish it myself when I got nothing but rejections. But the extent to which Ruth and her staff here got behind my novel was amazing to me, and touching. It gave me the courage to reach out to other booksellers and really build an audience, which was my goal."

"So what's next for you?"

"Well, I'm actually here to collect my books. I won't be selling my self-published novel here anymore. Or in any other stores for that matter."

She saw the frown on Ruth's face just as Lauren asked, "You're not giving up then, are you?"

"Oh no, quite the opposite. I've got a major book deal now with a top New York publisher. *A Quiet Wanting* is going to be published in hardcover next summer. And the novel I'm nearly finished with, *Confessions of a Poet*, will be published the following summer."

She couldn't help laughing as she watched Ruth's hands covering her mouth, shaking her head as if she couldn't believe it.

"You know, all along I wanted validation from the publishing industry, that my book was good enough. But I really had it all along, thanks to Ruth, and everyone here at The Book Lover."

"After a harrowing year and nearly closing shop, I'd call this a perfect ending for The Book Lover's 150th Anniversary," Lauren concluded, then switched off her microphone and turned to thank Lucy, but she was already running over to Ruth.

"I couldn't have done it without you," she whispered, pulling her into a tight hug. "You've been like a mother to me."

And now she really would be.

"There's just one more thing," Megan announced loudly, and they all turned to her in surprise. "As you all know, Ruth's essay won the Independent Booksellers contest for 'Why I'm a Bookseller.' I asked Lauren if I could read it now to close her program, because I think that'll be the perfect ending."

Lauren held up the microphone as Megan opened a folded sheet of paper. Lucy saw Thomas put his arm around Ruth and pull her close. Colin wheeled himself beside her, pulling her onto his lap. The store grew quiet and Megan began to read:

"I am a bookseller because it's everything I ever wanted to be. I wanted to be a social worker, so I take extra time helping those who are hurting to find an answer to their problems. I wanted to be a teacher, so I show children how to get excited about books. I wanted to be a writer, so I write reviews of books in the local papers.

I wanted to be an actress, so I give book talks and record radio commercials that let me reveal that hidden part of me. I wanted to be a community builder, so I take an active part in Downtown Revitalization. I wanted to be a preacher, so I choose uplifting books to feature in my advertising. I wanted to be a mother, so I keep in close touch with my grown children and grandchildren and call on their talents, when I need help in the store.

I am a bookseller because I love books, and love, and so I get to be a matchmaker and help orchestrate a proposal in my own store."

At that Megan paused and everyone gave a small round of applause to Larry and Angela, whose proposal Lucy had just missed. Then Megan continued:

"I am a bookseller because I love helping people find what they need in books,

from what to do with their lives, to how to solve a problem, to simply learning how to relax, and breathe.

I am a bookseller—it's everything I ever wanted to be."

They all turned to give Ruth a round of applause and a moment later were stunned to see her turn to Thomas and give him a long, tender kiss on the lips.

"Way to go, Mom," Jenny hooted.

"Way to go, Ruth," they all echoed.

EPILOGUE

SHE REMEMBERED LONG AGO WHEN SHE'D FIRST come to the lake and had no idea how her life would change, wondering what it would look like during winter. Its beauty exceeded her expectations.

On this cold January morning Lucy waited on the dock for them to arrive, breathing in the clean, frigid air. Part of the lake was frozen, its surface a dark shiny mirror, the shore scrimmed with a lacy edge of white crystal. The trees and mountains were brown and barren but you could see clear through the island now to the far shore. When she hiked, it was easier to spot deer and birds, although many had migrated south long ago. But robins and blue jays, a few cardinals and goldfinches still came to the feeders.

She heard the sound of cars then and turned toward the driveway to see Colin's Jeep, followed by three vans. She waited while they got out, as nearly half a dozen men and two women maneuvered themselves into wheelchairs and made their way across the frozen ground. Then she began walking toward them.

The decision of where to release the eagle had become an easy one. They needed a place where many wheelchairs would be able to maneuver without hazard. The Delaware Water Gap was a thought, of course, since that was where Kit was found. But in the end it would have been too difficult. And then Lucy asked Colin why they couldn't simply release the eagle right here? Their cove wasn't frozen thanks to a spring, and the water was deep, so a good source of fish if Kit decided to stay a while. There was no snow or bad weather in the coming week, another requirement. And freeing him in the early morning would give him all day to get his bearings before night set in.

So here they were, within flying distance of where Kit most likely nested and hopefully would return. Lucy hoped that if there was a mate, she was still waiting for him.

Randy and another man emerged from the van and pulled on the leather gloves, then walked to the back of the van. A moment later Randy began slowly walking toward them as he carried Kit, looking huge as he perched on one gloved arm. The eagle was still tethered to the glove with a leather strap, his yellow eyes searching as his head bobbed from side to side, a clear sign of nervousness, having no idea where he was headed. Lucy felt her heart soar at what was about to happen.

When she first came back to Colin in November and he told her that Kit might be released, she was stunned. On that final visit of hers, Susan was certain he would remain a display bird, that he would still have a purpose in helping them to educate the public. But his wing continued to improve while she was away, and Kit proved to be a fighter. He began to fly short distances, and then the length of the flight cage, 65 feet, with no difficulties. And so after careful consideration, the decision had been changed.

"Do you ever get attached to a bird?" she'd asked Susan when she found out. "I mean, after taking care of it."

"People who come here to work or volunteer sometimes want to have more of an emotional connection, but it'll never be like with a dog or cat," Susan had explained to her. "These are wild creatures, and even after being here for years, the birds still think of us as predators."

"I just feel such a bond with him," she'd said, watching him in the flight cage.

"Well, you and Colin are very responsible for saving his life, so that's understandable. But let me put it this way. Our personal affection or connection with a bird is one thing, that's a human response they can't reciprocate. For us, letting a bird go is the payoff. It's what we're here for. To respect, and celebrate, their wildness."

The Raptor Center's hope was always, when possible, to release a bird back out into the wild.

Now as they all waited, Lucy knew that for Colin, and these men and women, Kit symbolized their own second chance at life. At the educational program he'd given to this same group at the center yesterday, Colin had stressed just that thing.

"A raptor is defined by being a hunter, yet these birds will never hunt again," he'd said, after Lady and Scarlett were brought in, one after the other, to prove his point. "But they have another purpose now, something just as important that will define them."

As powerful as that had been for these soldiers, she knew that today's conclusion to the program would be even sweeter.

They all watched as the eagle was carried toward the edge of the clearing, near the water. Randy unhooked the tether. Lucy held her breath, glanced quickly and saw that each soldier was riveted to the eagle. Within seconds Kit's wings opened, fluttering several times as he hovered tentatively, just inches above the gloved arm. A moment later she heard hushed gasps as his wings stretched their full length and he caught the air, lifting higher and higher then soaring over them as he flew above the lake, with such grace, as if he'd done this very thing just yesterday. It had taken months for him to be rehabilitated and now, within short minutes, he skimmed treetops, circled once above the water, then turned toward the far ridge of hills, toward the Water Gap, until he disappeared.

It was only then that the men and women in wheelchairs turned to each other and began slapping high-fives. When they quieted down, she could see how pleased Colin was with his first veterans program, and knew he'd be doing more. Then he gave a few final words.

"Each of us here has a different purpose now," he said. "Find yours. Free yourself, just as this eagle has, from whatever it is that's holding you back. And believe that anything you aspire to is possible. That's what will define you now, and that's an order, soldiers."

His words were followed by a series of "Yes, Sir's" and salutes.

A moment later they were pushing toward the cars. Lucy stood there watching them, thinking about Colin's words. Knowing how true it was in her own life. Just a year and a half ago, her rejected manuscript had sat in a closet, all but forgotten. This coming June, a month after their baby was due, *A Quiet Wanting* would be published in hardcover and distributed all over the country. At that very moment it was being translated into Italian, Spanish, and French.

If you believed hard enough and refused to give up, dreams really could come true. Her book was proof of that.

So was their baby.

ACKNOWLEDGMENTS

W HEN I WAS A SELF-PUBLISHED AUTHOR, before my first novel, *The Richest Season*, was published by Hyperion books, I learned all aspects of the bookselling world. I was already familiar with the writing side of it. I began to speak about my experiences at book clubs and events, discovering that most readers have no idea of the mysterious, often perilous, journey a novel takes from the moment it begins in a writer's mind to when it eventually ends up in their hands.

Ironically, this book and I were also on a perilous journey, and it nearly didn't see print. Because it is such an honest look at the publishing world, most editors were uncomfortable with it. I was asked to "tone it down," but decided eventually that I didn't want to do that. I wanted to tell the very real story of what it's like to be a writer and a bookseller in today's world.

There are so many I need to thank who helped in making this a successful journey, after all:

All the booksellers who shared their stories with me, especially Harvey Finkel and Rob Dougherty. Also, Beth Carpenter, Tom Warner, Cathy Blanco, Ann Carlson, Susan Hinkle, and many more! A very special thank you to Betsy Rider of Otto's Bookstore, who shared her life, her home, and so much more that influenced this story. You are an amazing woman!

The United States Army, for help with uniforms, rankings, and general background. Lauren Butcher, Education Director at The Raptor Trust in Basking Ridge, New Jersey, for educating me further on the world of birds, especially bald eagles. If there are any errors in these storylines, they are mine alone.

Rory A. Cooper, PhD, U.S. Army Veteran, and Bill Hannigan, U.S. Army Veteran, for sharing their stories, and the life of a paraplegic, with such grace and honesty. I am forever indebted and inspired by you both. Donations to the Disabled American Veterans can be made at www.dav.org.

Susan Zuniga for help in researching Warwick. Any inaccuracies in portraying the Village of Warwick are for fictional purposes alone. And to the people of Upper Greenwood Lake, I've taken considerable liberties in altering your neighborhood for my story. I hope you don't mind.

A special thanks to Larry and Deb Portzline, for sharing the story of their proposal and allowing me to tweak it for this book.

My writer friends, Jenny Milchman, Judy Walters and Karyne Corum, who read countless drafts and provided me with an amazing support system any author would envy. Joshua Frank for his generous time and advice on all aspects of publishing. And Natalie Bejarano for helping to bring Three Women Press to life!

Peter Ryan for once again allowing me to borrow from his incredible life for one of my characters.

Alan Donaghey, extraordinary artist and generous friend, for designing my cover and my new website. Amy Neeley, for taking the gorgeous photos that became the cover.

To my friends and family who rallied behind me, and prayed for me and this book: Robin Abourizk, Lucy Heller, Vicki Malanga, Jennifer Kreh, Sue Burrows, Vicki Rossi, Helene and Tom Timbrook, Debora Messina, Lynn Vergano, Johnny Rout, Janet Bejarano, and Liz Cornett. Most especially my sister, Jacky Abromitis, and her partner, Kathy Ulisse, for going above and beyond in helping me with EVERYTHING!

To my parents, Jack and Angie Abromitis, my biggest fans, my best supporters, and my safe harbor still. Everyone should be so blessed.

To my incredible children Patrick and Marisa, who continue to inspire me to be all that I can be. And my beautiful little granddaughters, Alice, Lily, Julia and Phoebe, all book lovers already!

1. Do you think some of the things Ruth does to hold onto her store are
    obsessive? What about Lucy's efforts to get her book into stores and
    readers' hands?

2. Lucy sometimes tells little white lies to keep peace, or prevent someone
    getting upset. Have you ever done that? Do you think it's sometimes
    okay?

3. Were you surprised at the things Colin could and couldn't do as a
    paraplegic? Do you know, or have you had interaction, with a paraplegic
    personally?

4. How does the theme of nature, specifically the bald eagles, help Lucy to
    come to terms with her situation?

5. Did you find Thomas to be a sympathetic/realistic character? Did you
    understand why Ruth would not want to know what any of the prisoners
    did to be incarcerated?

6. Do you think Ruth's daughter is overprotective? Do you think Ruth is too
    easy going with her, or should she confront her about interfering?

7. Were you aware of the difficulties in being a writer or bookseller in
    today's world?

8. Were you surprised that Lucy didn't return to her husband? Why did she
    really marry him in the first place?

9. Was it wrong of Lucy to keep the contents of her new book a secret from
    Ruth? Colin? Why did she do it?

10. Were you surprised at the ending? Do you think Lucy atoned for her past transgressions? Do you think it's possible for Ruth to be happy with Thomas?

11. Have you ever thought of writing a book? Do you think it's true that everyone has a book inside them? Do you think everyone can write?

12. The author takes you behind the scenes of the publishing industry. Did this enhance, or take away from the story for you?